Tomorrow's, Today's [and] *Yesterday's Award-Winning* Science Fiction Authors Are Sure to be Among the Following:*

LARRY NIVEN
JOANNA RUSS
STEPHEN TALL
MICHAEL G. CONEY
POUL ANDERSON
CHRISTOPHER PRIEST
R. A. LAFFERTY
ALAN DEAN FOSTER
LEONARD TUSHNET
EDDY C. BERTIN
ARTHUR C. CLARKE
BARRY N. MALZBERG
HARLAN ELLISON
THEODORE STURGEON

They are all in this exciting expertly-selected collection of the finest fantastic fiction of the year.

* Hugos, Nebulas, Oscars, Edgars, Sfans, plaques, certificates . . . you name them. . . .

Anthologies from DAW

Wollheim's
WORLD'S
BEST
SF

Series One

Edited by
DONALD A. WOLLHEIM
with Arthur W. Saha

Formerly titled:
The 1972 Annual World's Best SF

DAW BOOKS, INC.
DONALD A. WOLLHEIM, PUBLISHER

1301 Avenue of the Americas
New York, N. Y.   10019

First Printing, May, 1972

4 5 6 7 8 9 10 11 12

PRINTED IN U.S.A.

INTRODUCTION

The essence of science fiction is that this is a changing world. In consequence science fiction reflects this. Though science fiction sets up stereotypes, they are stereotypes of that which may some day be or which might have been or could be, but they are always presentations of some form of a changed world.

The next three decades of the Twentieth Century are going to be enormously critical to the fate of this planet and its inhabitants—and maybe to the universe's future as well. In the Seventies the common people of the world are becoming aware of this. If we are to survive into that Infinite Future that science fiction writers of previous decades have managed to insinuate into the mental background of the world's dreams, then we are going to have to pay close political attention to what we have done with the products of science and their undesirable biproducts: pollution, overpopulation and atomic warfare.

Of course science fiction does not play solely the role of a Cassandra. It cannot afford to. It must, in occasional stories, point to these evils, but to rely on its enlarging audience, to keep the contentment of its constant readers, it must continue in the main to maintain a belief in human infinity. This, in the majority of its stories and novels, it does. To do otherwise would very soon cause science fiction itself—as a marketable category—to disappear. A steady diet of foreboding and horrifics would be palatable only to a misanthrope.

Science fiction readers are therefore generally youthful in mind, if not always in body, optimistic, even when occasionally dubious about the immediate future, favorable to human chances even when angered about individual political foibles, and believers in the beneficial uses of science even when protesting the commercial or military misuses of science.

It is in that sense that most of the material in this anthology is not gloomy—because this material has been selected from the primary sources of science fiction of of the past year, and the overwhelming majority of those sources, magazines, books, anthologies, are not publishing dire predictions. They are publishing that which science fiction has always published, primarily stories of men beating nature by men's wits. Which is the way civilization got to where it is now anyway. If we have some obstacles to overcome—well, as the song goes, "we shall overcome."

But this is no single-track collection. It is a careful effort to pick the best stories, and your editor would not like to state which stories are potentially gloomy and which are optimistic. The best stories are examples of fine narration—with wonder and power and human emotion. Let the reader determine for himself whether they are pure wish fulfillment or a mirror to a future that may come true.

Obviously a story like *Gleepsite* is hardly a tale one would wish to see come true, yet living in a great polluted metropolis, one has to say this is a vivid projection of one fork in the human near-future. Stories like Harlan Ellison's and Michael Coney's are other projections along paths not exactly the most pleasing.

Then we have Alan Dean Foster's story—a typical *Analog* theme in the best tradition of the late John W. Campbell who bought and published it during the last year of his life. Nothing polluted or depressed there. Man does overcome, and will overcome, and though your editor may personally have disputed John Campbell's unusual and arresting political views and his editorial comments (as we did in our critical study, *The Universe Makers*), the best tribute we can pay to John Campbell is to say that this story does somehow epitomize what he stood for.

That brings up again the subject of change. For as science fiction deals with change, and the next three decades will deal with really crisis changes, in our own little sector of literature the year past dealt with basic changes that will reflect on SF writing for the rest of this decade.

The death of John W. Campbell in 1971 was a major

marker of the changes that are to come. For Campbell, with his views and his brilliant editorial concern and great talent for directing writers, made his mark on the SF of the past firmly and strongly. It will be a long time before his hand is no longer felt in the styles and themes of the best writers, for he found many of them and set them on their way. *Analog* continues; who can say what alterations will slowly make themselves noticeable? 1971 was the last Campbell year of the magazine that has been said by many to have fathered modern science fiction (after the era of Gernsback and *Planet Stories*).

The passing of August Derleth was another sad milestone of 1971, for though Derleth was responsible through his Arkham House books for the popularization of the best in weird fantasy and especially for the boom and fame of H.P. Lovecraft, this was not without relevance to SF readers and writers.

As can be seen also change is reflected in this anthology itself. For our alteration of title reflects a modest admission of the break-up of the collaboration between Terry Carr and your editor in harvesting each year what we jointly agreed to be the best of the year. Both Mr. Carr and your editor have severed connections with the editorial staff or the publisher we formerly served. Mr. Carr to go his way as a writer and anthologist, I to go my way as an editor and publisher (this time for myself under the imprint of DAW Books).

In previous collections of the year's best the selection of stories was made by both of us and nothing appeared that did not have the agreement of Mr. Carr and myself. In general, though Terry Carr and I belong to different generations, our tastes were remarkably similar. We never disagreed on final choices. Suggestions made by one to the other were weighed and balanced—what resulted in agreement saw inclusion. But there really were almost no important points of conflict in our views. A good story could be recognized; a questionable one spotted as such.

The 1972 Annual World's Best SF is my continuation of the work done in the past year in reading and selecting from all the sources those SF stories which deserved the name of the best. I have not worked alone, for I have had the collaboration of an expert science fiction reader, collector and fan, Arthur W. Saha. Mr. Saha, who is a chemical engineer by profession, has been a devout reader of science fiction for over thirty years. A fan of some minor fame, attendee of most of the world conventions, an active member of science fiction clubs, and an avid collector, his name may not have been made familiar by publication of stories for he is not a story writer. But he is a capable and critical reader, and his help in the selection of this and forthcoming editions will be and has been invaluable.

The year past was marked by the growth of new forces along the lines predicted in the introduction to last year's Wollheim-Carr selection. The rise of books devoted entirely to new and original SF written directly at the behest of the anthologist continues unabated —a change which marks a further maturation of the field and a growing away from the category magazine sources. Five stories in this selection came from such books.

The rise of non-English language authors worthy of note continues, although more slowly, and still presenting difficulties in locating. One such story, by the talented Belgian writer, Eddy C. Bertin, made its way to us in time. We will be considering others in the year to come from other European writers. The writers and readers of Europe are gathering strength and beginning to be heard. This year will see the first All-European Convention of Science Fiction, in Trieste, Italy. Last year saw an even more remarkable occurrence, the holding of the first conference of science fiction writers of the socialist countries of Eastern Europe and the U.S.S.R., conducted in Budapest under the auspices of the Hungarian Writers Association. Recognizing that their work is virtually unknown to the Western literary world, this conference asked to be heard. One waits with interest the hearing, for almost all the names of the attending writers were unknown to the West.

There were also conventions and conferences of science fictionists in Japan, in Germany, in Sweden, in Belgium (where your editor was the Guest of Honor), in France, and other lands. There is a ferment in the world that is bringing science fiction to the fore. Foreboding may be present in this ferment, but a potential intoxication with the infinity opening up by scientific speculation is also very visible.

In 1957, men opened up space. In 1969, men opened up the Moon. And in 1971, the satellite-mapping of Mars was begun and two Earth-made objects now rest upon the sandy surface of the Red Planet.

How can anyone do otherwise but believe in the future? And is not the future the science fiction of today?

—*Donald A. Wollheim*

THE FOURTH PROFESSION

LARRY NIVEN

Larry Niven won both the Hugo and the Nebula awards last year for a grand space adventure novel in the best "Old Wave" tradition. It was therefore something of a surprise to find him appearing in probably the farthest out of the "New Wave" original collections, Chip Delany's *Quark*. However, reading *The Fourth Profession* reveals that Niven has not "sold out" the great tradition—instead he has shown how thoroughly superior good sound narrative writing can be.

The doorbell rang around noon on Wednesday.

I sat up in bed and—it was the oddest of hangovers. My head *didn't* spin. My sense of balance was quiveringly alert. At the same time my mind was clogged with the things I knew: facts that wouldn't relate, churning in my head.

It was like walking the high wire while simultaneously trying to solve an Agatha Christie mystery. Yet I was doing neither. I was just sitting up in bed, blinking.

I remembered the Monk, and the pills. How many pills?

The bell rang again.

Walking to the door was an eerie sensation. Most people pay no attention to their somesthetic senses. Mine were clamoring for attention, begging to be tested—by a backflip, for instance. I resisted. I don't have the muscles for doing backflips.

13

I couldn't remember taking any acrobatics pills.

The man outside my door was big and blond and blocky. He was holding an unfamiliar badge up to the lens of my spy-eye, in a wide hand with short, thick fingers, He had candid blue eyes, a square, honest face—a face I recognized. He'd been in the Long Spoon last night, at a single table in a corner.

Last night he had looked morose, introspective, like a man whose girl has left him for Mr. Wrong. A face guaranteed to get him left alone. I'd noticed him only because he wasn't drinking enough to match the face.

Today he looked patient, endlessly patient, with the patience of a dead man.

And he had a badge. I let him in.

"William Morris," he said, identifying himself. "Secret Service. Are you Edward Harley Frazer, owner of the Long Spoon Bar?"

"Part-owner."

"Yes, that's right. Sorry to bother you, Mr. Frazer. I see you keep bartender's hours." He was looking at the wrinkled pair of underpants I had on.

"Sit down," I said, waving at the chair. I badly needed to sit down myself. Standing, I couldn't think about anything but standing. My balance was all conscious. My heels would not rest solidly on the floor. They barely touched. My weight was all on my toes; my body insisted on standing that way.

So I dropped onto the edge of the bed, but it felt like I was giving a trampoline performance. The poise, the grace, the polished ease! Hell. "What do you want from me, Mr. Morris? Doesn't the Secret Service guard the President?"

His answer sounded like rote-memory. "Among other concerns, such as conterfeiting, we do guard the President and his immediate family and the President-elect, and the Vice-President if he asks us to." He paused. "We used to guard foreign dignitaries too."

That connected. "You're here about the Monk."

"Right." Morris looked down at his hands. He should have had an air of professional self-assurance to go with the badge. It wasn't there. "This is an odd case, Frazer. We took it because it used to be our job to protect foreign visitors, and because nobody else would touch it."

"So last night you were in the Long Spoon guarding a visitor from outer space."

"Just so."

"Where were you night before last?"

"Was that when he first appeared?"

"Yah," I said, remembering. "Monday night . . ."

He came in an hour after opening time. He seemed to glide, with the hem of his robe just brushing the floor. By his gait he might have been moving on wheels. His shape was wrong, in a way that made your eyes want to twist around to straighten it out.

There is something queer about the garment that gives a Monk his name. The hood is open in front, as if eyes might hide within its shadow, and the front of the robe is open too. But the loose cloth hides more than it ought to. There is too much shadow.

Once I thought the robe parted as he walked toward me. But there seemed to be nothing inside.

In the Long Spoon was utter silence. Every eye was on the Monk as he took a stool at one end of the bar, and ordered.

He looked alien, and was. But he *seemed* supernatural.

He used the oddest of drinking systems. I keep my house brands on three long shelves, more or less in order of type. The Monk moved down the top row of bottles, right to left, ordering a shot from each bottle. He took his liquor straight, at room temperature. He drank quietly, steadily, and with what seemed to be total concentration.

He spoke only to order.

He showed nothing of himself but one hand. That hand looked like a chicken's foot, but bigger, with lumpy-looking, very flexible joints, and with five toes instead of four.

At closing time the Monk was four bottles from the end of the row. He paid me in one-dollar bills and left, moving steadily, the hem of his robe just brushing the floor. I testify as an expert: he was sober. The alcohol had not affected him at all.

"Monday night," I said. "He shocked the hell out of us. Morris, what was a Monk doing in a bar in Hollywood? I thought all the Monks were in New York."

"So did we."

"Oh?"

"We didn't know he was on the West Coast until it hit the newspapers yesterday morning. That's why you didn't see more reporters yesterday. We kept them off your back.

I came in last night to question you, Frazer. I changed my mind when I saw that the Monk was already here."

"Question *me*. Why? All I did was serve him drinks."

"Okay, let's start there. Weren't you afraid the alcohol might kill a Monk?"

"It occurred to me."

"Well?"

"I served him what he asked for. It's the Monks' own doing that nobody knows anything about Monks. We don't even know what shape they are, let alone how they're put together. If liquor does things to a Monk, it's his own lookout. Let *him* check the chemistry."

"Sounds reasonable."

"Thanks."

"It's also the reason I'm here," said Morris. "We know too little about the Monks. We didn't even know they existed until something over two years ago."

"Oh?" I'd only started reading about them a month ago.

"It wouldn't be that long, except that all the astronomers were looking in that direction already, studying a recent nova in Sagittarius. So they caught the Monk starship a little sooner; but it was already inside Pluto's orbit.

"They've been communicating with us for over a year. Two weeks ago they took up orbit around the moon. There's only one Monk starship, and only one ground-to-orbit craft, as far as we know. The ground-to-orbit craft has been sitting in the ocean off Manhattan Island, convenient to the United Nations Building, for those same two weeks. Its crew are supposed to be all the Monks there are in the world.

"Mr. Frazer, we don't even know how your Monk got out here to the West Coast! Almost anything you could tell us would help. Did you notice anything odd about him, these last two nights?"

"Odd?" I grinned. "About a Monk?"

It took him a moment to get it, and then his answering smile was wan. "Odd for a Monk."

"Yah," I said, and tried to concentrate. It was the wrong move. Bits of fact buzzed about my skull, trying to fit themselves together.

Morris was saying, "Just talk, if you will. The Monk came back Tuesday night. About what time?"

"About four thirty. He had a case of—pills—RNA . . ."

It was no use. I knew too many things, all at once, all

unrelated. I knew the name of the Garment to Wear Among Strangers, its principle and its purpose. I knew about Monks and alcohol. I knew the names of the five primary colors, so that for a moment I was blind with the memory of the colors themselves, colors no man would ever see.

Morris was standing over me, looking worried. "What is it? What's wrong?"

"Ask me anything." My voice was high and strange and breathless with giddy laughter. "Monks have four limbs, all hands, each with a callus heel behind the fingers. I know their names, Morris. Each hand, each finger. I know how many eyes a Monk has. One. And the whole skull is an ear. There's no word for *ear*, but medical terms for each of the—resonating cavities—between the lobes of the brain . . ."

"You look dizzy. You don't sample your own wares, do you, Frazer?"

"I'm the opposite of dizzy. There's a compass in my head. I've got absolute direction. Morris, it must have been the pills."

"Pills?" Morris had small, squarish ears that couldn't possibly have come to point. But I got that impression.

"He had a sample case full of—education pills . . ."

"Easy now." He put a steadying hand on my shoulder. "Take it easy. Just start at the beginning, and talk. I'll make some coffee."

"Good." Coffee sounded wonderful, suddenly. "Pot's ready. Just plug it in. I fix it before I go to sleep."

Morris disappeared around the partition that marks off the kitchen alcove from the bedroom/living room in my small apartment. His voice floated back. "Start at the beginning. He came back Tuesday night."

"He came back Tuesday night," I repeated.

"Hey, your coffee's already perked. You must have plugged it in in your sleep. Keep talking."

"He started his drinking where he'd left off, four bottles from the end of the top row. I'd have sworn he was cold sober. His voice didn't give him away . . ."

His voice didn't give him away because it was only a whisper, too low to make out. His translator spoke like a computer, putting single words together from a man's recorded voice. It spoke slowly and with care. Why not? It was speaking an alien tongue.

The Monk had had five tonight. That put him through the ryes and the bourbons and the Irish whiskeys, and several of the liqueurs. Now he was tasting the vodkas.

At that point I worked up the courage to ask him what he was doing.

He explained at length. The Monk starship was a commercial venture, a trading mission following a daisy chain of stars. He was a sampler for the group. He was mightily pleased with some of the wares he had sampled here. Probably he would order great quantities of them, to be freeze-dried for easy storage. Add alcohol and water to reconstitute.

"Then you won't be wanting to test all the vodkas," I told him. "Vodka isn't much more than water and alcohol."

He thanked me.

"The same goes for most gins, except for flavorings." I lined up four gins in front of him. One was Tanqueray. One was a Dutch gin you have to keep chilled like some liqueurs. The others were fairly ordinary products. I left him with these while I served other customers.

I had expected a mob tonight. Word should have spread. *Have a drink in the Long Spoon, you'll see a Thing from Outer Space.* But the place was half empty. Louise was handling them nicely.

I was proud of Louise. As with last night, tonight she behaved as if nothing out of the ordinary was happening. The mood was contagious. I could almost hear the customers thinking: *We like our privacy when we drink. A Thing from Outer Space is entitled to the same consideration.*

It was strange to compare her present insouciance with the way her eyes had bugged at her first sight of a Monk.

The Monk finished tasting the gins. "I am concerned for the volatile fractions," he said. "Some of your liquors will lose taste from condensation."

I told him he was probably right. And I asked, "How do you pay for your cargos?"

"With knowledge."

"That's fair. What kind of knowledge?"

The Monk reached under his robe and produced a flat sample case. He opened it. It was full of pills. There was a large glass bottle full of a couple of hundred identical pills; and these were small and pink and triangular. But most of the sample case was given over to big, round pills of all colors, individually wrapped and individually labeled in the wandering Monk script.

No two labels were alike. Some of the notations looked hellishly complex.

"These are knowledge," said the Monk.

"Ah," I said, and wondered if I was being put on. An alien can have a sense of humor, can't he? And there's no way to tell if he's lying.

"A certain complex organic molecule has much to do with memory," said the Monk. "Ribonucleic acid. It is present and active in the nervous systems of most organic beings. Wish you to learn my language?"

I nodded.

He pulled a pill loose and stripped it of its wrapping, which fluttered to the bar like a shred of cellophane. The Monk put the pill in my hand and said, "You must swallow it now, before the air ruins it, now that it is out of its wrapping."

The pill was marked like a target in red and green circles. It was big and bulky going down.

"You must be crazy," Bill Morris said wonderingly.

"It looks that way to me, too, now. But think about it. This was a Monk, an alien, an ambassador to the whole human race. He wouldn't have fed me anything dangerous, not without carefully considering all the possible consequences.

"He wouldn't, would he?"

"That's the way it seemed." I remembered about Monks and alcohol. It was a pill memory, surfacing as if I had known it all my life. It came too late . . .

"A language says things about the person who speaks it, about the way he thinks and the way he lives. Morris, the Monk language says a lot about Monks."

"Call me Bill," he said irritably.

"Okay. Take Monks and alcohol. Alcohol works on a Monk the way it works on a man, by starving his brain cells a little. But in a Monk it gets absorbed more slowly. A Monk can stay high a week on a night's dedicated drinking.

"I knew he was sober when he left Monday night. By Tuesday night he must have been pretty high."

I sipped my coffee. Today it tasted different, and better, as if memories of some Monk staple foods had worked their way as overtones into my taste buds.

Morris said, "And you didn't know it."

"Know it? I was counting on his sense of responsibility!"

Morris shook his head in pity, except that he seemed to be grinning inside.

"We talked some more after that—and I took some more pills."

"Why?"

"I was high on the first one."

"It made you drunk?"

"Not drunk, but I couldn't think straight. My head was full of Monk words all trying to fit themselves to meanings. I was dizzy with nonhuman images and words I couldn't pronounce."

"Just how many pills did you take?"

"I don't remember."

"Swell."

An image surfaced. "I do remember saying, 'But how about something unusual? *Really* unusual.' "

Morris was no longer amused. "You're lucky you can still talk. The chances you took, you should be a drooling idiot this morning!"

"It seemed reasonable at the time."

"You don't remember how many pills you took?"

I shook my head. Maybe the motion jarred something loose. "That bottle of little triangular pills. I know what they were. Memory erasers."

"Good God! You didn't . . ."

"No, no, Morris. They don't erase your whole memory. They erase pill memories. The RNA in a Monk memory pill is tagged somehow, so the eraser pill can pick it out and break it down."

Morris gaped. Presently he said, "That's incredible. The education pills are wild enough, but *that* . . . You see what they must do, don't you? They hang a radical on each and every RNA molecule in each and every education pill. The active principle in the eraser pill is an enzyme for just that radical."

He saw my expression and said, "Never mind, just take my word for it. They must have had the education pills for a hundred years before they worked out the eraser principle."

"Probably. The pills must be very old."

He pounced. "How do you know that?"

"The name for the pill has only one syllable, like *fork*. There are dozens of words for kinds of pill reflexes, for swallowing the wrong pill, for side effects depending on what species is taking the pill. There's a special word for an animal training pill, and another one for a slave training pill. Morris, I think my memory is beginning to settle down."

"Good!"

"Anyway, the Monks must have been peddling pills to aliens for thousands of years. I'd guess tens of thousands."

"Just how many kinds of pill were in that case?"

I tried to remember. My head felt congested.

"I don't know if there was more than one of each kind of pill. There were four stiff flaps like the leaves of a book, and each flap had rows of little pouches with a pill in each one. The flaps were maybe sixteen pouches long by eight across. Maybe. Morris, we ought to call Louise. She probably remembers better than I do, even if she noticed less at the time."

"You mean Louise Schu, the barmaid? She might at that. Or she might jar something loose in your memory."

"Right."

"Call her. Tell her we'll meet her. Where's she live, Santa Monica?"

He'd done his homework, all right.

Her phone was still ringing when Morris said, "Wait a minute. Tell her we'll meet her at the Long Spoon. And tell her we'll pay her amply for her trouble."

Then Louise answered and told me I'd jarred her out of a sound sleep, and I told her she'd be paid amply for her trouble, and she said what the hell kind of a crack was *that?*

After I hung up I asked, "Why the Long Spoon?"

"I've thought of something. I was one of the last customers out last night. I don't think you cleaned up."

"I was feeling peculiar. We cleaned up a little, I think."

"Did you empty the wastebaskets?"

"We don't usually. There's a guy who comes in in the morning and mops the floors and empties the wastebaskets and so forth. The trouble is, he's been home with the flu the last couple of days. Louise and I have been going early."

"Good. Get dressed, Frazer. We'll go down to the Long Spoon and count the pieces of Monk cellophane in the wastebaskets. They shouldn't be too hard to identify. They'll tell us how many pills you took."

I noticed it while I was dressing. Morris's attitude had changed subtly. He had become proprietary. He tended to stand closer to me, as if someone might try to steal me, or as if I might try to steal away.

Imagination, maybe. But I began to wish I didn't know so much about Monks.

I stopped to empty the percolator before leaving. Habit. Every afternoon I put the percolator in the dishwasher before I leave. When I come home at three A.M. its's ready to load.

I poured out the dead coffee, took the machine part, and stared.

The grounds in the top were fresh coffee, barely damp from steam. They hadn't been used yet.

There was another Secret Service man outside my door, a tall Midwesterner with a toothy grin. His name was George Littleton. He spoke not a word after Bill Morris introduced us, probably because I looked like I'd bite him.

I would have. My balance nagged me like a sore tooth. I couldn't forget it for an instant.

Going down in the elevator, I could feel the universe shifting around me. There seemed to be a four-dimensional map in my head, with me in the center and the rest of the universe traveling around me at various changing velocities.

The car we used was a Lincoln Continental. George drove. My map became three times as active, recording every touch of brake and accelerator.

"We're putting you on salary," said Morris, "if that's agreeable. You know more about Monks than any living man. We'll class you as a consultant and pay you a thousand dollars a day to put down all you remember about Monks."

"I'd want the right to quit whenever I think I'm mined out."

"That seems all right," said Morris. He was lying. They would keep me just as long as they felt like it. But there wasn't a thing I could do about it at the moment.

I didn't even know what made me so sure.

So I asked, "What about Louise?"

"She spent most of her time waiting on tables, as I remember. She won't know much. We'll pay her a thousand a day for a couple of days. Anyway, for today, whether she knows anything or not."

"Okay," I said, and tried to settle back.

"You're the valuable one, Frazer. You've been fantastically lucky. That Monk language pill is going to give us a terrific advantage whenever we deal with Monks. They'll have to learn about us. We'll know about them already. Frazer, what does a Monk look like under the cowl and robe?"

"Not human," I said. "They only stand upright to make us feel at ease. And there's a swelling along one side that looks like equipment under the robe, but it isn't. It's part of the digestive system. And the head is as big as a basketball, but it's half hollow."

"They're natural quadrupeds?"

"Yah. Four-footed, but climbers. The animal they evolved from lives in forests of giant dandelions. They can throw rocks with any foot. They're still around on Center; that's the home planet. You're not writing this down."

"There's a tape recorder going."

"Really?" I'd been kidding.

"You'd better believe it. We can use anything you happen to remember. We still don't even know how your Monk got out her to California."

My Monk, forsooth.

"They briefed me pretty quickly yesterday. Did I tell you? I was visiting my parents in Carmel when my supvisor called me yesterday morning. Ten hours later I knew just about everything anyone knows about Monks. Except you, Frazer.

"Up until yesterday we thought that every Monk on Earth was either in the United Nations Building or aboard the Monk ground-to-orbit ship.

"We've been in that ship, Frazer. Several men have been through it, all trained astronauts wearing lunar exploration suits. Six Monks landed on Earth—unless more were hiding somewhere aboard the ground-to-orbit ship. Can you think of any reason why they should do that?"

"No."

"Neither can anyone else. And there are six Monks accounted for this morning. All in New York. Your Monk went home last night."

That jarred me. "How?"

"We don't know. We're checking plane flights, silly as that sounds. Wouldn't you think a stewardess would notice a Monk on her flight? Wouldn't you think she'd go to the newspapers?"

"Sure."

"We're also checking flying saucer sightings."

I laughed. But by now that sounded logical.

"If that doesn't pan out, we'll be seriously considering teleportation. Would you . . ."

"That's it," I said without surprise. It had come the way a memory comes, from the back of my mind, as if it had always been there. "He gave me a teleportation pill. That's why I've got absolute direction. To teleport I've got to know where in the universe I am."

Morris got bug-eyed. "You can teleport?"

"Not from a speeding car," I said with reflexive fear. "That's death. I'd keep the velocity."

"Oh." He was edging away as if I had sprouted horns.

More memory floated up, and and I said, "Humans can't teleport anyway. That pill was for another market."

Morris relaxed. "You might have said that right away."

"I only just remembered."

"Why did you take it, if it's for aliens?"

"Probably for the location talent. I don't remember. I used to get lost pretty easily. I never will again. Morris, I'd be safer on a high wire than you'd be crossing a street with the Walk sign."

"Could that have been you 'something unusual'?"

"Maybe," I said. At the same time I was somehow sure that it wasn't.

Louise was in the dirt parking lot next to the Long Spoon. She was getting out of her Mustang when we pulled up. She waved an arm like a semaphore and walked briskly toward us, already talking. "Alien creatures in the Long Spoon, forsooth!" I'd taught her that word. "Ed, I keep telling you the customers aren't human. Hello, are you Mr. Morris? I remember you. You were in last night. You had four drinks. All night."

Morris smiled. "Yes, but I tipped big. Call me Bill, okay?"

Louise Schu was a cheerful blonde, by choice, not birth. She'd been working in the Long Spoon for five years now. A few of my regulars knew my name; but they all knew hers.

Louise's deadliest enemy was the extra twenty pounds she carried as padding. She had been dieting for some decades. Two years back she had gotten serious about it and stopped cheating. She was *mean* for the next several months. But, clawing and scratching and half starved every second, she had worked her way down to one hundred and twenty-five pounds. She threw a terrific celebration that night and—to hear her tell it afterward—ate her way back to one-forty-five in a single night.

Padding or not, she'd have made someone a wonderful wife. I'd thought of marrying her myself. But my marriage had been too little fun, and was too recent, and the divorce had hurt too much. And the alimony. The alimony was why I was living in a cracker box, and also the reason I couldn't afford to get married again.

While Louise was opening up, Morris bought a paper from the coin rack.

The Long Spoon was a mess. Louise and I had cleaned off the tables and collected the dirty glasses and emptied the ashtrays into waste bins. But the collected glasses were still dirty and the waste bins were still full.

Morris began spreading newspaper over an area of floor.

And I stopped with my hand in my pocket.

Littleton came out from behind the bar, hefting both of the waste bins. He spilled one out onto the newspaper, then the other. He and Morris began spreading the trash apart.

My fingertips were brushing a scrap of Monk cellophane.

I'd worn these pants last night, under the apron.

Some impulse kept me from yelling out. I brought my hand out of my pocket, empty. Louise had gone to help the others sift the trash with their fingers. I joined them.

Presently Morris said, "Four. I hope that's all. We'll search the bar too."

And I thought: Five.

And I thought: I learned five new professions last night. What were the odds that I'll want to hide at least one of them?

If my judgment was bad enough to make me take a teleport pill intended for something with too many eyes, what else might I have swallowed last night?

I might be an advertising man, or a superbly trained thief, or a Palace Executioner skilled in the ways of torture. Or I might have asked for something really unpleasant, like the profession followed by Hitler or Alexander the Great.

"Nothing here," Morris said from behind the bar. Louise shrugged agreement. Morris handed the four scraps to Littleton and said, "Run these out to Douglass. Call us from there.

"We'll put them through chemical analysis," he said to Louise and me. "One of them may be real cellophane off a piece of candy. Or we might have missed one or two. For the moment, let's assume there were four."

"All right," I said.

"Does it sound right, Frazer? Should it be three, or five?"

"I don't know." As far as memory went, I really didn't.

"Four, then. We've identified two. One was a course in teleportation for aliens. The other was a language course. Right?"

"It looks that way."

"What else did he give you?"

I could feel the memories floating back there, but all scrambled together. I shook my head.

Morris looked frustrated.

"Excuse me," said Louise. "Do you drink on duty?"

"Yes," Morris said without hesitation.

And Louise and I weren't on duty. Louise mixed us three gin-and-tonics and brought them to us at one of the padded booths.

Morris had opened a flattish briefcase that turned out to be part tape recorder. He said, "We won't lose anything now. Louise, let's talk about last night."

"I hope I can help."

"Just what happened in here after Ed took his first pill?"

"Mmm." Louise looked at me askance. "I don't know when he took that first pill. About one I noticed that he was acting strange. He was slow on orders. He got drinks wrong.

"I remembered that he had done that for awhile last fall, when he got his divorce . . ."

I felt my face go stiff. That was unexpected pain, that memory. I am far from being my own best customer; but there had been a long lost weekend about a year ago. Louise had talked me out of trying to drink and bartend too. So I had gone drinking. When it was out of my system I had gone back to tending bar.

She was saying, "Last night I thought it might be the same problem. I covered for him, said the orders twice when I had to, watched him make the drinks so he'd get them right.

"He was spending most of his time talking to the Monk. But Ed was talking English, and the Monk was making whispery noises in his throat. Remember last week, when they put the Monk speech on television? It sounded like that.

"I saw Ed take a pill from the Monk and swallow it with a glass of water."

She turned to me, touched my arm. "I thought you were crazy. I tried to stop you."

"I don't remember."

"The place was practically empty by then. Well, you laughed at me and said that the pill would teach you not to get lost! I didn't believe it. But the Monk turned on his translator gadget and said the same thing."

"I wish you'd stopped me," I said.

She looked disturbed. "I wish you hadn't said that. I took a pill myself."

I started choking. She'd caught me with a mouthful of gin-and-tonic.

Louise pounded my back and saved my life, maybe. She said, "You don't remember that?"

"I don't remember much of anything coherent after I took the first pill."

"Really? You didn't seem loaded. Not after I'd watched you awhile."

Morris cut in. "Louise, the pill you took. What did the Monk say it would do?"

"He never did. We were talking about me." She stopped to think. Then, baffled and amused at herself, she said, "I don't know how it happened. All of a sudden I was telling the story of my young life. To a Monk. I had the idea he was sympathetic."

"The *Monk?*"

"Yes, the Monk. And at some point he picked out a pill and gave it to me. He said it would help me. I believed him. I don't know why, but I believed him, and I took it."

"Any symptoms? Have you learned anything new this morning?"

She shook her head, baffled and a little truculent now.

Taking that pill must have seemed sheer insanity in the cold gray light of afternoon.

"All right," said Morris. "Frazer, you took three pills. We knew what two of them were. Louise, you took one, and we have no idea what it taught you." He closed his eyes a moment, then looked at me. "Frazer, if you can't remember what you took, can you remember rejecting anything? Did the Monk offer you anything . . ." He saw my face and cut it off.

Because that had jarred something . . .

The Monk had been speaking his own language, in that alien whisper that doesn't need to be more than a whisper because the basic sounds of the Monk language are so unambiguous, so easily distinguished, even to a human ear. *This teaches proper swimming technique. A———can reach speeds of sixteen to twenty-four———per——— using these strokes. The course also teaches proper exercises . . .*

I said, "I turned down a swimming course for intelligent fish."

Louise giggled. Morris said, "You're kidding."

"I'm not. And there was something else." That swamped-in-data effect wasn't as bad as it had been at noon. Bits of data must be reaching cubbyholes in my head, linking up, finding their places.

"I was asking about the shapes of aliens. Not about Monks, because that's bad manners, especially from a race that hasn't yet proven its sentience. I wanted to know about other aliens. So the Monk offered me three courses in unarmed combat techniques. Each one involved extensive knowledge of basic anatomy."

"You didn't take them?"

"No. What for? Like, one was a pill to tell me how to kill an armed, intelligent worm, but only if I was an unarmed, intelligent worm. I wasn't *that* confused."

"Frazer, there are men who would give an arm and a leg for any of those pills you turned down."

"Sure. A couple of hours ago you were telling me I was crazy to swallow an alien's education pill."

"Sorry," said Morris.

"You were the one who said they should have driven me out of my mind. Maybe they did," I said, because my hypersensitive sense of balance was still bothering the hell out of me.

But Morris's reaction bothered me worse. *Frazer could*

start gibbering any minute. Better pump him for all he's worth while I've got the chance.

No, his face showed none of that. Was I going paranoid?

"Tell me more about the pills," Morris said. "It sounds like there's a lot of delayed reaction involved. How long do we have to wait before we know we've got it all?"

"He did say something . . ." I groped for it, and presently it came.

It works like a memory, the Monk had said. He'd turned off his translator and was speaking his own language, now that I could understand him. The sound of his translator had been bothering him. That was why he'd given me the pill.

But the whisper of his voice was low, and the language was new, and I'd had to listen carefully to get it all. I remembered it clearly.

The information in the pills will become part of your memory. You will not know all that you have learned until you need it. Then it will surface: Memory works by association, he'd said.

And: *There are things that cannot be taught by teachers. Always there is the difference between knowledge from school and knowledge from doing the work itself.*

"Theory and practice," I told Morris. "I know just what he meant. There's not a bartending course in the country that will teach you to leave the sugar out of an Old Fashioned during rush hour."

"*What* did you say?"

"It depends on the bar, of course. No posh bar would let itself get that crowded. But in an ordinary bar, anyone who orders a complicated drink during rush hour deserves what he gets. He's slowing the bartender down when it's crucial, when every second is money. So you leave the sugar out of an Old Fashioned. It's too much money."

"The guy won't come back."

"So what? He's not one of your regulars. He'd have better sense if he were."

I had to grin. Morris was shocked and horrified. I'd shown him a brand new sin. I said, "It's something every bartender ought to know about. Mind you, a bartending school is a trade school. They're teaching you to survive as a bartender. But the recipe calls for sugar, so at school you put in the sugar or you get ticked off."

Morris shook his head, tight-lipped. He said, "Then the

Monk was warning you that you were getting theory, not practice."

"Just the opposite. Look at it this way, Morris . . ."

"Bill."

"Listen, Bill. The teleport pill can't make a human nervous system capable of teleportation. Even my incredible balance, and it *is* incredible, won't give me the muscles to do ten quick backflips. But I do know what it *feels* like to teleport. That's what the Monk was warning me about. The pills give field training. What you have to watch out for are the reflexes. Because the pills don't change you physically."

"I hope you haven't become a trained assassin."

One must be wary of newly learned reflexes, the Monk had said.

Morris said, "Louise, we still don't know what kind of an education you got last night. Any ideas?"

"Maybe I repair time machines." She sipped her drink, eyed Morris demurely over the rim of the glass.

Morris smiled back. "I wouldn't be surprised."

The idiot. He meant it.

"If you really want to know what was in the pill," said Louise, "why not ask the Monk?" She gave Morris time to look startled, but no time to interrupt. "All we have to do is open up and wait. He didn't even get through the second shelf last night, did he, Ed?"

"No, by God, he didn't."

Louise swept an arm about her. "The place is a mess, of course. We'd never get it clean in time. Not without help. How about it, Bill? You're a government man. Could you get a team to work here in time to get this place cleaned up by five o'clock?"

"You know not what you ask. It's three-fifteen now!"

Truly, the Long Spoon was a disaster area. Bars are not meant to be seen by daylight anyway. Just because our worlds had been turned upside down, and just because the Long Spoon was clearly unfit for human habitation, we had been thinking in terms of staying closed tonight. Now it was too late . . .

"Tip-Top Cleaners," I remembered. "They send out a four-man team with its own mops. Fifteen bucks an hour. But we'd never get them here in time."

Morris stood up abruptly. "Are they in the phone book?"

"Sure."

Morris moved.

I waited until he was in the phone booth before I asked, "Any new thoughts on what you ate last night?"

Louise looked at me closely. "You mean the pill? Why so solemn?"

"We've got to find out before Morris does."

"Why?"

"If Morris has his way," I said, "they'll classify my head Top Secret. I know too much. I'm likely to be a political prisoner the rest of my life; and so are you, if you learned the wrong things last night."

What Louise did then, I found both flattering and comforting. She turned upon the phone booth where Morris was making his call, a look of such poisonous hatred that it should have withered the man where he stood.

She believed me. She needed no kind of proof, and she was utterly on my side.

Why was I so sure? I had spent too much of today guessing at other people's thoughts. Maybe it had something to do with my third and fourth professions . . .

I said, "We've got to find out what kind of pill you took. Otherwise Morris and the Secret Service will spend the rest of their lives following you around, just on the off chance that you know something useful. Like me. Only they *know* I know something useful. They'll be picking my brain until Hell freezes over."

Morris yelled from the phone booth. "They're coming! Forty bucks an hour, paid in advance when they get here!"

"Great!" I yelled.

"I want to call in. New York." He closed the folding door.

Louise leaned across the table. "Ed, what are we going to do?"

It was the way she said it. We were in it together, and there was a way out, and she was sure I'd find it—and she said it all in the sound of her voice, the way she leaned toward me, the pressure of her hand around my wrist. *We.* I felt power and confidence rising in me; and at the same time I thought: *She couldn't do that yesterday.*

I said, "We clean this place up so we can open for business. Meanwhile you try to remember what you learned last night. Maybe it was something harmless, like how to catch trilchies with a magnetic web."

"Tril . . . ?"

"Space butterflies, kind of."

"Oh. But suppose he taught me how to build a faster-than-light motor?"

"We'd bloody have to keep Morris from finding out. But you didn't. The English words for going faster than light—hyperdrive, space warp—they don't have Monk translations except in math. You can't even say 'faster than light' in Monk."

"Oh."

Morris came back grinning like an idiot. "You'll never guess what the Monks want from us now."

He looked from me to Louise to me, grinning, letting the suspense grow intolerable. He said, "A giant laser cannon."

Louise gasped "What?" and I asked, "You mean a launching laser?"

"Yes, a launching laser. They want us to build it on the moon. They'd feed our engineers pills to give them the specs and to teach them how to build it. They'd pay off in more pills."

I needed to remember something about launching lasers. And how had I known what to call it?

"They put the proposition to the United Nations," Morris was saying. "In fact, they'll be doing all of their business through the UN, to avoid charges of favoritism, they say, and to spread the knowledge as far as possible."

"But there are countries that don't belong to the UN," Louise objected.

"The Monks know that. They asked if any of those nations had space travel. None of them do, of course. And the Monks lost interest in them."

"Of course," I said, remembering. "A species that can't develop space flight is no better than animals."

"*Huh?*"

"According to a Monk."

Louise said, "But what *for?* Why would the Monks want a laser cannon? And on our moon!"

"That's a little complicated," said Morris. "Do you both remember when the Monk ship first appeared, two years ago?"

"No," we answered more or less together.

Morris was shaken. "You didn't notice? It was in all the papers. Noted Astronomer Says Alien Spacecraft Approaching Earth. No?"

"No."

"For Christ's sake! I was jumping up and down. It was like when the radio astronomers discovered pulsars, remember? I was just getting out of high school."

"Pulsars?"

"Excuse me," Morris said overpolitely. "My mistake. I tend to think that everybody I meet is a science fiction fan. Pulsars are stars that give off rhythmic pulses of radio energy. The radio astronomers thought at first that they were getting signals from outer space."

Louise said, "You're a science fiction fan?"

"Absolutely. My first gun was a Gyro-Jet rocket pistol. I bought it because I read Buck Rogers."

I said, "Buck who?" But then I couldn't keep a straight face. Morris raised his eyes to heaven. No doubt it was there that he found the strength to go on.

"The noted astronomer was Jerome Finney. Of course he hadn't said anything about Earth. Newspapers always get that kind of thing garbled. He'd said that an object of artificial, extraterrestrial origin had entered the solar system.

"What had happened was that several months earlier, Jodrell Bank had found a new star in Sagittarius. That's the direction of the galactic core. Yes, Frazer?"

We were back to last names because I wasn't a science fiction fan. I said, "That's right. The Monks came from the galactic hub." I remembered the blazing night sky of Center. My Monk customer couldn't possibly have seen it in his lifetime. He must have been shown the vision through an education pill, for patriotic reasons, like kids are taught what the Star Spangled Banner looks like.

"All right. The astronomers were studying a nearby nova, so they caught the intruder a little sooner. It showed a strange spectrum, radically different from a nova and much more constant. It even got stranger. The light was growing brighter at the same time the spectral lines were shifting toward the red.

"It was months before anyone identified the spectrum.

"Then one Jerome Finney finally caught wise. He showed that the spectrum was the light of our own sun, drastically blue-shifted. Some kind of mirror was coming at us, moving at a hell of a clip, but slowing as it came."

"Oh!" I got it then. "That would mean a light-sail!"

"Why the big deal, Frazer? I thought you already knew."

"No. This is the first I've heard of it. I don't read the Sunday supplements."

Morris was exasperated. "But you knew enough to call the laser cannon a launching laser!"

"I just now realized why it's called that."

Morris stared at me for several seconds. Then he said, "I forgot. You got it out of the Monk language course."

"I guess so."

He got back to business. "The newspapers gave poor Finney a terrible time. You didn't see the political cartoons either? Too bad. But when the Monk ship got closer it started sending signals. It *was* an interstellar sailing ship, riding the sunlight on a reflecting sail, and it was coming here."

"Signals. With dots and dashes? You could do that just by tacking the sail."

"You *must* have read about it."

"Why? It's so obvious."

Morris looked unaccountably ruffled. Whatever his reasons, he let it pass. "The sail is a few molecules thick and nearly five hundred miles across when it's extended. On light pressure alone they can build up to interstellar velocities—but it takes them a long time. The acceleration isn't high.

"It took them two years to slow down to solar system velocities. They must have done a lot of braking before our telescopes found them, but even so they were going far too fast when they passed Earth's orbit. They had to go inside Mercury's orbit and come up the other side of the sun's gravity well, backing all the way, before they could get near Earth."

I said, "Sure. Interstellar speeds have to be above half the speed of light, or you can't trade competitively."

"What?"

"There are ways to get the extra edge. You don't have to depend on sunlight, not if you're launching from a civilized system. Every civilized system has a moon-based launching laser. By the time the sun is too far away to give the ship a decent push, the beam from the laser cannon is spreading just enough to give the sail a hefty acceleration without vaporizing anything."

"Naturally," said Morris, but he seemed confused.

"So that if you're heading for a strange system, you'd naturally spend most of the trip decelerating. You can't count on a strange system having a launching laser. If you know your destination is civilized, that's a different matter."

Morris nodded.

"The lovely thing about the laser cannon is that if anything goes wrong with it, there's a civilized world right there to fix it. You go sailing out to the stars with trade goods, but you leave your launching motor safely at home. Why is everybody looking at me funny?"

"Don't take it wrong," said Morris. "But how does a paunchy bartender come to know so much about flying an interstellar trading ship?"

"What?" I didn't understand him.

"Why did the Monk ship have to dive so deep into the solar system?"

"Oh, that. That's the solar wind. You get the same problem around any yellow sun. With a light-sail you can get push from the solar wind as well as from light pressure. The trouble is, the solar wind is just stripped hydrogen atoms. Light bounces from a light-sail, but the solar wind just hits the sail and sticks."

Morris nodded thoughtfully. Louise was blinking as if she had double vision.

"You can't tack against it. Tilting the sail does from nothing. To use the solar wind for braking you have to bore straight in, straight toward the sun," I explained.

Morris nodded. I saw that his eyes were as glassy as Louise's eyes.

"Oh," I said. "Damn, I must be stupid today. Morris, that was the third pill."

"Right," said Morris, still nodding, still glassy-eyed. "That must have been the unusual, *really* unusual profession you wanted. Crewman on an interstellar liner. Jesus."

And he should have sounded disgusted, but he sounded envious.

His elbows were on the table, his chin rested on his fists. It is a position that distorts the mouth, making one's expression unreadable. But I didn't like what I could read in Morris's eyes.

There was nothing left of the square and honest man I had let into my apartment at noon. Morris was a patriot now, and an altruist, and a fanatic. He must have the stars for his nation and for all mankind. Nothing must stand in his way. Least of all, me.

Reading minds again, Frazer? Maybe being captain of an interstellar liner involves having to read the minds of the crew, to be able to put down a mutiny before some idiot can take a heat point to the *mpff glip habbabub*, or however a Monk would say it; it has something to do with straining ketones out of the breathing-air.

My urge to acrobatics had probably come out of the same pill. Free fall training. There was a lot in that pill.

This was the profession I should have hidden. Not the Palace Torturer, who was useless to a government grown too subtle to need such techniques; but the captain of an interstellar liner, a prize too valuable to men who have not yet reached beyond the moon.

And I had been the last to know it. Too late, Frazer.

"Captain," I said. "Not crew."

"Pity. A crewman would know more about how to put a ship together. Frazer, how big a crew are you equipped to rule?"

"Eight and five."

"Thirteen?"

"Yes."

"Then why did you say eight and five?"

The question caught me off balance. Hadn't I . . . ? Oh. "That's the Monk numbering system. Base eight. Actually, base two, but they group the digits in threes to get base eight."

"Base two. Computer numbers."

"Are they?"

"Yes. Frazer, they must have been using computers for a long time. Aeons."

"All right." I noticed for the first time that Louise had collected our glasses and gone to make fresh drinks. Good. I could use one. She'd left her own, which was half full. Knowing she wouldn't mind, I took a swallow.

It was soda water.

With a lime in it. It had looked just like our gin-and-tonics. She must be back on the diet. Except that when Louise resumed a diet, she generally announced it to all and sundry . . .

Morris was still on the subject. "You use a crew of thirteen. Are they Monk or human or something else?"

"Monk," I said without having to think.

"Too bad. Are there humans in space?"

"No. A lot of two-feet, but none of them are like any of the others, and none of them are quite like us."

Louise came back with our drinks, gave them to us, and sat down without a word.

"You said earlier that a species that can't develop space flight is no better than animals."

"According to the Monks," I reminded him.

"Right. It seems a little extreme even to me, but let it pass. What about a race that develops space flight and then loses it?"

"It happens. There are lots of ways a space-going species can revert to animal. Atomic war. Or they just can't live with the complexity. Or they breed themselves out of food, and the world famine wrecks everything. Or waste products from the new machinery ruins the ecology."

" 'Revert to animal.' All right. What about nations? Suppose you have two nations next door, same species, but one has space flight . . ."

"Right. Good point, too. Morris, there are just two countries on Earth that can deal with the Monks without dealing through the United Nations. Us, and Russia. If Rhodesia or Brazil or France tried it, they'd be publicly humiliated."

"That could cause an international incident." Morris's jaw tightened heroically. "We've got ways of passing the warning along so that it won't happen."

Louise said, "There are some countries I wouldn't mind seeing it happen to."

Morris got a thoughtful look—and I wondered if everybody would get the warning.

The cleaning team arrived then. We'd used Tip-Top Cleaners before, but these four dark women were not our usual team. We had to explain in detail just what we wanted done. Not their fault. They usually clean private homes, not bars.

Morris spent some time calling New York. He must have been using a credit card; he couldn't have that much change.

"That may have stopped a minor war," he said when he got back. And we returned to the padded booth. But Louise stayed to direct the cleaning team.

The four dark women moved about us with pails and spray bottles and dry rags, chattering in Spanish, leaving shiny surfaces wherever they went. And Morris resumed his inquisition.

"What powers the ground-to-orbit ship?"

"A slow H-bomb going off in a magnetic bottle."

"Fusion?"

"Yah. The attitude jets on the main starship use fusion power too. They all link to one magnetic bottle. I don't know just how it works. You get fuel from water or ice."

"Fusion. But don't you have to separate out the deuterium and tritium?"

"What for? You melt the ice, run a current through the water, and you've got hydrogen."

"Wow," Morris said softly. "Wow."

"The launching laser works the same way," I remembered. What else did I need to remember about launching lasers? Something dreadfully important.

"Wow. Frazer, if we could build the Monks their launching laser, we could use the same techniques to build other fusion plants. Couldn't we?"

"Sure." I was in dread. My mouth was dry, my heart was pounding. I almost knew why. "What do you mean, *if?*"

"And they'd pay us to do it! It's a damn shame. We just don't have the hardware."

"What do you mean? We've *got* to build the launching laser!"

Morris gaped. "Frazer, what's wrong with you?"

The terror had a name now. "My God! What have you told the Monks? Morris, listen to me. You've got to see to it that the Security Council promises to build the Monks' launching laser."

"Who do you think I am, the Secretary-General? We can't build it anyway, not with just Saturn launching configurations." Morris thought I'd gone mad at last. He wanted to back away through the wall of the booth.

"They'll do it when you tell them what's at stake. And we can build a launching laser, if the whole world goes in on it. Morris, look at the good it can do! Free power from seawater! And light-sails work *fine* within a system."

"Sure, it's a lovely picture. We could sail out to the moons of Jupiter and Saturn. We could smelt the asteroids for their metal ores, using laser power . . ." His eyes had momentarily taken on a vague, dreamy look. Now they snapped back to what Morris thought of as reality. "It's the kind of thing I day dreamed about when I was a kid. Someday we'll do it. Today—we just aren't ready."

"There are two sides to a coin," I said. "Now, I know how this is going to sound. Just remember there are reasons. Good reasons."

"Reasons? Reasons for what?"

"When a trading ship travels," I said, "it travels only from one civilized system to another. There are ways to tell whether a system has a civilization that can build a launching laser. Radio is one. The Earth puts out as much radio flux as a small star.

"When the Monks find that much radio energy coming from a nearby star, they send a trade ship. By the time the ship gets there, the planet that's putting out all the energy is generally civilized. But not so civilized that it can't use the knowledge a Monk trades for.

"Do you see that they *need* the launching laser? That ship out there came from a Monk colony. This far from the axis of the galaxy, the stars are too far apart. Ships launch by starlight and laser, but they brake by starlight alone, because they can't count on the target star having a launching laser. If they had to launch by starlight too, they probably wouldn't make it. A plant-and-animal cycle as small as the life-support system on a Monk starship can last only so long."

"You said yourself that the Monks can't always count on the target star staying civilized."

"No, of course not. Sometimes a civilization hits the level at which it can build a launching laser, stays there just long enough to send out a mass of radio waves, then reverts to animal. That's the point. If we tell them we can't build the laser, we'll be animals to the Monks."

"Suppose we just refuse? Not *can't* but *won't.*"

"That would be stupid. There are too many advantages. Controlled fusion . . ."

"Frazer, think about the cost." Morris looked grim. He wanted the laser. He didn't think he could get it. "Think about politicians thinking about the cost," he said. "Think about politicians thinking about explaining the cost to the taxpayers."

"Stupid," I repeated, "and inhospitable. Hospitality counts high with the Monks. You see, we're cooked either way. Either we're dumb animals, or we're guilty of a criminal breach of hospitality. And the Monk ship *still* needs more light for its light-sail than the sun can put out."

"So?"

"So the captain uses a gadget that makes the sun explode."

"The," said Morris, and "He," and "Explode?" He didn't know what to do. Then suddenly he burst out in great loud cheery guffaws, so that the women cleaning the

Long Spoon turned with answering smiles. He'd decided not to believe me.

I reached across and gently pushed his drink into his lap.

It was two-thirds empty, but it cut his laughter off in an instant. Before he could start swearing, I said, "I am not playing games. The Monks will make our sun explode if we don't build them a launching laser. Now go call your boss and tell him so."

The women were staring at us in horror. Louise started toward us, then stopped, uncertain.

Morris sounded almost calm. "Why the drink in my lap?"

"Shock treatment. And I wanted your full attention. Are you going to call New York?"

"Not yet." Morris swallowed. He looked down once at the spreading stain on his pants, then somehow put it out of his mind. "Remember, I'd have to convince him. I don't believe it myself. Nobody and nothing would blow up a sun for a breach of hospitality!"

"No, no, Morris. They have to blow up the sun to get to the next system. It's a serious thing, refusing to build the launching laser! It could wreck the *ship!*"

"Screw the ship! What about a whole planet?"

"You're just not looking at it right . . ."

"Hold it. Your ship is a trading ship, isn't it? What kind of idiots would the Monks be, to exterminate one market just to get on to the next?"

"If we can't build a launching laser, we aren't a market."

"But we might be a market on the next circuit!"

"What next circuit? You don't seem to grasp the *size* of the Monks' marketplace. The communications gap between Center and the nearest Monk colony is about . . ." I stopped to transpose . . ."sixty-four thousand years! By the time a ship finishes one circuit, most of the worlds she's visited have already forgotten her. And then what? The colony world that built her may have failed, or refitted the spaceport to service a different style of ship, or reverted to animal; even Monks do that. She'd have to go on to the next system for refitting.

"When you trade among the stars, *there is no repeat business.*"

"Oh," said Morris.

Louise had gotten the women back to work. With a

corner of my mind I heard their giggling discussion as to whether Morris would fight, whether he could whip me, etc.

Morris asked, "How does it work? How do you make a sun go nova?"

"There's a gadget the size of a locomotive fixed to the —main supporting strut, I guess you'd call it. It points straight astern, and it can swing sixteen degrees or so in any direction. You turn it on when you make departure orbit. The math man works out the intensity. You beam the sun for the first year or so, and when it blows, you're just far enough away to use the push without getting burned."

"But how does it work?"

"You just turn it on. The power comes from the fusion tube that feeds the attitude jet system . . . . Oh, you want to know why does it make a sun explode. I don't know that. Why should I?"

"Big as a locomotive. And it makes suns explode." Morris sounded slightly hysterical. Poor bastard, he was beginning to believe me. The shock had hardly touched me, because truly I had known it since last night.

He said, "When we first saw the Monk light-sail, it was just to one side of a recent nova in Sagittarius. By any wild chance, was that star a market that didn't work out?"

"I haven't the vaguest idea."

That convinced him. If I'd been making it up, I'd have said yes. Morris stood up and walked away without a word. He stopped to pick up a bar towel on his way to the phone booth.

I went behind the bar to make a fresh drink. Cutty over ice, splash of soda; I wanted to taste the burning power of it.

Through the glass door I saw Louise getting out of her car with her arms full of packages. I poured soda over ice, squeezed a lime in it, and had it ready when she walked in.

She dumped the load on the bar top. "Irish coffee makings," she said. I held the glass out to her and she said, "No thanks, Ed. One's enough."

"Taste it."

She gave me a funny look, but she tasted what I handed her. "Soda water. Well, you caught me."

"Back on the diet?"

"Yes."

"You never said *yes* to that question in your life. Don't you want to tell me all the details?"

She sipped at her drink. "Details of someone else's diet are boring. I should have known that a long time ago. To work! You'll notice we've only got twenty minutes."

I opened one of her paper bags and fed the refrigerator with cartons of whipping cream. Another bag held perking coffee. The flat, square package had to be a pizza.

"Pizza. Some diet," I said.

She was setting out the percolators. "That's for you and Bill."

I tore open the paper and bit into a pie-shaped slice. It was a deluxe, covered with everything from anchovies to salami. It was crisp and hot, and I was starving.

I snatched bites as I worked.

There aren't many bars that will keep the makings for Irish coffee handy. It's too much trouble. You need massive quantities of whipping cream and ground coffee, a refrigerator, a blender, a supply of those glass figure-eight-shaped coffee perkers, a line of hot plates, and—most expensive of all—room behind the bar for all of that. You learn to keep a line of glasses ready, which means putting the sugar in them at spare moments to save time later. Those spare moments are your smoking time, so you give that up. You learn not to wave your arms around because there are hot things that can burn you. You learn to half-whip the cream, a mere spin of the blender because you have to do it over and over again, and if you overdo it the cream turns to butter.

There aren't many bars that will go to all that trouble. That's why it pays off. Your average Irish coffee addict will drive an extra twenty minutes to reach the Long Spoon. He'll also down the drink in about five minutes, because otherwise it gets cold. He'd have spent half an hour over a Scotch and soda.

While we were getting the coffee ready, I found time to ask, "Have you remembered anything?"

"Yes," she said.

"Tell me."

"I don't mean I know what was in the pill. Just—I can do things I couldn't do before. I think my way of thinking has changed. Ed, I'm worried."

"Worried?"

She got the words out in a rush. "It feels like I've been falling in love with you for a very long time. But I haven't. Why should I feel that way so suddenly?"

The bottom dropped out of my stomach. I'd had thoughts like this—and put them out of my mind, and when they came back I did it again. I couldn't afford to fall in love. It would cost too much. It would hurt too much.

"It's been like this all day. It scares me, Ed. Suppose I feel like this about every man? What if the Monk thought I'd make a good call girl?"

I laughed much harder than I should have. Louise was getting really angry before I was able to stop.

"Wait a minute," I said. "Are you in love with Bill Morris too?"

"No, of course not!"

"Then forget the call girl bit. He's got more money than I do. A call girl would love him more, if she loved anyone, which she wouldn't, because call girls are generally frigid."

"How do you know?" she demanded.

"I read it in a magazine."

Louise began to relax. I began to see how tense she really had been. "All right," she said, "but that means I really am in love with you."

I pushed the crisis away from us. "Why didn't you ever get married?"

"Oh . . ." She was going to pass it off, but she changed her mind. "Every man I dated wanted to sleep with me. I thought that was wrong, so . . ."

She looked puzzled. "Why did I think that was wrong?"

"Way you were brought up."

"Yes, but . . ." She trailed off.

"How do you feel about it now?"

"Well, I wouldn't sleep with *any*one, but if a man was worth dating he might be worth marrying, and if he was worth marrying he'd certainly be worth sleeping with, wouldn't he? And I'd be crazy to marry someone I hadn't slept with, wouldn't I?"

"I did."

"And look how that turned out! Oh, Ed, I'm sorry. But you did bring it up."

"Yah," I said, breathing shallow.

"But I used to feel that way too. Something's changed."

We hadn't been talking fast. There had been pauses,

gaps, and we had worked through them. I had had time to eat three slices of pizza. Louise had had time to wrestle with her conscience, lose, and eat one.

Only she hadn't done it. There was the pizza, staring at her, and she hadn't given it a look or a smell. For Louise, that was unusual.

Half-joking, I said, "Try this as a theory. Years ago you must have sublimated your sex urge into an urge for food. Either that or the rest of us sublimated our appetites into a sex urge, and you didn't."

"Then the pill un-sublimated me, hmm?" She looked thoughtfully at the pizza. Clearly its lure was gone. "That's what I mean. I didn't used to be able to out-stare a pizza."

"Those olive eyes."

"Hypnotic, they were."

"A good call girl should be able to keep herself in shape." Immediately I regretted saying it. It wasn't funny. "Sorry," I said.

"It's all right." She picked up a tray of candles in red glass vases and moved away, depositing the candles on the small square tables. She moved with grace and beauty through the twilight of the Long Spoon, her hips swaying just enough to avoid the sharp corners of tables.

I'd hurt her. But she'd known me long enough; she must know I had foot-in-mouth disease . . .

I had seen Louise before and known that she was beautiful. But it seemed to me that she had never been beautiful with so little excuse.

She moved back by the same route, lighting the candles as she went. Finally she put the tray down, leaned across the bar and said, "I'm sorry. I can't joke about it when I don't *know*."

"Stop worrying, will you? Whatever the Monk fed you, he was trying to help you."

"I love you."

"What?"

"I love you."

"Okay. I love you too." I use those words so seldom that they clog in my throat, as if I'm lying, even when it's the truth. "Listen, I want to marry you. Don't shake your head. I want to marry you."

Our voices had dropped to whispers. In a tormented whisper, then, she said, "Not until I find out what I *do*, what was in the *pill*. Ed, I can't trust myself until then!"

"Me too," I said with great reluctance. "But we can't wait. We don't have time."

"What?"

"That's right, you weren't in earshot. Sometime between three and ten years from now, Monks may blow up our sun."

Louise said nothing. Her forehead wrinkled.

"It depends on how much time they spend trading. If we can't build them the launching laser, we can still con them into waiting for awhile, Monk expeditions have waited as long as . . ."

"Good Lord. You mean it. Is that what you and Bill were fighting over?"

"Yah."

Louise shuddered. Even in the dimness I saw how pale she had become. And she said a strange thing.

She said, "All right, I'll marry you."

"Good," I said. But I was suddenly shaking. Married. Again. Me. Louise stepped up and put her hands on my shoulders, and I kissed her.

I'd been wanting to do that for—five years? She fitted wonderfully into my arms. Her hands closed hard on the muscles of my shoulders, massaging. The tension went out of me, drained away somewhere. Married. Us. At least we could have three to ten years.

"Morris," I said.

She drew back a little. "He can't hold you. You haven't done anything. Oh, I *wish* I knew what was in that pill I took! Suppose I'm the trained assassin?"

"Suppose I am? We'll have to be careful of each other."

"Oh, we know all about you. You're a starship commander, an alien teleport, and a translator for Monks."

"And one thing more. There was a fourth profession. I took four pills last night, not three."

"Oh? Why didn't you tell Bill?"

"Are you kidding? Dizzy as I was last night, I probably took a course in how to lead a successful revolution. God help me if Morris found *that* out."

She smiled. "Do you really think that was what it was?"

"No, of course not."

"Why did we do it? Why did we swallow those pills? We should have known better."

"Maybe the Monk took a pill himself. Maybe there's

a pill that teaches a Monk how to look trustworthy to a generalized alien."

"I did trust him," said Louise. "I remember. He seemed so sympathetic. Would he really blow up our sun?"

"He really would."

"That fourth pill. Maybe it taught you a way to stop him."

"Let's see. We know I took a linguistics course, a course in teleportation for Martians, and a course in how to fly a light-sail ship. On that basis . . . I probably changed my mind and took a karate course for worms."

"It wouldn't hurt you, at least. Relax. . . . Ed, if you remember taking the pills, why don't you remember what was in them?"

"But I don't. I don't remember anything."

"How do you know you took four, then?"

"Here." I reached in my pocket and pulled out the scrap of Monk cellophane. And knew immediately that there was something in it. Something hard and round.

We were staring at it when Morris came back.

"I must have cleverly put it in my pocket," I told them. "Sometime last night, when I was feeling sneaky enough to steal from a Monk."

Morris turned the pill like a precious jewel in his fingers. Pale blue it was, marked on one side with a burnt orange triangle. "I don't know whether to get it analyzed or take it myself, now. We need a miracle. Maybe this will tell us—"

"Forget it. I wasn't clever enough to remember how fast a Monk pill deteriorates. The wrapping's torn. That pill has been bad for at least twelve hours."

Morris said a dirty thing.

"Analyze it," I said. "You'll find RNA, and you may even be able to tell what the Monks use as a matrix. Most of the memories are probably intact. But don't swallow the damn thing. It'll scramble your brains. All it takes is a few random changes in a tiny percentage of the RNA."

"We don't have time to send it to Douglass tonight. Can we put it in the freezer?"

"Good. Give it here."

I dropped the pill in a sandwich-size plastic Baggie, sucked the air out the top, tied the end, and dropped it in the freezer. Vacuum and cold would help preserve the thing. It was something I should have done last night.

"So much for miracles," Morris said bitterly. "Let's get

down to business. We'll have several men outside the place tonight, and a few more in here. You won't know who they are, but go ahead and guess if you like. A lot of your customers will be turned away tonight. They'll be told to watch the newspapers if they want to know why. I hope it won't cost you too much business."

"It may make our fortune. We'll be famous. Were you maybe doing the same thing last night?"

"Yes. We didn't want the place too crowded. The Monks might not like autograph hounds."

"So that's why the place was half empty."

Morris looked at his watch. "Opening time. Are we ready?"

"Take a seat at the bar. And look nonchalant, dammit."

Louise went to turn on the lights.

Morris took a seat to one side of the middle. One big square hand was closed very tightly on the bar edge. "Another gin-and-tonic. Weak. After that one, leave out the gin."

"Right."

"Nonchalant. Why should I be nonchalant? Frazer, I had to tell the President of the United States of America that the end of the world is coming unless he does something. I had to talk to him myself!"

"Did he buy it?"

"I hope so. He was so goddam calm and reassuring, I wanted to scream at him. God, Frazer, what if we can't build the laser? What if we try and fail?"

I gave him a very old and classic answer. "Stupidity is always a capital crime."

He screamed in my face. "Damn you and your supercilious attitude and your murdering monsters too!" The next second he was ice-water clam. "Never mind, Frazer. You're thinking like a starship captain."

"I'm what?"

"A starship captain has to be able to make a sun go nova to save the ship. You can't help it. It was in the pill."

Damn, he was right. I could *feel* that he was right. The pill had warped my way of thinking. Blowing up the sun that warms another race *had* to be immoral. Didn't it?

I couldn't trust my own sense of right and wrong!

Four men came in and took one of the bigger tables. Morris's men? No. Real estate men, here to do business.

"Something's been bothering me," said Morris. He

grimaced. "Among all the things that have been ruining my composure, such as the impending end of the world, there was one thing that kept nagging at me."

I set his gin-and-tonic in front of him. He tasted it and said, "Fine. And I finally realized what it was, waiting there in the phone booth for a chain of human snails to put the President on. Frazer, are you a college man?"

"No. Webster High."

"See, you don't really talk like a bartender. You use big words."

"I do?"

"Sometimes. And you talked about 'suns exploding,' but you knew what I meant when I said 'nova.' You talked about 'H-bomb power,' but you knew what fusion was."

"Sure."

"I got the possibly silly impression that you were learning the words the instant I said them. *Parlez-vous français?*"

"No. I don't speak any foreign languages."

"None at all?"

"Nope. What do you think they teach at Webster High?"

"*Je parle la langue un peu*, Frazer. *Et tu?*"

"*Merde de cochon!* Morris, *je vous dit*—oops."

He didn't give me a chance to think it over. He said, "What's fanac?"

My head had that *clogged* feeling again. I said, "Might be anything. Putting out a zine, writing to the lettercol, helping put on a Con—Morris, what *is* this?"

"That language course was more extensive than we thought."

"Sure as hell, it was. I just remembered. Those women on the cleaning team were speaking Spanish, but I understood them."

"Spanish, French, Monkish, technical languages, even fannish. What you got was a generalized course in how to understand languages the instant you hear them. I don't see how it could work without telepathy."

"Reading minds? Maybe." Several times today, it had felt like I was guessing with too much certainty at somebody's private thoughts.

"Can you read *my* mind?"

"That's not quite it. I get the feel of *how* you think, not *what* you're thinking. Morris, I don't like the idea of being a political prisoner."

"Well, we can talk that over later." *When my bargaining position is better,* Morris meant. *When I don't need the bartender's goodwill to con the Monk.* "What's important is that you might be able to read a Monk's mind. That could be crucial."

"And maybe he can read mine. And yours."

I let Morris sweat over that one while I set drinks on Louise's tray. Already there were customers at four tables. The Long Spoon was filling rapidly; and only two of them were Secret Service.

Morris said, "Any ideas on what Louise Schu ate last night? We've got *your* professions pretty well pegged down. Finally."

"I've got an idea. It's kind of vague." I looked around. Louise was taking more orders. "Sheer guesswork, in fact. Will you keep it to yourself for awhile?"

"Don't tell Louise? Sure—for awhile."

I made four drinks and Louise took them away. I told Morris, "I have a profession in mind. It doesn't have a simple one- or two-word name, like teleport or starship captain or translator. There's no reason why it should, is there? We're dealing with aliens."

Morris sipped at his drink. Waiting.

"Being a woman," I said, "can be a profession, in a way that being a man can never be. The word is *housewife,* but it doesn't cover all of it. Not nearly."

"Housewife. You're putting me on."

"No. You wouldn't notice the change. You never saw her before last night."

"Just what kind of change have you got in mind? Aside from the fact that she's beautiful, which I did notice."

"Yes, she is, Morris. But last night she was twenty pounds overweight. Do you think she lost it all this morning?"

"She *was* too heavy. Pretty, but also pretty well padded." Morris turned to look over his shoulder, casually turned back. "Damn. She's still well padded. Why didn't I notice before?"

"There's another thing. By the way. Have some pizza."

"Thanks." He bit into a slice. "Good, it's still hot. Well?"

"She's been staring at that pizza for half an hour. She bought it. But she hasn't tasted it. She couldn't possibly have done that yesterday."

"She may have had a big breakfast."

"Yah." I knew she hadn't. She'd eaten diet food. For years she'd kept a growing collection of diet food, but she'd never actively tried to survive on it before. But how could I make such a claim to Morris? I'd never even been in Louise's apartment.

"Anything else?"

"She's gotten good at nonverbal communication. It's a very womanly skill. She can say things just by the tone of her voice or the way she leans on an elbow or . . ."

"But if mind reading is one of *your* new skills . . ."

"Damn. Well—it used to make Louise nervous if someone touched her. And she never touched anyone else." I felt myself flushing. I don't talk easily of personal things.

Morris radiated skepticism. "It all sounds very subjective. In fact, it sounds like you're making yourself believe it. Frazer, why would Louise Schu want such a capsule course? Because you haven't described a housewife at all. You've described a woman looking to persuade a man to marry her." He saw my face change. "What's wrong?"

"Ten minutes ago we decided to get married."

"Congratulations," Morris said, and waited.

"All right, you win. Until ten minutes ago we'd never even kissed. I'd never made a pass, or vice versa. No, damn it, I don't believe it! I *know* she loves me; I ought to!"

"I don't deny it," Morris said quietly. "That would be why she took the pill. It must have been strong stuff, too, Frazer. We looked up some of your history. You're marriage-shy."

It was true enough. I said, "If she loved me before, I never knew it. I wonder how a Monk could know."

"How would he know about such a skill at all? Why would he have the pill on him? Come on, Frazer, you're the Monk expert!"

"He'd have to learn from human beings. Maybe by interviews, maybe by—well, the Monks can map an alien memory into a computer space, then interview that. They may have done that with some of your diplomats."

"Oh, *great*."

Louise appeared with an order. I made the drinks and set them on her tray. She winked and walked away, swaying deliciously, followed by many eyes.

"Morris. Most of your diplomats, the ones who deal with the Monks, they're men, aren't they?"

"Most of them. Why?"

"Just a thought."

It was a difficult thought, hard to grasp. It was only that the changes in Louise had been all to the good from a man's point of view. The Monks must have interviewed many men. Well, why not? It would make her more valuable to the man she caught—or to the lucky man who caught her . . .

"Got it."

Morris looked up quickly. "Well?"

"Falling in love with me was part of her pill learning. A *set*. They made a guinea pig of her."

"I wondered what she saw in you." Morris's grin faded. "You're serious. Frazer, that still doesn't answer . . ."

"It's a slave indoctrination course. It makes a woman love the first man she sees, permanently, and it trains her to be valuable to him. The Monks were going to make them in quantity and sell them to men."

Morris thought it over. Presently he said, "That's awful. What'll we do?"

"Well, we can't tell her she's been made into a domestic slave! Morris, I'll try to get a memory eraser pill. If I can't—I'll marry her, I guess. Don't look at me that way," I said, low and fierce. "I didn't do it. And I can't desert her now!"

"I know. It's just—oh, put gin in the next one."

"Don't look now," I said.

In the glass of the door there was darkness and motion. A hooded shape, shadow-on-shadow, supernatural, a human silhouette twisted out of true . . .

He came gliding in with the hem of his robe just brushing the floor. Nothing was to be seen of him but his flowing gray robe, the darkness in the hood, and the shadow where his robe parted. The real estate men broke off their talk of land and stared, popeyed, and one of them reached for his heart attack pills.

The Monk drifted toward me like a vengeful ghost. He took the stool we had saved him at one end of the bar.

It wasn't the same Monk.

In all respects he matched the Monk who had been here the last two nights. Louise and Morris must have been fooled completely. But it wasn't the same Monk.

"Good evening," I said.

He gave an equivalent greeting in the whispered Monk language. His translator was half on, translating my words into a Monk whisper, but letting his own speech alone. He said, "I believe we should begin with the Rock and Rye."

I turned to pour. The small of my back itched with danger.

When I turned back with the shot glass in my hand, he was holding a fist-sized tool that must have come out of his robe. It looked like a flattened softball, grooved deeply for five Monk claws, with two parallel tubes poking out in my direction. Lenses glinted in the ends of the tubes.

"Do you know this tool? It is a . . ." and he named it.

I knew the name. It was a beaming tool, a multi-frequency laser. One tube locked on the target; thereafter the aim was maintained by tiny flywheels in the body of the device.

Morris had seen it. He didn't recognize it, and he didn't know what to do about it, and I had no way to signal him.

"I know that tool," I confirmed.

"You must take two of these pills." The Monk had them ready in another hand. They were small and pink and triangular. He said, "I must be convinced that you have taken them. Otherwise you must take more than two. An overdose may affect your natural memory. Come closer."

I came closer. Every man and woman in the Long Spoon was staring at us, and each was afraid to move. Any kind of signal would have trained four guns on the Monk. And I'd be fried dead by a narrow beam of X rays.

The Monk reached out with a third hand/foot/claw. He closed the fingers/toes around my throat, not hard enough to strangle me, but hard enough.

Morris was cursing silently, helplessly. I could feel the agony in his soul.

The Monk whispered, "You know of the trigger mechanism. If my hand should relax now, the device will fire. Its target is yourself. If you can prevent four government agents from attacking me, you should do so."

I made a palm-up gesture toward Morris. *Don't do anything.* He caught it and nodded very slightly without looking at me.

"You can read minds," I said.

"Yes," said the Monk—and I knew instantly, what he was hiding. He could read everybody's mind, except mine.

So much for Morris's little games of deceit. But the

Monk could not read my mind, and I could see into his own soul.

And, reading his alien soul, I saw that I would die if I did not swallow the pills.

I placed the pink pills on my tongue, one at a time, and swallowed them dry. They went down hard. Morris watched it happen and could do nothing. The Monk felt them going down my throat, little lumps moving past his finger.

And when the pills had passed across the Monk's finger, I worked a miracle.

"Your pill-induced memories and skills will be gone within two hours," said the Monk. He picked up the shot glass of Rock and Rye and moved it into his hood. When it reappeared it was half empty.

I asked, "Why have you robbed me of my knowledge?"

"You never paid for it."

"But it was freely given."

"It was given by one who had no right," said the Monk. He was thinking about leaving. I had to do something. I knew now, because I had reasoned it out with great care, that the Monk was involved in an evil enterprise. But he must stay to hear me or I could not convince him.

Even then, it wouldn't be easy. He was a Monk crewman. His ethical attitudes had entered his brain through an RNA pill, along with his professional skills.

"You have spoken of rights," I said. In Monk. "Let us discuss rights." The whispery words buzzed oddly in my throat; they tickled; but my ears told me they were coming out right.

The Monk was startled. "I was told that you had been taught our speech, but not that you could speak it."

"Were you told what pill I was given?"

"A language pill. I had not known that he carried one in his case."

"He did not finish his tasting of the alcohols of Earth. Will you have another drink?"

I felt him guess at my motives, and guess wrong. He thought I was taking advantage of his curiosity to sell him my wares for cash. And what had he to fear from me? Whatever mental powers I had learned from Monk pills, they would be gone in two hours.

I set a shot glass before him. I asked him, "How do you feel about launching lasers?"

The discussion became highly technical. "Let us take a special case," I remember saying. "Suppose a culture has been capable of star flight for some sixty-fours of years— or even for eights of times that long. Then an asteroid slams into a major ocean, precipitates an ice age . . ." It had happened once, and well he knew it. "A natural disaster can't spell the difference between sentience and non-sentience, can it? Not unless it affects brain tissue directly."

At first it was his curiosity that held him. Later it was me. He couldn't tear himself loose. He never thought of it. He was a sailship crewman, and he was cold sober, and he argued with the frenzy of an evangelist.

"Then take the general case," I remember saying. "A world that cannot build a launching laser is a world of animals, yes? And Monks themselves can revert to animal."

Yes, he knew that.

"Then build your own launching laser. If you cannot, then your ship is captained and crewed by animals."

At the end I was doing all the talking. All in the whispery Monk tongue, whose sounds are so easily distinguished that even I, warping a human throat to my will, need only whisper. It was a good thing. I seemed to have been eating used razor blades.

Morris guessed right. He did not interfere. I could tell him nothing, not if I had had the power, not by word or gesture or mental contact. The Monk would read Morris's mind. But Morris sat quietly drinking his tonic-and-tonics, waiting for something to happen. While I argued in whispers with the Monk.

"But the ship!" he whispered. "What of the ship?" His agony was mine; for the ship must be protected . . .

At one fifteen the Monk had progressed halfway across the bottom row of bottles. He slid from the stool, paid for his drinks in one-dollar bills, and drifted to the door and out.

All he needed was a scythe and hourglass, I thought, watching him go. And what I needed was a long morning's sleep. And I wasn't going to get it.

"Be sure nobody stops him," I told Morris.

"Nobody will. But he'll be followed."

"No point. The Garment to Wear Among Strangers is a lot of things. It's bracing; it helps the Monk hold human shape. It's a shield and an air filter. And it's a cloak of invisibility."

"Oh?"

"I'll tell you about it if I have time. That's how he got out here, probably. One of the crewmen divided, and then one stayed and one walked. He had two weeks."

Morris stood up and tore off his sport jacket. His shirt was wet through. He said, "What about a stomach pump for you?"

"No good. Most of the RNA-enzyme must be in my blood by now. You'll be better off if you spend your time getting down everything I can remember about Monks, while I can remember anything at all. It'll be nine or ten hours before everything goes." Which was a flat-out lie, of course.

"Okay. Let me get the dictaphone going again."

"It'll cost you money."

Morris suddenly had a hard look. "Oh? How much?"

I'd thought about that most carefully. "One hundred thousand dollars. And if you're thinking of arguing me down, remember whose time we're wasting."

"I wasn't." He was, but he'd changed his mind.

"Good. We'll transfer the money now, while I can still read your mind."

"All right."

He offered to make room for me in the booth, but I declined. The glass wouldn't stop me from reading Mor-ris's soul.

He came out silent; for there was something he was afraid to know. Then: "What about the Monks? What about our sun?"

"I talked that one around. That's why I don't want him molested. He'll convince others."

"Talked him around? How?"

"It wasn't easy." And suddenly I would have given my soul to sleep. "The profession pill put it in his genes; he must protect the ship. It's in me too. I know how strong it is."

"Then . . ."

"Don't be an ass, Morris. The ship's perfectly safe where it is, in orbit around the moon. A sailship's only in danger when it's between stars, far from help."

"Oh."

"Not that that convinced him. It only let him consider the ethics of the situation rationally."

"Suppose someone else unconvinces him?"

"It could happen. That's why we'd better build the launching laser."

Morris nodded unhappily.

The next twelve hours were rough.

In the first four hours I gave them everything I could remember about the Monk teleport system, Monk technology, Monk family life, Monk ethics, relations between Monks and aliens, details on aliens, directions of various inhabited and uninhabited worlds—everything. Morris and the Secret Service men who had been posing as customers sat around me like boys around a campfire, listening to stories. But Louise made us fresh coffee, then went to sleep in one of the booths.

Then I let myself slack off.

By nine in the morning I was flat on my back, staring at the ceiling, dictating a random useless bit of information every thirty seconds or so. By eleven there was a great black pool of lukewarm coffee inside me, my eyes ached marginally more than the rest of me, and I was producing nothing.

I was convincing, and I knew it.

But Morris wouldn't let it go at that. He believed me. I felt him believing me. But he was going through the routine anyway, because it couldn't hurt. If I was useless to him, if I knew nothing, there was no point in playing soft. What could he lose?

He accused me of making everything up. He accused me of faking the pills. He made me sit up, and damn near caught me that way. He used obscure words and phrases from mathematics and Latin and fan vocabulary. He got nowhere. There wasn't any way to trick me.

At two in the afternoon he had someone drive me home.

Every muscle in me ached; but I had to fight to maintain my exhausted slump. Else my hindbrain would have lifted me onto my toes and poised me against a possible shift in artificial gravity. The strain was double, and it hurt. It had hurt for hours, sitting with my shoulders hunched and my head hanging. But now—if Morris saw me walking like a trampoline performer . . .

Morris's man got me to my room and left me.

I woke in darkness and sensed someone in my room. Someone who meant me no harm. In fact, Louise. I went back to sleep.

I woke again at dawn. Louise was in my easy chair, her feet propped on a corner of the bed. Her eyes were open. She said, "Breakfast?"

I said, "Yah. There isn't much in the fridge."

"I brought things."

"All right." I closed my eyes.

Five minutes later I decided I was all slept out. I got up and went to see how she was doing.

There was bacon frying, there was bread already buttered for toasting in the Toast-R-Oven, there was a pan hot for eggs, and the eggs scrambled in a bowl. Louise was filling the percolator.

"Give that here a minute," I said. It only had water in it. I held the pot in my hands, closed my eyes and tried to remember . . .

Ah.

I knew I'd done it right even before the heat touched my hands. The pot held hot, fragrant coffee.

"We were wrong about the first pill," I told Louise. She was looking at me very curiously. "What happened that second night was this. The Monk had a translator gadget, but he wasn't too happy with it. It kept screaming in his ear. Screaming English, too loud, for my benefit.

"He could turn off the part that was shouting English at me, and it would still whisper a Monk translation of what *I* was saying. But first he had to teach me the Monk language. He didn't have a pill to do that. He didn't have a generalized language-learning course either, if there is one, which I doubt.

"He was pretty drunk, but he found something that would serve. The profession it taught me was an old one, and it doesn't have a one- or two-word name. But if it did, the word would be *prophet!*"

"Prophet," said Louise. "Prophet?" She was doing a remarkable thing. She was listening with all her concentration, and scrambling eggs at the same time.

"Or disciple. Maybe *apostle* comes closer. Anyway, it included the Gift of Tongues, which was what the Monk was after. But it included other talents too."

"Like turning cold water into hot coffee?"

"Miracles, right. I used the same talent to make the

little pink amnesia pills disappear before they hit my stomach. But an apostle's major talent is persuasion.

"Last night I convinced a Monk crewman that blowing up suns is an evil thing.

"Morris is afraid that someone might convert him back. I don't think that's possible. The mind-reading talent that goes with the prophet pill goes deeper than just reading minds. I read souls. The Monk is my apostle. Maybe he'll convince the whole crew that I'm right.

"Or he may just curse the *hachiroph shisp,* the little old nova maker. Which is what I intend to do."

"Curse it?"

"Do you think I'm kidding or something?"

"Oh, no." She poured our coffee. "Will that stop it working?"

"Yes."

"Good," said Louise. And I felt the power of her own faith, her faith in me. It gave her the serenity of an idealized nun.

When she turned back to serve the eggs, I dropped a pink triangular pill in her coffee.

She finished setting breakfast and we sat down. Louise said, "Then that's it. It's all over."

"All over." I swallowed some orange juice. Wonderful, what fourteen hours' sleep will do for a man's appetite. "All over. I can go back to my fourth profession, the only one that counts."

She looked up quickly.

"Bartender. First, last, and foremost, I'm a bartender. You're going to marry a bartender."

"Good," she said, relaxing.

In two hours or so the slave sets would be gone from her mind. She would be herself again: free, independent, unable to diet, and somewhat shy.

But the pink pill would not destroy real memories. Two hours from now, Louise would still know that I loved her, and perhaps she would marry me after all.

I said, "We'll have to hire an assistant. And raise our prices. They'll be fighting their way in when the story gets out."

Louise had pursued her own thoughts. "Bill Morris looked awful when I left. You ought to tell him he can stop worrying."

"Oh, no. I *want* him scared. Morris has got to talk the rest of the world into building a launching laser, instead of just throwing bombs at the Monk ship. And we *need* the launching laser."

"Mmm! That's good coffee. Why do we need a launching laser?"

"To get to the stars."

"That's Morris's bag. You're a bartender, remember? The fourth profession."

I shook my head. "You and Morris. You don't see how *big* the Monk marketplace is, or how thin the Monks are scattered. How many novas have you seen in your lifetime?

"Damn few," I said. "There are damn few trading ships in a godawful lot of sky. There are things out there besides Monks. Things the Monks are afraid of, and probably others they don't know about.

"Things so dangerous that the only protection is to be somewhere else, circling some other star, when it happens here! The Monk drive is our lifeline and our immortality. It would be cheap at any price . . ."

"Your eyes are glowing," she breathed. She looked half hypnotized, and utterly convinced. And I knew that for the rest of my life, I would have to keep a tight rein on my tendency to preach.

GLEEPSITE

JOANNA RUSS

After you have read this story, read it over again, and perhaps read it a third time. Then, like the editor, you may find that you will see things here you did not notice before. This short tale is like an exquisitely designed miniaturization—it contains a great deal in a small space. We still do not know the meaning of the title, though.

I try to make my sales at night during the night shift in office buildings; it works better that way. Resistance- is gone at night. The lobbies are deserted, the air filters on half power; here and there a woman stays up late amid piles of paper; things blow down the halls just out of the range of vision of the watch-ladies who turn their keys in the doors of unused rooms, who insert the keys hanging from chains around their necks in the apertures of empty clocks, or polish with their polishing rags the surfaces of desks, the bare tops of tables. You make some astonishing sales that way.

I came up my thirty floors and found on the thirty-first Kira and Lira, the only night staff: two fiftyish identical twins in the same gray cardigan sweaters, the same pink dresses, the same blue rinse on their gray sausage-curls. But Kira wore on her blouse (over the name tag) the emblem of the senior secretary, the Tree of Life pin with the cultured pearl, while Lira went without, so I addressed myself to the (minutes-) younger sister.

"We're closed," they said.

Nevertheless, knowing that they worked at night, knowing that they worked for a travel agency whose hints of imaginary faraway places (Honolulu, Hawaii—they don't exist) must eventually exacerbate the longings of even the most passive sister, I addressed myself to them again, standing in front of the semicircular partition over which they peered (alarmed but bland), keeping my gaze on the sans-serif script over the desk—or is it roses!—and avoiding very carefully any glance at the polarized vitryl panels beyond which rages hell's own stew of hot winds and sulfuric acid, it gets worse and worse. I don't like false marble floors, so I changed it.

Ladies.

"We're closed!" cried Miss Lira.

Here I usually make some little illusion so they will know who I am; I stopped Miss Kira from pressing the safety button, which always hangs on the wall, and made appear beyond the nearest vitryl panel a bat's face as big as a man's: protruding muzzle, pointed fangs, cocked ears, and rats' shiny eyes, here and gone. I snapped my fingers and the wind tore it off.

No, no, no, no! cried the sisters.

May I call you Flora and Dora? I said. *Flora and Dora in memory of that glorious time centuries past when ladies like yourselves danced on tables to the applause of admiring gentlemen, when ladies wore, like yourselves, scarlet petticoats, ruby stomachers, chokers and bibs of red velvet, pearls and maroon high-heeled boots, though they did not always keep their petticoats decorously about their ankles.*

What you have just seen, ladies, is a small demonstration of the power of electrical brain stimulation—mine, in this case—and the field which transmitted it to you was generated by the booster I wear about my neck, metallic in this case, though they come in other colors, and tuned to the frequency of the apparatus which I wear in this ring. You will notice that it is inconspicuous and well designed. I am allowed to wear the booster only at work. In the year blank-blank, when the great neurosurgical genius, Blank, working with Blank and Blank, discovered in the human forebrain what has been so poetically termed the Circle of Illusion, it occurred to another great innova-

*tor, Blank, whom you know, to combine these two great
discoveries, resulting in a Device that has proved to be of
inestimable benefit to the human race. (We just call it the
Device.) Why not, thought Blank, employ the common,
everyday power of electricity for the stimulation, the
energization, the concretization of the Center of Illusion
or (to put it bluntly) an* aide-mémoire, *crutch, companion, and record-keeping book for that universal human
talent, daydreaming? Do you daydream, ladies? Then you
know that daydreaming is harmless. Daydreaming is vol-
untary. Day dreaming is not night dreaming. Daydreaming
is normal. It is not hallucination or delusion or deception
but creation. It is an accepted form of mild escape. No
more than in a daydream or reverie is it possible to con-
fuse the real and the ideal; try it and see. The Device
simply supplements the power of your own human brain.
If Miss Kira—*

"No, no!" cried Miss Lira, but Miss Kira had already
taken my sample ring, the setting scrambled to erase the
last customer's residual charge.

*You have the choice of ten scenes. No two persons will
see the same thing, of course, but the parameters remain
fairly constant. Further choices on request. Sound, smell,
taste, touch, and kinesthesia optional. We are strictly pro-
hibited from employing illegal settings or the use of variable condensers with fluctuating parameters. Tampering
with the machinery is punishable by law.*

"But it's so hard!" said Miss Kira in surprise. "And it's
not real at all!" That always reassures them. At first.

*It takes considerable effort to operate the Circle of
Illusion even with mechanical aid. Voltage beyond that required for threshold stimulation is banned by law; even
when employed, it does not diminish the necessity for
effort, but in fact increases it proportionately. No more
than in life, ladies, can you get something for nothing.*

Practice makes perfect.

Miss Kira, as I knew she would, had chosen a flowery
meadow with a suggestion of honeymoon; Miss Lira
chose a waterfall in a glade. Neither had put in a Man,
although an idealized figure of a Man is standard equipment for our pastoral choices (misty, idealized, in the
distance, some even see him with wings) and I don't
imagine either sister would ever get much closer.

Miss Lira said they actually had a niece who was actually married to a man.

Miss Kira said a half-niece.

Miss Lira said they had a cousin who worked in the children's nursery with real children and they had holidays coming *and if I use a variable condenser, what's it to you?*

Behind me, though I cannot imagine why, is a full-length mirror, and in this piece of inconstancy I see myself as I was when I left home tonight, or perhaps not, I don't remember: beautiful, chocolate-colored, naked, gold braided into my white hair. Behind me, bats' wings.

A mirror, ladies, produces a virtual image, and so does the Device.

Bats' faces.

Hermaphroditic.

It is no more addicting than thought.

Little snakes waving up from the counter, a forest of them. Unable to stand the sisters' eyes swimming behind their glasses, myopic Flora and Dora, I changed the office for them, gave them a rug, hung behind them on the wall original Rembrandts, made them younger, erased them, let the whole room slide, and provided for Dora a bedroom beyond the travel office, a bordello in white and gold baroque, embroidered canopy, goldfish pool, chihuahuas on the marble and bats in the belfry.

I have two heads.

Flora's quite a whore.

The younger sister, not quite willing to touch the ring again, said they'd think about it, and Kira, in a quarrel that must have gone back years, began in a low, vapid whisper—

Why, they're not bats at all, I said, over at the nearest vitryl panel; *I was mistaken,* and Lira, Don't open that! We'll suffocate!

No one who is sane, of course, opens anything any more into that hell outside, but this old, old, old place had real locks on the vitryl and real seams between, and a narrow balcony where someone had gone out perhaps fifty years ago (in a diving suit) to admire the updrafts between the dead canyons where papers danced on the driving murk and shapes fluttered between the raw lights; one could see several streets over to other spires, other shafts, the hurricane tearing through the poisoned air. Nighttime makes a kind of inferno out of this and every once in a while someone decides on a gaudy exit: the lungs eaten away, the room reeking of hydrosulfurous acid, torn paper settling on the discolored rug.

When you have traveled in the tubes as much as I have, when you have seen the playground in Antarctica time after time, when your features have melted enough between black and brown and white, man and woman, as plastic as the lazy twist of a thought, you get notions. You get ideas. I saw once in a much more elegant office building a piece of polished wood, so large, so lovely, a curve fully six feet long and so beautiful that if you could have made out of that wood an idea and out of that idea a bed, you could have slept on that bed. When you put your hand on the vitryl panels at night, the heat makes your hand sweat onto the surface; my hand's melted through many times, like oil on water. I stood before the window, twisting shapes for fun, seeing myself stand on the narrow balcony, bored with Kira and Lira, poor Kira, poor Lira, poor as-I-once-was, discussing whether they can afford it.

". . . an outlet for creativity . . ."

". . . she *said* it's only . . ."

What effort it takes, and what an athlete of illusion you become! able to descend to the bottom of the sea (where we might as well be, come to think of it), to the manless moon, to the Southern Hemisphere where the men stay, dreaming about us; but no, they did away with themselves years ago, they were inefficient, the famous Blank and Blank (both men) saw that men were inefficient and did themselves in (I mean all the men except themselves) in blank-blank. Only three percent of the population male, my word!

". . . legal . . ."

". . . never . . ."

"Don't!" cried Miss Kira.

They know what I'm going to do. Ever since I found out those weren't bats' faces. As Miss Kira and Miss Lira sign the contract (thumbsy-up, thumbsy-down) I wrench the lock off the vitryl and squeeze through, what a foul, screaming wind! shoving desperately at the panels, and stumble off the narrow, railless balcony, feeling as I go my legs contract, my fingers grow, my sternum arch like the prow of a boat, little bat-man—woman with sketchy turned-out legs and grasping toes, and hollow bones and fingers down to my ankles, a thumb-and-forefinger grasper at the end of each wing, and that massive wraparound of the huge, hollow chest, all covered with blond fur; in the middle of it all, sunk between the shoulders, is the human face. Miss Kira would faint. I would come up to Miss Lira's waist. Falling down the nasty night air until I shrug up hard, hard, hard, into a steep upward glide and ride down the currents of hell past the man-made cliff where Kira and Lira, weeping with pain, push the vitryl panel back into place. The walls inside are blackening, the fake marble floor is singed. It is comfy-cold, it is comfy-nice, I'm going to mate in midair, I'm going to give shuddering birth on the ledge of a cliff, I'm going to scream at the windows when I like. They found no corpse, no body.

Kira and Lira, mouths like O's, stare out as I climb past. They do a little dance.

> She was a Floradora baby
> With a chance to meet the best,
> But she had to go and marry Abie,
> The drummer with the fancy vest!

Tampering with the machinery is punishable by law, says Kira.

Oh my dear, we'll tinker a bit, says Lira.

And so they will.

THE BEAR WITH THE KNOT ON HIS TAIL

STEPHEN TALL

If you sit around and think about it (after reading it, we trust) you might decide that the plot of this is not unique. But you would also have to agree that the depth of feeling for the characters and the poetic undertone of this novelette of an interstellar S. O. S. raise it high above the level of the field.

We swept in comfortable wide orbit around Earth, thirty thousand miles beyond the Moon. Cap'n Jules Griffin kept us in the Moon shadow, the umbra, a pleasanter location in which to drift and listen than out in the raw yellow radiance of Sol. Only a few degrees away from the Moon's vast shadowy disc the full Earth hung like a color plate, blue, cloud-shrouded, the most majestic object I've ever seen from space.

And I've been around. We all have. It's our job.

Ultraspan made us possible. A discovery that must have been an accident—or almost. How can matter move faster than energy? Or can it? Ultraspan eliminates time; so our position in space can be anything Cap'n Jules wills it to be. Not that he understands what he does. Especially not that. He knows every pulse of the timonium engines that move us in finite space, but Ultraspan he takes on faith. Like religion. Like magic. Like the things that happen in dreams.

We've tested it. For the past nine years the research ship

Stardust has done with ease what was not possible before Willoughby's Hypothesis, that strange variant of an Einsteinian concept that divorces space from time. You don't know what I'm talking about? Neither do I—but it works. Harnessed, implemented, it's Ultraspan.

Life aboard the *Stardust* is comfortable, but for me it's not the good life. I really come alive when we drop in, break out of orbit, and drift down to the surface of some unknown world, some planet that from space shows that it will tolerate us long enough for a look-see. And I did say drift down. The searing outpourings of combustion energy that first took us into and out of space are all a part of our history now. Gravity is no longer a problem. If the conditions required it, Cap'n Jules could bring our fifteen-hundred-foot laboratory-home down over any planet surface at ten miles an hour. We have conquered the attraction of mass for mass.

"Dreaming, Roscoe?"

I don't like to be touched or backslapped, but the hand on my shoulder now was a notable exception to that. Especially when the owner slipped around my easy chair and plumped her luscious self into my lap. I put my arms around her, and we both sat watching the wide screen on which the Earth hung in misty glory.

"The Old Homestead," Lindy said. "If I can just see it once in a while, like now, I'm perfectly content with space. But that's the ultimate, that beautiful blue-green marble out there. We can search all our lives and we'll never find anything like it."

"It's a point of view," I admitted. "Statistically, though, probably not defensible. Somewhere in our Galaxy of hundreds of millions of stars, with space only knows how many planets around them, the Earth has to have a twin. We're still babes in the cosmic woods, and already we've come close. You haven't—say you haven't!—forgotten Cyrene?"

She hadn't forgotten. How could she? And the star Cyrene was a Sol-type sun. Its yellow rays on the surface of its fourth planet could easily have been mistaken for Sol's rays. But Planet Four had had a strange and simple ecology, and life forms so different that they had made me famous. Yes, I'm that Kissinger. *A Different Evolutionary System*, by Roscoe Kissinger. The lettuce-cube-mill-wheel food chain. So now when I'm on Earth, I have to make speeches. And I don't much like to speak. I'm a field ecologist. I like to do.

But that's not why Lindy remembered Planet Four. It was there, after many invitations, that she finally decided that to be Mrs. Kissinger might be a good thing. Maybe it was the homelike atmosphere. For Planet Four of the star Cyrene *was* Earthlike.

Lindy twisted in my lap and faced me, her classic features, green eyes, and red lips not six inches from my more or less Neanderthal visage. So I did what any man in the Galaxy would have done, and when I had finished she was properly breathless.

"Necking again!" Pegleg Williams growled. He came rolling across the lounge, his slight limp accentuated. He does that when he wants to attract attention. He took the chair next ours.

"Don't you two ever fight, like normal couples? You'll both develop space diabetes, living in a sea of sugar like you do."

Lindy giggled. I kept my grin down to respectable proportions.

"You're in good form," I said. "So what's bugging you?"

Pegleg shrugged and hunched down in the chair. After a moment he waved a hand at the screen.

"Ennui!" he said. "Boredom! We've been lying doggo out here in the Moon shadow for a month. We've listened and we've listened—and if anybody has learned anything, they've carefully kept it from me!"

We're used to Pegleg. We wouldn't even like him any way but the way he is. Occasionally he'll put your teeth on edge, but whenever I undertake a field mission where the chips are really down, Pegleg's the other man. We complement each other like salt and vinegar. Pegleg's one of the great geologists—and as an ecologist, I'm not so bad. So I knew what he meant.

"Don't blame it on Mother Earth." I said. "Blame Johnny Rasmussen. He has an itch. You know that. And he's never had one yet where the scratching didn't turn out to be fun."

Pegleg sprawled deeper in the chair. Reflectively he stared at the screen and automatically flexed his plastic knee joint. He does this when he's thinking. It was while we were scratching one of Rasmussen's itches that he lost that leg, bitten off smooth by a plesiosaur-like critter in a little lagoon on a planet I'd just as soon forget. That one had been only partly fun.

But as I said, I knew what he meant. A geologist hasn't got much going for him in space. He's got to have something to set his feet on, rocks to swing his hammer against. And the ecologist is no better off. Oh, I suppose I could get concerned about the space biome. But it's not me. I need my habitats tangible, my biota solid enough to feel and see.

Lindy rolled out of my lap and stood looking down on us both.

"I think," she said casually, "that I've become supernumerary. I recognize the symptoms. You two want to sit and deplore your respective futile situations. You may forget that I, too, am temporarily unemployed."

Lindy's genius with extraterrestrial microforms is such that we wouldn't dare a landing without her. She was Dr. Linda Peterson, microbiologist extraordinary, long before she was Mrs. Roscoe Kissinger. In fact, Johnny Rasmussen has never recognized the marriage, even though he performed the ceremony. He still carries her on the roster as Dr. Peterson.

"Sit down, Lindy," Pegleg said. "We couldn't gripe with effect without you."

"No," said my gorgeous wife. "When discontent's the topic, it's still a man's world. Or should I say universe? I think I'll go run a diabetes test on myself."

Even Pegleg grinned.

But it started then, and almost unwillingly we listened. Not that it was unpleasant. It wasn't at all. It was strange, weird, haunting. The sounds came rolling out of the speakers with a curious lack of rhythm, with no pattern that could be pinned down. In fact, that was what was driving the sound boys out of their skulls.

Here were no pulsars, no monotonously repeated patterns of any of the several types of sound we're getting now from space. Here was infinite sound variety, constantly changing tone and pitch, sometimes like soft music, sometimes raucous, but with a compelling completeness, point and counterpoint. It went from laughter to pleading, from murmur to roar. And yet the overall feel of it was alien. As sophisticated and endlessly changing as it was, no one even considered that it might have human origin. It was from space, from deep space, and no tests that we had yet made could tell us even the direction from whence it came.

I say "we" because that was the way Dr. Johannes Rasmussen regarded every mission the *Stardust* undertook. Each job was a team job. Sitting out here in the Moon shadow, swinging with the Moon in its orbit around Earth, an elaborate organization of explorer specialists, Earth's finest space teams, had only one mandate, one directive. Everyone, regardless of concern or training, was asked to listen to the sounds, to the always different medley our energy dish was picking up from the great disc on the Moon.

At intervals that never varied, nineteen hours and thirteen minutes thirty-seven seconds, the cosmic broadcasts poured from the speakers. They lasted exactly fourteen minutes seven seconds. From the first decibel they had been carefully and completely recorded, and each staff member was urged, in addition to his other duties, to listen to the tapes whenever he had the chance. Since our duties were minimal, to be charitable, we had heard a lot of replays. They hadn't helped a bit.

So we listened now. Lindy dropped back into my lap, and we held hands and sat quietly while the speakers gurgled and cried and moaned.

"They're unhappy," Lindy murmured. "They're in danger and frightened and alone. They're begging for help. They're not frantic yet, but they hope we'll hear them. They know they can't help themselves."

"They?" Pegleg and I said it together.

"They!" Lindy said firmly.

" 'One giant step'," Pegleg quoted. "Have you told Johnny Rasmussen? He'll be delighted. He'll be especially interested in how you know."

Lindy gestured helplessly and squirmed on my lap.

"He'll be like you," she said in disgust. "Literal. Obtuse. But I *feel* it! That's not just contact. That's urgent contact. They need us!"

Pegleg shifted his gaze to me.

"Your wife makes a nice appearance in public, but she's subject to hallucinations. I hope it doesn't interfere with your home life."

"Helps, really," I deadpanned. "She thinks I'm handsome."

"That proves my point," Pegleg said.

If this dialogue seems out of character to you, just know

that it's the way we are. It's the smoke screen behind which we think. We've been doing it our way for years, and in general things have come out all right. See the thick sheaf of research papers under each of our names in any library worthy to be called a library. We've all got oak-leaf clusters on our Ph.D.s.

But we weren't trained for this. And the sound boys and the cryptographers and the language experts were beginning to suspect that they weren't either. Especially befuddled were the communications specialists. For the medley of sounds, picked up by the fifty-acre reception disc on the Moon as though it were originating just beyond the next hill, was directionless. After a full month of trying, they still had no clue. The great disc received the sounds equally well whether phased for north or south, east or west; whether focused critically on Polaris, Deneb or Arcturus. And we, hanging in space thirty thousand miles away, found that even their relay was hard to orient.

We listened until the end. As always, there were familiar elements in the broadcast that I felt the cryptographers should have been able to use. But each transmission was different, and since Lindy had suggested it, I fancied that the tone of each was special. Somewhere, beings with an advanced technology were telling a story to the Galaxy. Hoping, hoping, that somewhere there were beings who could hear. These were feelings, too. My feelings. Only the variety, complexity and timing of the broadcasts could be used for support for them. So I kept them to myself.

The last notes of the transmission, a plaintive, appealing series of wails, died away.

Lindy shifted in my arms. She sighed gently.

"The Music of the Spheres," she said.

Pegleg and I were silent. There was nothing to say.

Of the personnel of the *Stardust,* of all the assorted specialists that made up the Earth's most elaborate space organization, one person was never out of a job. Pegleg and I could gripe; Lindy could sigh for new space bugs; Bud Merani could fidget because there was nothing for an archaeologist to explore out there in the Moon shadow. But Ursula Potts was busy.

Ursula was nothing you'd expect to find in a starship. Little, skinny, old, with weasel features and a great bun of gray hair, she looked like her usual mode of transportation ought to be a broom. To see her strolling the corridors in sneakers, knee-length shorts of red or yellow or green, and an old gray sweater that she wore inside or out, hot planet or cold, was enough to make you wonder if it wasn't time for your annual checkup. I mean you, of course. Not us. We knew her well; knew her and respected her, and sometimes were even a little afraid of her.

Ursula painted. Painters are traditionally kooks, and Ursula abused even that privilege, but she also was a mystic —and a genius. Johnny Rasmussen spent more time looking at Ursula's paintings than he did reading my reports. And I didn't resent it. Somehow, Ursula saw things nobody else saw. She pulled together the results of a look-see.

She beckoned to me as I passed her studio door. She didn't do that to everybody. But we'd seen some strange things together, she and Lindy and Pegleg and I. She was with us at Armageddon on Cyrene Four. So I slid back the door and stepped out into the studio; out into the raw depths of space. Or so it seemed.

"What do you see, Roscoe?"

No greeting. No nothing. She didn't even wave at the big painting on her easel. But that's what she wanted me to look at. Her strange eyes were glinting in a way I recognized. Ursula was excited about something.

A big, decorated star map. That was my first impression of Ursula's painting. Not her usual thing at all. But when I looked closer, I could see what she'd done. It wasn't a star map. Actually, it was a series of isolated sketches on one canvas. They would have been familiar to any schoolchild.

The old constellations. From our position out there in the Moon shadow, they showed little distortion, and Ursula had simply noted them down, perhaps almost idly, as little dots of yellow and blue and red and white. But then she'd done more. Around the clusters she had sketched the old mythological figures, filling them in as her interest grew, supplying detail and emphasizing it with color until each sketch seemed almost alive.

Old Orion seemed just ready to step off, his club held high, his lion's skin across his shoulder, and the short blade gleaming in his belt. Behind him prowled the Greater and Lesser Dogs, tongues lolling, eyes eager. One was a German shepherd and one was a Great Dane. Pegasus swept his great wings across more than his share of the canvas as he stretched out into what seemed to be a level run, nostrils flared, foam flying from his mouth. In spite of the wings, he wouldn't have been out of place at Churchill Downs.

I chuckled as I skipped from figure to figure. They were clever, done with the technique only a great artist can command, but I couldn't see anything more. They were superficial. I enjoyed them, but that was all.

I looked at Ursula, and her insistent gaze sent me back to the painting again. I was missing something. There sat Cassiopeia on her throne. Draco pushed his ugly head up toward where the northern bears hung with their ridiculous tails pointing to and away from the Pole Star. And then I got it. The Little Bear looked plump and contented, and Ursula had skillfully painted a honeycomb in his mouth. But old Ursa Major was unhappy. He was gaunt and thin. His lips writhed back from his fangs as though in pain. And no wonder! Out near the end of his long, unbear-like tail Ursula had painted a big, livid, and obviously uncomfortable knot.

"I see it," I said. "Why?"

"Don't know," Ursula said. "Just happened. Didn't look right any other way."

I peered at the knot. Two visuals gleamed in the middle of the bruised and purple lump, one yellowish and one white.

"Mizar and Alcor," I said. "Could be three visuals. A little magnification will bring out another one."

"Know it. Put in another one. Didn't look right. Took it out."

"It would scarcely be visible," I protested. "It couldn't make any real difference in the picture, could it?"

"Did, though. Wasn't happy with it in."

I have mentioned stepping out into Ursula's studio. That was literal. When we were in space, Ursula painted in a transparent bubble, a small, room-sized blister that could be extruded from the apparently featureless side of the *Stardust*. There, in radiation-shielded, air-conditioned comfort, Ursula interpreted the Galaxy.

From deep in the umbra of the Moon, the constellations gleamed like on a summer night on Earth, but with far greater scope. The Great Bear literally hung before us. I picked up Ursula's binoculars, a 12x pair she had evidently been using to verify visuals. I focused on Mizar and Alcor, the region of the knot, the Horse and Rider of some mythology. The third visual came faintly into view, just as I remembered.

"It's there," I said. "Hasn't changed a bit."

"Know it," Ursula said. "Still can't put it in. Doesn't feel right."

"And the knot?"

"Belongs. Got to be. Don't know why."

She looked at me for a moment, then suddenly turned back to her easel, her skinny fingers unerringly selecting the right brush from the collection thrust handle-end first into the large gray bun on the back of her head. It was dismissal. But as I slid back the door, she looked up briefly.

"Think about it, Roscoe."

She didn't have to say it. I was thinking.

There hadn't been one for all the time we had spent in the Moon shadow; so when it came, it was overdue. After looking at Ursula's picture, though, I knew I had been expecting it.

"Ladies and gentlemen!" The voice of Stony Price, communications chief, purred sedately out of our speakers. It was evident that he had been given a formal communique and told to stick with it. "Dr. Rasmussen requests the pleasure of the company of all senior and supervisory staff at dinner this evening. Appetizers at 1800. —Be it known I've consulted the cook. It's a good menu!"

The last, of course, was pure Stony Price. He never stuck to a script in his life.

Johnny Rasmussen's dinners were a tradition aboard the *Stardust*. They all had the same format, the same formal lack of formality. That doesn't sound right. But it says what I want. And a dinner always meant more than it appeared to mean. It always preceded a crisis, or a big decision, or with the same deadpan gentility, it occasinally was a celebration. The *raison d'être* was never mentioned. Attendance wasn't compulsory. But nobody missed Rasmussen's dinners. They were where big things happened.

"I feel twitchy," Lindy said. "My radar is jumping. This dinner is going to be a weirdy!"

She was selecting a dinner gown, of course. She was busy at that ten minutes after the communique came through.

I knew what she meant. The dinner would be toothsome, as always, the company familiar and comfortable. It was the reason for it that she was talking about.

She strolled back and forth between two creations she had hung on opposite sides of her dressing table. One was gray, a living, almost ominous gray, streaked through with long diagonal flashes of vivid blue. The other was like a flame hung on the wall. And that was the one she turned to, more and more often.

No red-haired, green-eyed woman can wear a blazing red formal and get away with it. False. One can. She did, too; and with her curls piled high in a strange coiffure, a rope of milk pearls across the scenic splendor of her breasts, and a white orchid at her left shoulder, she looked like some barbaric princess on a world we'd just discovered. Actually, that's literary fudging. Since the *Stardust* first passed Pluto, we've found plenty of life, but none of it human or humanoid. Certainly nothing that remotely resembled Lindy.

I seated her proudly, as I always do. The women all tried, and several of them looked pretty spectacular, but I had the queen and everybody knew it. And that's fair to good going for a guy who looks as rough as I do. Even a dinner jacket and a close shave can do only so much for a body like a storage tank, long, thick arms, pillar legs, and black hair showing everywhere hair *can* show except on the top of my head. Add a face that could have been chopped out with a dull hatchet—and you wonder about Lindy. It must be my beautiful eyes.

Dr. Johannes Rasmussen made his entrance, on cue, exactly at 1800 hours. Tall, slender, tanned, immaculate, his mustaches waxed to points, he stood behind his chair and gazed with pleasure down the long table. Then, starting at his right, he named names:

"Captain Griffin, Mr. Cheng, Miss Potts, Dr. Kissinger," —on around the table. When he got back to himself he said, "I'm happy to have you here this evening. Won't you please be seated?" He could have done the whole bit in his sleep. And so could most of us.

The men sat, and we all pitched in without ceremony. Utensils clinked. Conversation builded from a polite murmur to a contented waterfall roar, punctuated occasionally by a deep laugh, or perhaps Lindy's high-pitched giggle.

Next to me Ursula Potts dug into her baked fish like a hungry terrier. Ursula loves to eat as well as I do, which is no faint praise. Ursula's dinner dress was a sullen russet, with no ornamentation. Her skinny finger were heavy with rings. But her wizened face and strange eyes were the same against any backdrop. She flicked those eyes up and down the table and chewed steadily. She wasn't missing a thing.

"Good fish, Ursula," I said. "Must be Friday."

She licked her thin lips.

"Barbaric reference, Roscoe. No connection between food and the days of the week."

"Not to me," I admitted. "I eat anything any day. But a lot of people still connect Friday and fish."

"Day of mourning among the fish," Ursula said drily. "Quit beating around the bush, Roscoe."

"Okay." I shifted my tone. "What's this bash about, Ursula? Any premonitions? Better still, any information?"

Ursula slurped her Chablis with appreciation.

"Don't know. Can guess, though."

"Give!"

"We're going out."

Rasmussen's seating seemed to confirm it. Cap'n Jules Griffin was on his right, and he wasn't there for his sparkling conversation. Cap'n Jules is the dullest man in space. I can't talk to him for five minutes. Usually he sits far down the table. But he's the genius who implements Ultraspan. He gets us where we want to go.

And Moe Cheng sat next to him, a big-nosed, slant-eyed little man who knows more about the Galaxy than any man has ever known. So it *was* logistics! But Ursula was next, and then I. We weren't there by accident either. Johnny never does anything at random.

We ate, and Rasmussen exchanged polite amenities with those of us within range, like the correct, formal English gentleman he is. I did say English. Forget the name. In the nineteenth century he would have been one of the boys. To him, dinner wouldn't taste right if he weren't dressed for it. Dinner jacket. Black tie.

When the coffee arrived, big fragrant cups of it, and delicate shells of good brandy on the side, Johnny unwrapped the baby. Without seeming to do so, he raised his genteel voice, just enough so that the people at the far end of the table could hear him clearly.

"Ladies and gentleman, a brief but important announcement."

He paused, and the talk died.

"Miss Potts has painted a picture."

Again that pause, but this time the silence was from astonishment.

"Well, good for her!" Pegleg's sour voice was low, but it carried. "But that is Miss Potts' business, painting pictures. If Miss Potts had won the high jump, that might be news!"

Rasmussen's eyes twinkled, but he kept the faith. He didn't smile.

"This particular picture is important to all of us," he said. "On the basis of it I have made a decision. Dr. Kissinger, you have seen the picture. Would you describe it, please?"

I was as out of it as anybody, but I can go along with a gag.

"I suppose you mean the knot on the bear's tail," I said.

"Proceed."

So I went over the picture verbally and wound up with gaunt old Ursa Major, with his unhappy look and the painful lump on his caudal appendage. I played it straight, but people began to snicker. Everybody thought it was a yuk. For that matter, so did I.

"I would prefer tangible data," the chief said, "but we don't have them. We tried everything we know. With the help of the Luna Reception Center—the Big Dish, if you will—we have monitored and analyzed and been frustrated by the sounds from space that Dr. Peterson has called the Music of the Spheres. It has been impossible to determine direction of origin."

Johnny had curled his long fingers around his brandy glass, warming it, and now he raised it, barely wetting his lips.

"Miss Potts has sensed a disturbance in Ursa Major. She has even been specific as to location. Now we know that this is not evidence admissible anywhere in any scientific context. But most of us also know that Miss Potts has—shall we say—unique gifts." (What he meant was that the old witch *was* a witch!) "She has been a staff member on every flight of the *Stardust*, and I have never known her painted analyses to be entirely without foundation."

A delicate sip of coffee, then more brandy.

"I have therefore notified the International Space Council that the sounds appear to emanate from *zeta Ursae*

Majoris, colloquially called Mizar, and have received clearance to proceed there to investigate."

There wasn't even a murmur the entire length of the table.

"The distance is eighty-eight light-years. Captain Griffin has assured me that we have the capacity to span it in seven stages. Mr. Cheng has plotted these stages. For seventy-two hours we will renew supplies at Tycho Base on Luna, during which time R. and R. leave will be granted to all personnel not involved in these activities. If any individual feels disinclined to make this voyage, he may separate without prejudice, and we will understand. That *is* a very angry-looking knot on the bear's tail!"

He couldn't have bound them any closer to the ship if he had put chains on them. And well he knew it.

He rose and stood tall, the brandy glass still in his hand.

"It has been a pleasure to have you here this evening. There will be further refreshment in the main lounge, where the picture is on display for your examination. Good evening!"

The old formula again. He didn't wait to take a bow, just slipped out the way he always does. And the press toward the lounge was faster than usual. If space people didn't have curiosity, they probably wouldn't be space people.

Well, that was the program, and that's the way it happened. The *Stardust* bestirred herself, swept out of the Moon shadow in a long ellipse and into the bright unfiltered glare of Sol. Cap'n Jules took the scenic route, orbiting the Moon once as we spiraled in to our spot at the Tycho docks.

The landscape below us hadn't changed much. The dome clusters were few and far between. For the most part the long stretches of bleak, jumbled, cratered surface were just as three billion years had left them. I had been over them hundreds of times, but I still took a moment to stand straight and mentally salute two truly brave men in a tiny, flimsy, spider-legged craft who came safely to rest for the first time in that empty wilderness below. Countless messages have come to Earth from space since 1969, but none will ever again have the thrilling impact of the cheerful announcement:

"The Eagle has landed!"

But enough of reminiscence and history. The *Stardust* eased gently into her slip, her thousands of tons completely nullified by her new timonium antigravs. Cap'n Jules brought her in like a feather on a breeze. She lay full length, a vast metal sausage, blunt-nosed, blunt-sterned and featureless. No onlooker could have imagined the variety of handy little gadgets that could be extruded at need from her glistening hide, from jumper platforms to Ursula Potts' studio. Nor was there any hint of the full fifty openings that could be activated; personnel ports, cargo ports, great shutter-like openings that could each discharge a four-man scoutboat into space.

The personnel ports were promptly put to use as all but a handful of our researchers and crew streamed into the pressurized corridors and out into the big-city attractions and fleshpots of Tycho Base. Pegleg and Lindy and I went along. I couldn't have cared less about Tycho's charms, but it did feel good to get my feet back on terra firma once again. I said as much.

"Luna firma," Lindy corrected. "Terra is thataway."

And so it was, hanging resplendent, high in the Lunar northern sky. The great central dome of Tycho arched over the sector of shops and hotels and entertainment places in one graceful, lofty sweep. It filtered out hard radiation and gave a soft, ghostlike quality to the sunlight it allowed to come through. And it changed the celestial view. We looked up at a luminous green Earth, and behind it the northern constellations were picked out in icy dots. The Great Bear was in view. For a moment I could almost see his gaunt, unhappy look, and the swelling knot on his long tail.

We prowled the grass-bordered streets, looked into shop windows, sniffed at the doors of eating places. We sat on the benches in Tycho's famous Aldrin Park, where oaks and beeches and pines and dogwoods pretended, like the people, that they were still on Earth. A mockingbird sang from a holly tree near where we sat. Cardinals and bluebirds flashed as they flew. I wondered what effect the lessened gravity had on their flight. They seemed happy and normal.

It was a pleasant little interlude. Pegleg left us on affairs of his own, which I suspected had to do with a slumberous-eyed, darkhaired little stewardess he knew on one of the shuttle runs to Earth. The nature of man changeth not. I felt smug, for I'd put all that behind me. Or, to put it more correctly, I liked my arrangement better.

Lindy and I had dinner at the Earthview, not Tycho's biggest or grandest restaurant, but I knew from experience that you couldn't beat the food. And that's why I go to eating places. We had oysters Luna, a pale green soup that smelled like a breath of the jungle, reindeer steaks from Lapland, artichokes and spinach from Texas, and three kinds of wine. There were fruits from Malaya, a French dessert, and finally coffee and a heavenly clear liqueur, a specialty of the house. And all served by a blonde goddess six feet tall and magnificently topless!

"Eyes are for looking," Lindy said, "but don't neglect your food. Would you like to bet I couldn't take her job?"

"Why," I asked reproachfully, "would you want to put a poor girl out of work? You already have a job. One that's yours as long as you want it, and when you don't want it any more, I'll close the position out for good. Now may I look?"

Her green eyes danced. She reached across the little table to put a hand on mine.

"Stare away," my wife said. "I don't see how it can hurt you."

If you're thinking that this is irrelevant, that it's all digression, don't you believe it. That little touch of R. and R. was important. We needed the supplies they were loading into the *Stardust,* but no more than we needed that touch of solid ground beneath our feet, the renewed contact with the substrate that periodically we all have to have. Still, the seventy-two hours were enough. When the *Stardust,* herself rested, lifted gently like a living thing from her berth and the Moon dropped away, we were all aboard, and we were all glad.

Earth was in our viewports for a brief while. Then, under full timonium drive we flashed across the Solar System and into deep interstellar space beyond Pluto's orbit. Yet we were simply checking, getting ready for the journey. Light-minutes were nothing, even at the terrific finite speeds of which we were capable. Light-years were ahead of us. Eighty-eight of them. And that meant Ultraspan.

We were in the hands of three unlikely geniuses—they

abound on the *Stardust*—and I'm sure I've been more concerned for my life in a Paris taxi.

Moe Cheng planned the stages. Cap'n Jules stood by to implement them, one by one. Johnny Rasmussen structured the patterns at the end of each stage, move by move. This was new space, and we were tracking sounds in a direction not determined by any scientific data. We could never have justified ourselves to any logical inquiry. Still, that didn't disturb me either. Computers can goof, but I'd never known Ursula's weird sixth sense to be entirely wrong.

An Ultraspan stage can't be described. Nevertheless, I'll try. You are conscious in stage, but nothing has either importance or meaning. In effect, according to one school, during the jump you cease to exist as an entity, and the Nirvana-like consciousness is like a shadow projected forward, your id stripped of all concerns and without a home. I don't know. There is a perceptible time-span in stage, and you know it's there. Yet theoretically time does not exist, and with the effect of time suspended, one space is as likely as another. Still, stages can be plotted and the target space occupied. We've been doing it for years.

Lindy and I held hands for the first stage, programmed for ten light-years. I was nothing and she did not exist, yet somehow I knew that we were sitting in our quarters in the *Stardust,* and that we were holding hands. It seemed days and weeks, and yet it seemed only a minute or two. Our view screen showed an alien pattern of stars. My wife's hand was warm in mine. The starship barely had headway, perhaps no more than a thousand miles an hour. We were in pattern after the stage, orienting, checking, verifying. And the life of the ship went on as though it had not been interrupted. Which, indeed, perhaps it had not. We use Ultraspan, but we may never really understand it.

"There'll come a day," Lindy said, "when I won't want to tolerate that any more."

She got up and walked restlessly across the room.

"It's painless," I said.

"Of course. It isn't that. It's—it's just that it seems to take me away from me! You dig? With all my problems solved, all my curiosities satisfied, all my challenges met, maybe sometime I won't want to come back. To go ten light-years in space without time lapse isn't for man. It's—it's ag'in nature!"

"Karma," I said. "Nirvana. Maybe we have found the way. And what, after all, is ag'in nature? What's nature?"

Lindy turned, and suddenly she smiled at me. It was the quick change of mood that all women show. Or I suppose they all do. I could see the strain go out of her face, the confidence return.

"You and me together! That's nature, friend. Pay me no attention, Roscoe. I go gloomy, but I'll always come back."

I rose and started for her. And our speaker rattled, cleared its throat, and the Music of the Spheres poured out of it.

It was different. There was more discord, more harshness, than in any broadcast before. It throbbed and pulsed and wailed. Where before only Lindy could detect urgency, now it seemed to me that anyone could. And I thought I knew why. We were closer. Whatever was impending, whatever motivated those calls to the Galaxy, to whomever or whatever would listen—whatever it was, it was nearer. If we had stayed at our base near Earth, we wouldn't have heard this broadcast for ten years yet.

The signal was no stronger. It came in plainly, though, and here we were dependent on our own sensors. We didn't have the enormous backing of the Big Dish on the Moon. As I listened, conviction grew. We were headed exactly right. We were on the beam.

After an Ultraspan stage, Rasmussen always activated a twenty-four hour pattern. This gave time for a rest period, time for all data to be processed, time for all personnel to adjust. For the feel of one sector of space is not the feel of another. I can't explain that. But it's so.

We staged again, fourteen light-years. There was no star pattern on our view screens then. They were awash with brilliant light, all radiation screens were activated, and not twenty-five million miles away lay the awesome grandeur and tossing energy of a flaring sun. It was as close as we had ever come to a primary energy unit, but it was no mistake. We were where Moe Cheng intended we should be.

The broadcast came through fragmented by the roiling radiation, we still picked up most of it. And fourteen years had made a difference. There was panic in the music now, fear, desperation, and the first faint threads of despair. If anyone had doubted that our direction was right, they didn't any more.

Five stages later—five memorable stages—and the *Stardust* drifted at the edge of a spectacular star system. Not large, as such systems go, not as colorful as the red giants are, but with an attraction for us that I suppose was at least partly historical. Since man first had raised his eyes toward the heavens, he had known this little twinkling dot in space. It was a part of the complex by which travelers found their way. Ancients had used it as an eye test. For this was Mizar.

I don't have to instruct you. Any schoolboy knows the double-triple systems of this brighter one of the Alcor-Mizar duo. But no schoolboy or anyone else of human origin had ever had our view of them. The first human visitation. And the last.

Our astronomers probed and measured and explored and verified, while we sat impatiently watching the view screens. They made it easy for us. The triple system of Mizar B, three bluish suns, moved slowly along the paths of their complex orbits around their common center in space. From Earth they simply melded to form a dim blue point. But it was Mizar A, the double, that had been our objective, though we had not known it. Here, somewhere here, was the point of origin of the Music of the Spheres.

The smaller component of Mizar A lay far in the distance across the system, a blue-white sun that glimmered cheerily and normally. Its relatively giant twin, a bright yellow on the charts, was no longer that. It hung in space before us, an ominous, shifting, sullen orange, a vast, savage celestial furnace, unstable and threatening. We knew its nature and its fate before the sounds came through once more, exactly on time.

You have listened to a requiem. You know the sounds of a dirge. The Music of the Spheres was still music, but there was in it no hope, no calls for help, no panic and no fear. The time was past for these. Whatever made the music was saying good-bye, was expressing thankfulness for having lived, for the wonders of having been sentient. There was even a gentle speculation that this was not the end after all—that somewhere, in an unimaginable future, there might be something more.

Now I'm not sensitive, as Lindy is. Certainly I have no touch of the mysticism that allowed Ursula Potts to feel crisis across the light-years. And Pegleg is worse. Yet all of us, sitting in the small lounge listening to that broadcast, all of us heard just what I've described. We felt it so plainly that we could put it into words, as I've done here. And there was one thing more we could detect. It was regret. Regret that before life ended it had not known other life, other beings that knew the joys of thought and achievement, beings that it believed existed, and to whom it had sent its music pulsing out among the stars.

Ursula Potts sat small and still in her chair as the broadcast ended, her strange eyes glowing. Tears flowed down Lindy's cheeks. Pegleg twisted uncomfortably as he sat. Automatically he flexed his plastic knee joint. I got up and paced.

"All personnel, attention please!"

Dr. Johannes Rasmussen never speaks on intercom, but they were his cultured tones that came out of the speakers now.

"This is a summary, for your information. The sun Mizar A-1 is in unstable condition, prenova. It will disintegrate in thirty-three hours. It has a single planet. Dr. Frost has recorded all vital physical data; so let it suffice to say that it is appreciably larger than Earth, has an atmosphere, and every evidence of varied and complex life. The music has originated there."

Johnny paused, and I could imagine him sitting, his face calm and apparently untroubled, reflecting on how to phrase his next sentence.

"We have time. We will proceed immediately to the planet, orbit and descend to the surface unless conditions make that impossible. Radiation is already high, many times human tolerance, but far less than the shielding capacities of our ship, or even our spacesuits. Unless the music is mechanically produced, life still exists on the planet's surface. But probably you all detected finality in the last broadcast. Remarkable, really!"

Johnny seemed to be saying the last two words to himself.

"The planet is now on your screens. We will keep it there during approach. Please consider what part you would care to play in our brief reconnaissance. The brevity is occasion for regret, but it is fortunate that we have arrived before the system destroys itself. We will allow ourselves a safety margin of three hours, and we will stage thirty hours from this time. Thank you."

Nobody but Rasmussen could have made the most

dramatic experience man had ever known sound as routine as a weather report.

The planet was a small bright dot on our screens as we flashed toward it and toward its glowering sun. It grew steadily, though. Cap'n Jules wasn't wasting time. Before long the dot was a sphere; shadows showed and drifted on its surface; colors glowed. Finally it hung before us in majestic blue-white splendor, suffused over all by the deepening orange light of the sullen sun. Doomed planet!

"What a pity!" Lindy murmured. "What a terrible, horrible, hard-to-understand, unbelievable fate! Roscoe, if I didn't remember Earth, *that* would be the grandest object we've ever seen from space!"

"Location, distance from its primary, rotation rate, revolution rate, light quality and intensity, all ideal." I said. "And there's plenty of water, and oxygen atmosphere, a deep and varied planetary crust. Just the kind of cradle life would have to have."

I had been running down Doug Frost's physical data tables. Like I said, everything was perfect. If you had set out to build a model planet, this was probably how it would have looked when you had finished. Then add countless eons of evolution! The results at least were life forms so sophisticated, so learned, that they could send complicated musical messages far into the Galazy. How far, we had no way of knowing.

And now the source of its life was sick, stricken with an incurable illness, a slowly progressing loss of balance in its atomic furnaces. In thirty-three hours the story would end. Thirty-one hours, now. We had taken two hours to approach the planet. For the life on that beautiful world out there, thirty-one hours until the end of time!

As we swept into high orbit, three thousand miles above the planet's surface, speakers came alive all over the ship. Johnny Rasmussen was calling the makers of music, and he wanted us all to hear. Every characteristic of the celestial broadcasts had long ago been analyzed. I could imagine the care with which Stony Price was matching element to element, intensity to intensity, frequency to frequency. But it was Rasmussen's voice that was going out. His message was simple. He knew that if it was detected it would not be understood, but his neat soul squirmed if all ends were not carefully tied.

"This is the starship *Stardust*, from the Sol system,

eighty-eight light-years from your own. We have come in response to your messages. We see the condition of your sun. We will meet with you if it is possible. Please respond."

The speakers were silent. I probably held my breath for a full minute before I remembered to exhale. But nothing happened. After a brief time lapse Johnny repeated his message. Again nothing. Then he spoke to us, to the personnel of the *Stardust.*

"I had hoped that we might establish the location of the transmitting installations and home directly on them. It was a remote hope, at best. Some hours remain before the next scheduled broadcast, if in fact another ever will be made. A pity. As you may now see from the building complexes on your screens, life has indeed reached a high level here. We have not before encountered any forms so advanced."

He paused, doubtless rearranging his next sentence into a form that pleased him better. He never got a chance to use it.

The music came softly, hesitantly, wonderingly, as if its maker or makers didn't really believe. To our knowledge, they had been sending their calls out across the Galaxy for nearly a hundred years. And now, when time had almost run out, they were answered! The tones deepened, strengthened. We could hear the exultant questions in them: *"Who are you? Where are you? Speak to us again!"*

Pegleg was at our screen, adjusting for a better view, and we all could see the image whirl as the *Stardust* changed direction. Cap'n Jules had shifted course with the first pulse of sound.

"This is the *Stardust,*" Rasmussen said. "We hear you. Speak again! Speak again! Speak again!"

The response poured from the speakers like a hymn of thanksgiving, like the sound of a choir in a great cathedral. I'm no musician, but any field man can sort our sounds. I could tell that that volume came from many sources. Then it died away into soft, happy whispers and only one tone remained, a clear, resonant soloist. That tone went up and down the scale, repeated and doubled back on itself in amazing patterns. And I knew, everybody knew, that it was speech.

The *Stardust* swept down into the atmosphere in a fluid, ever-decreasing glide. She knew where she was going,

now. The computer had solved the location of the transmitter in seconds, for the unrelayed sound no longer
lacked direction. Clouds briefly blurred the view screens.
Then we were cruising smoothly and slowly over a landscape like nothing we had ever seen before. Still, it was
familiar. All the elements of cultured, civilized occupancy
were there. Only the forms were different.

It was not Earthlike. There were no trees, no grass,
no flowers. Color was there, and variety, and I suppose
I sorted things out pretty quickly. In the presence of
proper stimuli I began to function automatically. If you
put food before a hungry animal, it will salivate. Put
an ecologist in a new ecosystem and he will start to
analyze. Pavlovian. Inevitable.

All over the ship the same thing going on. Johnny
Rasmussen issued no orders. It wasn't necessary. Every
researcher, every team, has gone into a structured behavior pattern, preparing, planning, anticipating. Each
knew better than anyone else what his own part should
be in this strange, brief, and tragic exploration.

I was in my lab, without remembering how I got there.
Lindy undoubtedly was scooping up samples, assaying
the life in the atmosphere. Pegleg was readying to go out
at first touch down. And there was no doubt that Ursula's
studio was extruded and that she was hard at work.

My view screen flickered as the scoutboats went out.
Four Swishes. Sixteen men. Geographers and meteorologists probably. They would range for hundreds of miles
around the mother ship, their cameras recording everything from horizon to horizon, packing in raw data about
this world that would be studied and analyzed long after
the planet had ceased to be. We knew this. We all faced
it. But there was no other thing we could do. Here
life had evolved to high level—but all life must end
sometime.

I changed into field gear. It wasn't much, just shorts,
a jersey, sandals and a gear harness. Outside was going
to be awkward and tricky, for we would be in spacesuits.
The strange landscape looked tranquil and peaceful, but
the radiation was lethal. We'd never worked under such
conditions before. The suits anticipated them, though. We
had a wide margin of safety.

"Shame about that blasted radiation." Pegleg read my
mind. I hadn't even noticed him come into the lab. I
was scooting my chair on its track back and forth along

the row of sensor consoles that reported and recorded a variety of basic abiotic data. "As you can see, the air is sweet. More oxygen than we're used to."

"I've been checking the sources," I said. "Photosynthesis, as you'd expect from all the green. Funny thing, though. *Everything* seems to be photosynthesizing. Haven't picked up a flicker of what you might call animal life."

"Nothing looks like it either."

Pegleg studied my screen. We were cruising at two thousand feet and at fifty miles an hour. First reconnaissance pattern. As eager as we were to contact the dominant life, the makers of music, still Johnny Rasmussen held to the pattern. We had time. We learned as we went. By now we all knew that the transmitter was a thousand miles away, but we'd spend an hour in this pattern, then flash to our destination in minutes. It was midmorning on the land below us, the last midmorning it would ever see.

"Animals are more sensitive to radiation," I suggested. "Could be they're already dead."

"The broadcast boys are still on the ball. Are you hinting that they're plants too?"

"We're shielded," I pointed out. "Why shouldn't they be? Somehow they haven't developed the know-how to escape their planet, but I predict that in many ways they'll be as advanced as we are. We couldn't have sent out the Music of the Spheres."

Pegleg's narrow face had its usual suspicious expression, as though he smelled a dead mouse.

"Smart enough, maybe, to take over the *Stardust*, and leave us here in their places to face Eternity in the morning?"

"This is a planet bigger than Earth," I said drily. "The *Stardust* would be just a mite overloaded."

Pegleg snorted.

"Genghis Khan would only have picked a few passengers. Hitler wouldn't have taken everybody. Just a lady friend, maybe, and a few zealots to do the work. Don't be an ass, Roscoe. Even so-called kindly life forms want to keep on living. It's a pretty basic urge. The hand of brotherhood should be backed up by a club, just in case."

"If I know Johnny Rasmussen, it will be. He doesn't look or act as ornery as you do, but I do sometimes get the impression that he's sadly lacking in faith. Taking the

Stardust would require a gambit we can't even imagine. You know that as well as I do."

"A comforting thought." Pegleg subsided, but he still grumbled. "Just the same, when we finally go, that'll be the reason. 'Love thy neighbor' is an impossible assignment. All it does is to leave the door unlocked so he can knock you on the head or steal you blind."

This was standard Pegleg philosophy, and how much of it he actually believed I suppose I'll never know. What I do know is that if and when I ever do get trapped in a last extremity, there's no man I'd rather have backing me up than Pegleg Williams.

We concentrated on the view screen. The ship was traversing a tremendously wide valley, and in length it seemed to go on and on. There were surfaced roads that swept in sinuous curves, water courses that undulated, and wherever road met river there was a gracefully arching bridge. Everything was curved. There wasn't an angle anywhere.

Nothing seemed to fit the specifications of a town. There were buildings, always in clusters, always piled masses of brightly colored domes. Too big for family dwellings, as we understand families, I still felt that they housed the builders and users of the roads and bridges. The green mounds arranged in orderly curved patterns over wide areas became plants in fields in my thinking. The green was chlorophyll. So the life pattern was below us, at least for this portion of the planet, but never a sign of the dominant forms, never a hint of movement. Either they were already dead from the radiation, or the *Stardust* had spooked them. If they were alive, they must have heard that their space broadcasts had been answered. So I reasoned, but nothing I could see gave much support to my speculations.

The first reconnaissance hour passed. Johnny Rasmussen gave the word, the ship nosed upward slightly, and the land below us began to blur. In an hour we had traveled fifty miles. In the next few minutes we went almost twenty times that far. Then the *Stardust* cut speed and peeled off in a long sweeping glide. The structure we had come eighty-eight light-years to seek spread out ahead of us. It was, it had to be, the transmitter complex, and just to see it was worth the trip.

It rose out of a level plain, row on row and tier on tier of multicolored domes, piled on and against each other in a fashion that looked fearfully unstable, but which must have represented the ultimate in fine engineering. From a distance it looked like an oriental fan or a peacock's tail, spreading outward and upward from a narrow base, the cantilevered domes like beads on strings, thousands and thousands of them, each as large as family dwellings on Earth. Two miles into the sky the great fan spread, the weirdest and most beautiful artifact of my experience.

We swung slowly around it, drifting in a twenty-mile circle. Cameras and sensors were probing and recording the whole improbable complex. My info board also told me that the *Stardust* was enveloped in a force field that would require incredible energy to penetrate. Pegleg needn't have worried. Rasmussen wasn't underestimating anybody—or anything.

Our peerless leader was at his microphone.

"We're here, friends. We're coming in for a landing. Do you see us? Give us a sign! Can you hear us? Give us a sign!"

Perhaps the last was because we had heard nothing since we dropped into the atmosphere. And I found myself wearing a humorless grin. Even in this last extremity, they mistrusted us as well.

The domed dwellings were scattered in patterns outward from the base of the fan, multicolored, brilliant. There were many hundreds of them, and roads curved in from all directions. Everything was there—except the life forms, except the "people."

Cap'n Jules picked the closest empty spot and set the *Stardust* down gently, without a jar. Pegleg and I were suiting up, checking again and again the shielded protective coverings we had never had a chance to use before. Johnny's voice came at intervals from the speakers. No response. Suddenly we were too strange, too alien for the inhabitants of this world, some of whom had to be still alive and watching us at this moment. But they gave no sign.

Rasmussen has imagination. He wasn't getting through and he knew he was being heard. He changed tactics. The next sound that came from the speakers was very familiar and soothing to me. I had heard it under many circumstances, and on at least twenty worlds. Often in my quarters, after a good meal, it relaxes me as nothing else ever could. For Lindy strummed her guitar and sang softly, sang a baby lullaby from old Earth, eighty-eight light-years away.

That did it. Throbbing musical chords broke from the speakers. Sounds ran up the scales and peaked in little questioning tones. Lindy answered with chords of her own, always gentle, always changing. We could feel the answering excitement as the responses caught up each note, elaborated it, and flung it back, every time with the question so plain it was almost in words.

"I wonder what I'm really saying to them," Lindy murmured. "I do hope it's not insulting." She struck a series of soft notes and crooned a paraphrase of an old movie song, a fairy tale from back in the twentieth century: *"Come out, little people, wherever you are, and see the nice spaceship that came from a star!"*

But the little people did not come out. The musical dialogue continued, but nothing moved. By now, though, we had more information about them. The physiologists had activated their delicate metabolic probes and were searching the dwellings and working their way up and down the fan. There were life forms behind every wall, forms with complicated metabolisms, apparently all one species. They were shy or frightened or suspicious, but they were there.

Pegleg and I were ready. Johnny gave his okay and we went out through the locks, the first human beings to walk on this doomed world. We barely beat out Bud Merani and his team of archaeologists. If Merani can't find ruins, new, strange buildings will do. They swarmed out behind us, spread toward the nearer dwellings. In our bulky white suits and gleaming helmets we may have looked like a pretty formidable invasion, if Lindy's continuing concert wasn't reassuring enough. I rather hoped she wouldn't accidentally say the wrong thing. Undoubtedly the local inhabitants could use energy concentrations, if they chose. We each were protected by a force field, but as you would expect, it was minimal. It would be a minor deterrent, at best.

Pegleg saw them first.

"Roscoe! Bud! Heads up!" Pegleg's communicator was set for universal output; so he rasped in everyone's earphones.

Large oval doors were sliding open all along the base of the transmitter complex. Out of them small cars came rolling, one after another, a vertible fleet of them. Like the houses, their colors glistened. They came steadily toward the starship, falling into lines as the roads fanned out.

We had set down between two wide highways. In a few minutes each was choked with the little vehicles for the entire length of the *Stardust*. There were hundreds, maybe thousands of them, identical except for color, and each with its single occupant. And the reason for that was simple enough. One was all a car could hold. A hitch-hiker would have been out of luck.

Each little car moved on four fat, balloon-like wheels. Each car body was a short, thick flat oval, and the driver fitted down into it like an egg into an eggcup. You'd be surprised how apt that was. The driver *looked* like an egg. Well, maybe not exactly, but they were the same shape. The old idea that intelligent life forms would inevitably be human or humanoid just hasn't panned out for us. We've never found any that *were*. Thinking it over, why should they be?

I walked slowly over to the nearest line of cars, the idea forming in the back of my mind that perhaps the beings couldn't leave their transportation. I could see no limbs, no outgrowths of any sort. They had them, though, as one of them quickly proved. It extended tentacles, pushed itself up out of its nest between the wheels, and climbed down, shooting out extensions wherever it needed them, retracting them again when the need passed. It rolled toward me on multiple outgrowths, each flattening at the tip as weight was put on it.

The thing was perhaps five feet tall. It was a uniform pale olive-green. Longitudinal striations showed on the body surface from top to bottom. Across the upper third of the body, on the side kept toward me, was a conspicuous, eight-inch ribbon-like strip, delicate and glistening and rosy pink in color. It came to a halt six feet away, raised itself up on three stiffened tentacles, tripod-like, and a well-defined oval section in its middle began to vibrate. The flute-like tones were familiar enough. We had been listening to them for many weeks. They were pleasing, varied, and the being produced them in what was evidently a formal manner. We were being welcomed. Or I hoped we were.

"The keys to the city, Roscoe." Pegleg seemed to have the same impression.

I bowed to the egg-like dignity.

"We thank you very much, sir or madam, as the case

may be. We understand you're having some trouble with
your sun. I regret to say that there's not a blasted thing
we can do about it, but we're at your service if you can
think of something. Johnny, do you have any suggestions
for dealing with our little friends?''

"Play it by ear. You're doing fine!" Rasmussen's voice
was in my earphone. The egg couldn't hear him. It was
already speaking again. Its voice was rich with overtones
and rose and fell with undoubted emotion. Then it paused
and stood as high as it tripod would allow, the pink
strip across its upper front rippling and intensifying. I
suspected that this was an organ of vision, as suspicion
later verified.

I bowed again.

"It has made some kind of a profound pronouncement."
I spoke clearly. "I think Lindy's guitar can give the best
answer. Play something, Lindy." I turned and gestured
toward the spaceship.

From twenty speakers Lindy's series of musical chords
flooded out. Then, one note at a time, she picked out
the first phrase of a simple tune, totally inappropriate and
three hundred years out of date:

"Oh, the Moon shines bright tonight along the Wabash!"

Out of date or not, it was a sensation. The beings all
swiveled back and forth in their cars, their vision strips
rippled, and a whole array of tentacles sprouted and
waved and were retracted again.

"Oh, dear!" Lindy sang. "I hope I haven't promised
them anything we can't deliver. Would you say they're
pleased or angry?"

"If I had a month, I'd be able to tell you." I glanced
upward at the savage, sullen sun, and once again was
aware of the murderous orange overglow. "This is a
shame! To us they look ridiculous, but they know what
the problems are. Here's culture and learning and joy of
living—and this time tomorrow it will all be gone. They
know we know. And they know we can't help. Kismet!"

"In that case," Johnny Rasmussen said in my ear, "they'll
find satisfaction in knowing about us. Invite him in!"

A lot of things were happening. Squads of white-suited,
helmeted figures were pouring out of the exits as team
after special team implemented its investigation pattern.
They expected full cooperation from the inhabitants,
which had nothing at all to lose, and certainly knew it.
There was no time for diplomatic sparring, for evidences

of good faith. The only verity was the dwindling time.

The little cars left the roads and scurried like beetles over the fields around the *Stardust*. The featureless hide of the ship changed. Rasmussen opened viewpoints, extruded platforms and a veritable forest of sensors, anything he could make visible without danger from the deadly radiation. I saw a whole circlet of the small vehicles ranged around Ursula's transparent studio, the vision strips of the drivers fixed on the strange figure dabbing away at the big canvas. What they must have thought unfortunately will never be known.

The first of the returning scoutboats circled the transmitter and planed in to ease itself into its slip through a briefly opened orifice. Each boat would be decontaminated as it entered. That the boat caused excited comment from the egg-beings was obvious, for the volume of sound rose and peaked as it came in. They were talking among themselves continuously now, like a vast orchestra tuning up.

Three more beings had left their cars and came rolling across to join the official greeter, if that is what he/she was. I beckoned, waved toward the starship, took a few steps. They got it immediately. They faced each other in a circle, fluted softly back and forth, then turned again to me. I led on and they followed.

As we went through decontamination, I worried. What it would do to them we couldn't even guess. But we were all lethally hot and it had to be done. As it happened, I was wasting my concern. It didn't inconvenience them in the least.

They were more concerned when Pegleg and I shucked our spacesuits and appeared as vastly different creatures emerging, like insects, from our bulky white chrysalides. They twittered and fluted in what was without doubt astonishment. The four of them rolled around and around us, nervously extruding and extending tentacles, almost touching us, but never quite making contact. When the purple all-clear light showed in the little room, we led them through the sphincter into the locker room beyond and then into the corridors of the *Stardust*.

"Bring them up to main."

Rasmussen's voice came from a speaker on the wall, and our guests responded with a series of organ tones. Evidently they recognized the voice. The corridors were empty; the automatic lift opened when we needed it, and there were no sounds. The ship was quiet. Since the egg-beings had no faces, it was pretty hard to read their reactions, but their vision strips were rippling and pulsing wildly, changing from palest pink to cloudy violet.

Dignity is a universal trait. Don't think of it as human. You've seen it in the confident pace of a fine horse, in the gracious, condescending mien of a full-fed lion, in a tabby cat lying in the sun. Dignity projects and demands respect. And our guests, or hosts, depending on how you look at it, had it in full measure.

We ushered them into the big main lounge, with its easy chairs scattered as in a retirement club and wide multiview screens everywhere. Just about every chair was occupied. All rose to their feet as we entered. Johnny Rasmussen came forward with the brand of dignity that is *his* special trademark, tall and well-groomed and elegant. And the egg-beings matched him, gesture for gesture, tone for tone. They knew he was The Man.

"Welcome aboard the *Stardust*," the chief said.

The egg-beings responded in unison, a pleasing medley of sounds.

Johnny hesitated for a moment, then lowered himself into the nearest chair. He had nothing comparable to offer to them, but it was an experiment, just the same. It meant: *Let's communicate.* And they weren't at a loss. They ranged themselves in a half-circle before him, retracted all extrusions, flattened themselves on their bases, and sat, after their fashion. They looked like a half-moon of outsized paperweights, motionless except for their rippling vision strips.

Communication, though, wasn't that easy. Somehow, we hadn't been able to stumble on the key that would give meaning to their music. It was reasonable to suppose that they were trying and had had no better luck with our speech. Except for gestures, it was a stalemate. And there was no time.

After a few minutes of unintelligible amenities, Ramussen made his decision.

"We will show them the ship, Dr. Kissinger." He still seemed to be chatting with his guests. "We'll show them quarters, labs, machinery, communications, libraries. We'll make things work. Project a tape for them. Show them how we prepare food and eat it. Let them look at view screens and through telescopes. Everything we can think of. Many physical principles are universal. They're bound to recognize something. Sooner or later we'll get a common denominator."

I could hear Pegleg's almost inaudible growl beside me. Rasmussen sensed it.

"Don't worry, Dr. Williams. We'll stay alert."

"See that we do, Johnny," Pegleg said "No dopes built that transmitter out there. They may have us pretty well cased already."

"A possibility," Rasmussen admitted, "and a chance we have to take. You've never been exactly the conservative type, Pegleg."

Johnny *never* uses Pegleg's nickname.

"I'm almost tempted to hope," Pegleg said, "that I get a chance to say 'I told you so!' It doesn't make sense that they will cheerily tell us good-bye and then sit flat on their bottoms like they're doing now and await disintegration. 'Tain't lifelike. 'Tain't human!"

"Neither are they," I said.

We showed them the ship. As we progressed, I could sense the astonishment that they first exhibited give way to keen, understanding scrutiny. I was sure that they grasped the purposes of most equipment we showed them. They twittered and whistled and fluted over each new situation, with an occasional chord thrown in. When I spoke into a microphone and indicated by gestures that my voice was being heard by the thousands outside, they made the connection immediately. As you'd expect. Communication was probably their area of greatest technical competence.

One of them, perhaps the First Greeter, though I never could be sure, rolled before the mike and showed plainly that he wanted to use it.

"Oh, oh!" Pegleg said.

But Johnny waved a hand. The egg-being seemed to swell; his vision strip flickered frantically; and he launched into a long series of clear tones, modulated, muted, and then occasionally ringing. It was quite a speech, and it took him several minutes.

"Complete report," Pegleg said in disgust. "Those boys now know more about how this ship ticks than I do. May I timidly suggest that you don't show them Ultraspan?"

"I always like to hold something back," Rasmussen said drily. "It would take perfect communication even to project the idea of Ultraspan. No, I think we're safe. There was another reason for that speech. Look at them."

The panoramic view screen in the communications room showed the base of the great transmitter, the roads leading from it, and all the car-packed area between it and the ship. Our four visitors clustered around the screen, flattened their bottoms, and sat watching.

The little cars swirled and circled like colony ants. Many of them swung about and rolled back toward the entrances in the base of the complex. The roads cleared. The traffic departments in some of our Earth cities could have learned a lot from the neatness and dispatch with which they sorted themselves out.

By the time the roads were open, cars were again issuing from the transmitter base. They came slowly, each pulling a small four-wheeled trailer behind it, and each trailer was piled high with multicolored oval packages. Without hesitation they rolled toward the ship and on up to the port through which we had entered.

Our four visitors tried earnestly to explain. Their fluting notes were persuasive and pleading. They extruded more tentacles than we had yet seen, rolled around the communications room, paused to harangue each of us in turn.

"Well, I'll be——!" Pegleg said. "That's a cold-blooded bit. They want to load on supplies and go along. To heck with the peasants!"

Somehow that didn't seem valid to me. Rasmussen, too, looked dubious. Lindy had joined us on our tour of the ship but had stayed in the background. Now she moved forward, her guitar slung into position, her green eyes and bright hair shining. I felt it a shame that our guests had no basis for appreciating her.

They felt her sympathy, though. They clustered around her, all speaking together, a medley of musical frustration. She plucked single, somehow questioning notes. They responded with a flood of sound.

"I don't know what I'm saying," she said, "but maybe it will give them ideas. They make no sense at all out of our vocal sounds. They're more at home with the strings."

She pointed to the loaded trailers on the screen, then to the egg-beings themselves, then swept her hand in a wide arc to indicate the ship. She plucked a single sharp inquiring note on the A string. And the visitors grew completely quiet. There was no way to substantiate it, but to me they seemed appalled.

Suddenly one of them, surely the First Greeter, extruded tentacles in clusters and rolled swiftly to the wall of record files the rows and rows of cabinets from which we had taken the tapes we had projected. He touched them, rolled to the screen, and pointed to the carts. A single, infinitely dignified tone came from him.

"Records," Lindy said. "They're giving us their history. They're doomed, but they'd like the Universe to know that they've lived, that they've learned and achieved and enjoyed. They're willing to go. They just don't want to be forgotten."

I don't know how she does it. But we all sensed that she was right. The egg-beings sensed it too. They had got through. Their soft medley of sound was thankful and contented.

"Run out a loading belt, bring in a trailer load," Johnny ordered. "We'll have a look."

"A *good* look," Pegleg muttered.

But that's what they were. Many of the bright boxes were filled with tapes, rolls and rolls of them, each inscribed with wavering lines in bewildering and complete confusion. Some were packed with metallic sheets thinner than the thinnest paper, but sturdy and resistant. From edge to edge they were covered with symbols in many colors. Records. The records of a planet. Of a race. Of an evolution. A Galactic treasure beyond imagining.

Rasmussen gave the order; loading belts ran out all along the ship, and hour after hour the little trailers rolled up and discharged their loads onto the endless moving surfaces. We're an explorer ship. We have space for the specimens, the artifacts of an intensive look-see. So storage was no problem. I could imagine how eagerly the archaeologists, the historians, the mathematicians, the cryptologists were eyeing this treasure trove. But it depressed me. When we got down to the point of interpreting them, the beings who had recorded, compiled and packed them would be no more, would be part of a tenuous mass of gas outrushing into the depths of the Galaxy.

"I want to see!" Lindy said. "They'll show me. I'm special. I'm sure they will."

She got it across to them, too. At the screen she pointed to the great fan of the transmitter complex, to them and then to herself. They fluted with understanding—and beckoned. It was the last thing we could do, and most of the field units took advantage of it. Time remained. Rest and sleep could wait, while a planet lived its last hours.

Spacesuited again, we followed our guests, now our hosts, through the exit ports. Long lines of white-clad members of field teams swarmed out behind us. The egg-beings seemed not to object. There was no possible reason why they should. But we, as Lindy said, were special.

Our four guides climbed back into their little cars, fluted positive notes into the medley of sounds rising from their countrymen, and presto—we had transportation. A car with a trailer ranged alongside each of us, and we were beckoned to climb aboard. The flat trailer beds seemed as soft as sponge rubber, but they held us, one person to a vehicle. Promptly we rolled toward the great fan at a dizzying five miles an hour.

A description of that tour does not belong here. You've read it in Rasmussen's official report (*ISC Annals, Vol. 72, A. D. 2119. The Log of the Stardust*), or you've had it piecemeal in a hundred news media items. It's here only because it's part of a sequence, or an order of happenings, when we had to explore a star system, a planet, and a civilization in less than thirty hours. It's significant because it gave us the beginnings of our understanding of the level of technology which these odd little egg-beings had achieved.

For hours the little cars rolled noisely up the gently sloping ramps, switching back, detouring into lofty chambers packed with mazes of strange machinery, occasionally debouching onto the wide outlook window spaces from which the country stretched away to a far horizon. The metallic length of the *Stardust* on the ground below grew smaller and smaller as we climbed, and the tiny cars were beetles swarming around it. We spent half an hour on the highest point, on the very crest of the fan, a flat parking area that might have held a hundred or more of the little cars. And as I think back, we said almost nothing during the whole unreal experience.

The roiling, pulsing, unhappy sun was setting. This world would never see it set again. We watched it for a brief while, then followed our guides back down through the miles of sloping corridors, glowing with multicolored illumination, and finally out into an early darkness sprinkled with an alien canopy of stars.

The night seemed long. The *Stardust* teams worked with the structured efficiency that makes us the best, each team the extended arm of a master scientist. The *Stardust* gleamed like a giant glowworm. The brilliance of magna-flashes lit up the countryside for miles. Scoutboats darted in and away again. And over all, the many colors of the lights of the transmitter complex cast a strange, somber glow. In spite of the seething activity, it all seemed like an enormous wake. Which, in a way, I suppose it was.

I was glad when the night thinned, and finally the sullen orange sun climbed into view. I welcomed Stony Price's solemn announcement on intercom, "Official. Nova minus two hours. Staging minus thirty minutes." A sober Stony Price. No clowning with communiques now.

Outside the little cars still swarmed and scurried about in their thousands. But the last of our people came in. Personnel check was complete. The many checklists were finished and verified. We were ready.

"Staging minus sixty seconds!"

Lindy and I sat side by side, holding hands, watching the second sweep of the chronometer approach the sixty mark, waiting for the antigrav lift that would precede the familiar Nirvana-like state of Ultraspan.

And nothing happened.

Our fingers still clung while the chronometer made another sixty-second circle. The *Stardust* lay inert. No lift. No motion. Then the shaken voice of Stony Price on intercom. "Revision. Staging minus twenty minutes. A small difficulty."

In crisis, I am one of Johnny Rasmussen's four first-line replacements. Any one of us, in emergency, could take over operations and run the ship. Cap'n Jules Griffin, Moe Cheng and Pegleg are the others. I arrived at the control room last, but only by about a couple of seconds.

Cap'n Jules sat in his control chair as always, his square face unchanging. Rasmussen reported.

"There is an energy hold on the antigrav units. We can't lift."

Moe Cheng's slits of eyes gleamed with anger, but Pegleg looked almost happy. Or least he looked vindicated.

"Outside energy! Applied where it counts! We showed them too much!"

"But why?" I protested. "We have their records. They want them saved. They want the Galaxy to know. I'd swear it!"

"Play-acting," Pegleg said. "If they can't live, why should we? They've analyzed our lift-off mechanism and nullified it. All the while that we've been gathering data, so have they. In an hour and a half, we all go together."

I've never admired Johnny Rasmussen more than at that moment. Impeccably dressed as always, his mustaches newly waxed, he could have been considering a minor detail of operation. His tanned face showed no stress. He seated himself, punched for a brandy from the console alongside. He said nothing until he'd had a sip.

"Cap'n Jules," he said quietly, "I think I know the answer but why not Ultraspan direct? It has no relation to conventional energy application."

Cap'n Jules shook his white head stolidly.

"We're in contact; so essentially the *Stardust* is a part of the mass of the planet. Even Ultraspan couldn't stage a planet."

"So,"

"We'd disintegrate," the captain said. "Or theory says we would. Never been tried, of course."

"In an hour and twenty minutes we disintegrate anyway. That'll be our last resort, our last experiment. Meanwhile, we try to get them to release us. How, Roscoe?"

"I always get the easy assignments." I tried to keep a calm face, but it was a job to hold my voice steady. "Still, when I'm in deep trouble, I always look in the same direction. This time I think it's practical. Call my wife. Call Lindy—and her guitar."

"Of course." Rasmussen looked like he should have thought of it himself. He made the call. In a few minutes she came into the control room, a quiet, pale Lindy, but with live green eyes sparkling, and a faint wink for me as she passed.

"They're holding us, Dr. Peterson," Rasmussen said. "Somehow they've nullified the antigravs. Do you think you could find out why?"

Lindy looked from face to face. She saw nothing but chagrin and disillusionment, I'm afraid.

"Maybe I can't," she said slowly, "but if they're doing it, there *is* a reason. They don't want us destroyed."

"All the little atoms and ions that used to be me will take satisfaction in that as they blow out across the Universe," Pegleg said.

Lindy's eyes crinkled suddenly, deeply. She turned toward the waiting microphone. Johnny Rasmussen sipped his brandy, and his lean face was faintly quizzical. Pegleg's very sourness had lifted our spirits a little.

Lindy worked. How she worked! Her guitar queried and scolded and pled. The egg-beings crowded around the starship, row on row and rank on rank of little cars. The illusion of the tuning orchestra was more complete than it had ever been. They answered her with flutings and bell tones and deep, majestic chords. But they showed no indication that they understood what she wanted. We couldn't detect any concern that we were overstaying our time. And all the while that time grew shorter.

At nova minus thirty minutes, Rasmussen admitted defeat.

"Thank you, Dr. Peterson. I'm afraid they've won. Our outlook now seems to be the same as theirs. But at nova minus ten we'll try our last experiment. Even in contact with the planet, we'll try Ultraspan."

I don't think Lindy heard the last part of that. Excitedly she grasped Johnny Rasmussen by the arm, almost spilling his brandy. And, even with disintegration staring you in the face, you just don't *do* that!

"That's it!" she cried. "Oh, of course that's it! The one thing we couldn't take away before! They want us to *feel* like they feel, to know what it's like to face the certainty of Eternity! They'll let us go, Johnny! They don't plan for us to die!"

And they proved it for her. Through the packed masses of little cars somehow a roadway opened. A pale blue car came through, hauling a blue trailer. On the trailer sat a large blue casket. The whole blue unit drew up at the location of the port nearest us. That was sealed, of course. No sign of it from outside. But they knew.

A single high clear note came from the thousands of diaphragms, a snaky forest of tentacles sprouted, waved and retracted.

"That's for Lindy," I said. I'd heard that note again and again.

Rasmussen gave the order; a loading belt extruded, and the blue casket came aboard. We broke the simple fastenings, and Lindy opened it there in the control room.

For a brief moment the contents of the casket made no sense at all. Then suddenly we knew. Even Cap'n Jules left his chair to join the circle looking down at the smooth, slightly quivering mass of clear gelatin that filled the box to the brim. Embedded in it were rows and rows of tiny green capsules, layer on layer of them. Thousands.

"They don't want to die," Lindy breathed. "They're saying, 'Find us a planet; find us a home with a healthy sun. Let our race and our culture and our knowledge live on.' "

"I don't understand, Dr. Peterson." Cap'n Jules Griffin's heavy, colorless voice was evidence that he didn't. Cap'n Jules is a genius, but he has no imagination whatever.

"These are their spawn, their babies." Lindy looked ready for tears. "Probably the most highly selected genes they could arrange for in a hurry. They themselves will die, of course. But their race is here in this box. We can lift off now, Cap'n Jules. The antigravs are free. They want us to go."

And a moment later the *Stardust* stirred gently, raised herself like a soap bubble on a breeze, and swept slowly in a great circle around the magnificent fan of the transmitter, the thousands of tiny, colorful cars and their occupants dwindling to insect size.

"Nova minus fifteen minutes! Staging minus sixty seconds!" Stony Price sounded vastly relieved.

A sound began and grew and poured from our speakers, a single pure deep organ-tone. Benediction and good-bye!

Lindy and I held hands there in the control room; Pegleg and Rasmussen and Moe Cheng settled into chairs. Our senses blurred into the timeless nothingness of Ultraspan. Then reality returned. The *Stardust* floated in alien space. On our screens, four light-years away, the twin stars of Mizar A gleamed cheerily, although one of them seemed somewhat smudged and murky. But our view was four years old. We all winced when the chronometers swept past nova zero, then sat for a few minutes in a sort of numb sadness.

"They're gone," Lindy said. "Sun and planet snuffed out. Perhaps the other twin rendered unstable by the energy release. But the life and the wisdom it all made possible have escaped." She patted the blue casket.

It was tragedy. We knew them briefly, but they were our friends and we mourned. Yet we knew that such things happened often even in our Galaxy. How much more so across the Universe?

In perspective, this was simply a single blink of the Celestial Eye.

THE SHARKS OF PENTREATH

MICHAEL G. CONEY

Combine the problem of overpopulation with
the problem of vacationing "away from the
madding crowd," and you have one solution in
this tale of the quaint resort town of Pentreath.
Michael G. Coney should know something of
all this first hand for he himself is a resort
proprietor on the isolated Caribbean island of
Antigua.

During the night there was a thunderstorm and I lay
awake for some time as the scarlet curtains flared again
and again to the incessant lightning. I got out of bed
once and looked out across the harbor to the open sea
flashing silver between the jagged black teeth of the twin
headlands. I saw the boats heaving restlessly at anchor
as the long waves rolled in and smashed against the stone
quay, throwing high plumes of spray across the narrow
waterfront street. I worried about the boats because two
of them were assigned to me for my current Fulltime;
I had rented them with good money.

Then I thought about Gordon Ewell's jerry-built Grotto
down the road, and I felt better. He had not allowed
for this sort of weather in May.

I went back to bed. As I shrugged my head deeper into
the pillow I saw Sylvia's eyes flicker open in alarm when
another crack of thunder shook the village. Thunder
frightened her; I knew she was thinking of suggesting

she get into my bed. So I turned the other way and went to sleep.

By breakfast time the storm had passed over and a watery sun glinted from the puddles and sea with unnatural brilliance. We concluded our usual silent meal and I left Sylvia to wash up the things while I took a stroll down the street. Pentreath looked good that May morning and I hoped the weather would stay fine for the opening of the official tourist season. The facades of the buildings, freshly painted and gleaming with rain, looked much as they must have in the twentieth century and earlier; a rambling row of dissimilar stone and brick structures, some overhanging the street, some with jutting bow windows packed with curios, all restored with painstaking detail garnered from old photographs and picture postcards. Come to quaint Pentreath, the resort with character.

Nearly all totally fake, of course—the stone and brick mostly recreated from modern materials—the facades are just that; behind the solid-looking fronts are prefabricated rooms decked out with imitation oak and plaster, extraordinarily convincing. But my place is real—The Treasure Trove Gifte Shoppe and Tea Rooms is the identical building which has stood for centuries on Pentreath quay, a genuine ancient monument.

I had rented the Treasure Trove in the earlier days; in successive Fulltime years I had come here, and Sylvia and I had worked damned hard. After four years of this, punctuated by eight years of careful Shelflife, I had bought the place. Now we should be set for life. During our periods of Shelflife I let the place out; on the income we are able to send our remotors almost anywhere we please to enliven the enforced idleness. But we seldom go together. In December of last year I had my remotor adapted for skiing and enjoyed the winter sports at St. Moritz while I lay in comfort at the Shelflife Center, secure in my steel cabinet. Sylvia, however, monitored the Christmas festivities at the Center; her remotor never stirred out of the building but sat chattering to the other machines belonging to those people on Rotomation One too impoverished to remotravel. I can never understand why Sylvia likes people so much.

I crossed the street to the quayside and checked the rope that secured my dinghy. A glance across the harbor satisfied me that *Daffodil* and *Skylark* still rode smoothly at anchor—their chains had held fast during the night. I didn't expect any boat customers today but in a week or two, when the season warmed up, the carft would be in use continuously, trotting remotors around the bay on fishing trips.

Turning, I walked over to Ewell's Grotto. Ewell himself was busy with a broom, ineffectively sweeping water out of the entrance in muddy waves,

"Much damage last night?" I inquired.

He looked up. His young, weak face was flushed with effort.

"Could be worse, Mr. Green," he replied. "One or two rips in the canvas, that's all." He hesitated. "I wonder—could Mrs. Green lend me a hand and stitch things up a bit?"

I didn't reply but strolled inside to inspect the damage. Fiberglass stalagmites lay around in confusion and the canvas hung awry. A gaping hole in one wall had allowed leaves and twigs to blow in and the fairy pool was full of muck. The place was a mess.

Ewell's Grotto is a temporary structure; he dismantles it at the end of each Fulltime year and packs it away while he takes his two years Shelflife. Consequently he doesn't pay local siterates. I find this sort of situation annoying; people of Ewell's type are parasites feeding off gullible remotourists while the rest of us foot the bill. My own siterates are heavy.

"Oh, dear. What a shame." I swung around on hearing Sylvia's voice. She was standing at the entrance, regarding the devastation with dismay. Ewell hovered at her side, eager for sympathy. "Look, Gordon," she continued, "I'll slip home and fetch the sail-making things and get the canvas sewn up while John helps you clear up the mess. I won't be a minute."

She departed, leaving me in helpless irritation. It wasn't the first time she had volunteered my services to help a competitor. Ewell was grinning at me gratefully—being unmarried, he is insensitive to nuances of behavior between married couples.

"Thanks a lot, Mr. Green," he said as we started to tidy the place up.

It took about an hour to get the Grotto presentable and set up Ewell's ridiculous little gift shop, a rough imitation-rock counter at the back of the tent complex which Sylvia and he loaded carefully with worthless trinkets and postcards. I left Sylvia to help with the finishing touches and went out to see to the Herefords.

The Herefords are another of those touches of authenticity of which I am rather proud. The herd numbers twenty white-faced brown brutes of no practical purpose save to stand around the large field at the back of the waterfront street and look picturesquely rustic. Sylvia once tried making genuine Cornish Beef Pies for the Tea Room but the experiment was a failure. The few Fulltime tourists we get, together with the locals, found the variable consistency of real meat repulsive and quickly reverted to synthetics. The remotors, which constitute the vast majority of tourists, do not eat and seemed reluctant to burden themselves with perishable pies to take back to the Shelflife Centers.

On the strength of the Herefords, however, they do buy our Olde Englishe Clotted Cream which, laughably, is synthetic.

In the bright sun this morning the Herefords looked wonderful, posing in powerful attitudes against the background of grass, hillside and puffclouded sky—like a nineteenth-century oil painting. One of the animals, a large cow under a tall cedar, was bellowing realistically. For a moment I toyed with the idea of herding them down outside the back windows of the Tea Room but decided to leave that until later. In their present position they could be seen from the coach park at the top of the village.

I unlocked my small shed and took out the signs. Labeling the cattle is a long job but worthwhile from an advertising point of view. The signs are large and heavy and I can only cary two at a time, so it was an hour before I had finished; but by ten o'clock each cow carried, slung across its broad back and hanging down either flank, twin boards reading: THE SHELFLIFE OF GREEN'S CREAM IS AS LONG AS YOUR OWN.

I surveyed the field and was satisfied. In the distance, over the crest of the hill, the sun reflected from the roofs of the approaching coaches.

By the time I reached the coach park the vehicles were arriving, groaning and spewing archaic diesel smoke. There were two, each about eight feet wide and thirty long with deep, unnecessary windows running the length

of the sides. Painted scarlet, they bore the words MID-
LAND RED along their sides. In front, just below the roof
line, were placards reading ROTOMATION 2 and ROTO-
MATION 3.

They pulled into the park and halted side by side. The
din of internal combustion ceased. The drivers jumped out,
carrying lists, held a leisurely conversation, then strolled
to the rear of the vehicles. I followed. I like to know
the worst, right away.

I needn't have worried. The coaches were packed with
remotourists. The driver of Rotomation 2 jerked open
the twin doors and began to hand down the metallic
boxes to his companion, who laid them carefully on the
ground. I positioned myself above the first box, a cube
with dimensions something under two feet, and waited
while it shifted, lifted itself three feet from the ground on
telescopic legs, then extended a slender, gleaming neck
from the center of the cube. At the top of the neck
was the head, cylindrical and about six inches in diameter, about level with my own.

The robot spoke, "Good morning," it said politely.

"Are you in charge of Rotomation Two?" I asked.

"That's right. Name's Tom Lynch. Gloucester Shelflife
Center."

"John Green," I said, grasping the stubby hand pro-
jecting from the side of the cube, "of the Treasure
Trove Gifte Shoppe and Tea Rooms." I produced my
handout. "Here you are. You'll find us about halfway
along the waterfront. I'll make it worth your while."

"Ah, Mr. Green." If it were possible for a remotor to
stiffen, Lynch would have stiffened. "This tour is in no
way regimented. I don't shepherd these people around.
The idea is, they do what they want for the day."

I meet this type sometimes. "I'm aware of that." I
tried to match his air of dignity. "But you're in a position
to make suggestions. That's all I meant."

"Yes," replied the remotor ambiguously, turning away
and allowing my handout to flutter to the ground. "On
your feet, folks!" His voice became jovial as he addressed
the gangling forms lurching around, getting used to their
legs. "We've only got a day here. Get set to enjoy yourselves! Hurry! Hurry—"

Within a short while both coaches were unloaded.

"That's progress for you." The driver of Rotomation
2 spoke; he leaned against the side of his coach, smoking.

"This used to be a forty-seater. Now it holds three hundred. Pack 'em in—" He chuckled cynically.

"That's the story of Rotomation," I agreed. "Why do you use these old vehicles?"

"Adds color to the deal. My company, we've got fifty of these. Used to take Fulltime tourists about but it didn't pay, not at forty to a coach. Even though the coaches are authentic and we charged accordingly. So we switched to remotors and advertised at the Shelflife Centers. Genuine tours just like grandpa used to take. Those your cows?"

"Yes."

"Nice touch. One thing I miss, though. I'm sixty, been driving all my life. Time was, years ago, I drove real tourists around, before Rotomation. Used to get girls, unaccompanied like." He sniggered. "Nowadays, how do I know what they look like, one remotor is just like the next? You can't even tell the age, not unless you ask a remotor straight out. Look a bit silly when you find you're chatting up an old dear of seventy." He sighed. "Anyway, I'm getting a bit old for that game."

He looked it. Thin gray hair straggled across the parchment skin of his lined brow. Suddenly I tired of his reminiscences. The remotourists were pouring down the village in a silver tide and I had work to do. I walked away, leaving him staring ruminatively at his moist cigarette.

The coach park belongs to a friend of mine by the name of Charles Judd. He charges by the head and makes a good living from this and his remotor repair shop. He picked up the coach park cheap, too, from an old fellow disheartened by the fall in land values following Rotomation.

In order that the appearance of Pentreath remain unspoiled the local council insists on Charles' site at the clifftop being the only coach park near the village. Well away from the cluster of buildings at the waterfront, the park has a rough path leading down to the main street. The view is superb and gives a good initial impression to the remotourist.

Charles has an interesting sideline; he has affixed at the seaward side of the park a notice which states that persons descending to the beach by the cliff path do so at their own risk. The cliff path, as distinct from the proper path to the village, is barely negotiable.

The remotourist is naturally adventurous. He has little to lose; should his remotor be damaged in some stupid escapade he merely pays to have it repaired, while himself lying in comfort at the Shelflife Center, experiencing exciting events through his imperiled robot's senses. I do quite well in heavy seas that way; the boats are comprehensively insured.

As a result many remotourists, rather than take the safe road to the village, will see Charles' sign and attempt the cliff path. A Fulltime human can manage it if he has a strong head for heights, but remotors are not so agile.

And sure enough, as I passed the sign grinning to myself as always at the shrewdness of Charles' idea, I heard cries for help.

I hurried to the repair shop, a wooden shack at the village end of the park, and banged on the door. Charles appeared with a telescopic leg in his hand.

"You've got customers on the cliff path," I informed him.

His expression brightened. "Thanks," he said. He fetched a rope from inside the shack and hurried to the cliff-top. I tagged along to watch the fun.

"Hang on to this, will you, John?" He tied the rope about his waist and handed me the end. "Take a turn around that post. Not that I expect to fall; I could climb this cliff blindfold." He chuckled and scrambled over the edge. I paid the rope out, keeping it taut around the post. Presently there was a jerk. I began to pull in. Charles reappeared with a pair of remotors in tow. The rescue operation was slickly complete. "Fine," he said, dusting himself down. "That'll be twenty-five for the two of you, please." The remotors paid up without a murmur, digging the notes out of a large yellow bag.

I accompanied the robots down the sensible path to the village. They seemed not to be suffering from any shortage of cash. I wanted to get them into the Treasure Trove among the souvenirs.

"What a nice man," remarked one of the remotors. I saw from the name tag that it was woman, Lucy Allbright. "How lucky that he happened to be around, Al."

Albert Allbright laughed. "Don't kid yourself, Lucy. He

makes useful money from his rescue setup. And I wouldn't be surprised if our friend here were in on it, too."

"Not me," I said hastily. "I own a gift shop. My name's Green, by the way."

"Glad to meet you, Mr. Green." They introduced themselves unnecessarily. "You must be Green's Cream," remarked Al.

"We have to take some of that back," added Lucy.

"All genuine stuff," I murmured.

"I'm sure. We first came here over forty years ago, you know." I couldn't tell whether the statement was intended to be significant. "Haven't been back since. From where we are now, it looks much the same, doesn't it, Lucy?"

This couple must be pretty old, I decided. They were the sort of tourists we wanted. Sentimental and with money to spare.

I took them to the Treasure Trove and introduced them to Sylvia. In minutes they were chatting with her like old friends—Sylvia has this effect on people—so I left the three of them at the table. The Tea Room seats about twenty-five and there were one or two Fulltime villagers in, drinking coffee and eating buns, generally adding a touch of local color. This is very necessary. Remotors do not, obviously, eat or drink—but remotorists like to sit down from time to time in an authentic atmosphere and watch other folks or chat with locals. The Tea Room, basically, serves as a meeting place where remotorists get to know each other in attractive surroundings, buy Green's Cream, and then wander around the Treasure Trove, spending the rest of their budget for the day.

I passed through the doorway that separates the Tea Room from the Shoppe and was pleased to find the latter full of chattering remotors lurching among the counters on spindly legs, spending freely.

Well satisfied, I let myself out and strolled along the waterfront to the Smugglers' Arms. The public bar at this hour was almost empty; Jack Rivers was swabbing the counter in desultory fashion, the air smelled of disinfectant and the parrot was muttering unpleasantly to itself, occasionally plucking at the bars of its cage like an ill-tempered harpist. I ordered a pint and sat down.

"Aah, it be a fine mornin', stranger."

"For God's sake, Bert," I snapped. "It's me, Green."

"Oh, I beg your pardon, Mr. Green." The old man's eyes focused with rheumy difficulty. "All the same, I'll have a pint, please."

"Not from me you won't. Wait till the tourists start coming in."

Bert Jennings is the village character and quite good at it. His line is to trade homespun philosophy and weather forecasts for drinks while sitting in an ancient wheelback chair in the corner of the bar. The remotorists spot him and cluster around as he clutches an empty mug in both mittened, arthritic hands and tells them the history of the village in a quavering voice. After a while the remotors buy him a drink and move away, pick up a stone jar of homemade Cornish Mead to take back to the Center, and drift out into the street, to be replaced by further seekers after information. We have an arrangement in Pentreath. If a remotorist wants details of village history, we send them to Bert. While the rest of us sell souvenirs and experiences, he sells words.

I often wonder what happens while we are all on Shelflife and the village is in the hands of Rotomation 2 and 3. Do they, too, have their village sage? Once or twice while at the Center I have contemplated sending my remotor to Pentreath to find out exactly what goes on, but I have never gotten around to it; there are too many other places to see.

"Hi, John. Thanks for the customers." Charles Judd was standing at the bar. He handed me a beer.

"Thanks. I took them into the Tea Room after, and let Sylvia loose on them."

Charles smiled. "A wife in a million. She makes more money with her personality than you with all your schemes."

"I'm not too sure about that." I frowned. They don't know what it's like to live with somebody who seems to like everyone except me. "She sometimes forgets that we do all this for money."

"Come off it, John. You know you couldn't do without her."

I fought back my irritation. Barroom banter is not my line. "Sometimes I wish it were permissible to exchange Rotomations. I'd like to see some new faces."

"Fine," he chuckled. "Leave her with me. Oh, by the way—" He sat down, pulled his chair close. "I heard some disturbing news today. From a fellow on Rotomation Two, who came here last year while Rotomation Three was in charge."

"Oh?"

"It seems they dropped prices all around and advertised the fact. It's the first I've heard about it. I don't think it'll be the last. This guy on Two wanted a small repair job done this morning. He called me a crook when I told him the price."

"What?" This was serious. Those of us who own our businesses let them to other Rotomations on the strict understandings that prices be maintained. "We'll have to put this before the Chamber of Commerce," I said.

"And I tell you another thing. Ewell's selling cream in his Grotto."

"What?" Poaching on one another's preserves is something we don't do. I got to my feet. "I'll deal with this right away. I'll have that little swine thrown out of the Chamber!"

"Hold it. He's not a member. His is a temporary structure. He doesn't pay local siterates either."

"I know that." I charged out of the bar, incensed. I had to see Sylvia immediately. She had helped Ewell set up his stall this morning. She must have seen the cream. What the hell was she thinking of?

I stormed into the Tea Room to find Sylvia still seated at a table with the Allbrights. This did not improve my temper. She should have been showing them around the Treasure Trove by now. She looked up as I entered.

"Oh, John." She smiled at me brightly, insensitive to my mood. "Mr. Allbright was just telling me. Did you know—he knew this place before Rotomation? They spent their honeymoon here. He says the place has hardly changed."

"Sit down, Mr. Green." The remotourist waved me to a vacant chair. "That's right, Sylvia. Mind you, the people have changed. I don't suppose any of the old ones are left now."

"I wonder if you knew Bert Jennings," Sylvia said.

"Had you thought of taking a fishing trip?" I asked hastily.

"Bert Jennings? That wouldn't be young Bert—do you remember, Lucy? He showed us how to catch bass? I wonder now—" The remotor fell silent, thinking then: "Where can we find him?"

"He'll be in the Smugglers'. He's alway there at this

hour." Sylvia seemed determined to send our customers elsewhere.

"What luck," exclaimed Allbright. "We must have a word with him. I'm sure it's the same man. You know"—He looked around, cylindrical head pivoting—"you've done a wonderful job with this place. It's almost exactly as I remember it. You can't know what it means to Lucy and me to come back here and see it all again."

"Last time I suppose the village was packed with Full-time tourists," Sylvia remarked.

"You can't imagine the crowds—of course, everyone was Fulltime then. It was two years before Rotomation came in—earth was crowded, believe me. You could hardly move. The roads were one solid traffic jam. But now, well, look at the coaches we came in. Three hundred people in such a small space. Oh, yes—Rotomation was a wonderful idea."

"And it solved the food problem, Al. Don't forget that," Lucy pointed out.

"Oh, yes. Things were getting difficult. I won't say we were starving—but some of us were hungry. Now—in two years Shelflife a person only consumes a few gallons of drip. Of course, we all eat during our Full-time year but that's only one-third of the population."

"How do you enjoy Shelflife?" asked Sylvia. "After having known what it was like before."

"Fine. I'm packed away comfortably in Gloucester. I'm conscious of my mind and body being there but only when I think about it. In my first two years Shelflife I adapted completely. It seemed strange to go on Fulltime again when my Rotomation came round."

"The remotors are good," said Lucy, nodding her shining head in a way which somehow betrayed her real age.

I was still trembling with rage; I wanted to get Sylvia alone. I think they sensed it.

"Well." Allbright stood up suddenly. "We must be going. My, it feels good to be young again. My real body's pretty feeble now, you know."

In an effort to be polite I managed to join the conversation at last. "You won't try to take your wife down that cliff in your next Fulltime, then?"

I had been tactless. I could tell by the pause before he replied but I was too mad at Sylvia to care.

"We're truly young only once," he replied at last quietly.

"It's always as well to make the best of things while you can, Mr. Green." He glanced from Sylvia to myself. "Remotors are good but they're no substitute for flesh and blood. We climbed that cliff over forty years ago. We won't do it again."

His wife spoke. "Where do you recommend we go now, dear?" she asked Sylvia.

"You must see Gordon Ewell's Grotto," she replied at once. "And then why not slip into the Smugglers' and have a word with Bert Jennings?"

"Fine. That would be interesting. Oh, and before we go, I must have some of your cream to take back."

"I shouldn't bother now," said Sylvia. "You don't want to carry it about all day. You can pick it up later. The Grotto sells it as well, if that's nearer for you."

The sight of a woman crying moves me to fury. It is unnecessary; an attempt to take unfair advantage, calculated to turn logical defeat into a moral victory. I suppose she expected me to apologize.

"And you can cut out the tears," I told her. "Once and for all, get it into your head that we're in this for the money. To save for our Shelflife so that we can send our remotors out anywhere we like and enjoy ourselves. We get people in and we *sell*. Is that clear?"

"But why can't we enjoy ourselves all the time?" she asked. "Do we have to behave like the other sharks in the village? Like your friend Charles?"

"Charles is okay. He's a good businessman. What about your friend Ewell and his fake Grotto?"

"John, everyone knows Gordon's Grotto is fake. The tourists know it. There's no pretense about it. Gordon's a nice fellow."

I could feel the rage boiling up again, a sick volcano in my stomach. "By God, anyone would think you were in love with that lousy little creep." I was losing control of myself; I seized her by the shoulders and shook her. "Are you, Sylvia? Are you?"

She bit her lip and gave me a patient look; I very nearly slapped her face. "You know I'm not, John," she said quietly. "I'm in love with you. But sometimes I wish you could be a bit less—hard. This isn't dog eat dog—that sort of life finished when Rotomation came in. There's plenty for all of us."

"And how the hell did he get to selling cream?" I

raged. "You helped him this morning. You must have seen it."

"I didn't think——"

"Where does he get it from? Where does he get this fake cream he sells in his fake Grotto?"

"I believe it's the same brand as ours. He just puts a different label on it, as we do."

"What? He doesn't even have any cows——" My head was spinning; I felt dizzy with rage and frustration. I swung around and left Sylvia standing there, her cheeks wet, her eyes wide and stupid. I slammed out the back way and strode into the field. The Herefords were grouped around the rear of the building. My gun was in the wooden shed. The canvas of Ewell's Grotto shone white in the sun. My hands were wet and shaking.

They say a thunderstorm clears the air. This may be so in other parts of the country but it doesn't usually apply to Pentreath. Here a fine spell may be broken by a storm, which is often the precursor of further storms and endless drizzling rain, day after day.

But the late afternoon of the first day of the tourist season was still delightful. The sun continued to shine unabated and as I climbed the cliff path life seemed pretty good. I reached the grassy knoll at the top and turned to admire the view. Across the tiny bay, on the opposite headland, were the two coaches, children's toys in the hard light. The village lay beneath me, the boats bobbing at anchor as the ebbing remnants of last night's heavy seas slapped against the quay. The village street glittered with promenading remotors; the wreckage of Ewell's Grotto lay at the near end, canvas flattened and tent poles askew. There had been no customers for my boats but I was not particularly bothered; the Treasure Trove was doing well and I had decided to take the afternoon off; Sylvia and the assistants could cope.

"Lovely afternoon, Mr. Green."

I jumped, startled, and turned round. Two remoters were sitting farther along the cliff, telescopic legs dangling over the edge.

"Oh, hello, Mr. Allbright—Mrs. Allbright. Yes, it's very nice," I replied none too enthusiastically. I find I am happiest when alone—inane conversation bores me. I leave that to Sylvia.

"It must be very pleasant living here for your Fulltime," remarked Mrs. A. "You're very lucky."

I don't like being told I'm lucky. "What do you do?" I asked.

"I work in a synthetics plant," replied Allbright. "Hard work for a man of my age. You have to watch the machinery. Particularly in January after the previous Rotomation goes off. There's never much maintenance done in December. They're too busy thinking what they're going to do with their Shelflife."

Across the bay a hooter brayed.

"Time to be getting back to the coaches," observed Allbright. They stood up. "Would you mind walking back with us, Mr. Green? I've got an idea which might interest you."

Together we descended to the village. "The Grotto looks a mess," I observed. "It's better to build solidly even if it does mean paying local siterates."

"I think it's a shame," said Mrs. Allbright. "You can tell a lot of work's gone into that place. When I saw those cows stampeding through and smashing it all up, I could have cried for the poor man."

"I wonder what set those cattle running," speculated her husband. "You could have lost a lot of money yourself, Mr. Green. Herefords are valuable beasts."

"I was lucky," I said. "You know, they've never done it before. I expect they were nervous after last night's storm and some sudden noise startled them. Although I can't say I'm too sorry about the Grotto. It's a fake. I feel it lowers the tone of the village."

"I think it's fun," said the old woman. "And how do you mean, a fake?"

"Well—it's not genuine."

She laughed. "Oh, dear. Well now, just tell me what is."

"My Herefords are genuine."

"In what way? Do they have any practical use as cows used to? Do the boats and the Smugglers' Arms and your Tea Room—and Bert Jennings?"

"Bert Jennings?" I was puzzled and a little annoyed.

"Which is the real Bert Jennings?" she asked. "The old character who sits in the bar for one year out of three, putting on his act, or the remotor who goes skiing and flying and climbs Everest for the other two years? On a time basis it ought to be the remotor."

"Don't worry about it, Mr. Green." Allbright chuckled.

"Lucy gets these moods. She has few illusions—both of us have. The point is, we came here on our honeymoon—ages ago—and we had a wonderful time. Today, after all these years, we thought we'd come back and see the old place. We didn't expect to find it quite the same and it wasn't. But it's still wonderful. You've all done a great job of maintaining the appearance; the sea is still here—and the beach and the harbor and the cliffs. It's still Pentreath. And as for fake souvenirs and synthetic cream and shabby sideshows, well, they had those forty years ago, too. I tell you, nothing's changed very much. There's no need to feel defensive about things here."

The path narrowed and they moved ahead. I saw they were actually holding hands. Two remotors holding hands, for God's sake, like a couple of starcrossed lovers. I thought about Sylvia and myself in forty years' time. . . .

We were passing the Treasure Trove when he made his suggestion. The narrow street was full of gleaming remotors stilting their way toward the coaches.

"It used to be a guest house, you know. They put people up for the night as the Smugglers' did. Have you ever thought of doing so again in those bedrooms upstairs? Nobody else in the village does. I've asked."

"But we don't get guests," I objected. "Everyone works during Fulltime except the very rich and they go abroad."

"I mean putting remotors up in proper rooms, in beds, instead of just packing them away for the night. It'd be a novel idea. You could advertise all-inclusive fishing weeks."

"Remotors in beds?" I couldn't help laughing—the idea seemed so ridiculous.

"No, I'm serious. Lucy and I would have enjoyed staying in a real bedroom and having a whole week here. Delivery could be arranged with the coach people. After all, even remotourists get tired of rushing from place to place all the time, particularly the older ones like us."

Most tourists, if you allow yourself to get drawn into conversation, will make suggestions as to how trade could be improved. I thought I'd heard it all—from paddle steamers to traveling circuses. But I'd never before heard of letting furnished bedrooms to remotors. They cannot experience discomfort, so what's wrong with the trundling coach, which saves overnight time between one stop and the next? And in any case, why should anyone want to spend more than one day in any place? The truth of the matter was, they were a couple of sentimentalists who wanted to relive their ancient honeymoon in as much detail as possible. Fulltime traveling is expensive and cuts into valuable money-earning days.

I was still chuckling to myself as, hand in steel hand, they climbed the hill to the coach park. The shadow of the setting sun pursued us up the slope; the village was in dusk against the crimson-capped black hillside.

We reached the coaches. Allbright extended a silver claw. "Good-bye, Mr. Green," he said. "Would you say thank you to Sylvia for us for making our day so pleasant."

He turned to his wife. "Bye, Lucy," he said.

"See you in Bristol, Al." They stood in silence for a moment, then slowly Mrs. Allbright withdrew herself into a cube. The coach driver, damp cigarette adhering to his lower lip, picked up the remotor and slid it into the rear entrance to the vehicle.

Allbright turned away and stalked across to the other coach. I followed, puzzled. "What goes on?" I asked.

"This is my coach," he replied shortly.

"I don't understand," I muttered. I suddenly got an inkling of something I didn't want to know.

"It's quite simple, Mr. Green. Lucy and I married young and hastily. Soon we fought. I think you know how married couples can fight. We thought we hated each other. In two years we were divorced. Single people again. Free. You understand?"

"No." But I understood. Oh, God, I understood.

"Rotomation came along. They put us on different shifts. We kept in touch and met again as remotors. There are certain things in life we find out too late. Mistakes we cannot correct."

It is not permissible to exchange Rotomations.

"I haven't seen Lucy—*seen* her—for forty years."

He stiffened and began to sink to the ground. I watched.

At my feet was a silver box with hairline cracks on the top.

An inert, lifeless silver box; the driver lifted it into the coach.

A piece of precision machinery.

A cube.

I turned and ran toward the setting sun, toward the village, Sylvia. The sun must have been strong because my eyes were smarting.

A LITTLE KNOWLEDGE

POUL ANDERSON

For mastery of the science of star journeying and the art and business of making money out of interstellar trade, Poul Anderson cannot be beat, as he demonstrates in this, perhaps tongue-in-cheek, example.

They found the planet during the first Grand Survey. An expedition to it was organized very soon after the report appeared; for this looked like an impossibility.

It orbited its G9 sun at an average distance of some three astronomical units, thus receiving about one eighteenth the radiation Earth gets. Under such a condition —and others, e.g., the magnetic field strength which was present—a subJovian ought to have formed; and indeed it had fifteen times the terrestrial mass. But—that mass was concentrated in a solid globe. The atmosphere was only half again as dense as on man's home, and breathable by him.

"Where 'ave h'all the H'atoms gone?" became the standing joke of the research team. Big worlds are supposed to keep enough of their primordial hydrogen and helium to completely dominate the chemistry. Paradox, as it was unofficially christened, did retain some of the latter gas, to a total of eight percent of its air. This posed certain technical problems which had to be solved before anyone dared land. However, land the men must; the puzzle they confronted was so delightfully baffling.

A nearly circular ocean basin suggested an answer which studies of its bottom seemed to confirm. Paradox had begun existence as a fairly standard specimen, complete with four moons. But the largest of these, probably a captured asteroid, had had an eccentric orbit. At last perturbation brought it into the upper atmosphere, which at that time extended beyond Roche's limit. Shock waves, repeated each time one of those ever-deeper grazings was made, blew vast quantities of gas off into space: especially the lighter molecules. Breakup of the moon hastened this process and made it more violent, by presenting more solid surface. Thus at the final crash, most of those meteoroids fell as one body, to form that gigantic astrobleme. Perhaps metallic atoms, thermally ripped free of their ores and splashed as an incandescent fog across half the planet, locked onto the bulk of what hydrogen was left, if any was.

Be that as it may, Paradox now had only a mixture of what had hitherto been comparatively insignificant impurities, carbon dioxide, water vapor, methane, ammonia, and other materials. In short, except for a small amount of helium, it had become rather like the young Earth. It got less heat and light, but greenhouse effect kept most of its water liquid. Life evolved, went into the photosynthesis business, and turned the air into the oxynitrogen common on terrestrials.

The helium had certain interesting biological effects. These were not studied in detail. After all, with the hyperdrive opening endless wonders to them, spacefarers tended to choose the most obviously glamorous. Paradox lay a hundred parsecs from Sol. Thousands upon thousands of worlds were more easily reached; many were more pleasant and less dangerous to walk on. The expedition departed and had no successors.

First it called briefly at a neighboring star, on one of whose planets were intelligent beings that had developed a promising set of civilizations. But, again, quite a few such lay closer to home.

The era of scientific expansion was followed by the era of commercial aggrandizement. Merchant adventurers began to appear in the sector. They ignored Paradox, which had nothing to make a profit on, but investigated the inhabited globe in the nearby system. In the language dominant there at the time, it was called something like Trillia, which thus became its name in League Latin. The speakers of that language were undergoing their equivalent of the First Industrial Evolution, and eager to leap into the modern age.

Unfortunately, they had little to offer that was in demand elsewhere. And even in the spacious terms of the Polesotechnic League, they lived at the far end of a long haul. Their charming arts and crafts made Trillia marginally worth a visit, on those rare occasions when a trader was on such a route that the detour wasn't great. Besides, it was as well to keep an eye on the natives. Lacking the means to buy the important gadgets of Technic society, they had set about developing these for themselves.

Bryce Harker pushed through flowering vines which covered an otherwise doorless entrance. They rustled back into place behind him, smelling like allspice, trapping gold-yellow sunlight in their leaves. That light also slanted through ogive windows in a curving wall, to glow off the grain of the wooden floor. Furniture was sparse: a few stools, a low table bearing an intricately faceted piece of rock crystal. By Trillian standards the ceiling was high; but Harker, who was of average human size, must stoop.

Witweet bounced from an inner room, laid down the book of poems he had been reading, and piped, "Why, be welcome, dear boy—Oo-oo-ooh!"

He looked down the muzzle of a blaster.

The man showed teeth. "Stay right where you are," he commanded. The vocalizer on his breast rendered the sounds he made into soprano cadenzas and arpeggios, the speech of Lenidel. It could do nothing about his vocabulary and grammar. His knowledge did include the fact that, by omitting all honorifics and circumlocutions without apology, he was uttering a deadly insult.

That was the effect he wanted—deadliness.

"My, my, my dear good friend from the revered Solar Commonwealth," Witweet stammered, "is this a, a jest too subtle for a mere pilot like myself to comprehend? I will gladly laugh if you wish, and then we shall enjoy tea and cakes. I have genuine Lapsang Soochong tea from Earth, and have just found the most darling recipe for sweet cakes—"

"Quiet!" Harker rapped. His glance flickered to the windows. Outside, flower colors exploded beneath reddish tree trunks; small bright wings went fluttering past; The Waterfall That Rings Like Glass Bells could be heard in the distance. Annanna was akin to most cities of Lenidel, the principal nation on Trillia, in being spread through an immensity of forest and parkscape. Nevertheless, Annanna had a couple of million population, who kept busy. Three aircraft were crossing heaven. At any moment, a pedestrian or cyclist might come along The Pathway Of The Beautiful Blossoms And The Bridge That Arches Like A Note Of Music, and wonder why two humans stood tense outside number 1337.

Witweet regarded the man's skinsuit and boots, the pack on his shoulders, the tightly-drawn sharp features behind the weapon. Tears blurred the blue of Witweet's great eyes. "I fear you are engaged in some desperate undertaking which distorts the natural goodness that, I feel certain, still inheres," he quavered. "May I beg the honor of being graciously let help you relieve whatever your distress may be?"

Harker squinted back at the Trillian. *How much do we really know about his breed, anyway? Damned nonhuman thing—Though I never resented his existence till now—* His pulse knocked; his skin was wet and stank, his mouth was dry and cottony-tasting.

Yet his prisoner looked altogether helpless. Witweet was an erect biped; but his tubby frame reached to barely a meter, from the padded feet to the big, scalloped ears. The two arms were broomstick thin, the four fingers on either hand suggested straws. The head was practically spherical, bearing a pug muzzle, moist black nose, tiny mouth, quivering whiskers, upward-slanting tufty brows. That, the tail, and the fluffy silver-gray fur which covered the whole skin, had made Olafsson remark that the only danger to be expected from this race was that eventually their cuteness would become unendurable.

Witweet had nothing upon him except an ornately embroidered kimono and a sash tied in a pink bow. He surely owned no weapons, and probably wouldn't know what to do with any. The Trillians were omnivores, but did not seem to have gone through a hunting stage in their evolution. They had never fought wars, and personal violence was limited to an infrequent scuffle.

Still, Harker thought, *they've shown the guts to push*

into deep space. I daresay even an unarmed policeman—
Courtesy Monitor—could use his vehicle against us, like by
ramming.

Hurry!

"Listen," he said. "Listen carefully. You've heard that
most intelligent species have members who don't mind using brute force, outright killing, for other ends than self-
defense. Haven't you?"

Witweet waved his tail in assent. "Truly I am baffled
by that statement, concerning as it does races whose
achievements are of incomparable magnificence. However,
not only my poor mind, but those of our most eminent
thinkers have been engaged in fruitless endeavors to—"

"Dog your hatch!" The vocalizer made meaningless
noises and Harker realized he had shouted in Anglic. He
went back to Lenidellian-equivalent. "I don't propose to
waste time. My partners and I did not come here to trade
as we announced. We came to get a Trillian spaceship.
The project is important enough that we'll kill if we must.
Make trouble, and I'll blast you to greasy ash. It won't
bother me. And you aren't the only possible pilot we can
work through, so don't imagine you can block us by sacri-
ficing yourself. I admit you are our best prospect. Obey,
cooperate fully, and you'll live. We'll have no reason to
destroy you." He paused. "We may even send you home
with a good piece of money. We'll be able to afford
that."

The bottling of his fur might have made Witweet im-
pressive to another Trillian. To Harker, he became a ball of
fuzz in a kimono, an agitated tail and a sound of colora-
tura anguish. "But this is insanity . . . if I may say that to a
respected guest . . . One of *our* awkward, lumbering,
fragile, unreliable prototype ships—when you came in a
vessel representing centuries of advancement—? Why,
why, why, in the name of multiple sacredness, why?"

"I'll tell you later," the man said. "You're due for a
routine supply trip to, uh, Gwinsai Base, starting tomorrow,
right? You'll board this afternoon, to make final inspection and settle in. We're coming along. You'll be leaving in
about an hour's time. Your things must already be packed.
I didn't cultivate your friendship for nothing, you see!
Now, walk slowly ahead of me, bring your luggage back
here and open it so I can make sure what you've got.
Then we're on our way."

Witweet stared into the blaster. A shudder went

through him. His fur collapsed. Tail dragging, he turned toward the inner rooms.

Stocky Leo Dolgorov and ash-blond Einar Olafsson gusted simultaneous oaths of relief when their leader and his prisoner came out onto the path. "What took you that time?" the first demanded. "Were you having a nap?"

"Nah, he entered one of their bowing, scraping, and unction-smearing contests." Olafsson's grin held scant mirth.

"Trouble?" Harker asked.

"N-no . . . three, four passers-by stopped to talk—we told them the story and they went on," Dolgorov said. Harker nodded. He'd put a good deal of thought into that excuse for his guards' standing around—that they were about to pay a social call on Witweet but were waiting until the pilot's special friend Harker had made him a gift. A lie must be plausible, and the Trillian mind was not human.

"We sure hung on the hook, though." Olafsson started as a bicyclist came around a bend in the path and fluted a string of greetings.

Dwarfed beneath the men, Witweet made reply. No gun was pointed at him now, but one rested in each of the holsters near his brain. (Harker and companions had striven to convince everybody that the bearing of arms was a peaceful but highly symbolic custom in *their* part of Technic society, that without their weapons they would feel more indecent than a shaven Trillian.) As far as Harker's wire-taut attention registered, Witweet's answer was routine. But probably some forlornness crept into the overtones, for the neighbor stopped.

"Do you feel quite radiantly well, dear boy?" he asked.

"Indeed I do, honored Pwiddy, and thank you in my prettiest thoughts for your ever-sweet consideration," the pilot replied. "I . . . well, these good visitors from the starfaring culture of splendor have been describing some of their experiences—oh, I simply must relate them to you later, dear boy!—and naturally, since I am about to embark on another trip, I have been made pensive by this." Hands, tail, whiskers gesticulated. *Meaning what?* wondered Harker in a chill; and clamping jaws together: *Well, you knew you'd have to take risks to win a kingdom.* "Forgive me, I pray you of your overflowing generosity, that I rush off after such curt words. But I have promises to keep, and considerable distances to go before I sleep."

"Understood." Pwiddy spent a mere five minutes bidding farewell all around before he pedaled off. Meanwhile several others passed by. However, since no well-mannered person would interrupt a conversation even to make salute, they created no problem.

"Let's go." It grated in Dolgorov's throat.

Behind the little witch-hatted house was a pergola wherein rested Witweet's personal flitter. It was large and flashy—large enough for three humans to squeeze into the back—which fact had become an element in Harker's plan. The car that the men had used during their stay on Trillia, they abandoned. It was unmistakably an off-planet vehicle.

"Get started!" Dolgorov cuffed at Witweet.

Olafsson caught his arm and snapped: "Control your emotions! Want to tear his head off?"

Hunched over the dashboard, Witweet squeezed his eyes shut and shivered till Harker prodded him. "Pull out of that funk," the man said.

"I . . . I beg your pardon. The brutality so appalled me—" Witweet flinched from their laughter. His fingers gripped levers and twisted knobs. Here was no steering by gestures in a lightfield, let alone simply speaking an order to an autopilot. The overloaded flitter crawled skyward. Harker detected a flutter in its grav unit, but decided nothing was likely to fail before they reached the spaceport. And after that, nothing would matter except getting off this planet.

Not that it was a bad place, he reflected. Almost Earthlike in size, gravity, air, deliciously edible life forms—an Earth that no longer was and perhaps never had been, wide horizons and big skies, caressed by light and rain. Looking out, he saw woodlands in a thousand hues of green, meadows, river-gleam, an occasional dollhouse dwelling, grainfields ripening tawny and the soft gaudiness of a flower ranch. Ahead lifted The Mountain Which Presides Over Moonrise In Lenidel, a snowpeak pure as Fuji's. The sun, yellower than Sol, turned it and a few clouds into gold.

A gentle world for a gentle people. Too gentle.

Too bad. For them.

Besides, after six months of it, three city-bred men

were about ready to climb screaming out of their skulls. Harker drew forth a cigarette, inhaled it into lighting and filled his lungs with harshness. *I'd almost welcome a fight,* he thought savagely.

But none happened. Half a year of hard, patient study paid richly off. It helped that the Trillians were—well, you couldn't say lax about security, because the need for it had never occurred to them. Witweet radioed to the portmaster as he approached, was informed that everything looked O.K., and took his flitter straight through an open cargo lock into a hold of the ship he was to pilot.

The port was like nothing in Technic civilization, unless on the remotest, least visited of outposts. After all, the Trillians had gone in a bare fifty years from propeller-driven aircraft to interstellar spaceships. Such concentration on research and development had necessarily been at the expense of production and exploitation. What few vessels they had were still mostly experimental. The scientific bases they had established on planets of next-door stars needed no more than three or four freighters for their maintenance.

Thus a couple of buildings and a ground-control tower bounded a stretch of ferrocrete on a high, chilly plateau; and that was Trillia's spaceport. Two ships were in. One was being serviced, half its hull plates removed and furry shapes swarming over the emptiness within. The other, assigned to Witweet, stood on landing jacks at the far end of the field. Shaped like a fat torpedo, decorated in floral designs of pink and baby blue, it was as big as a Dromond-class hauler. Yet its payload was under a thousand tons. The primitive systems for drive, control, and life support took up that much room.

"I wish you a just too, too delightful voyage," said the portmaster's voice from the radio. "Would you honor me by accepting an invitation to dinner? My wife has, if I may boast, discovered remarkable culinary attributes of certain sea weeds brought back from Gwinsai; and for my part, dear boy, I would be so interested to hear your opinion of a new verse form with which I am currently experimenting."

"No . . . I thank you, no, impossible, I beg indulgence—" It was hard to tell whether the unevenness of Witweet's response came from terror or from the tobacco smoke that had kept him coughting. He almost flung his vehicle into the spaceship.

Clearance granted, *The Serenity of the Estimable Philosopher Ittypu* lifted into a dawn sky. When Trillia was a dwindling cloud-marbled sapphire among the stars, Harker let out a breath. "We can relax now."

"Where?" Olafsson grumbled. The single cabin barely allowed three humans to crowd together. They'd have to take turns sleeping in the hall that ran aft to the engine room. And their voyage was going to be long. Top pseudovelocity under the snail-powdered hyperdrive of this craft would be less than one light-year per day.

"Oh, we can admire the darling murals," Dolgorov fleered. He kicked an intricately painted bulkhead.

Witweet, crouched miserable at the control board, flinched. "I beg you, dear, kind sir, do not scuff the artwork," he said.

"Why should you care?" Dolgorov asked. "You won't be keeping this junk heap."

Witweet wrung his hands. "Defacement is still very wicked. Perhaps the consignee will appreciate my patterns? I spent *such* a time on them, trying to get every teensiest detail correct."

"Is that why your freighters have a single person aboard?" Olafsson laughed. "Always seemed reckless to me, not taking a backup pilot at least. But I suppose two Trillians would get into so fierce an argument about the interior decor that they'd each stalk off in an absolute snit."

"Why, no," said Witweet, a trifle calmer. "We keep personnel down to one because more are not really needed. Piloting between stars is automatic, and the crewbeing is trained in servicing functions. Should he suffer harm en route, the ship will put itself into orbit around the destination planet and can be boarded by others. An extra would thus uselessly occupy space which is often needed for passengers. I am surprised that you, sir, who have set a powerful intellect to prolonged consideration of our astronautical practices, should not have been aware—"

"I was, I was!" Olafsson threw up his hands as far as the overhead permitted. "Ask a rhetorical question and get an oratorical answer."

"May I, in turn, humbly request enlightenment as to your reason for . . . sequestering . . . a spacecraft ludicrously inadequate by every standard of your oh, so sophisticated society?"

"You may." Harker's spirits bubbled from relief of tension. They'd pulled it off. They really had. He sat down—the deck was padded and perfumed—and started a cigarette. Through his bones beat the throb of the gravity drive: energy wasted by a clumsy system. The weight it made underfoot fluctuated slightly in a rhythm that felt wavelike.

"I suppose we may as well call ourselves criminals," he said; the Lenidellian word he must use had milder connotations. "There are people back home who wouldn't leave us alive if they knew who'd done certain things. But we never got rich off them. Now we will."

He had no need for recapitulating except the need to gloat: "You know we came to Trillia half a standard year ago, on a League ship that was paying a short visit to buy art. We had goods of our own to barter with, and announced we were going to settle down for a while and look into the possibility of establishing a permanent trading post with a regular shuttle service to some of the Technic planets. That's what the captain of the ship thought, too. He advised us against it, said it couldn't pay and we'd simply be stuck on Trillia till the next League vessel chanced by, which wouldn't likely be for more than a year. But when we insisted, and gave him passage money, he shrugged," as did Harker.

"You have told me this," Witweet said. "I thrilled to the ecstasy of what I believed was your friendship."

"Well, I did enjoy your company," Harker smiled. "You're not a bad little osco. Mainly, though, we concentrated on you because we'd learned you qualified for our uses—a regular freighter pilot, a bachelor so we needn't fuss with a family, a chatterer who could be pumped for any information we wanted. Seems we gauged well."

"We better have," Dolgorov said gloomily. "Those trade goods cost us everything we could scratch together. I took a steady job for two years, and lived like a lama, to get my share."

"And now we'll be living like fakirs," said Olafsson. "But, afterward—afterward!"

"Evidently your whole aim was to acquire a Trillian ship," Witweet said. "My bemusement at this endures."

"We don't actually want the ship as such, except for demonstration purposes," Harker said. "What we want are the plans, the design. Between the vessel itself, and the service manuals aboard, we have that in effect."

Witweet's ears quivered. "Do you mean to publish the data for scientific interest? Surely, to beings whose ancestors went on to better models centuries ago—if, indeed, they ever burdened themselves with something this crude —surely the interest is nil. Unless . . . you think many will pay to see, in order to enjoy mirth at the spectacle of our fumbling efforts?" He spread his arms. "Why, you could have bought complete specifications most cheaply; or, indeed, had you requested of me, I would have been bubbly-happy to obtain a set and make you a gift." On a note of timid hope: "Thus you see, dear boy, drastic action is quite unnecessary. Let us return. I will state you remained aboard by mistake—"

Olafsson guffawed. Dolgorov said, "Not even your authorities can be that sloppy-thinking." Harker ground out his cigarette on the deck, which made the pilot wince, and explained at leisured length:

"We want this ship precisely because it's primitive. Your people weren't in the electronic era when the first human explorers contacted you. They, or some later visitors, brought you texts on physics. Then your bright lads had the theory of such things as gravity control and hyperdrive. But the engineering practice was something else again.

"You didn't have plans for a starship. When you finally got an opportunity to inquire, you found that the idealistic period of Technic civilization was over and you must deal with hardheaded entrepreneurs. And the price was set 'way beyond what your whole planet could hope to save in League currency. That was just the price for diagrams, not to speak of an actual vessel. I don't know if you are personally aware of the fact—it's no secret—but this is League policy. The member companies are bound by an agreement.

"They won't prevent anyone from entering space on his own. But take your case on Trillia. You had learned in a general way about, oh, transistors, for instance. But that did not set you up to manufacture them. An entire industrial complex is needed for that and for the million other necessary items. To design and build one, with the inevitable mistakes en route, would take decades at a minimum, and would involve regimenting your entire species and living in poverty because every bit of capital has to be reinvested. Well, you Trillians were too sensible to pay that price. You'd proceed more gradually. Yet at the same time, your scientists, all your more adventurous species, were burning to get out into space.

"I agree your decision about that was intelligent, too. You saw you couldn't go directly from your earliest hydrocarbon-fueled engines to a modern starship—to a completely integrated system of thermonuclear power plant, initiative-grade navigation and engineering computers, full-cycle life support, the whole works, using solid-state circuits, molecular-level and nuclear-level transitions, force fields instead of moving parts—an *organism* more energy than matter. No, you wouldn't be able to build that for generations, probably.

"But you could go ahead and develop huge, clumsy, but workable fission-power units. You could use vacuum tubes, glass rectifiers, kilometers of wire, to generate and regulate the necessary forces. You could store data on tape if not in single molecules, retrieve with a cathode-ray scanner if not with a quantum-field pulse, compute with miniaturized gas-filled units that react in microseconds if not with photon interplays that take a nanosecond.

"You're like islanders who had nothing better than canoes till someone stopped by in a nuclear-powered submarine. They couldn't copy that, but they might invent a reciprocating steam engine turning a screw—they might attach an airpipe so it could submerge—and it wouldn't impress the outsiders, but it would cross the ocean too, at its own pace; and it would overawe any neighboring tribes."

He stopped for breath.

"I see," Witweet murmured slowly. His tail switched back and forth. "You can sell our designs to sophonts in a proto-industrial stage of technological development. The idea comes from an excellent brain. But why could you not simply buy the plans for resale elsewhere?"

"The damned busybody League." Dolgorov spat.

"The fact is," Olafsson said, "spacecraft—of advanced type—have been sold to, ah, less advanced peoples in the past. Some of those weren't near industrialization, they were Iron Age barbarians, whose only thought was plundering and conquering. They could do that, given ships which are practically self-piloting, self-maintaining, self-everything. It's cost a good many lives and heavy material losses on border planets. But at least none of the barbarians have been able to duplicate the craft thus far. Hunt every pirate and warlord down, and that ends the problem. Or so the League hopes. It's banned any more such trades."

He cleared his throat. "I don't refer to races like the Trillians, who're obviously capable of reaching the stars by themselves and unlikely to be a menace when they do," he said. "You're free to buy anything you can pay for. The price of certain things is set astronomical mainly to keep you from beginning overnight to compete with the old-established outfits. They prefer a gradual phasing-in of newcomers, so they can adjust.

"But aggressive, warlike cultures, that'd not be interested in reaching a peaceful accommodation—they're something else again. There's a total prohibition on supplying their sort with anything that might help them to get off their planets in less than centuries. If League agents catch you at it, they don't fool around with rehabilitation like a regular government. They shoot you."

Harker grimaced. "I saw once on a telescreen interview," he remarked, "Old Nick van Rijn said he wouldn't shoot that kind of offenders. He'd hang them. A rope is reusable."

"And this ship *can* be copied," Witweet breathed. "A low industrial technology, lower than ours, could tool up to produce a modified design, in a comparatively short time, if guided by a few engineers from the core civilization."

"I trained as an engineer," Harker said. "Likewise Leo; and Einar spent several years on a planet where one royal family has grandiose ambitions."

"But the horror you would unleash!" wailed the Trillian. He stared into their stoniness. "You would never dare go home," he said.

"Don't want to anyway," Harker answered. "Power, wealth, yes, and everything those will buy—we'll have more than we can use up in our lifetimes, at the court of the Militants. Fun, too." He smiled. "A challenge, you know, to build a space navy from zero. I expect to enjoy my work."

"Will not the . . . the Polesotechnic League take measures?"

"That's why we must operate as we have done. They'd learn about a sale of plans, and then they wouldn't stop till they'd found and suppressed our project. But a non-Technic ship that never reported in won't interest them. Our destination is well outside their sphere of normal operations. They needn't discover any hint of what's going on—till an interstellar empire too big for them to break is there. Meanwhile, as we gain resources, we'll have been modernizing our industry and fleet."

"It's all arranged," Olafsson said. "The day we show up in the land of the Militants, bringing the ship we described to them, we'll become princes."

"Kings, later." Dolgorov added. "Behave accordingly, you xeno. We don't need you much. I'd soon as not boot you through an air lock."

Witweet spent minutes just shuddering.

The Serenity, et cetera moved on away from Trillia's golden sun. It had to reach a weaker gravitational field than a human craft would have needed, before its hyperdrive would function.

Harker spent part of that period being shown around, top to bottom and end to end. He'd toured a sister ship before, but hadn't dared ask for demonstrations as thorough as he now demanded. "I want to know this monstrosity we've got, inside out," he said while personally tearing down and rebuilding a cumbersome oxygen renewer. He could do this because most equipment was paired, against the expectation of eventual in-flight down time.

In a hold, among cases of supplies for the research team on Gwinsai, he was surprised to recognize a lean cylindroid, one hundred twenty centimenters long. "But here's a Solar-built courier!" he exclaimed.

Witweet made eager gestures of agreement. He'd been falling over himself to oblige his captors. "For messages in case of emergency, magnificent sir," he babbled. "A hyperdrive unit, an autopilot, a radio to call at journey's end till someone comes and retrieves the enclosed letter—"

"I know, I know. But why not build your own?"

"Well, if you will deign to reflect upon the matter, you will realize that anything we could build would be too slow and unreliable to afford very probable help. Especially since it is most unlikely that, at any given time, another spaceship would be ready to depart Trillia on the instant. Therefore, this courier is set, as you can see if you wish to examine the program, to go a considerably greater distance—though nevertheless not taking long, your human constructions being superlatively fast—to the planet called, ah, Oasis . . . an Anglic word meaning a lovely, cool, refreshing haven, am I correct?"

Harker nodded impatiently. "You are right. One of the League companies does keep a small base there."

"We have arranged that they will send aid if requested. At a price, to be sure. However, for our poor economy, as ridiculous a hulk as this is still a heavy investment, worth insuring."

"I see. I didn't know you bought such gadgets—not that there'd be a pegged price on them; they don't matter any more than spices or medical equipment. Of course, I couldn't find out every detail in advance, especially not things you people take so for granted that you didn't think to mention them." On impulse, Harker patted the round head. "You know, Witweet, I guess I do like you. I will see you're rewarded for your help."

"Passage home will suffice," the Trillian said quietly, "though I do not know how I can face my kinfolk after having been the instrument of death and ruin for millions of innocents."

"Then don't go home," Harker suggested. "We can't release you for years in any case, to blab our scheme and our coordinates. But we could, however, smuggle in whatever and whoever you wanted, same as for ourselves."

The head rose beneath his palm as the slight form straightened. "Very well," Witweet declared.

That fast? jarred through Harker. *He is nonhuman, yes, but*— The wondering was dissipated by the continuing voice:

"Actually, dear boy, I must disabuse you. We did not buy our couriers, we salvaged them."

"What? Where?"

"Have you heard of a planet named, by its human discoverers, Paradox?"

Harker searched his memory. Before leaving Earth he had consulted every record he could find about this entire stellar neighborhood. Poorly known though it was to men, there had been a huge mass of data—suns, worlds . . . "I think so. Big, isn't it? With a freaky atmosphere."

"Yes." Witweet spoke rapidly. "It gave the original impetus to Technic exploration of our vicinity. But later the men departed. In recent years, when we ourselves became able to pay visits, we found their abandoned camp. A great deal of gear had been left behind, presumably because it was designed for Paradox only and would be of no use elsewhere, hence not worth hauling back. Among these machines we came upon a few couriers. I suppose they had been overlooked. Your civilization can afford profligacy, if I may use that term in due respectfulness."

He crouched, as if expecting a blow. His eyes glittered in the gloom of the hold.

"Hm-m-m." Harker frowned. "I suppose by now you've stripped the place."

"Well, no." Witweet brushed nervously at his rising fur. "Like the men, we saw no use in, for example, tractors designed for a gravity of two-point-eight terrestrial. They can operate well and cheaply on Paradox, since their fuel is crude oil, of which an abundant supply exists near the campsite. But we already had electric-celled grav motors, however archaic they are by your standards. And we do not need weapons like those we found, presumably for protection against animals. We certainly have no intention of colonizing Paradox!"

"Hm-m-m." The human waved, as if to brush off the chattering voice. He slouched off, hands in pockets, pondering.

In the time that followed, he consulted the navigator's bible. His reading knowledge of Lenidellian was fair. The entry for Paradox was as laconic as it would have been in a Technic reference; despite the limited range of their operations, the Trillians had already encountered too many worlds to allow flowery descriptions. Star type and coordinates, orbital elements, mass, density, atmospheric composition, temperature ranges, and the usual rest were listed. There was no notation about habitability, but none was needed. The original explorers hadn't been poisoned or come down with disease, and Trillian metabolism was similar to theirs.

The gravity field was not too strong for this ship to make landing and, later, ascent. Weather shouldn't pose any hazards, given reasonable care in choosing one's path; that was a weakly energized environment. Besides, the vessel was meant for planetfalls, and Witweet was a skilled pilot in his fashion . . .

Harker discussed the idea with Olafsson and Dolgorov. "It won't take but a few days," he said, "and we might pick up something really good. You know I've not been too happy about the Militants' prospects of building an ample industrial base fast enough to suit us. Well, a few machines like this, simple things they can easily copy but designed by good engineers . . . could make a big difference."

"They're probably rust heaps," Dolgorov snorted. "That was long ago."

"No, durable alloys were available then." Olafsson said. "I like the notion intrinsically. I don't like the thought of our xeno taking us down. He might crash us on purpose."

"That sniveling faggot?" Dolgorov gibed. He jerked his head backward at Witweet, who sat enormous-eyed in the pilot chair listening to a language he did not understand. "By accident, maybe, seeing how scared he is!"

"It's a risk we take at journey's end," Harker reminded them. "Not a real risk. The ship has some ingenious fail-safes built in. Anyhow, I intend to stand over him the whole way down. If he does a single thing wrong, I'll kill him. The controls aren't made for me, but I can get us aloft again, and afterward we can rerig."

Olafsson nodded. "Seems worth a try," he said. "What can we lose except a little time and sweat?"

Paradox rolled enormous in the viewscreen, a darkling world, the sky-band along its sunrise horizon redder than Earth's, polar caps and winter snowfields gashed by the teeth of mountains, tropical forests and pampas a yellow-brown fading into raw deserts on one side and chopped off on another side by the furious surf of an ocean where three moons fought their tidal wars. The sun was distance-dwarfed, more dull in hue than Sol, nevertheless too bright to look near. Elsewhere, stars filled illimitable blackness.

It was very quiet aboard, save for the mutter of power-plant and ventilators, the breathing of men, their restless shuffling about in the cramped cabin. The air was blued and fouled by cigarette smoke; Witweet would have fled into the corridor, but they made him stay, clutching a perfume-dripping kerchief to his nose.

Harker straightened from the observation screen. Even at full magnification, the rudimentary electro-optical system gave little except blurriness. But he'd practiced on it, while orbiting a satellite, till he felt he could read those wavering traces.

"Campsite and machinery, all right," he said. "No details. Brush has covered everything. When were your people here last. Witweet?"

"Several years back," the Trillian wheezed. "Evidently vegetation grows apace. Do you agree on the safety of a landing?"

"Yes. We may snap a few branches, as well as flatten a lot of shrubs, but we'll back down slowly, the last hundred meters, and we'll keep the radar, sonar, and gravar sweeps going." Harker glanced at his men. "Next thing is to compute our descent pattern," he said. "But first I want to spell out again, point by point, exactly what each of us is to do under exactly what circumstances. I don't aim to take chances."

"Oh, no," Witweet squeaked. "I beg you, dear boy, I beg you the prettiest I can, please don't!"

After the tension of transit, landing was an anticlimax. All at once the engine fell silent. A wind whistled around the hull. Viewscreens showed low, thick-boled trees; fronded brownish leaves; tawny undergrowth; shadowy glimpses of metal objects beneath vines and amidst tall, whipping stalks. The sun stood at late afternoon in a sky almost purple.

Witweet checked the indicators while Harker studied them over his head. "Air breathable, of course," the pilot said, "which frees us of the handicap of having to wear smelly old spacesuits. We should bleed it in gradually, since the pressure is greater than ours at present and we don't want earaches, do we? Temperature—" He shivered delicately. "Be certain you are wrapped up snug before you venture outside."

"You're venturing first," Harker informed him.

"What? Oo-ooh, my good, sweet, darling friend, no, please, no! It is *cold* out there, scarcely above freezing. And once on the ground, no gravity generator to help, why, weight will be tripled. What could I possibly, possibly do? No, let me stay inside, keep the home fires burning —I mean keep the thermostat at a cozy temperature—and, yes, I will make you the nicest pot of tea . . ."

"If you don't stop fluttering and do what you're told, I'll tear your head off," Dolgorov said. "Guess what I'll use your skin for."

"Let's get cracking," Olafsson said. "I don't want to stay in this Helheim any longer than you."

They opened a hatch the least bit. While Paradoxian air seeped in, they dressed as warmly as might be, except for Harker. He intended to stand by the controls for the first investigatory period. The entering gases added a whine to the wind-noise. Their helium content made speech and other sounds higher-pitched, not quite natural; and this would have to be endured for the rest of the journey, since the ship had insufficient reserve tanks to flush out the new atmosphere. A breath of cold got by the heaters, and a rank smell of alien growth.

But you could get used to hearing funny, Harker thought. And the native life might stink, but it was harmless. You couldn't eat it and be nourished, but neither could its germs live off your body. If heavy weapons had been needed here, they were far more likely against large, blundering herbivores than against local tigers.

That didn't mean they couldn't be used in war.

Trembling, eyes squinched half shut, tail wrapped around his muzzle, the rest of him bundled in four layers of kimono, Witweet crept to the personnel lock. Its outer valve swung wide. The gangway went down. Harker grinned to see the dwarfish shape descend, step by step under the sudden harsh hauling of the planet.

"Sure you can move around in that pull?" he asked his companions.

"Sure," Dolgorov grunted. "An extra hundred-fifty kilos? I can backpack more than that, and then it's less well distributed."

"Stay cautious, though. Too damned easy to fall and break bones."

"I'd worry more about the cardiovascular system," Olafsson said. "One can stand three Gs for a while, but not for a very long while. Fluid begins seeping out of the cell walls, the heart feels the strain too much—and we've no gravanol along as the first expedition must have had."

"We'll only be here a few days at most," Harker said, "with plenty of chances to rest inboard."

"Right," Olafsson agreed. "Forward!"

Gripping his blaster, he shuffled onto the gangway. Dolgorov followed. Below, Witweet huddled. Harker looked out at bleakness, felt the wind slap his face with chill, and was glad he could stay behind. Later he must take his turn outdoors, but for now he could enjoy warmth, decent weight—

The world reached up and grabbed him. Off balance, he fell to the deck. His left hand struck first, pain gushed, he saw the wrist and arm splinter. He screamed. The sound came weak as well as shrill, out of a breast laboring against thrice the heaviness it should have had. At the same time, the lights in the ship went out.

Witweet perched on a boulder. His back was straight in spite of the drag on him, which made his robes hang stiff as if carved on an idol of some minor god of justice. His tail, erect, blew jauntily in the bitter sunset wind; the colors of his garments were bold against murk that rose in the forest round the dead spacecraft.

He looked into the guns of three men, and into the terror that had taken them behind the eyes; and Witweet laughed.

"Put those toys away before you hurt yourselves," he said, using no circumlocutions or honorifics.

"You swine, you filthy treacherous xeno, I'll kill you," Dolgorov groaned. "Slowly."

"First you must catch me," Witweet answered. "By virtue of being small, I have a larger surface-to-volume ratio than you. My bones, my muscles, my veins and capillaries and cell membranes suffer less force per square centimeter than do yours. I can move faster than you, here. I can survive longer."

"You can't outrun a blaster bolt," Olafsson said.

"No. You can kill me with that—a quick, clean death which does not frighten me. Really, because we of Lenidel observe certain customs of courtesy, use certain turns of speech—because our males in particular are encouraged to develop aesthetic interests and compassion—does that mean we are cowardly or effeminate?" The Trillian clicked his tongue. "If you supposed so, you committed an elementary logical fallacy which our philosophers name the does-not-follow."

"Why shouldn't we kill you?"

"That is inadvisable. You see, your only hope is quick rescue by a League ship. The courier can operate here, being a solid-state device. It can reach Oasis and summon a vessel which, itself of similar construction, can also land on Paradox and take off again . . . in time. This would be impossible for a Trillian craft. Even if one were ready to leave, I doubt the Astronautical Senate would permit the pilot to risk descent.

"Well, rescuers will naturally ask questions. I cannot imagine any story which you three men, alone, might concoct that would stand up under the subsequent, inevitable investigation. On the other hand, I can explain to the

League's agents that you were only coming along to look into trade possibilities and that we were trapped on Paradox by a faulty autopilot which threw us into a descent curve. I can do this *in detail,* which you could not if you killed me. They will return us all to Trillia, where there is no death penalty."

Witweet smoothed his wind-ruffled whiskers. "The alternative," he finished, "is to die where you are, in a most unpleasant fashion."

Harker's splinted arm gestured back the incoherent Dolgorov. He set an example by holstering his own gun. "I . . . guess we're outsmarted," he said, word by foul-tasting word. "But what happened? Why's the ship inoperable?"

"Helium in the atmosphere," Witweet explained calmly. "The monatomic helium molecule is ooh-how-small. It diffuses through almost every material. Vacuum tubes, glass rectifiers, electronic switches dependent on pure gases, any such device soon becomes poisoned. You, who were used to a technology that had long left this kind of thing behind, did not know the fact, and it did not occur to you as a possibility. We Trillians are, of course, rather acutely aware of the problem. I am the first who ever set foot on Paradox. You should have noted that my courier is a present-day model."

"I see," Olafsson mumbled.

"The sooner we get our message off, the better," Witweet said. "By the way. I assume you are not so foolish as to contemplate the piratical takeover of a vessel of the Polesotechnic League."

"Oh, no!" they said, including Dolgorov, and the other two blasters were sheathed.

"One thing, though," Harker said. A part of him wondered if the pain in him was responsible for his own abnormal self-possession. Counter-irritant against dismay? Would he weep after it wore off? "You bargain for your life by promising to have ours spared. How do we know we want your terms? What'll they do to us on Trillia?"

"Entertain no fears," Witweet assured him. "We are not vindictive, as I have heard some species are; nor have we any officious concept of 'rehabilitation.' Wrongdoers are required to make amends to the fullest extent possible. You three have cost my people a valuable ship and whatever cargo cannot be salvaged. You must have technological knowledge to convey, of equal worth. The working conditions will not be intolerable. Probably you can make restitution and win release before you reach old age.

"Now, come, get busy. First we dispatch that courier, then we prepare what is necessary for our survival until rescue."

He hopped down from the rock, which none of them would have been able to do unscathed, and approached them through gathering cold twilight with the stride of a conquerer.

REAL-TIME WORLD

CHRISTOPHER PRIEST

If you stand in the center of a room whose floor, ceiling, and four walls are all mirrors, how large is the room? Do you think you could tell? And if you take up habitation in a place where there is no night and no day, no sunset and no sunrise, and no horizon, what time is it? How could you be sure? There is a problem posed in this unusual story which is going to have to be answered some day soon by the space-flight agencies.

This is not relevant, but it serves to illustrate the pedantic and languid attitude to life we have all developed on the observatory.

The accommodation cabins of the observatory have been built on the periphery, in such a way that each cabin has at least one wall against vacuum. As the laboratory is moved from place to place, structural tensions come out in the form of cracks in the outer shell.

In the cabin I share with my wife, Clare, there are twenty-three cracks, each one of which would be capable of evacuating our cabin of its air if it were not periodically checked and resealed. This number of cracks is fairly typical; there is no cabin which does not have at least half a dozen.

The largest crack in the wall opened one night while we were asleep and, in spite of the fact that we had rigged elaborate pressure-reduction alarms, we were in an advanced state of hypoxia before we were awakened. That crack affected several other cabins at the same time, and it was after this that there was a move among some of the staff to abandon the accommodation section altogether and sleep in one of the common rooms.

Nothing came of the idea: on the observatory the twin evils of boredom and lethargy go hand in hand.

Thorensen came into my office and dumped a handwritten report on my desk. He is a large, ugly man, with graceless mannerisms. He has participated heavily in the social side of life on the observatory and it is rumored that he is an alcoholic. No one cares much about these things under normal circumstances, but when Thorensen is drunk he is boorish and noisy. Ordinarily, he is slow-moving, virtually reactionless.

"Here," he said. "Observed reproductive cycle in one of the echinoderms. Don't bother to try to understand it. You'll get the gist."

"Thanks," I said. I have grown accustomed to the intellectual snobbery of some of the scientists. I'm the only nonspecialist on the observatory. "Does it have to be dealt with today?"

"Suit yourself. I don't suppose anyone is waiting for it."

"I'll do it tomorrow."

"OK." He turned to leave.

"I've got your daily sheet for you," I said. "Do you want it?"

He turned back. "Let's have it."

He glanced at it uninterestedly, looking quickly across the two or three lines of print-out. I watched his expression, not sure exactly what I was trying to glean from it. Some of the staff don't read the sheets in my presence, but fold them up, place them in a pocket and read them in private. That is how it was expected they would be read, but not everyone reacts the same.

Thorensen had perhaps less to worry about at home, or less interest.

I waited for him to finish.

Then I said: "Marriott was in here yesterday. He says that a fire killed seven hundred people in New York."

Interest came into Thorensen's eyes. "Yes, I heard that too. Do you know anything more about it?"

"Only what Marriott told me. Apparently it was in a block of apartments. The fire started on the fourth floor and no one above it could escape."

"Isn't that fascinating? Seven hundred people, just like that."

"It was a terrible disaster," I said.

"Yes, yes. Terrible. But not as bad as that . . ." He leaned forward and put the palms of his hands on the far side of my desk. "Did you hear that? There was a riot somewhere in South America. Bolivia, I think. They called in troops to deal with it, things got out of hand and nearly two thousand people died."

This was new to me.

I said: "Who told you this?"

"One of the others. Norbert, I think."

"Two thousand," I said. "That's fascinating . . ."

Thorensen straightened.

"Anyway, I've got to get back. Will you be down in the bar this evening?"

"Probably," I said.

When Thorensen had left I looked at the report he had brought in. My function was to absorb the sense of the report, rewrite it into nontechnical language as far as possible, then prepare it for transmission back to Earth via the transor. Thorensen's original would then be photostated and returned to him, the copy being filed away in my office until our return to Earth.

I had a dozen other reports outstanding and Thorensen's would have to go to the bottom of the pile. Neither he nor the people on Earth would care when it was sent.

And in any event there was no hurry. The next transor-conjunction was that same evening and it was obvious I wouldn't have it ready by then. The conjunction after this was four weeks away.

Putting aside the report, I went to the door of my office and locked it, switching on the electric sign on the outside which said. TRANSOR ROOM—DO NOT DISTURB. Then I unlocked one of my cabinets and removed from it the rumor dissemination file.

I wrote down: "Thorensen/New York/700 deaths/apartment building. Ex Marriott/ditto." Then underneath: "Thorensen/Bolivia (?)/2000 deaths/riot. Ex Norbert Colston (?)."

As the Bolivian story was a new one to me, I had to

conduct a search through the Affectance Quotient 84 files. This would take some time. I had checked out the New York story the day before and found that it probably related to a fire in an office-building in Boston three days earlier, when 683 people had died. None of them was related in any way to members of the staff of the observatory.

In the AQ 84 files, I searched first through entries for Bolivia. There had been no major riots or public disorders there in the last four weeks. It was possible that the rumor related to an event earlier than this, but not probable. After Bolivia, I tried the other South American countries, but again drew a negative.

There had been a demonstration in Brazil the week before, but only a few people had been injured, and no one killed.

I shifted to Central America and ran similar checks in the various republics there. I chose to discount countries in North America or Europe, since it was not likely that if two thousand people had died, there would be no connection with any of the staff here.

I finally found the reference in Africa; under Tanzania. Nine hundred and sixty people massacred by panicking police when a hunger march degenerated into a riot. I looked at the transor report dispassionately, seeing the event as a statistic, another entry in my dissemination file. Before putting away the report, I took a note of the AQ. 27. Comparatively high.

In my rumor dissemination file I wrote: "Thorensen/ Bolivia . . . read Tanzania? Await confirmation."

I then added the date, and initialed it.

When I unlocked the office door Clare, my wife, was waiting outside. She was crying.

I have this problem with which I must live: in some respects I'm on my own at the observatory. Let me try to explain that.

If there is a group of people all basically similar, or even if there is a group of individuals making up a coherent and recognizable social unit, then there is companionship. If, on the other hand, there is no form of intercourse between the individuals, then a different kind of social structure exists. I wouldn't know what to call it, but it certainly does not constitute a unit. Something of the sort happens in big cities: millions of people coexisting on a few hundred square miles of land and yet, with certain exceptions, there is no real unitary construction to their society. Two people can live next door to one another and yet never know each other's name. People living alone in a building full of others can die of loneliness.

But there's another kind of solitude when in a group and that's what is happening to me. It's one of sanity. Or intellect. Or awareness.

In cold factual language: I'm a sane man in an insane society.

But the particular thing is that everyone on the observatory is *individually* just as sane as I am. But collectively, they're not.

Now there's a reason for this, and it accounts for my presence on the observatory. For the benefit of the others I have been given this other work of rewriting their reports and acting in general as press officer.

But the real reason is one of far greater importance. I'm the observer of the observatory.

I watch the staff, I take notes on their behavior and I channel information about them back to Earth. Not the most desirable of jobs, it may seem.

One of the staff I must observe, spy upon, treat clinically, is my wife.

Clare and I no longer get on with each other. There is nothing tempestuous between us; we've reached a state of acceptance of the mutual hostility and there it stays. I won't dwell on the less pleasant incidents between us. The cabin walls of the accommodation section are thin and any hatred to be vented must be done in near-silence. The observatory has made us like this; we are a product of our environment. Before the observatory we lived together in peace—perhaps when we get back home we may once more do so. But for the moment that is how it is.

I have said enough.

But Clare was crying . . . and she had come to me.

I opened the door, let her in.

"Dan," she said, "it's terrible about those children."

It registered at once. When Clare comes to me in my office, I do not know straight away whether she comes as a wife or as a member of the staff. This time, she was the latter.

"I know, I know," I said, as soothingly as I could manage. "But they will be doing verything they can."

"I feel so *helpless* here. If only I could do something."

"How are the others taking the news?"

She shrugged. "Melinda told me. She seemed to be very upset. But not——"

"Not as much as you? But then she hasn't been so involved with children." I had guessed that when the story of the refugees reached Clare it would upset her. Before coming to the observatory with me she had been a child-care welfare officer. Now she had to be content with study of the humanoid children outside.

"I hope the people responsible are satisfied," she said.

"Have you heard any more details?" I prompted her.

"No. But Melinda said that Jackson, the doctor who works with her, told her that the New Zealand authorities were calling in the United Nations."

I nodded. I'd heard this earlier in the day from Clifford Makin, the arachnologist. I had expected the further detail to be in full currency by about this time.

I said: "You heard about that fire in New York?"

"No?"

I told her about it, in substantially the same detail as Thorensen had told me.

When I'd finished she stood still for a while, her head bent forward.

"I wish we could go home," she said in the end. I had my wife in the office now.

I said: "So do I. Just as soon as we finish . . ."

She glared at me. I knew as well as she that the progress of the work had no bearing on the length of our stay here. And in any case, I was doing nothing to further that work. Only I, of all the staff, contribute nothing to the progress.

"Forget it, Dan," she said. "There's nothing at home for either of us now."

"What makes you say that?"

"If you don't know, I'm not going to spell it out for you."

A veiled reference to our crumbling relationship. I wondered, as I had done many times before, if even a break with the closed environment of the observatory would ever restore what we had had.

"All right," I said, "let's leave it at that."

"Anyway, with all these things we hear, I'm not sure I want to go back."

"Not ever?"

"I don't know. I hear—I hear that things on Earth are worse, far worse, than we are told about."

I found myself breaking out of my role as husband, became the observer once again.

"What do you mean? That there's some form of censorship?"

She nodded. "Only I don't see what harm it would do for us to know what is going on."

"Well, that's your best argument against censorship."

She nodded again.

I had on my desk a small pile of unclaimed daily sheets. I would leave the pile to mount up for a few days, then take them round myself and deliver them. I wasn't too keen on the idea of delivering them. The attitude of several of the staff toward the sheets was casual anyway, and if they got the idea I would deliver them then they wouldn't collect them at all.

The worst offender in this respect was Mike Querrel, who had never, to my knowledge, come of his own accord to collect his sheets. A gloomy bachelor whose parents had died while he was still a child, he had told me once that he had nothing at home of which to receive news, so why did he have to bother about the sheets.

True enough, his daily sheets had the least news on them of anybody's, but there was no point in the experiment unless everyone took his sheets.

I sifted through the pile before me. There were eleven of Mike's, two or three others which had not been claimed, and those of Sebastian, the only man who had so far died on the Observatory. Sebastian's death had been one of the factors that had gone unanticipated, and there was no way for me to de-program the computer on board. On the real-time simulator back on Earth, Sebastian's identity had been removed.

Once every twenty-four hours the computer would print out the daily news sheets, one for each person on board. The staff had been told that the news came up every day through the transor, but this was not the truth.

The news came in once in every four weeks, was fed direct into the computer, and then released in twenty-nine daily installments, roughly in the order in which it had occurred. This day, as I have said, there was to be another transor-conjunction and the next four weeks' news would arrive. I would have access to the unprocessed bulk of it at once if I wished, but for the rest of the staff the news would have to trickle out at daily intervals.

There was no way of short-circuiting the system; even I could not get out of the computer the personal sheets of the "next" day until the appropriate time.

Every person on board, including myself, had one sheet of personalized news, once a day, every day.

I decided to clear the accumulated pile and took them around the observatory, delivering them as necessary. Then I returned to my office.

Some time before the expedition in the observatory had been conceived, a man named Tolneuve had invented a system for classifying news of current events into a graded table of what he called Affectance Quotients. This ran from nought to one hundred; from nil affectance to complete affectance.

Tolneuve's argument was that in the normal course news of current affairs had little relevance—or affectance—to personal life. One could read of distant wars, or social disturbances, or disasters,-or one could experience them vicariously through the visual media, but one was not *affected* in any way.

On the other hand, some items of news did have relevance, even if it was only of a very long term, or in a very indirect way.

Tolneuve once cited an example of this.

While one's life could be measurably affected by the news, say, of the demise of a well-loved and well-endowed uncle, it would not be so easy to estimate the impact of a rise in the price of some industrial commodity such as manganese. If the cost of living of one individual could be ultimately affected and measured, then the same could be said of everybody's. Large numbers of people would have low AQs for most news and only a small proportion of the population would have very high ones.

Tolneuve acknowledged this and derived his graded table. Applied to an individual whose entire social situation could be established, it was possible to apply an AQ to any item of news. To one man, the rich uncle's legacy might produce a 95 percent AQ or higher; more expensive manganese a 10 percent AQ or lower. To another man (for example, a distant relative of the first man who was a broker in industrial metals) the same two items might have exactly opposite percentages.

It was an almost entirely useless piece of sociological

research. It was played around with for a year or two by the news dissemination agencies, then put aside. It just had no practical use.

But then the observatory was conceived and a use for it was found.

It would be secondary to a main purpose of the scientific work to be conducted, but an entirely closed social structure composed of intelligent and trained personnel, and one depending exclusively on one source for its news of the outside world, would be a perfect way of putting to experimental use what Tolneuve had theorized.

The intention of the scheme was specific: what, *precisely* what, would be the effect on a community deprived of news?

Or in another sense: does an awareness of current events really matter?

It was the kind of social experiment which in absolute terms would not be worthwhile unless other circumstances suited it. In the case of the Joliot–Curie observatory, it was decided they would. Provided that such a scheme did not interfere with the normal work of the scientists, there could be no possible objection.

How the details were worked out is not fully known to me, as I was brought in as a collaborator only toward the end. However, what was done was as follows.

During the selection of the observatory personnel, detailed dossiers on each potential member were raised. At the end of the selections, those of the people not joining the staff were destroyed. The others were analyzed by computer, and Tolneuve ratings established for each person.

During training for the mission, dummy runs were carried out, but the scheme was not properly initiated until the laboratory was in full operation. Then, when we began our observations, the system of personalized news sheets was introduced and the experiment began.

The news-sheet of each person carried only that news which had an AQ of 85 percent or higher, for that person. All other news with a lower percentage was printed out on to what I came to call the 84 file, and stored in my office.

Thus, each person received information on external events only to a level of high personal concern. Family news came through, and local news; word of social changes in his country of origin, or where he had made his home. And news from Earth, of course, of the reactions to the work of the observatory.

But more general information—national or international events, sporting results, disasters, political changes, criminal news—passed into the 84 file.

Of all the people on the observatory only I had access to that information. My function was to record what happened, if anything, and pass the information back to Earth. Because Tolneuve's theory was that people raised in a high-stimulus environment became a product of their society and could not keep their orientation without some knowledge of what was outside their sphere.

I often sought, and found, companionship with Mike Querrel. Although he held a master's degree in bacteriology and was a part of the microorganism survey team, he spent much of his time working on the central power generators. This gave him something of the manner of a nonspecialist, and in fact he and I managed to get along surprisingly well.

On this day, though, Querrel was in one of his moods of deliberate reticence. When I had passed him his accumulated pile of news sheets, he took them from me and turned away without comment.

"Is anything wrong, Mike?" I said.

"No. But this place gets me down."

"It affects all of us."

"You too?"

I nodded.

"That's odd. I didn't think you were the type."

I said: "That's a matter of viewpoint. I live with the same prospect of metal walls as anybody. I eat the same food, hear the same stories, see the same faces."

"Would it help if you had something more constructive to do? If you wanted, I could fit you in on some of the research."

His manner of fellowship as a nonspecialist was only superficial. He saw the social difference between me and the others exactly the same as any of them.

Back in my office, I pulled one of the reports across and skimmed through it. Then I found some clean paper, put it in the typewriter and began to rewrite the report into lay English.

I wondered how the present situation with Clare had arisen. A variety of possibilities presented themselves.

We had grown over-familiar with each other in the claustrophobic environment of the observatory;

We were not and never had been "suited" for one another—I disliked the word, distrusted the concept—and the environment had merely brought things to a head earlier than would have been normal;

It was merely a phase, ending either naturally or when we left the observatory;

I had unwittingly behaved in such a manner as to initiate a vicious circle . . . or Clare had unwittingly done so;

Clare had taken a lover . . . or she suspected me of doing so;

There was some other factor I had not anticipated.

Such were the possibilities. The awkward thing with such a situation is that only those two people involved are aware of the true state of affairs. And through no fault of their own, they are incapable of assessing it objectively or reliably. Much as I could recognize the breach between Clare and myself, I was helpless to do anything about it. While there was no overt love between us, paradoxically there remained a surface level of interaction where we could behave acceptably with one another in company. And on the observatory there was always company.

One of the reports I rewrote was from Mike Querrel, on the current state of the main generators.

As I have said, the generators were not Querrel's main interest, but he had by and large done all the research work in his own particular line that he had intended to do. As our tour of duty on the observatory had been extended indefinitely, he had been left with time to spare and had involved himself with the servicing of the engines.

These were intended to be fully automatic, requiring no attention. It was fortunate, therefore, that Querrel had taken the interest he did, as he discovered a fault that might, had it been left unattended, have created a great deal of danger to all of us.

After this, he had received formal authority from mission headquarters on Earth and had been submitting regular reports ever since.

The generators were crucial to the existence of the observatory, for in addition to providing all electrical power —and thus all heat, motor power, light, and life supports

—they also provided the field which produced the elocation effect which kept us alive and operating on this
planet.

Elocation had about as much relation to time travel as
a flight of stairs has to space travel. That should give you
some idea of the relative scale. All the elocation field can
do is to push the observatory back in time by about one
nanosecond—but that was enough, and more would be
equally unnecessary and inconvenient.

One nanosecond of elocated time allows the observatory
to move about the surface of this planet in what amounts
to complete invisibility to the inhabitants, in a state of re-
curring nonexistence. Practically, it is ideal for the work
of ecological surveys, as it allows complete freedom of
movement without any pollution of or interference with
the external environment. By use of localized field abroga-
tors it is possible to view chosen pieces of the outside—
such as a plant or animal, or a piece of soil or rock—and
thus conduct the scientific work of the observatory.

That is the official version, the one the staff know . . .
and for the moment that will do.

Querrel's report was not much more than a listing of
various readings taken from the equipment. These would
be used on Earth to update the real-time simulators, and
allow the controllers to keep accurate note of our progress. Most of the automatic readings would be transored
back by the computers, but Querrel's figures covered the
parts of the equipment which had had manual override.

Bored with thinking about the observatory, bored with
being confined inescapably in the observatory, bored
through and through *with* the observatory, I left my office
and wandered around one or two of the viewing ports.

Here, although I could see what was being observed of
the outside, I came into closer contact with the scientists.
It is not paranoia which causes me to say that I am not
liked. I know it for a fact. I would be liked even less if the
true nature of my duties were known.

The problem about Clare was still nagging at me, as it
always did. It was not made easier by the awareness—
growing by the day—that our protracted stay in the
laboratory was futile. Whatever purpose may have been
served within the originally intended tour of duty certainly
could not justify this extension. Though many of the scientists—including Clare—claimed that their work could not
be finished in the foreseeable future, I knew that everything

on the observatory would be ultimately unavailing.

I passed through five of the observation bays. Conversations stopped, resumed behind me as I passed. I exist in a world of silence: forcing another silence on those around me.

The results of the Tolneuve experiment are known, but the final inferences have yet to be drawn. Through my confusions the simple beauty of what has happened shines through. What is to come is not so clear. I can show you the results (without the conclusions) in the form of a chart.

I like that chart—it is of my own devising. But it is not complete, for things are going wrong.

The REALITY line represents what is true, what is real. It symbolizes sanity and reason, what we hope we may ultimately return to. The FANTASY line we have reached and moved away from. That was where the observatory society passed into an insane state.

The result of the Tolneuve experiment was now apparent: deprive a community of news of the outside world, and the community finds a replacement. In short, it develops a network of rumors based on speculation, imagination, and wish-fulfilment.

This is reflected in my chart.

For the first six months or so, everyone was reacting to the fresh stimulus of the observatory. Their interests were oriented around themselves and their work. Interest in the outside world was at a minimum. What conversations I overheard in that time, or participated in, were based broadly on what was known or remembered.

By the end of the first year—four-week cycle No. 13—the situation had changed.

The environment and society of the observatory were not enough to sustain the imaginations of these highly intelligent people. Curiosity about what was happening back on Earth led to direct conversations about it. Speculation . . . guesses . . . gossip . . . I detected exaggerated stories of past exploits. The system of fact orientation was being broken down.

In the following months, up until approximately the end of the twentieth cycle, this became extreme.

The network of rumors became the main obsession of the staff, and by and large their formal work suffered. During this period, the controllers on Earth became

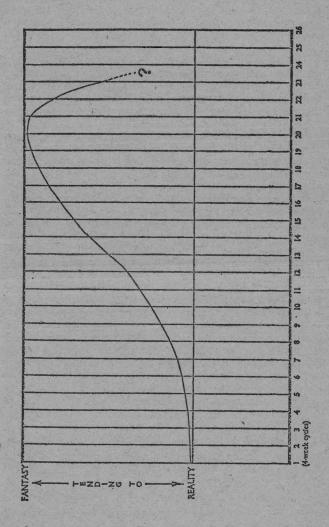

alarmed and it was thought for a time that the experiment would have to be curtailed.

The rumors lost any basis in reality, became fantastic, wild, demented. And the staff—cool, logical scientists— believed in them profoundly. It was asserted as fact that black became white, that the impossible became the possible . . . that governments fell, that wars had been fought and won, that cities had burned, that life went on after death . . . that God was alive, God was dead, that continents had sunk. It wasn't the assumptions in themselves that were so incredible as the way in which they were accepted.

During this time, life went on as normal on the observatory and on Earth, and the regular daily sheets were handed out to the staff. And the work proceeded—erratically, but still there was progress.

And then . . . Then the fantastic aspects of the rumors diminished. Traces of fact crept back into what was being said. By the end of the twenty-third cycle, eight weeks ago, it was clear that the speculation was returning, spontaneously, to reality.

And incredibly, the rumors began to anticipate fact.

Word would go round, stemming unprompted from God knew where, about some clearly defined event: a natural disaster, a sporting result, the death of a statesman. And when I checked through the 84 file, I would find that it had a collateral in reality.

A rumored landslide in Greece would be an earth-tremor in Yugoslavia; a rumored change of government in Southeast Asia would correspond with a coup somewhere else; a rumored policy change in the attitude of the public toward this very mission would be nearly accurate. And then there were other stories that I could not check. Things like unexpected famines, or increasing crime rates, or social dissent—events which would not normally get into the news anyway.

With this change, a conclusion came into sight: that in due course the rootless network of rumor would return of its own accord to reality. Reflecting it accurately, anticipating it accurately. If this happened, the social consequences—in the broadest sense—would be unprecedented.

But for some reason this conclusion was not in sight. The network had stagnated. The return to reality had been postponed. My beautiful chart ended in a query.

The transor-conjunction was scheduled for 23:30 hours and I had the whole evening to kill. We followed real-time days for the sake of convenience. Had we adapted to the day cycles of the planet, the simulators on Earth would have had to be continually modified.

I stayed in my office until 20:00 hours, working on a few more of the reports. I sent out for food and this was brought to me by Caroline Newison, botanist wife of one of the bacteriological team.

She told me the rumor about the Bolivian riot, fleshing it out with the detail that just over a thousand people had died. This was nearer the actual figure and it pleased me. In turn, I passed on the word about the New York fire, but she had already heard this.

It always struck me as curious that individual members of the staff were friendlier to me than they were as a whole. It was consistent, though, with the overall behavior of the staff: this difference between individual and collective behavior or attitudes.

Later, I locked my filing cabinets, closed my desk and went in search of Clare. I had ready all the necessary work for the time of the conjunction.

What I could not understand about the postponement of what I had reasoned would be a return to reality-based conjecture was that most of the other factors in Tolneuve's theory held good.

But the rumoring had not progressed. The staff were still passing word about events of the same kind as they had been doing eight weeks ago. And there was less speculative activity.

Could it be that the lethargy which affected us all was similarly causing a renewed lack of interest in the outside world?

If the flow of my chart had gone as I had extrapolated, by now—the end of the twenty-fifth cycle—we would be again aware of what was happening on Earth. The sensation ability to anticipate what could not otherwise be known would be established.

Thorensen was holding forth when I went into the bar. He was slightly drunk.

". . . and I think we shouldn't. He's the only one who can talk with them. I don't trust it."

He turned as I walked toward him.

"Will you have a drink, Dan?" he said.

"No, thanks. I'm looking for Clare. Has she been here?"

"She was in a little earlier. We thought she was with you."

The group of four or five men with Thorensen listened to the exchange without expression.

"I've only just left my office," I said. "I haven't seen her since this morning."

O'Brien, standing next to Thorensen, said: "I think she was going back to your room. She said she had a headache."

I thanked him and moved out of the bar. I knew Clare's headaches. She often used some minor physical symptom as a cover for a deeper emotion and though she had been genuinely upset earlier, I didn't think the rumored death of the children in New Zealand would be still affecting her. The reaction of all members of the staff to the stories they generated, however disastrous or seemingly important, was superficial.

When I reached our room, she was not there. As far as I could recall, the room looked much as it had done when we had left it in the morning. There was no sign that Clare had been back.

I walked around the observatory, growing increasingly puzzled at her absence. There were not all that many places in which she could be, unless she was deliberately avoiding me. I tried all the observation ports, all the social and communal rooms, and even, in the end, the generators. She was there with Mike Querrel, and they were kissing.

The truth of it was that by all accounts the situation on Earth was in a very delicate state. In a political sense the division between the East and the West had widened and in the uncommitted territories in which the different ideologies met there was continuous tension. In a social sense, the environment had exhausted itself. Here it was the developed and underdeveloped countries which had grown apart.

When we had left Earth two years before, the situation had been very bad and in the intervening period things had worsened. Crop failures were widespread—soil exhaustion and unbalanced atmospheric ecology being the main factors. Consequently, any country not attuned to a high level of technology suffered famine and disease.

Large areas of land which had been irrigated and cultivated fell into disuse. There was an increasing blind
dependence on technology. In the developed countries,
pollution was the main social problem, with interracial
conflict running a close second. These internal factors
aggravated the international political situation; each side
blamed the other for its contribution, but neither could
afford practical help either for itself or for its economic
dependencies. There were too many complexities involved: too many vested interests in uncommitted nations
from too many sides. All this was reflected in the news
sheets which came up to the observatory; none of it directly affected the members of the staff and none of it got into
their personalized daily sheets. If I scanned through my
84 file, from any one of the two dozen transors we had
had since being here, I would see the facts reflected there:
strikes, famines, riots, civil uprisings, territorial demands
by one state on another, conventions of environmental
pundits who could see what was coming but were power-
less to do anything about it, disasters in the cities caused
be the fine tuning of technology, and fighting in the
streets, and murder of security forces, and bomb outrages,
and sabotage, and political assassinations, and breakdown
of diplomatic relationships, and the ending of trade agreements, and the stockpiling of weapons . . . and over it all
a growing awareness of and a clamoring for the war
which was now inevitable. . . .

And no one except me on the observatory had any
formal access to this information, and I had felt that their
speculations would have developed to it, and they hadn't,
and I didn't know why.

Later, when Clare had gone, I stood alone with Querrel
by the main generators.

The scene that had just taken place could have happened only on the observatory. Each of us knew the mental
and physical strains being undergone by the others, as
each of us was subjected to the same. That Clare had
gone to another man did not surprise me . . . it was only
the shock of discovering it was Querrel. As far as he and
Clare were concerned, I assumed that each of them must
have known that their *affaire* could not have gone on for
long before I discovered it. So there could be no genuine
shame there. Nor could they have hoped to continue it if
and when we left the observatory.

We had said very little. Clare pulled away from Querrel, I tried to grab her but she evaded me. Querrel turned away and Clare said she was going up to our room.

When she had gone, I lit a cigarette.

"How long has this been going on?" I said, aware of the honor time had lent to the phrase.

"It doesn't matter," Querrel said.

"It does to me."

"Long enough. About seven weeks."

"Are you sure that's all?"

"Seven weeks. You know it was your fault, Winter. Clare really resents what you are doing to her."

"What do you mean?"

He didn't reply, but sat down on the edge of one of the machine housings. Around us, the generators worked on smoothly.

"Come on," I said. "What did you mean?"

He shrugged. "Clare will tell you. I can't."

I said: "Who started it? You or Clare?"

"She did. Though it comes back to you. She said it was a reaction against you."

"And you didn't mind being used like that."

He didn't reply. I wasn't so blind as to be unaware that when a marriage is betrayed both parties are equally to blame. Though what Querrel meant by Clare's resentment was lost on me. I had not to my knowledge done anything that would cause this reaction. Just then, Clare came back into the generator room with Andrew Jenson, the chief ecologist on board the observatory.

He nodded briefly at Querrel, then looked at me. "Has Querrel told you?"

"Told me what?"

Querrel said: "No, I haven't. This hasn't exactly been a convenient moment."

In spite of my involvement, I registered the understatement. I said to Jenson: "Did you know about this?"

"I think we must be talking about something else."

I had wondered what connection Jenson had with the *affair*e between Querrel and my wife.

Querrel got up from his perch on the edge of the housing, and went toward the door. "Excuse me for copping out of this," he said. "I've had enough for one day."

I stared after him as he left us.

It will have been noticed that during my descriptions of the work on the observatory there had been a certain amount of circumspectness as regards detail. There are reasons for this.

It could be said, for instance, that in an environment where one's whole existence is centered around some activity such as scientific study of an alien planet, then one's behavior should be very much colored by what is going on. I have remained in this account remarkably free of the excitement of the staff over the various discoveries of minerals, bacteria, and various higher life forms.

The main reason for my reluctance to go into detail is that there is a disparity between the activities of the staff and what I know to be their true function here.

This is a necessarily cryptic state of affairs; not altogether without analogy to Tolneuve's theories.

But consider: the year is 2019, the planet we are supposed to be exploring cannot logically be within our solar system, mankind has not developed his technology to a point which would enable him to reach such a planet. A vacuum surrounds our observatory—unarguably there, as the air leaks from our cabins continually testify—and yet outside there appears to be life. None of the staff has ever queried these things.

Jenson went to the intercom and spoke for a few minutes to one or two other people. Taking advantage of the fact that we were alone, Clare and I exchanged a few words. At first she was sullen and unforthcoming. Then she let go, and spoke to me freely.

She said that for several weeks she had been bored and depressed, anxious about me. That she had been unable to communicate with me. That I would not respond. She had suspected, for a time, that I had taken up with another woman, but discreet investigations had ruled this out to her own satisfaction. She said that she had been forced by the attitude of other scientists to separate herself from me in certain respects and that her personal attitude to me had changed in a parallel way. I asked her what she meant by this and she said that that was what Jenson was here for. She said that she and Querrel had started their *affaire* more or less as a consequence of this and that had I not acted in such a secretive way it would have never happened.

"So you mean you think I'm holding something back?" I said.

"Yes."

"But I'm not. At least, not as far as you and I are concerned."

She turned away. "I don't believe you."

Jenson put down the intercom handset for the last time and came back to us. His face bore an expression, the like of which I had rarely seen on the observatory. One commonly sees a kind of blankness in the faces, but Jenson's showed purpose, intent.

"You've got one of your transor-conjunctions tonight, haven't you?"

"At eleven thirty, real-time."

"OK. As soon as that's finished, we're leaving the observatory. Are you coming with us?"

I gaped at him. What he had just said amounted almost to treason against his own identity. It was impossible for him, or any other members of the staff, to conceive independently of the notion of leaving the observatory. Every member of the staff had been fully conditioned *against* such a concept.

Clare said: "This is what I meant. We've been planning to get out for several weeks. The others told me not to talk to you about it."

"But that's impossible."

"To get out?" Jenson smiled at me as if I were to be patronized. "We intend to use the abort mode. Nothing could be simpler."

Whatever may or may not be outside the observatory— whether you accept the official rationale of the observatory or, like me, you are aware of the true state of affairs—there is certainly a great deal of hard vacuum. Either the vacuum of elocated space, or the other and more common kind. No human being could hope to exist outside without full, portable, life supports. Jenson knew this; everyone knew it.

"You're insane," I said. "You're incapable of assessing the true state of affairs." I meant this emotionally and literally. He was acting in a deranged way and by definition, by the way he and all the others behaved in the sense of group response, he was insane. "You don't know what's outside."

Clare said: "We do, Dan. We've known for some time."

"The planet's uninhabitable," I said. "The lifeforms

you've been observing are incompatible with the hydro-carbon cycle. Even if you could get through the elocation field, you'd never survive."

I was sticking to the official line. Jenson and Clare glanced at each other. Even as I spoke, I realized that none of this was their intention.

This is relevant:

The moon orbits the Earth at a distance of roughly a quarter-million miles. As it completes one orbit, so its own period of revolution ends. Result—we see only one face. However, the orbital path of the moon is elliptical and thus its speed in orbit varies depending on its distance from Earth. Result—an observer on Earth sees the face of the moon moving very slightly from side to side as if it were shaking its head. It is therefore possible to see frac-tionally more of the moon's surface than that on the side facing Earth. This movement is known as libration. On the northeast edge of the moon's near side, as viewed from the Earth, is a crater named Joliot–Curic. For just over twenty-eight days of every lunar month the crater is in-visible from Earth. But for a few hours every month an observer inside the crater would see the Earth creep into sight over the horizon.

On the floor of the crater, operating in a narrow strip of land from which the earth can be seen at this time, is the observatory.

I glanced at my wrist watch. I said: "What has the next transor-conjunction to do with this?"

"Some of the others want to have a look at the whole communication as it arrives. This is a genuine transor, isn't it?"

"As opposed to . . . ?"

"Those times when you close your office to get up to God only knows what. We know that there's only one transor every four weeks, Winter. And that the observa-tory is run from Earth on a real-time basis of four-weekly cycles."

"How do you know that?"

"We're not entirely subject to the controllers' whims," said Clare. "We have some access to what's going on."

"I wouldn't be too sure of that," I said. It had been comforting to be the only person on the observatory with the knowledge of what was really going on. Now it looked as if the others had somehow found out.

"Look, Winter," said Jenson. "Will you accept that we *do* know what the real situation is? You don't run the observatory, you know."

"But I do have control of information," I said.

Jenson gestured impatiently. "You had," he corrected. "It's been common knowledge for some time that the mission's purpose has had to be changed. We know about the troubles on Earth."

I thought about that for a moment.

"Why do you want to get out of the observatory just at this moment?"

Jenson shrugged. "This is the time," he said. "We're tired of being cooped up in here. Now we know exactly what's going on, we especially resent being here for no good reason. Some of us have members of our families on Earth . . . with the trouble brewing up, not unnaturally we want to be with them. Also, there is a strong current of feeling that if a war does break out on Earth, we may well be stranded inside here. It's apparent that the experiment as it was has come to an end."

Clare had moved across to me. Now she laid a hand on my arm. The touch of her felt vaguely alien, yet also reassuring.

"We must get out of here, Dan," she said. "For both of us."

I tried to give her a cold look; the memory of what I had found her doing with Querrel still a disconcerting thought in the back of my mind.

"You say you know what's happening. I don't believe you do."

Jenson said: "It isn't just me. Everyone on board knows. There's no point in arguing about it."

"I'm not arguing."

"OK. But for God's sake let's forget the official line about surveying an alien planet."

By the manner in which Jenson was talking, I knew that he wasn't trying to extract information from me . . . though at another time this might have been an acceptable motive within the terms of the experiment. Rather, it was as if we were both living with a falsehood, both knew it, and both should abandon it.

I said: "All right. We're not on an alien planet. What do you think the observatory is?"

"We don't think," said Clare. "We know."

Jenson nodded to her. "We know that what we are expected to believe is a series of implanted reactions to preprogramed stimuli. That the scientific reports we give to you to relay to Earth are in fact viewed in the sense of how well we have reacted rather than what our reaction has actually been. We also know that a large number of our assumptions about the observatory are artificial and were conditioned into us before we came here."

I said: "I'll concede you that so far."

"What we don't know, on the other hand, is the exact purpose of the experiment, though there have been several speculations that we are a kind of control group. In the same way that we have been told that this mission is simulated on Earth by computers, so we are ourselves a kind of simulation for some other expedition . . . perhaps one even on another planet. Or an expedition which is intended to go to another planet."

I had no idea how they had reached this knowledge, but what Jenson was saying was almost exactly so.

"There is also some other kind of experiment going on, but of this we have no knowledge at all. We think, though, that it is connected with you, and accounts for your presence here."

I said: "How have you found this out?"

"By common deduction."

"There's just one more thing," I said. "You are proposing to leave the observatory. Do you *know* what's outside?"

Clare glanced up at Jenson, and he laughed.

"Office-blocks, motels, smog, grass . . . I don't know, anything you like."

"If you try to get outside the observatory you'll die," I said. "There's literally nothing outside. No air . . . certainly no grass or smog."

"What do you mean?"

"We're on the moon," I said. "Earth's moon. You've been right in everything you've said so far . . . but you're wrong about this. The observatory is on the moon."

They exchanged glances again. "I don't believe it," Clare said. "We've never left Earth. Everyone knows that."

"I can prove it," I said.

I turned to an equipment bay behind me and took a steel lever from its rack. I held it in my hand before them, then let go. It floated gently to the floor . . . one-sixth gee, lun r gravity.

"What does that prove?" Jenson said. "You've dropped a lever. So what?"

"So we're in the lunar field of gravity."

Jenson picked up the lever, dropped it again. "Does this look to you as if it's falling slowly?" he said.

I nodded.

"What about you, Clare?"

She said with a slight frown, "It looks perfectly normal to me."

I put my hands on Jenson's shoulders, pushed backwards. He moved away lightly, recovered easily.

"On Earth," I said, "you would have fallen heavily."

"On the moon," Jenson replied, "you couldn't have pushed so hard."

We picked up the lever and dropped it again and again to the floor. Each time it fell smoothly and gently to the floor, bouncing two or three times with light ringing noises. And yet they maintained that it fell as if under normal gravity.

Who, I began to wonder, was imagining what?

Before the escalation of the troubles on Earth, an expedition had been planned. I don't know where it was intended to go, nor how it was supposed it would be transported there. The members of the expedition would live and work in a mobile laboratory, carrying out various facets of ecological research.

The Joliot–Curie observatory was a practice run—deliberately placed in a relatively inaccessible area of the moon, deliberately rigged to mislead the occupants into believing they were working in the field.

So conditioned were they that no one until this moment had ever questioned the mission, or speculated as to its purpose. What they saw of the unnamed planet was pre-recorded films, prepared slides, pretaped responses on the EEGs. What was observed at the observatory was the observer.

We moved along the main corridor to my office. At Jenson's request, several of the others had joined us. I noticed Thorensen was among them, but not Querrel. We walked with the habitual slow grace of the observatory . . . light, bounding steps to get the most out of the lunar gravity.

But the distracting thought persisted: if no one else but I could detect the effects of the low gravity, how did their bodies' metabolism compensate? It was a new development to me and one that should have occurred before. I knew that they had been conditioned to ignore the low gravity, to react to it as if it were normal, but I had not seen before that if one's mind and one's body are oriented around differing physical phenomena, then at the very lowest level of reaction there would be inefficient synchronization of movement, and at the highest level there would be ultimate mental breakdown.

We arrived at the office about six minutes before the transor-conjunction was due to commence.

The conjunction begins as the edge of the Earth rises slowly over the southwestern horizon. It takes a few minutes for a direct line-of-sight tight-beam to be locked on. As soon as this has been accomplished, the stored data in our computers is fed back to Earth. This takes around twenty seconds. Immediately after, the controllers on Earth send up the various messages and information direct into our computer. This can take anything between five minutes and three hours.

I said nothing about the files in my cabinets and showed the staff the equipment for the transor, and how it may be monitored. Very few of them showed interest.

At 23:32 hours, the conjunction began. A series of red pilot lights along the console showed that we had locked on to the automatic tracking equipment on Earth. Exactly where the equipment was situated I never knew, as it depended on the configuration of the Earth and the moon at the time of the conjunction. There were twelve stations situated at various parts of the globe.

I switched in the data transmitter and we waited while this was sent to Earth. There was an uncomfortable silence in the office; neither from concentration nor anticipation, but more a kind of patient waiting.

When the console showed that our transmission was concluded, I switched in the acquisition circuit. And we waited.

Ten minutes later, we were still waiting. The circuit was dead.

Jenson said: "I think that confirms it."

"It didn't need to be confirmed," said one of the others.

I looked at Thorensen, then Clare. Their faces showed no surprise, still that expression of patience.

"The experiment's over," Jenson said. "We can go home."

"What do you mean?' I said.

"You know about the war on Earth? It's been threatening for months. Now it has started."

"Ten days ago," Thorensen said. "Or at least, that was what we heard."

I said: "But there's been no news of it."

Jenson shrugged. "You won't be getting any more from that," he said, nodding toward the console. "You might as well turn the bloody thing off."

"How did you know about the war?" I said.

"We've known for some time. In fact, we anticipated it by several days."

"Why didn't anyone say anything?"

Thorensen said bluntly: "They did . . . but not to you."

Clare came over and stood by my side. "We had to be careful, Dan. We knew you were holding back information from us, and we didn't know what would happen if we told you we knew."

I said: "Thanks, Clare."

On one of the sides of the observatory is a tunnel large enough to accommodate at one time the entire staff. It is the abort mode. It has been designed to stay provisioned and airtight long enough to keep everyone alive in the event of an emergency until help can be sent from Earth.

It is also the only access point to the inside of the observatory, and had the experiment ended at the originally designated time, we would have passed down the tunnel on our way to the relief modules.

We periodically pressurized and checked out the abort tunnel and everyone on the observatory knew how to operate it.

Jenson said: "We're getting out."

"You can't."

The others looked around at each other. Two of the men moved toward the door.

"We have a choice," Jenson said. "We can die in here, or we can get outside. What the conditions are like out there, we don't know. Probably there is a high level of radioactivity. But we do know that the observatory is somewhere on Earth. Last night we took a vote on it and it was unanimously agreed that we're not staying here."

"What about you, Clare?"

She said: "I'm going too."

I sat at my desk, staring at the 84 file. Everything was in here. All the pieces that made up a picture of the world committing suicide. I had had those pieces, but the staff hadn't. And yet the absence of that information had somehow generated an awareness of its existence and they had known what was happening. But I hadn't.

I thought again of my chart which, had it finished, would have returned to the line of reality about now. I could see what had gone wrong with the chart—that the staff had deliberately excluded me from the more important of their rumors. That as their stories drew nearer and nearer to what was real, they had said nothing to me.

So they had built reality from speculation in exactly the way I had theorized, yet had hardly dared to believe.

Jenson came back to my office about an hour later.

"Are you going to come, Winter?" he said.

I shook my head. "You don't know what you are doing. You're going to step out of that tunnel into the moon's vacuum. You'll die instantly."

"You're wrong," he said. "About this and other things. You say we've been conditioned—well, we'll accept that. But what about you? How can you tell that everything you think about the observatory is accurate?"

"But I know," I said.

"And a madman knows he is the only one sane."

"If you like."

Jenson extended his hand to shake mine. "Well, see you outside, then."

"I'm not going to go."

"Perhaps not now, but later maybe."

I shook my head again, emphatically. "Is Clare going with you?"

"Yes."

"Will you ask her to come in here for a moment?"

He said: "She's already in the tunnel. She said it would not be a good thing to see you at the moment."

I shook his hand, and he left the office.

A few minutes ago I went down to the abort tunnel. The outer door was open and the tunnel was empty. I closed the door with the remote-control wheel and repressurized the tunnel.

I have been right through the observatory and I have confirmed that I am alone. It is very quiet in here. I sit at my desk, holding a part of my 84 file. Every now and again I hold it out from the desk and watch it fall slowly to the floor. Its movement is gentle and very graceful. I could watch it for hours.

ALL PIECES OF A RIVER SHORE

R. A. LAFFERTY

By now so much has been said by so many about R. A. Lafferty's ability to dream up new ideas that all one can say about this marvelous tale is that it, too, contains a new idea.

It had been a very long and ragged and incredibly interlocked and detailed river shore. Then a funny thing had happened to it. It had been broken up, sliced up into pieces. Some of the pieces had been folded and compressed into bales. Some of them had been rolled up on rollers. Some of them had been cut into still smaller pieces and used for ornaments and as Indian medicine. Rolled and baled pieces of the shore came to rest in barns and old warehouses, in attics, in caves. Some were buried in the ground.

And yet the river itself still exists physically, as do its shores, and you may go and examine them. But the shore you will see along the river now is not quite the same as that old shore that was broken up and baled into bales and rolled onto rollers, not quite the same as the pieces you will find in attics and caves.

His name was Leo Nation and he was known as a rich Indian. But such wealth as he had now was in his collections, for he was an examining and acquiring man. He had cattle, he had wheat, he had a little oil, and he

171

spent everything that came in. Had he had more income he would have collected even more.

He collected old pistols, old ball shot, grindstones, early windmills, walking-horse threshing machines, flax combs, Conestoga wagons, brass-bound barrels, buffalo robes, Mexican saddles, slick horn saddles, anvils, Argand lamps, rush holders, hay-burning stoves, hackamores, branding irons, chuck wagons, longhorn horns, beaded serapes, Mexican and Indian leatherwork, buckskins, beads, feathers, squirrel-tail anklets, arrowheads, deerskin shirts, locomotives, streetcars, mill wheels, keelboats, buggies, ox yokes, old parlor organs, blood-and-thunder novels, old circus posters, harness bells, Mexican oxcarts, wooden cigar-store Indians, cable-twist tobacco a hundred years old and mighty strong, cuspidors (four hundred of them), Ferris wheels, carnival wagons, carnival props of various sorts, carnival proclamations painted big on canvas. Now he was going to collect something else. He was talking about it to one of his friends, Charles Longbank, who knew everything.

"Charley," he said, "do you know anything about 'The Longest Pictures in the World' which used to be shown by carnivals and in hippodromes?"

"Yes, I know a little about them, Leo. They are an interesting bit of Americana: a bit of nineteenth-century back-country mania. They were supposed to be pictures of the Mississippi River shore. They were advertised as one mile long, five miles long, nine miles long. One of them, I believe, was actually over a hundred yards long. They were badly painted on bad canvas, crude trees and mudbank and water ripples, simplistic figures and all as repetitious as wallpaper. A strong-armed man with a big brush and plenty of barn paint of three colors could have painted quite a few yards of such in one day. Yet they are truly Americana. Are you going to collect them, Leo?"

"Yes. But the real ones aren't like you say."

"Leo, I saw one. There is nothing to them but very large crude painting."

"I have twenty that are like you say, Charley. I have three that are very different. Here's an old carnival poster that mentions one."

Leo Nation talked eloquently with his hands while he also talked with his mouth, and now he spread out an old browned poster with loving hands:

The Arkansas Traveler, World's Finest Carnival, Eight Wagons, Wheel, Beasts, Dancing Girls, Baffling Acts, Monsters, Games of Chance. And Featuring the World's Longest Picture, Four Miles of Exquisite Painting. This is from the Original Panorama; it is Not a Cheap-Jack Imitation.

"So you see, Charley, there was a distinction: there were the original pieces, and there were the crude imitations."

"Possibly some were done a little better than others, Leo; they could hardly have been done worse. Certainly, collect them if you want to. You've collected lots of less interesting things."

"Charley, I have a section of that panoramic picture that once belonged to the Arkansas Traveler Carnival. I'll show it to you. Here's another poster:

King Carnival, The King of them All. Fourteen Wagons. Ten Thousand Wonders. See the Rubber Man. See the Fire Divers. See the Longest Picture in the World, see Elephants on the Mississippi River. This is a Genuine Shore Depictment, not the Botches that Others show.

"You say that you have twenty of the ordinary pictures, Leo, and three that are different?"

"Yes I have, Charley. I hope to get more of the genuine. I hope to get the whole river."

"Let's go look at one, Leo, and see what the difference is."

They went out to one of the hay barns. Leo Nation kept his collections in a row of hay barns. "What would I do?" he had asked once, "call in a carpenter and tell him to build me a museum? He'd say, 'Leo, I can't build a museum without plans and stuff. Get me some plans.' And where would I get plans? So I always tell him to build me another hay barn one hundred feet by sixty feet and fifty feet high. Then I always put in four or five decks myself and floor them, and leave open vaults for the tall stuff. Besides, I believe a hay barn won't cost as much as a museum."

"This will be a big field, Charley," Leo Nation said now as they came to one of the hay-barn museums. "It will take all your science in every field to figure it out. Of the three genuine ones I have, each is about a hundred and eighty yards long. I believe this is about the standard length, though some may be multiples of these. They passed for paintings in the years of their display, Charley, *but they are not paintings"*

"What are they then, Leo?"

"I hire you to figure this out. You are the man who knows everything."

Well, there were two barrel reels there, each the height of a man, and several more were set farther back.

"The old turning mechanism is likely worth a lot more than the picture," Charles Longbank told Leo Nation. "This was turned by a mule on a treadmill, or by a mule taking a mill pole round and round. It might even be eighteenth century."

"Yeah, but I use an electric motor on it," Leo said. "The only mule I have left is a personal friend of mine. I'd no more make him turn that than he'd make me if I was the mule. I line it up like I think it was, Charley, the full reel north and the empty one south. Then we run it. So we travel, we scan, from south to north, going upstream as we face west."

"It's funny canvas and funny paint, much better than the one I saw," said Charles Longbank, "and it doesn't seem worn at all by the years."

"It isn't either one, canvas or paint," said Ginger Nation, Leo's wife, as she appeared from somewhere. "It is picture."

Leo Nation started the reeling and ran it. It was the wooded bank of a river. It was a gravel and limestone bank with mud overlay and the mud undercut a little. And it was thick timber to the very edge of the shore.

"It is certainly well done," Charles Longbank admitted. "From the one I saw and from what I had read about these, I wasn't prepared for this." The rolling picture was certainly not repetitious, but one had the feeling that the riverbank itself might have been a little so, to lesser eyes than those of the picture.

"It is a virgin forest, mostly deciduous," said Charles Longbank, "and I do not believe that there is any such temperate forest on any large river in the world today. It would have been logged out. I do not believe that there were many such stretches even in the nineteenth century. Yet I have the feeling that it is a faithful copy of something, and not imaginary."

The rolling shores: cottonwood trees, slash pine, sycamore, slippery elm, hackberry, pine again.

"When I get very many of the pictures, Charley, you

will put them on film and analyze them or have some kind of computer do it. You will be able to tell from the sun's angle what order the pictures should have been in, and how big are the gaps between."

"No, Leo, they would all have to reflect the same hour of the same day to do that."

"But it *was* all the same hour of the same day," Ginger Nation cut in. "How would you take one picture at two hours of two days?"

"She's right, Charley," Leo Nation said. "All the pictures of the genuine sort are pieces of one original authentic picture. I've known that all along."

Rolling shore of pine, laurel oak, butternut, persimmon, pine again.

"It is a striking reproduction, whatever it is," Charles Longbank said, "But I'm afraid that after a while even this would become as monotonous as repeating wallpaper."

"Hah," said Leo. "For a smart man you have dumb eyes, Charley. Every tree is different, every leaf is different. All the trees are in young leaf too. It's about a last-week-of-March picture. What it hangs on, though, is what part of the river it is. It might be a third-week-in-March picture, or a first-week-in-April. The birds, old Charley who know everything, why don't we pick up more birds in this section? And what birds are those there?"

"Passenger pigeons, Leo, and they've been gone for quite a few decades. Why don't we see more birds there? I've a humorous answer to that, but it implies that this thing is early and authentic. We don't see more birds because they are too well camouflaged. North America is today a bird watchers' paradise because very many of its bright birds are later European intrusions that have replaced native varieties. They have not yet adjusted to the native backgrounds, so they stand out against them visually. Really, Leo, that is a fact. A bird can't adapt in a short four or five hundred years. And there are birds, birds, birds in that, Leo, if you look sharp enough."

"I look sharp to begin with, Charley; I just wanted you to look sharp."

"This rolling ribbon of canvas or whatever is about six feet high, Leo, and I believe the scale is about one to ten, going by the height of mature trees and other things."

"Yeah, I think so, Charley. I believe there's about a mile of river shore in each of my good pictures. There's things about these pictures though, Charley, that I'm almost afraid to tell you. I've never been quite sure of your nerves. But you'll see them for yourself when you come to examine the pictures closely."

"Tell me the things now, Leo, so I'll know what to look for."

"It's all there, Charley, every leaf, every knob of bark, every spread of moss. I've put parts of it under a microscope, ten power, fifty power, four hundred power. There's detail there that you couldn't see with your bare eyes if you had your nose right in the middle of it. You can even see cells of leaf and moss. You put a regular painting under that magnification and all you see is details of pigment, and canyons and mountains of brush strokes. Charley, you can't find a brush stroke in that whole picture! Not in any of the real ones."

It was rather pleasant to travel up that river at the leisurely equivalent rate of maybe four miles an hour, figuring a one to ten ratio. Actually the picture rolled past them at about half a mile an hour. Rolling bank and rolling trees, pin oak, American elm, pine, black willow, shining willow.

"How come there is shining willow, Charley, and no white willow, you tell me that?" Leo asked.

"If this *is* the Mississippi, Leo, and if it is authentic, then this must be a far northern sector of it."

"Naw. It's Arkansas, Charley. I can tell Arkansas anywhere. How come there was shining willow in Arkansas?"

"If that is Arkansas, and if the picture is authentic, it was colder then."

"Why aren't there any white willow?"

"The white willow is a European introduction, though a very early one, and it spread rapidly. There are things in this picture that check *too* well. The three good pictures that you have, are they pretty much alike?"

"Yeah, but not quite the same stretch of the river. The sun's angle is a little different in each of them, and the sod and the low plants are a little different."

"You think you will be able to get more of the pictures?"

"Yeah. I think more than a thousand miles of river was in the picture. I think I get more than a thousand sections if I know where to look."

"Probably most have been destroyed long ago, Leo, if there ever were more than the dozen or so that were advertised by the carnivals. And probably there were duplications in that dozen or so. Carnivals changed their features often, and your three pictures may be all that there ever were. Each could have been exhibited by several carnivals and in several hippodromes at different times."

"Nah, there were more, Charley. I don't have the one with the elephants in it yet. I think there are more than a thousand of them somewhere. I advertise for them (for originals, not the cheap-jack imitations), and I will begin to get answers."

"How many there were, there still are," said Ginger Nation. "They will not destroy. One of ours has the reel burned by fire, but the picture did not burn. And they won't burn."

"You might spend a lot of money on a lot of old canvas, Leo," said Charles Longbank. "But I will analyze them for you: now, or when you think you have enough of them for it."

"Wait till I get more, Charley," said Leo Nation. "I will make a clever advertisement. 'I take those things off your hands,' I will say, and I believe that people will be glad to get rid of the old things that won't burn and won't destroy, and weigh a ton each with reels. It's the real ones that won't destroy. Look at that big catfish just under the surface there, Charley! Look at the mean eyes of that catfish! The river wasn't as muddy then as it is now, even if it was springtime and the water was high."

Rolling shore and trees: pine, dogwood, red cedar, bur oak, pecan, pine again, shagbark hickory. Then the rolling picture came to an end.

"A little over twenty minutes I timed it," said Charles Longbank. "Yes, a yokel of the past century might have believed that the picture was a mile long, or even five or nine miles long."

"Nah," said Leo. "They were smarter then, Charley; they were smarter then. Most likely that yokel would have believed that it was a little less than a furlong long, as it is. He'd have liked it, though. And there may be pieces that are five miles long or nine miles long. Why else would they have advertised them? I think I can hit the road and smell out where a lot of those pictures are. And I will call in sometimes and Ginger can tell me who have answered the advertisements. Come here again in six months, Charley, and I will have enough sections of the river for you to analyze. You won't get lonesome in six months, will you, Ginger?"

"No. There will be the hay cutters, and the men from the cattle auctions, and the oil gaugers, and Charley Longbank here when he comes out, and the men in town and the men in the Hill-Top Tavern. I won't get lonesome."

"She jokes, Charley," said Leo. "She doesn't really fool around with the fellows."

"I do not joke," said Ginger. "Stay gone seven months, I don't care."

Leo Nation did a lot of traveling for about five months. He acquired more than fifty genuine sections of the river and he spent quite a few thousands of dollars on them. He went a couple of years into hock for them. It would have been much worse had not many people given him the things and many others sold them to him for very small amounts. But there were certain stubborn men and women who insisted on a good price. This is always the hazard of collecting, the thing that takes most of the fun out of it. All these expensively acquired sections were really prime pieces and Leo could not let himself pass them by.

How he located so many pieces is his own mystery, but Leo Nation did really have a nose for these things. He smelt them out; and all collectors of all things must have such long noses.

There was a professor man in Rolla, Missouri, who had rugged his whole house with pieces of a genuine section.

"That sure is tough stuff, Nation," the man said. "I've been using it for rugs for forty years and it isn't worn at all. She how fresh the trees still are! I had to cut it up with a chain saw, and I tell you that it's tougher than any wood in the world for all that it's nice and flexible."

"How much for all the rugs, for all the pieces of pieces that you have?" Leo asked uneasily. There seemed something wrong in using the pieces for rugs, and yet this didn't seem like a wrong man.

"Oh, I won't sell you any of my rugs, but I will give you pieces of it, since you're interested, and I'll give you the big piece I have left. I never could get anyone much interested in it. We analyzed the material out at the college. It is very sophisticated plastic material. We could reproduce it, or something very like it, but it would be impossibly expensive, and plastics two thirds as tough are quite cheap. The funny thing, though, I can trace the history of the thing back to quite a few decades before any plastic was first manufactured in the world. There is a big puzzle there, for some man with enough curiosity to latch onto it."

"I have enough curiosity; I have already latched onto it," Leo Nation said. "That piece you have on the wall—it looks like—if I could only see it under magnification—"

"Certainly, certainly, Nation. It looks like a swarm of bees there, and it is. I've a slide prepared from a fringe of it. Come and study it. I've shown it to lots of intelligent people and they all say 'So what?' It's an attitude that I can't understand."

Leo Nation studied the magnification with delight. "Yeah" he said. "I can even see the hairs on the bees' legs. In one flaking-off piece there I can even make out the cells of a hair." He fiddled with low and high magnification for a long while. "But the bees sure are funny ones," he said. "My father told me about bees like that once and I thought he lied."

"Our present honeybees are of late European origin, Nation," the man said. "The native American bees *were* funny and inefficient from a human viewpoint. They are not quite extinct even yet, though. There are older-seeming creatures in some of the scenes."

"What are the clown animals in the piece on your kitchen floor?" Leo asked. "Say, those clowns are big!"

"Ground sloths, Nation. They set things as pretty old. If they are a hoax, they are the grandest hoax I ever ran into. A man would have to have a pretty good imagination to give a peculiar hair form to an extinct animal—a hair form that living sloths in the tropics do not have . . . a hair form that sloths of a colder climate just possibly might have. But how many lifetimes would it have taken to paint even a square foot of this in such microscopic detail? There is no letdown anywhere, Nation; there is prodigious detail in every square centimeter of it."

"Why are the horses so small and the buffaloes so big?"

"I don't know, Nation. It would take a man with a hundred sciences to figure it out, unless a man with a hundred sciences had hoaxed it. And where was such a man two hundred and fifty years ago?"

"You trace your piece that far back?"

"Yes. And the scene itself might well be fifteen thousand years old. I tell you that this is a mystery. Yes, you can carry those scraps with you if you wish, and I'll have the bale that's the remaining big piece freighted up to your place."

There was a man in Arkansas who had a section of the picture stored in a cave. It was a tourist-attraction cave, but the river-shore picture had proved a sour attraction.

"The people all think it is some sort of movie projection I have set up in my cave here," he said. " 'Who wants to come down in a cave to see movies,' they say. 'If we want to see a river shore we will go see a river shore,' they say, 'we won't come down in a cave to see it.' Well, I thought it would be a good attraction, but it wasn't."

"How did you ever get it in here, man?" Leo Nation asked him. "That passage just isn't big enough to bring it in."

"Oh, it was already here, rock rollers and all, fifteen years ago when I broke out that little section to crawl through."

"Then it had to be here a very long time. That wall has formed since."

"Nah, not very long," the man said. "These limestone curtains form fast, what with all the moisture trickling down here. The thing could have been brought in here as recent as five hundred years ago. Sure, I'll sell it. I'll even break out a section so we can get it out. I have to make the passage big enough for people to walk in anyhow. Tourists don't like to crawl on their bellies in caves. I don't know why. I always liked to crawl on my belly in caves."

This was one of the most expensive sections of the picture that Nation bought. It would have been even more expensive if he had shown any interest in certain things seen through trees in one sequence of the picture. Leo's heart had come up into his mouth when he had noticed those things, and he'd had to swallow it again and maintain his wooden look. This was a section that had elephants on the Mississippi River.

The elephant (*Mammut americanum*) was really a

mastodon, Leo had learned that much from Charles Longbank. Ah, but now he owned elephants; now he had one of the key pieces of the puzzle.

You find a lot of them in Mexico. Everything drifts down to Mexico when it gets a little age on it. Leo Nation was talking with a rich Mexican man who was as Indian as himself.

"No, I don't know where the Long Picture first came from," the man said, "but it did come from the north, somewhere in the region of the river itself. In the time of De Soto (a little less than five hundred years ago) there was still Indian legend of the Long Pictures, which he didn't understand. Yourselves of the north, of course, are like children. Even the remembering tribes of you like the Caddos have memories no longer than five hundred years.

"We ourselves remember longer. But as to this, all that we remember is that each great family of us took a section of the Long Picture along when we came south to Mexico. That was, perhaps, eight hundred years ago that we came south as conquerors. These pictures are now like treasures, to the old great Indian families, like hidden treasures, memories of one of our former homes. Others of the old families will not talk to you about them. They will even deny that they have them. I talk to you about it, I show it to you, I even given it to you because I am a dissident, a sour man, not like the others."

"The early Indian legends, Don Caetano, did they say where the Long Picture first came from or who painted it?"

"Sure. They say it was painted by a very peculiar great being, and his name (hold onto your *capelo*) was Great River Shore Picture Painter. I'm sure that will help you. About the false or cheap-jack imitations for which you seem to have contempt, don't. They are not what they seem to you, and they were not done for money. These cheap-jack imitations are of Mexican origin, just as the shining originals were born in the States. They were done for the new great families in their aping the old great families, in the hope of also sharing in ancient treasure and ancient luck. Having myself just left off aping great families of another sort, I have a bitter understanding of these imitations. Unfortunately they were done in a late age that lacked art, but the contrast would have been as great in any case: all art would seem insufficient beside that of the Great River Shore Picture Painter himself.

"The cheap-jack imitation pictures were looted by gringo soldiers of the U.S. Army during the Mexican War, as they seemed to be valued by certain Mexican families. From the looters they found their way to mid-century carnivals in the States."

"Don Caetano, do you know that the picture segments stand up under great magnification, that there are details in them far too fine to be seen by the unaided eye?"

"I am glad you say so. I have always had this on faith but I've never had enough faith to put it to the test. Yes, we have always believed that the pictures contained depths within depths."

"Why are there Mexican wild pigs in this view, Don Caetano? It's as though this one had a peculiar Mexican slant to it."

"No. The peccary was an all-American pig, Leo. It went all the way north to the ice. But it's been replaced by the European pig everywhere but in our own wilds. You want the picture? I will have my man load it and ship it to your place."

"Ah, I would give you something for it surely——"

"No, Leo, I give it freely. You are a man that I like. Receive it, and God be with you! Ah, Leo, in parting, and since you collect strange things, I have here a box of bright things that I think you might like. I believe they are no more than worthless garnets, but are they not pretty?"

Garnets? They were not garnets. Worthless? Then why did Leo Nation's eyes dazzle and his heart come up in his throat? With trembling hands he turned the stones over and worshiped. And when Don Caetano gave them to him for the token price of one thousand dollars, his heart rejoiced.

You know what? They really were worthless garnets. But what had Leo Nation thought that they were in that fateful moment? What spell had Don Caetano put on him to make him think that they were something else?

Oh well, you win here and you lose there. And Don Caetano really did ship the treasured picture to him free.

Leo Nation came home after five months of wandering and collecting.

"I stand it without you for five months," Ginger said.

"I could not have stood it for six months, I sure could not have stood it for seven. I kidded. I didn't really fool around with the fellows. I had the carpenter build another hay barn to hold all the pieces of picture you sent in. There were more than fifty of them."

Leo Nation had his friend Charles Longbank come out.

"Fifty-seven new ones, Charley," Leo said. "That makes sixty with what I had before. Sixty miles of river shore I have now, I think. Analyze them, Charley. Get the data out of them somehow and feed it to your computers. First I want to know what order they go in, south to north, and how big the gaps between them are."

"Leo, I tried to explain before, that would require (besides the presumption of authenticity) that they were all done at the same hour of the same day."

"Presume it all, Charley. They *were* all done at the same time, or we will assume that they were. We will work on that presumption."

"Leo, ah—I had hoped that you would fail in your collecting. I still believe we should drop it all."

"Me, I hoped I would succeed, Charley, and I hoped harder. Why are you afraid of spooks? Me, I meet them every hour of my life. They're what keeps the air fresh."

"I'm afraid of it, Leo. All right, I'll get some equipment out here tomorrow, but I'm afraid of it. Damn it, Leo, *who was here?*"

"Wasn't anybody here," Ginger said. "I tell you like I tell Charley, I was only kidding, I don't really fool around with the fellows."

Charles Longbank got some equipment out there the next day. Charles himself was looking bad, maybe whiskeyed up a little bit, jerky, and looking over his shoulder all the time as though he had an owl perched on the back of his neck. But he did work several days running the picture segments and got them all down on scan film. Then he would program his computer and feed the data from the scan films to it.

"There's like a shadow, like a thin cloud on several of the pictures," Leo Nation said. "You any idea what it is, Charley?"

"Leo, I got out of bed late last night and ran two miles up and down that rocky back road of yours to shake myself up. I was afraid I was *getting* an idea of what those thin clouds were. Lord, Leo, who was here?"

Charles Longbank took the data in to town and fed it to his computers.

He was back in several days with the answers.

"Leo, this spooks me more than ever," he said, and he looked as if the spooks had chewed him from end to end. "Let's drop the whole thing. I'll even give you back your retainer fee."

"No, man, no. You took the retainer fee and you are re-tained. Have you the order they go in, Charley, south to north?"

"Yes, here it is. But don't do it, Leo, don't do it."

"Charley, I only shuffle them around with my lift fork and put them in order. I'll have it done in an hour."

And in an hour he had it done.

"Now, let's look at the south one first, and then the north one, Charley."

"No, Leo, no, no! Don't do it."

"Why not?"

"Because it scares me. They really *do* fall into an order. They really could have been done all at the same hour of the same day. Who was here, Leo? Who is the giant look-ing over my shoulder?"

"Yeah, he's a big one, isn't he, Charley? But he was a good artist and artists have the right to be a little peculiar. He looks over my shoulder a lot too."

Leo Nation ran the southernmost segment of the Long Picture. It was mixed land and water, island, bayou and swamp, estuary and ocean mixed with muddy river.

"It's pretty, but it isn't the Mississippi," said Leo as it ran. "It's that other river down there. I'd know it after all these years too."

"Yes," Charles Longbank gulped. "It's the Atchafalaya River. By the comparative sun angle of the pieces that had been closely identified, the computer was able to give close bearings on all the segments. This is the mouth of the Atchafalaya River which has several times in the geological past been the main mouth of the Missippippi. But how did he know it if he wasn't here? Gah, the ogre is looking over my shoulder again. It scares me, Leo."

"Yeah, Charley, I say a man ought to be really scared at least once a day so he can sleep that night. Me, I'm scared for at least a week now, and I like the big guy. Well, that's one end of it, or mighty close to it. Now we take the north end.

"Yes, Charley, yes. The only thing that scares you is

that they're real. I don't know why he has to look over our shoulders when we run them, though. If he's who I think he is he's already seen it all."

Leo Nation began to run the northernmost segment of the river that he had.

"How far north are we in this, Charley?" he asked.

"Along about where the Cedar River and the Iowa River later came in."

"That all the farther north? Then I don't have any segments of the north third of the river?"

"Yes, this is the farthest north it went, Leo. Oh God, this is the last one."

"A cloud on this segment too, Charley? What are they anyhow? Say, this is a pretty crisp scene for springtime on the Mississippi."

"You look sick, Long-Charley-Bank," Ginger Nation said. "You think a little whiskey with possum's blood would help you?"

"Could I have the one without the other? Oh, yes, both together, that may be what I need. Hurry, Ginger."

"It bedevils me still how any painting could be so wonderful," Leo wondered.

"Haven't you caught on yet, Leo?" Charles shivered. "It isn't a painting."

"I tell you that at the beginning if you only listen to me," Ginger Nation said. "I tell you it isn't either one, canvas or paint, it is only picture. And Leo said the same thing once, but then he forgets. Drink this, old Charley."

Charles Longbank drank the healing mixture of good whiskey and possum's blood, and the northernmost segment of the river rolled on.

"Another cloud on the picture, Charley," Leo said. "It's like a big smudge in the air between us and the shore."

"Yes, and there will be another," Charles moaned. "It means we're getting near the end. Who were they, Leo? How long ago was it? Ah—I'm afraid I know that part pretty close—but they couldn't have been human then, could they? Leo, if this was just an inferior throwaway, why are they still hanging in the air?"

"Easy, old Charley, easy. Man, that river gets chalky and foamy! Charley, couldn't you transfer all this to microfilm and feed it into your computers for all sorts of answers?"

"Oh, God, Leo, it already *is*!"

"Already is what? Hey, what's the fog, what's the

mist? What is it that bulks up behind the mist? Man, what kind of blue fog-mountain—?"

"The glacier, you dummy, the glacier," Charles Long-bank groaned. And the northernmost segment of the river came to an end.

"Mix up a little more of that good whiskey and pos-sum's blood, Ginger," Leo Nation said. "I think we're all going to need it."

"That old, is it?" Leo asked a little later as they were all strangling on the very strong stuff.

"Yes, that old," Charles Longbank jittered. "Oh, who was here, Leo?"

"And, Charley, it already is *what?*"

"It already *is* microfilm, Leo, to them. A rejected strip, I believe."

"Ah, I can understand why whiskey and possum's blood never caught on as a drink," Leo said. "Was old possum here then?"

"Old possum was, we weren't." Charles Longbank shivered. "But it seems to me that something older than possum is snuffing around again, and with a bigger snuf-ter."

Charles Longbank was shaking badly. One more thing and he would crack.

"The clouds on the—ah—film, Charley, what are they?" Leo Nation asked.

And Charles Longbank cracked.

"God over my head," he moaned out of a shivering face, "I wish they *were* clouds on the film. Ah, Leo, Leo who were they here, who were they?"

"I'm cold, Charley," said Leo Nation. "There's bone-chill draft from somewhere."

The marks . . . too exactly like something, and too big to be: the loops and whorls that were eighteen feet long . . .

WITH FRIENDS LIKE THESE . . .

ALAN DEAN FOSTER

This is in some ways a perfect example of the best type of *Analog* story and it represents what may be the primary underlying thought that brought that magazine, under the late John W. Campbell, to its leadership. Which is that humanity, come hell or high water, is basically unbeatable.

As she commenced her first approach to the Go-type sun, the light cruiser *Tpin's* velocity began to decrease from the impossible to the merely incredible. Her multidrive engines put forth the barely audible whine that signified slowdown, and she once more assumed a real mass that the normal universe could and would notice.

Visual observation at the organic level became possible as the great ship cut the orbit of the last gas giant. Those of the vessel's complement took the never dull opportunity to rush the ports for a glimpse of a new solar system; those whose functions did not include the actual maneuvering of the craft. Curiosity was a fairly universal characteristic among space-going races. The crew of the *Tpin*, although a grim lot, were no exception.

Within the protected confines of the fore control room of the half-kilometer long bubble of metal and plastic, Communicator First Phrnnx shifted his vestigial wings and asked Commander First Rappan for the millionth time what the hell-equivalent they hoped to find.

"Phrnnx," Rappan sighed, "if you haven't been sufficiently enlightened as to the content of the legends by now, I fail to see how I can aid you. Instead of repeating yourself for the sake of hearing yourself oralize, I suggest you bend a membrane to your detection apparatus and see if you can pick up any traces of that *murfled* Yop battleship!"

Phrnnx riffled his eyelids in a manner indicative of mild denial, with two degrees of respectful impatience. "We lost those inept yipdips five parsecs ago, sir. I am fully capable of performing my duties without any well-intentioned suggestions from the bureaucracy. Do I tell you how to fly the ship?"

"A task," began Rappan heatedly, "so far beyond your level of comprehension that . . . !"

"Gentlebeings, gentlebeings, please!" said the Professor. Subordinate and commander alike quieted.

The "Professor"—his real title was unpronounceable to most of the crew—was both the guiding force and the real reason behind the whole insane expedition. It was he who rediscovered the secret of breaking the Terran Shield. He came from a modest three-system cluster nearly halfway to the Rim—far removed from their own worlds. Due to the distance from things and to their own quiet, retiring nature, his folk took little part in the perpetual cataclysm of the Federation-Yop wars. What small—if important—role they did deign to play in the conflict was not occasioned by choice. Rather, it was engendered by the Yop policy of regarding all those peoples, who were not allies of the Yop, as mortal enemies of the Yop. There was room in neither Yop culture, nor Yop language, for the concept of a "neutral." Yop temperament was such that their total complement of allies came to a grand total of zero. The members of the Federation had matured beyond prejudice, but it was admitted in most quarters that the Yops were not nice people. Possibly some of this attitude stemmed from the Yop habit of eating everything organic that moved, without regard for such minor inconveniences as, say, the intelligence of the dinner, or his desire to be not-eaten.

Against them was allied the total remaining strength of the organized galaxy; some two hundred and twelve federated races.

However—due to diet, perhaps—there were a lot of Yops.

The avowed purpose of the expedition was to make that latter total two hundred and thirteen.

The Professor continued in a less stern tone. "If you *must* fight among yourselves, kindly do so at a civilized level. At least out of deference to me. I am an old being, and I possess a perhaps unreasonable allergy to loud and raucous noises."

The others in the room immediately lowered their voices in respect. In the Federation age was a revered commodity, to be conserved as such. And there was no denying the Professor's age. His antennae drooled noticeably, his chiton was growing more and more translucent, losing its healthy purple iridescence, and his back plates were exfoliating in thin, shallow flakes. That he had held up as well as he had on this trip, with its sometimes strenuous dodging of Yop warships, was in itself remarkable. He seemed to grow stronger as they neared their objective, and now his eyes, at least, glowed with a semblance of vitality.

All eyes were trained on the great mottled sphere turning slowly and majestically below them.

"Planet Three," intoned Navigator First. "Primary colors blue, white, brown, green. Atmosphere . . .", and he dropped off to a low mumbling. At last, "It checks, sir."

"And the gold overlay?" asked Communicator Phrnnx, for being among the youngest of the crew, his curiosity quotient was naturally among the highest.

"That, gentlebeings, means that the Shield is still up. After all these years I'd thought perhaps . . ." The Professor made what passed for a shrug among his people. He turned from the port to the others.

"As you all recall, I hope, the phenomenon below us, the 'Shield,' is the direct result of the Old Empire-Terran Wars of ages ago. At that time, the inhabitants of this planet first broke free of their own system and started to come out to the stars.

"They found there a multi-racial empire nominally ruled by a race known to us as the Veen. The Terrans were invited to join the empire, accruing the same rights and privileges as had historically been granted to all new space-going races for thousands and thousands of years."

"And they refused," put in Rappan.

"Yes, they refused. It became quickly apparent to the Veen that the Terrans intended to carve out a little pocket empire of their own in another sector of space. Since Terra was so far away from the center of things, so to speak, the Veen decided that for the sake of peace . . . and the Veen . . . this could not be allowed to take place. Accordingly, there was a war, or rather, a series of wars. These lasted for centuries, despite the overwhelming numerical superiority of the Veen. Gradually the Terrans were pushed back to their own home world. A standoff ensued, as the Veen and their allies were unable to break the ultimate defenses of the Terrans.

"Then a great scientist of one of the allied races of the Veen discovered, quite by accident, the quasi-mathematical principle behind the Shield. The nature of the Shield forbade its use on anything smaller than a good-sized moon. It was thus useless for such obvious military applications as, for example, a ship defensive screen. Then someone got the bright idea of enveloping the entire planet of Terra in one huge Shield, making it into an impenetrable cage. At worst, it would provide the Empire with a breathing spell in which to marshal its sorely battered forces. At best it would restrict the Terrans to their own fortress until such time as the Veen saw fit to let them out. The chances of the Terrans accidentally stumbling onto the same principle was considered to be slight. As you can now see, this indeed has been the case." The Professor sighed again, a high, whistling sound.

"However, the wars with Terra had also depleted the resources of the Veen tremendously. Those races which had been allied to them only by virtue of the Veen's superior knowledge and strength saw an irresistible opportunity to supplant the Veen in the hierarchy of Empire. The result? The Time of Conflicts, which resulted in the breakdown of the Empire, the final elimination of the once-proud Veen, and after considerable bickering and fighting, the formation of our present Federation—in a much more primitive form, of course."

He returned his gaze once again to the blue-white planet circling below, its land areas blurred in the shifting golden haze which was the by-product of the Shield. They had already locked in to the Shield station on the planet's only satellite. "Unfortunately, the Ban still remains."

Rappan broke away from his console for a moment. "Look, we've been through all that. The supposed rule states that the penalty for breaking the Shield either partially, or completely, is death, for all those concerned. But that *murfled* law is millennia old!"

"And still on the books," retorted old Alo, the Commander Second.

"I know, I know!", said Rappan, adjusting a meter. "Which is one reason why every being on this ship is a volunteer. And if I thought we had a choice I'd never have commandeered the *Tpin* for this trip. But you know as well as I, Alo, we *have* no choice! We've been fighting the Yops now for nearly three hundred *sestes*, and been losing ever since we started. Oh, I know how it looks, but the signs are all there. One of these days we'll turn around for the customary reinforcement and *piff!*, they won't be there! That's why it's imperative we find new allies . . . even if we have to try Terra. When I was a cub, my den parents would scare us away from the *Grininl*-fruit groves by saying: 'the Terrans will get you if you don't watch out.' "

" 'Ginst the Edict," murmured Alo, not to be put off.

Navigator First Zinin broke in on the heavy bass-rumbling of his heavy-planet civilization. "There will be no Edicts, old one, if the Yops crush the Federation. We must take *some* risks. If the Terrans are willing to aid us . . . and are still capable of it . . . I do believe that GalCen will agree to some slight modification of the rules. And, if these creatures have fallen back to the point where they can be of no help to us, then they will not be a threat to us either. GalCen will not be concerned."

"And if by chance mebbee they should be a bit angry at us and decide to renew an ancient grudge?" put in the ever pessimistic Alo.

"Then the inevitable," put in Zinin, "will only be hastened."

Philosophizing was of needs broken off. The *Tpin* was entering the Shield.

Green, thought Phrnnx. *It is the greenest nontropical planet I have ever seen.*

He was standing by the end of the ramp which led out from the belly of the cruiser. The rest of the First Contact party was nearby. They had landed near a great mountain range, in a lush section of foothills and gently rolling green. Tall growths of brown and emerald dominated two sides of their view. In front of them stretched low hillocks covered with what was obviously cultivated vegetation. Behind the ship, great silver-gray mountains thrust white-haloed crowns into the sky. Had the *Tpin* been an air vessel, the updrafts sweeping up the sides of those crags would have given them trouble. As it was, they merely added another touch to the records the meteorologists were assembling.

Somewhere in the tall growths—which they later learned were call *trees*—a brook of liquid H_2O made gurgling sounds. Overhead, orinthorphs circled lazily in the not unpleasant heat of morning. Phrnnx was meditating on how drastically the Shield had affected the normal climate of this world when he became aware of Alo and Zinin strolling up behind him.

"A peaceful world, certainly," said Zinin. "Rather light on the oxygen and argon, and all that nitrogen gives it a bit of odor, but on the whole a most pleasant ball of dirt."

"Humph! From one who burns almost as much fuel as the ship I wouldn't have expected compliments," grumbled Alo. "Still, I'll grant you 'tis a quiet locale we've chosen to search out allies. I wonder if such a world did indeed spawn such a warlike race, or were they perhaps immigrants from elsewhere?"

"They weren't, and it didn't," interposed the Professor. He had relinquished the high point to the commander and his military advisers, as their conversation had bored him.

"Mind explaining that a mite, Professor?" asked Alo.

The Professor bent suddenly and dug gently in the soft earth with a claw. He came up with a small wiggling thing. This he proceeded to pop into his mouth and chew with vigor.

"Hm-m-m. A bit bitter, But intriguing. I believe there is at least one basis for trade here."

"Be intriguing if it poisons you," said Phrnnx with some relish.

The Professor moved his antennae in a gesture indicative of negativity, with one degree of mild reproach. "Nope. Sorry to disappoint you, youngster, but Bio has already pronounced most of the organics on this planet nontoxic. Watch out for the vegetation, though. Full of acids and things. As to your question, Alo. When the Terrans . . ."

"Speaking of Terrans," put in Zinin, "I'd like to see one of these mythical creatures I don't recall seeing any cities on our descent."

"Neither did Survey. Oh, don't look so smug, Navigator. Survey reports their presence . . . Terrans, not cities . . . but they estimate no more than a hundred million of them on the planet. The only signs of any really large clusterings are vague outlines that could be the sites of ancient ruins. Might have expected something of the sort. People change in a few *Ipas*, you know."

"*My* question," prompted Alo once more.

"Well, when the Terrans went out into extra-solar space and began setting up their own empire, the Veen decided at first to leave them alone. Not only was there no precedent for a space-faring race not accepting citizenship in the empire, but the Terrans weren't bothering anyone. They were also willing to sign all kinds of trade agreements and such. Anything of a nonrestrictive and nonmilitary nature."

"Why'd the Veen change their minds, then?" asked the now interested Phrnnx.

"Some bright lad in the Veen government made a few computer readings, extrapolating from what was known of Terran scientific developments, rate of expansion, galactic acclimatization, and so on."

"And the result?"

"According to the machines . . . and the Veen had *good* ones . . . in only one hundred *Ipas* the Veen would have to start becoming acclimatized to Terra."

Zinin was the only one of the three listeners who expressed his reaction audibly. Surprisingly, it was by means of a long, drawn-out whistle.

"Yes, that's about how the Veen took it. So they decided to cut the Terrans down to where they would no longer be even an indirect threat."

"Seems they did," said Alo, gazing up at the goldflecked Shield sky.

The Professor spared a glance the same way. "Yes, it would seem so." He stared off in the direction of the commander's post where a force-lift was depositing a ground car. "But it's enlightening to keep one other little thing in mind."

"Which is?" said Alo belligerently.

"There *are* no more Veen."

Survey had detected what appeared to be a small, artificial edifice down in the slight dip between the foothills. It was, therefore, decided that a party consisting of

Commander Rappan, Navigator Zinin, Communicator Phrnnx, a philologist, a xenologist, and of course, the Professor, would take a ground car down to the structure and attempt a First Contact. Despite vigorous protests, Commander Second Alo was restricted to acting captain.

"Give the crew land-leave," instructed Rappan. "Shifts of the usual six. Maintain a semialert guard at all times until further notice. I know this place looks about as dangerous as a *mufti*-bug after stuffing, but I intend to take no chances. At the first sign of hostilities, raise ship and get out. That is a first-degree order. You have others on board who can operate the remote Shield equipment. In the event that all is not what it seems, I don't want to leave these creatures a way out."

"Noted and integrated, sir," replied Alo stiffly. And then in a lower voice, "Watch yourself, sir. This place smells funny to me, and I am not referring to the nitro in the atmosphere, either!"

Rappan essayed a third-level smile, with two degrees of mild affection, nonsexual. "You've said that now on . . . let's see . . . thirty-nine planet-falls to date. But rest assured I will take no chances. We know too little of this place, including the Professor."

"Anyway, legends are notoriously nonfactual."

The little car hummed softly to itself as it buzzed over the dark soil. A cleared path is unmistakable on any planet, and this one ran straight as an *Opsith* through the fields of low, irrigated plants. Phrnnx had wondered idly what they were, and if they would appeal to his palate. The Professor had replied by reminding him of Bio's warning about plant acids and added that stealing the native's food would be a poor way to open friendly negotiations. Phrnnx discarded the notion. Besides, the vegetation of this area appeared to be disgustingly heavy in cellulose content—doubtlessly bland in flavor, if any. And there had been no sign of domesticated food animals. Was it possible these people existed solely on wood fibers? It was a discouraging thought.

He had no chance to elaborate on it, for as the car rounded the first turn they had come to, they were confronted by the sight of their first native. The car slowed and settled to the earth with a faint sigh.

In the nearby field a shortish biped was walking smoothly behind a large brown quadruped. Together they were engaged in driving a wedge of some bright metal through the soft soil, turning it over on itself in big loamy chunks. The name of this particular biped happened to be Jones, Alexis. The name of the quadruped was Dobbin, period.

The two natives apparently caught sight of the visitors. Both paused in their work to stare solemnly at the outlandish collection of aliens in the ground car. The aliens, pop-eyed, stared back. The biped wore some kind of animal skin shirt. This was partly hidden by some form of artificial fabric coveralls and boots. Seeing this, it occurred to Phrnnx that they must have *some* kind of manufacturing facilities somewhere. The quadruped wore only a harness, again artificial, which was attached to the metal wedge. It soon grew bored in its survey of the aliens and dropped its head to crop patiently at the few sparse bits of grass that had so far managed to avoid the plow.

Commander Rappan's instinctive reaction to this first move was to reach for his pistol. He was momentarily abashed to find it missing from its customary place in his shell. The Professor had insisted that all contact was to be open and trusting from the first. Consequently, all weapons had been left back on the ship. The Professor had also looked longingly at the bristling gunports of the *Tpin,* but the commander and his advisers had adamantly refused to leave the ship unprotected. The Professor had patiently explained that if the Terrans were going to be any real help against the Yops, then the guns of the *Tpin* would hardly be effective against them. And if they weren't going to be, then the guns weren't needed. As might be expected, this argument went far over the heads of the soldiers.

But Rappan still felt naked, somehow.

The native made no threatening gestures. In fact, he made no guestures at all, but instead continued to stare placidly at the pertrified load of explorers. After several minutes of this, Rappan decided it was time things got moving. Besides, the native's unbroken stare was beginning to make him feel a bit fidgety, not to mention silly.

"You, philologist! Can you talk to that thing?" Commander Rappan asked.

The philologist, a meter-tall being from a Ko star near Cen-Cluster, essayed a nervous reply. "It remains to be seen, sir. We have no records of their speech patterns, and there were few broadcasts to monitor the computers to as we descended." His voice was faintly disapproving. "I am not even sure which of the two creatures is the dominant form."

"The large one in the lead, certainly," said the xenologist.

"I believe the Terrans are described in the legends, when not as hundred *foomp* high fire-breathing monsters, as bipeds," said the Professor quietly. "Although it also has four limbs, two are obviously manipulative. I suggest that one."

"I shall have to work from next to nothing," protested the philologist.

"I don't care if you do it holding your breath, but get out there and do *something!* I feel like an idiot sitting here."

"Yes, sir."

"Yes, sir—*what?*"

The philologist decided that this would be an auspicious time to essay a First Contact. He hurried out the door. At least, he thought, the native couldn't be much more difficult to communicate with than the commander. He wished fervently that he was back in the community nest.

Trailing the philologist, the party made its way to the two natives.

"Uh," began the philologist, straining over the guttural syllables, "we come in peace, Terran. Friends. Buddies. Comrades. Blut-burderhood. We good-guys. You comprende?"

"Me, Tarzan; you Jane," said the Terran.

The philologist turned worriedly to Rappan. "I'm afraid I can't place his answer, sir. The reference is obscure. Shall I try again?"

"Skip it," said the Terran, in fluent, if archaic, Galactico. "Ancient humorism. Surprising how old jokes stand time better than most monuments." He seemed to sigh a little.

"You speak!" blurted the xenologist.

"An unfortunate malady of which I seem incapable of breaking myself. Sic transit gloryoski. Up the Veen. But come on down to the house. Maria's making some ice cream . . . I hope you like chocolate . . . you're welcome to try it, although I don't think we'd have enough for King Kong, here."

Zinin decided to regard this unfamiliar aphorism as

a neutral compliment. There wasn't much else he could do. He tried to hunch his three-meter bulk lower, gave it up when he realized that he didn't know whether the promised ice cream was a food, a paint, or a mild corrosive for cleaning out reluctant teeth.

"We appreciate your hospitality, sir. We've come to discuss a very ungent matter with your superiors. It involves perhaps more than you can comprehend." Here the Professor peered hard at the native, who looked back at him with placid assurance. "Although I have a hunch you might have some idea what I mean."

If the Terran noticed a change in the Professor's glance he gave no sign, but instead smiled apologetically.

"Ice cream first."

The Terran's residence, when seen from close up, was a ultilitarian yet not unbeautiful structure. It appeared to be made mostly from native woods, with a hint of metal only here and there. A small quadruped was lying on its entrance step. It raised its head to gaze mournfully at the arrivals, with wise eyes, before returning it to its former position on its forepaws. Had the Professor known anything about the history of Terran canines, this quiet greeting would have been interesting indeed.

The building proved to admit more light and air than had seemed probable from the outside. Furniture appeared to be mostly of the handmade variety, with here and there an occasional hint of something machine-turned. Bright colors predominated but did not clash, not that the Terran color-scheme meant anything to the visitors anyway. At least the place was big enough to hold all.

The Jones's mate was a sprightly little dark woman of indeterminate age, much like her husband. A single male sibling by the name of Flip stared solemnly from a window seat at the grouping of guests assembled in his parent's den. He had a twig, or stick, which he would sometimes tap on the floor.

"Now, Alex . . ." said the woman, fussing with a large wooden ice cream maker, "you didn't tell me we were having visitors. How am I supposed to prepare for these things if you don't tell me about them in advance?"

The native smiled. "Sorry, hon, but these, um, gentlemen, just sort of dropped in on us. I promised them some ice cream."

"I hope they like chocolate," she said.

When they had been seated around the room, each being curling up according to the style fitting to its own physiognomy, Commander Rappan decided to break into the cheerful dialogue and get down to business. Fraternizing with the natives was all very well and good. No doubt the Xeno Department would approve. However, he was not so sure that his colleagues, hard-pressed to hold off the Yop waves, would see things in the same way.

Unfortunately, this thing called *ice cream* got quite a grip on one's attention.

Zinin was one of the few present to whom the concoction had proved unappealing. He leaned over and whispered to Phrnnx, "These are the deadly fighters we are supposed to enlist? Conquerors of the Veen fleets? Stuff of horror tales? Why, they look positively soft! I could crush that male under one paw. He hardly comes up to my eyes!"

"Few of us do, oh hulking one," replied Phrnnx, adding a gesture indicative of second-degree ironic humor. "But that is hardly an indication one way or the other. Although I admit they *do* seem a bit on the pastoral side."

Zinin snorted.

"What star system are you folks from? Not all from the same, surely!"

"Indeed," said the Professor. It occurred to him what had troubled his thoughts ever since they had met these natives. For a race that had not had extraplanetary contact for umpti-thousand *Ipas* they were treating the crew of the *Tpin* like next-next neighbors who popped over for a visit every time-period. Even the sibling . . . where had *he* disappeared to? . . . had been fully self-possessed when confronted by what must be to him utterly strange beings. It was just a touch unnerving. "You might be interested to know that the Veen have been extinct for some 450,000 of your time-revolutions."

The biped nodded understandingly. "We guessed as much. When so much time passed and nothing happened, one way or the other, friendly or hostile . . . we assumed that we'd been forgotten and filed away somewhere."

"Not forgotten," said the Professor. "Legends persist longer than their creators, sometimes. There was a period of . . . confusion . . . at the end of the Veen-Terran wars." (Was that a twitch of reaction in the native's face? Yes? No?) "When the bureaucracy set up by the Veen was submerged by a wave of would-be empire-builders, interstellar government pretty well collapsed. It took a while for things to straighten themselves out. Which is why we have not contacted you till now. (Could he read the lie?) Another problem has arisen."

The biped sighed again. "I was afraid this mightn't be a social call. What is your problem, Professor?"

Backed at certain intervals by succinct comments from Rappan, he began to outline the present desperate situation with respect to the Yops, ending with a plea to forget any past differences and come to the aid of the Federation.

The Terran had listened quietly to their arguments, unmoving. Now he sat in a attitude of intense concentration, seeming to listen to voices and thoughts outside their ken. When he at last raised his face to them again he wore a serious smile.

"I must, of course, consult with and deliver your message to my . . . 'superiors.' Such a decision would be difficult for us to make. As you can see for yourselves"—he made an all-encompassing gesture—"we have changed our mode of existence somewhat since we fought the Veen. We are no longer geared to the production of war material. Incidentally, we hold no grudge against any of you. I have no idea if my ancestors and yours ever met, let alone battled with one another. We never even really held animosity towards the Veen. In fact, I'd give a lot to know exactly *why* they went to war with us in the first place."

Phrnnx had heard the Professor's explanation and looked expectantly in his direction, but that worthy remained silent.

"Of course," continued the Terran after a while, "as a gesture of your goodwill we would naturally expect you to lower the Shield. Despite a hell of a lot of scribbling and figuring, that's one thing we could never quite do."

"Of course," said Rappan determinedly.

The biped stood. "It will take me a while to convey your message to my superiors. In the meantime, do feel free to enjoy the countryside and my poor home." He turned and walked into another room.

The female eyed them speculatively.

"I don't suppose any of you gentlemen play bridge?"

Phrnnx was wandering through the nearby forest, following the path made by the cheerful stream. He had quickly grown bored with studying the simple native household, and, unlike the Professor or Commander Rappan, the intricacies of Terran "bridge" were a touch more intellectual a pastime than he wished for. The two scientists had found plenty to keep them occupied profitably, but after reporting to the ship their accumulated data and the word that things seemed to be progressing satisfactorily, there had remained little for a communicator to do.

The dense undergrowth led away from the house at a right angle. With the sense of direction his kind possessed he was not afraid of getting lost, and the damp coolness of the place was the closest thing he'd found to the rain forests of home. It was full of interesting sounds and new smells. The native female had assured him that no dangerous creatures lurked within its inviting shadows. He was thoroughly enjoying himself. Orinthorphs and small invertebrates . . . "insects," they were called . . . flitted rapidly from growth to growth. He could have snatched them easily in midair with his long suckers, but was mindful of strange foods despite the Professor's assurance that the native organics were edible. Besides, he was not hungry. He strode on in high spirits.

The hike was about to come to an unpleasant end.

The trees appeared to cease abruptly off to one side. Espying what seemed to be a glint of sunlight on water he turned in that direction. His supposition was correct. In front of him was a large clearing which bordered on a good-sized lake. In the foreground stood the diminutive figure of Flip, the native's offspring. He was gazing at a pair of massive, glowering figures in space armor. These did not fit into the picture.

Yops!

Phrnnx stood paralyzed with shock. The Yop battleship that he thought they had lost near that red dwarf sat half-in, half-out of the blue-green lake. He assumed it was the same one. Its gunports were wide open. Troops were clustering around a landing portal on one side of the kilometer-and-a-half-long monster. Dirt had been gouged out on all sides by the sheer mass of the huge vessel. These two figures in the foreground were doubtlessly scouts.

How in the central chaos had they slipped in past the

cruiser's screens? Unless they, too, had found a way to negate the Shield—and this seemed unlikely—then they must have entered by way of the temporary hole made by the *Tpin*. A quick glance at the sky showed the now familiar gold tinge still strong. So they hadn't destroyed the generating equipment on the planet's satellite, then. Yop invisibility screens were known to be good, but this good? . . . His speculations were interrupted by what happened next.

The nearest Yop reached down and lifted the Flip in one massive, knobby claw. It held it like that, steady, while it examined the youngster along with its partner. The boy, in turn, appeared to be examining them with its wide, deep-gray eyes. Both were making the motions and gestures which Phrnnx knew indicated Yop laughter.

What followed occurred so rapidly that Phrnnx, afterwards, had difficulty in reconstructing the incident.

The Yop raised the youngster over its horned head and swung it towards the ground with every intention of smashing the child's brains out. But the boy abruptly slowed in midair, turned, and landed gently on its feet. The Yop was staring at its now empty hand in surprise. The expression of placid innocence, which had heretofore been the child's sole visage, shifted all at once into a strong frown that was somehow more terrifying than any contortion of rage could have been. It said, in a very unchildlike tone of voice, two words.

"Bad mans!"

And gestured with the twig.

The two Yops glowed briefly an intolerable silver-white, shading to blue. It was the color of nova—a chrome nova. The two scouts "popped" loudly, once, and disappeared. In their places two clouds of fine gray ash sifted slowly to the ground. They boy pointed his stick at the multi-ton Yop warship. "More bad mans," he said. The ship abruptly glowed with the same intolerable radiance. It "popped" with a considerably louder and much more satisfying bang! The boy then turned and went over to the brook. He began slowly stirring the water with his stick.

Phrnnx found he could breathe again. The feathers on his back, however, did not lie down. All that remained of the invincible Yop battlewagon was the faint smell of ozone and a very large pile of fine multi-colored ash. This was patiently being removed by a small breeze.

The boy suddenly looked up, turned, and stared straight at where Phrnnx was crouching behind the bole of a large pine. He started to stroll over.

Phrnnx ran. He ran hard, fast, and unthinkingly. He was not sure what a "bad mans" was but he had no wish to be included in that category—none whatsoever. No sirree. He ran in a blind panic with all four legs and a great sorrow that his ancestors had traded their wings for intelligence. Ahead, a dark, cavelike depression appeared in the ground. Without breaking stride, he instinctively threw himself into the protective opening.

And into the closet of the world.

Phrnnx awoke with the equivalent of a throbbing headache. He almost panicked again when he remembered that last moment before blacking out. A touch of the hard, unresisting metal underneath reassured and calmed him. He had thrown himself into a cave . . . only it hadn't been a cave. It had been a hole. A hole filled with machinery. Yes, that's right! He remembered falling past machinery—levels and levels and levels of it. He did not know it, but he had fallen only a mile before the first of the automatic safety devices had analyzed his alien body chemistry, pronounced him organic, alive, and reasonably worth saving, and brought him to a comfortable resting place at the fifty-third level.

He staggered to his feet, becoming aware of a faint susurration around him. Warm air, and the faint sounds of the almost silent machines. A slow look around confirmed the evidence of his other senses . . . and he almost wished it hadn't. Machines. Machine upon Machine. Massive and unnoticing, they throbbed with life and power all around him. He could not see the end of the broad aisle he stood on. He turned and staggered over to the edge of the shaft he had obviously fallen into, following the current of fresh air.

A quick look over the side made him draw back involuntarily. His race was not subject to vertigo, but there are situations and occasions where the reality transcends the experience. There is too much relativity in a cavern, even an artificial one.

Above stretched over a mile of levels, seemingly much like this one. Very faintly and far away he could just make out the tiny circle of light that marked the surface and his entranceway to this frighteningly silent metal world.

He could not see the bottom.

He found himself giggling. Oh yes, pastoral indeed! Quite. Not prepared to turn out war material. Certainly not. No capability whatsoever. No cities, remember? Handmade furniture. Quaint way to live. Didn't say by what kind of hands, though. Poor, degenerated natives! Cannon fodder, he'd seen it in Commander Rappan's eyes.

But the commander hadn't peeked in the basement.

When the hysteria had worked itself out, he took several deep gulps of the fresh air. There had to be a manual way out. Stairs, a lift, something! He had to get back and warn the others. He tried his pocket communicator, suspecting that it wouldn't work. It didn't. A communicator who couldn't communicate. He almost started giggling again, but caught himself this time. He began to search for a way out. He did not know it, and probably would not have cared anyway, but his situation was remarkably analogous to that of a very ancient and very imaginary Terran female named Alice.

"I am pleased to say," began the native known as Alexis Jones, "that the committee . . . government . . . ruling body? I forget the relevant term. Anyway, we have agreed to do what we can to aid your Federation. These Yops . . ." and he paused momentarily, "do not sound like very nice people . . ."

"They're not!" added Zinin fervently.

". . . And even if we only add a bit of manpower to your gallant effort, we will be happy to be of assistance. We are a bit," he added apologetically, "out of practice."

"That's all right," beamed the commander. At first he had regarded these disgustingly peaceful and soft-seeming bipeds more of a liability than an asset. Then it occurred to him that the Yops, too, were familiar with the Terran legends. Could be the materialization of a real legend might disconcert them a bit. Of course these peaceful mammals would have to be thoroughly instructed, or their appearance would merely make the Yops go into fits of laugheter, but . . . "We appreciate your desire to aid in this great crusade. I am certain this historic arrangement will go down in history as one of exceptional benefit to all the races concerned. As a prelude to further discussion, I have ordered . . ."

He paused, open-mouthed, concentration broken. The Terran was staring upwards. His face had . . . changed. It was brightening, expanding, opening hitherto unsuspecting vistas to their startled gaze, like a night-blooming flower. Within those two small oculars, previously so gray and limpid, there now glowed a deep-down fire that seemed to pierce upwards and spread over all present like a nerve-deadening drug. It made the commander draw back and Zinin hiss involuntarily.

"The Shield is Down!" shouted the native, flinging its arms wide.

"The Shield is Down!" answered his wife.

And all over the planet, among all the members, large and small, of the Brotherhood of Warmblood; the dogs, the mice, the cats and orcas, birds and shrews; ungulates, carnivores, herbivores, and omnivores, the great telepathic shout went up.

"THE SHIELD IS DOWN!"

And in the field Dobbin and the small brown dog began to discuss the ramifications at length.

The man turned to face his visitors, who were silent.

"You have done us a very large favor, gentlebeings, and we are oh, so grateful! How many years we labored to find the answer to the Shield, how many years, only to discover that it could only be applied, or retracted, *from an outside source.* Now that it is down, we will *not* make the error of allowing it to be put up again. Once again, gentlebeings, we are in your debt. Our agreement still holds. If you will return to your ship we will . . . commence preparations to follow in ours." The native smiled, and it was at once a lovely and terrible thing to see. (Among the known creatures of the universe, only the Terran human bares its fangs to express friendship.)

"It has been *so* long," the Jones sighed wistfully, "since we have had a decent war!"

Back on the *Tpin* it was a thoughtful yet jubilant Rappan who confronted a very bedraggled Communicator First.

"Commander," panted Phrnnx, "listen! You mustn't drop the Shield! This whole world . . . it's a sham, sir! A fake. We've been fooled, and badly. These natives aren't as primitive as they'd like us to think. I *saw*, sir! Machines, automatic factories, synthetic food-processing plants . . . the *whole planet*, Commander . . . it's

filled with their machines! I fell into it . . . accident
. . . the machines down there are programmed to answer
questions . . . I asked . . ." He paused for breath, became
aware then that no one in the happy control cabin was
paying any attention to him. Most of the crew were
telling jokes, patting each other contently on their back-
equivalents, and preparing for a lift-off. Only the Professor seemed unaffected by the otherwise universal gid-
diness. Phrnnx turned to the elder.

"Professor, I'm telling the truth! Tell them, make them
listen, we've got to . . . !"

The Professor turned a spare eye on him. "Oh, I
believe you, youngster. Yes, I believe you. If those
muftis could control their glee long enough to listen
to you, they'd no doubt believe you, too." he paused.
"Have you looked at the sky recently?"

Phrnnx ran to a port and stared wildly upwards.

"The Shield's gone!"

The Professor favored his announcement with a first-
degree nod, indicating positive acknowledgment. "Indeed it is. Commander Rappan had left orders with
Commander Second Alo to drop it as a sign of good
faith the moment the Terrans agreed to sign the mutual
defense pact edicts with us." He looked thoughtfully at
the port. "The Jones and his mate seemed to know exactly
when the generating machinery on the satellite cut off.
Even the animals were acting in a most peculiar fashion as we returned to the ship." He shivered slightly.

"I, for one, shall be less unhappy than I first thought
at the prospect of leaving this place."

"What makes you think that, now with the Shield off,
they'll hold to their agreement to help us?"

"Two reasons, youngster. First of all, the Jones said that
they would, and I have a hunch that they are the kind
of folk who put much in store by their word. And also,
I kind of think they could have turned it off any time
they wanted to, after our initial penetration."

Phrnnx did not answer. He was watching the sky grow
darker outside the port as the ship rose beyond the
atmosphere, watching the stars come out, remembering a
picture . . . a little boy, two Yop scouts, and a battleship.
Then a little boy and a battleship. Then just a little boy.
And the machine that had soothed his traumas, deep
under the crust of the planet.

"Sir," began Zinin to the commander, and his great

voice was strangely muffled, "they're coming . . . in their ship, like they said they would."

Phrnnx yanked himself back to reality—if such it still could be called—and joined the others who were not occupied at the fore port.

Below. Great masses of puffy white clouds. Brown and green land masses, unchanged. Blue oceans, unchanged.

Except one.

In the middle of the planet's second ocean, great, impossible masses of thick columnar crystals began to leap upwards from the waters. Translucent at first, the chalcedony towers began to pulse with deep inner fires: blue, purple, gold, carmine, and finally a strange, yet familiar, silver-gray. The ionosphere, tickled, began to surround the flashing needles with auroras, clothing them in blankets of coruscating radiance.

Following, the planet began to move after the *Tpin*.

On board the cruiser it was very quiet.

"I see," whispered Rappan idly, "that they are bringing their moon along also."

"You get accustomed to something like that," breathed an engineer. "A moon, I mean."

Old Alo was making mystic signs with his tentacles. "Egg of the Code, I almost feel sorry for the Yops!"

The crew picked up this thread of awed enthusiasm as they began to relate the impossible sight to their own personal views of the war. In no time the mood of jubilation was back again, stronger than ever. Stimulants were broken out and passed among those who indulged in them. The communicators—excepting one Phrnnx—began to ply the spacewaves with brazen, challenging messages, daring the Yops to locate them.

"Poor old Yops," whispered Phrnnx. "I can almost see Alo's point."

"Yes," replied the Professor. "There is only one thing that is worrying me."

"What is worrying you?" asked Phrnnx.

The Professor turned old eyes on him. They held irony, and they held musing.

"What," he said, "are we going to do with them when there are no more Yops?"

AUNT JENNIE'S TONIC

LEONARD TUSHNET

We had two good reasons for selecting this as one of the best of the year—it has an "ethnic" background which is genuine and human—and it deals with a subject very few sf writers have handled or can handle—the origins of modern medicine from primitive folk remedy.

Aunt Jennie was a witch or a saint. Or an ignorant old woman. The first two descriptions were subjective, depending on your dealings with her. The last was more objective, except for the "ignorant" part.

Aunt Jennie was nobody's aunt, as far as I know. The title was purely honorific, given in recognition of her advanced age, 108 the year she died an untimely death. She would have been called "Grandma" if she'd had children. I was the closest thing to offspring that she had. I recall her as an old woman, rambling in her talk, going back and forth in time and space, giving irrelevant details and omitting important ones, getting sidetracked into reminiscences and then skipping ahead so much that I got lost and had to have her repeat herself.

That often made her angry. Once she sneered at my notebook on the kitchen table. "You went to college and you can't remember from here to there. Me, I never learned even the Aleph-Beth and I could recite out of

my head books and books you would take twenty years
to write down."

She was probably right. Unfortunately for me, I had
double trouble in my interviews with her. I had to mentally
translate her barbarous Yiddish dialect, interlarded as it
was with Hungarian and Slovak words, and then retrans-
late it into anatomical and chemical terms before putting
it down on paper.

Those people who called Aunt Jennie a witch used
the word metaphorically. They disbelieved in her charmed
potions. They were rational doctors, rabbis, social work-
ers. They railed at her followers as superstitious fools.
They tried to influence the Board of Health, the City Law
Department, and the Jewish Community Council to have
her put away in a nice safe place like the Home for
the Aged.

They were unsuccessful because those who called her
a saint meant what they said. The parents of girls "in
trouble," the relatives of lunatics, the senior citizens who
came to her for tonics were grateful. They saw to it
that her frame house on Avenue K near the abattoirs
was fireproofed and a sprinkler system installed; they
provided her with matzos for Passover; they arranged
for weekly deliveries of food.

Aunt Jennie was old, very old. She was small, her neck
bent by arthritis, her hands gnarled. She kept a coal
stove going winter and summer in her little three-room
house with its bedroom, a large kitchen, and another
room whose door was always locked. She wore a
babushka that hid her dark-brown hair, a shawl, a
shapeless cardigan sweater buttoned up to the neck, and
a heavy woolen skirt over several petticoats. She was
never without an apron, and she never wore shoes but
padded about in heavy felt slippers.

She was really 108 years old when she died, give or
take a year. I know because my great-grandmother was
eight years old when she came to this country in 1873.
The ticket of entry at Philadelphia from Trieste is still in
the family scrapbook. My great-grandmother was born in
Homona (then Hungary, now Slovakia). She was orphaned
in one of the epidemics that periodically swept the outly-
ing areas of Franz Josef's empire. She was sent for by a
well-to-do relative in Newark who also sent enough money
for a traveling companion. That companion was Aunt
Jennie. Great-grandma's ticket says "in charge of Shaindel

Weiss," giving Shaindel's age as twenty. My great-grand-mother died at 96, active, bright, alert, not a white hair on her head, her skin rosy and smooth as a teen-ager's. Her death was by accident—she tripped over a toy left on the stairs by one of my cousin's children, fell down-stairs, and broke her neck.

Aunt Jennie died only a month later, not by accident. She was killed, not surprising in view of where she lived. The kids who killed her were caught when they tried to spend the multilated gold pieces and the silver dollars. They hadn't meant to suffocate her, they said. They just wanted to keep her quiet while they searched her house for the fortune she was supposed to have. But the gag they used was a rag she had in her hand, saturated with metal polish, and they stuffed it too far down her throat.

The first time I saw Aunt Jennie I was already in college. I'd heard of her as part of the family lore, always spoken of with respect, except by Dr. Allan, Aunt Rose's husband. He pooh-poohed her "miracles" as the results of suggestion therapy, quoting Freud's statement: "There are more cures effected at Lourdes than by psychoanalysis." The family paid no attention to him. They told of Mollie Frohlich, a violent maniac until Aunt Jennie took her in hand, and of Lawyer Greenbaum's son who didn't grow until he followed Aunt Jennie's advice, and of Sarah Miller, given up by doctors but brought back to health by Aunt Jennie. I also heard whisperings about other treatments Aunt Jennie gave, treatments adjudged unfit for children to hear about.

My great-grandmother attributed her own good health to Aunt Jennie's tonic, a thick brown-black foul-smelling liquid. Every Friday night, after she lit the candles, great-grandma would take a tablespoonful of her tonic, shudder, and quickly chew on celery to get the taste out of her mouth. Then she'd lament, "Ai, if my husband (let him rest in peace!) wouldn't have been so stubborn he would be here today! But he was an Apikouros." Epicurean is the generic Yiddish word for an atheist, an unbeliever. In this case, an unbeliever in Aunt Jennie's tonic. Great-grandma's four sons, my great-uncles and my grandfather also took the tonic. My grandmother never had; she died in childbirth. My father, an Apikouros too, refused it; he said he preferred gray hairs to a sick stomach.

The tonic came in a one-ounce bottle, enough for a

month. When the bottle was empty, Aunt Jennie would refill it at a cost of a bottle of cherry brandy, one of almond extract, and a five-dollar gold piece. Five-dollar gold pieces became worth much more than their face value, but Aunt Jennie refused other payment. The family grumbled but paid up when my grandfather or his brothers asked rhetorically, "Will it be cheaper for you if I were like old man Abramowitz in the Daughters of Israel Home or like Hochberg laying in bed, filthy like an animal and blind? Or like poor Mrs. Weinstein, wandering around the streets the police always have to bring her home and you'll have to tip them?"

One day there was nobody to go for great-grandma's tonic but me. A big blue Cadillac was parked outside Aunt Jennie's house. I knocked at the door, was told to enter, and saw as astonishing scene. Aunt Jennie was holding a brown paper bag, and a middle-aged well-dressed man was interpreting her instructions to the mayor and his wife. (I recognized them from newspaper pictures.) "Everything will continue to be good," Aunt Jennie was saying. "Don't forget—no salt in his food and no food made with salt. Let him take every night one teaspoon of the powder mixed with pure spring water." Mrs. Callaghan dropped to her knees and kissed Aunt Jennie's hand. "May the Holy Mother and all the saints in Heaven watch over you!" Mayor Callaghan, tears streaming down his face, handed Aunt Jennie a little cloth bag. "I can't thank you enough. You've saved us all." Aunt Jennie hefted the bag. "It's all there," he went on, "and all in gold, and if you want twice as much, just let me know. I'll clean out every coin store in town for you. And if anybody ever bothers you about anything, just let me know." The interpreter looked at me, shrugged, and then translated only the mayor's remarks.

The Callaghans left. I grabbed the interpreter's arm. "What's this all about?" I asked.

"They have a son, he was *meshuga*, and she cured him," he answered.

I introduced myself to Aunt Jennie. She grimaced in what she supposed was a smile. "So you're Tsilli's great-grandson? And for what are you studying?" (Studying was taken for granted in one of my age.)

"To be a chemist." I explained to her what a chemist did.

She kept nodding but I didn't think she was listening.

When I finished, she said, "You speak a beautiful Yiddish. So many young people come here they don't know a word."

I told her my Yiddish was the result of six years at a Sholom Aleichem school. I didn't tell her I was forced to go there by my father, a rabid secularist who equated Hebrew with the synagogue.

She patted my hand. "It's good to learn the mother tongue. Sit down a while and talk to me. People come but they run right away. All they want is my medicines."

I sat down. While she carefully filled the little bottle I asked. "What was the mayor so happy about?"

Aunt Jennie screwed the cap on the bottle. "He has a son, went crazy like a dybbuk was in him. With my powders he's now better." She looked at me shrewdly. "My child, I'm a bit of a chemist, too. I make special medicines. Only a few, but good. I learned from a wise man in Nagy Arok the time I ran away from home." She rambled on with a very romantic tale of a betrothal when she was fourteen to a man she didn't like. It was interesting at first, but the unnecessary details with which she embroidered her story became boring after a while. I got up and excused myself, saying I had to go on other errands for my great-grandmother.

"Go, then," she said. "You're a good boy to do what your elders want. Come again next month."

I didn't see her for several months. That time I met in her kitchen a weeping girl with her embittered mother. The mother was arguing with Aunt Jennie. "Ten silver dollars! There's no bank open now. Where will I get silver dollars? Here's a twenty-dollar bill. Take it and give me the pill."

Aunt Jennie shook her head. "Not for fifty pieces of paper like that." The woman flounced out, dragging the girl with her.

I was curious. "Why didn't you take the twenty dollars?" I asked.

"Because I need the silver. And the gold. You're a chemist. You should know. Can you you use paper when you need metal?" We chatted. She asked about great-grandma and her friend, Mr. Gottfried, and complained that nobody came to visit with her any more. "With automobiles they're afraid. With horses and wagons they didn't worry about the bad street." Indeed, Avenue K was in poor shape. Rubble from the buildings demolished to make way for the new skyway lay all around, and trucks from the nearby slaughterhouses had rutted the streets. Everyone but Aunt Jennie had already left the neighborhood.

She took a liking to me. She made coffee and gave me sweet hard cinnamon cookies. She told about her life with the wise man of Nagy Arok. "What he had in his little finger a dozen professors don't have in their heads." I was polite, not letting Aunt Jennie know what I thought she was—a herb doctor convinced of the efficacy of her concoctions and mysterious enough to convince others.

I didn't see her for a long time. I got my degree, my Master's, and then my Ph.D. I got married. I had a son. Aunt Jennie, Great-uncle Bernard said, often inquired about me and was pleased with my progress.

Shortly after I began work as a junior pharmacologist at Reinhard and Kessel, my Cousin Estelle attempted suicide. This was her fourth try; and when she got out of her depression, she promptly entered the manic stage of her psychosis. The doctors advised commitment to an institution. Great-grandma intervened. "You've spent a fortune already and no results. Why don't you try Aunt Jennie?" Aunt Bessie hopelessly agreed.

Estelle's cure was the talk of the family circle. "She was better in one week," Aunt Bessie said. "In one week! And just from a no-salt diet and a plain white powder! We get spring water delivered for Estelle from the health-foods store."

I paid little attention to the talk. I'm not a physician, not a psychiatrist, but I knew that patients with manic-depressive psychosis could have long periods of normal behavior between their swings of mood. But less than a year later came the word that lithium salts were very effective in the treatment of mania. I recalled the Callaghan episode. I begged a little of the powder from Aunt Bessie and analyzed it. It was an impure lithium salicylate.

I was a scientist, and an ambitious man. Not stupid, either. Paracelsus had said that the best materia medica came from herbalists, wise women, and shepherds. I knew of the drugs that had entered therapeutics through folk medicine: the Peruvian bark for malaria, ephedrine from the Chinese *Ma Huang* for asthma, the tranquilizer reserpine from the Indian snakeroot, and many others. I knew that witch doctors and herb healers would not have achieved their eminence in primitive societies had their remedies been totally worthless.

Here was an opportunity to advance science—and myself. Aunt Jennie knew that lithium salts were effective in mania. How did she get her powder? What else did she know?

I wasn't dishonest with her. She was too clever not to see through any dissembling I could try. I told her straight-forwardly, "Aunt Jennie, may you live and be well, but accidents happen to all of us, like with my neighbor who was run over by a car. Who is going to carry on after you're gone? Who is going to help these poor people who come to you? I want to become your pupil. You teach me what you know so that your wisdom won't be lost with you."

Aunt Jennie was flattered. "You want an old woman like me to teach you? And you went to a university?"

"Some things we don't learn in school. Some things we learn from people like you." And I told her of how quinine was developed from cinchona and of how right now doctors at the National Cancer Institute were investigating a plant from Guatemala that the natives there used to cure cancer.

Aunt Jennie shook her head in amazement. "Is that so? Big doctors in Washington listen to people like me? A blessing on Columbus!" She got excited. "I can tell you how to make a pill that only one will bring on a woman's time, and a powder for weak blood, and another for lunatics, and a medicine to make boys into men, and one to make barren women bear, and another to straighten crooked bones and another to stop hair from getting gray, and another for a bad cough, and another for swelling of the feet, and salves for all kinds of sores, and—"

I held up my hand. "One at a time, Aunt Jennie, one at a time, Aunt Jennie, one at a time! Let's start with the powder for lunatics." I figured that would be a touch-stone. If she'd made the lithium salicylate by chance, then her folk knowledge would be worthless to me, but if she knew what she was doing, well. . . .

"Come." She unlocked the door to the third room. Shelves filled with jars were on the far wall. On the right was a large table on which lay cigar boxes and piles of drying herbs, flowers, and grasses. On the left was a heap of what appeared to be a crystalline gravel. The odor in the room was a mixture of aromatics, decay, must, and dust. Near the door were several large earthenware crocks. Aunt Jennie lifted the lid off one of them. I smelled vinegar. "That's where I age my gold and silver."

Woe is me! I thought to myself. I'm wasting my time. Gold doesn't age or combine with acetic acid, and silver acetate can't be prepared by pickling.

Aunt Jennie picked up a handful of the glittering coarse stones. "Now I'll show you how I make the powder." In the kitchen she had me pound the stones with a brass pestle in a mortar, the kind we have as a showpiece at home. She went back into the little room and returned with two bottles clearly labeled, one OIL OF WINTERGREEN and the other OIL OF VITRIOL. I kept a straight face. My herb doctor was an amateur chemist!

She poured the now fine powder into a glass pie plate and added the sulfuric acid slowly, stirring it into the powder with a glass rod. She shook up her stove and carefully lowered the plate onto the red-hot coals. "Now I say the words." She muttered some garbled Hebrew for a few minutes. She lifted out the pie plate with two pairs of tongs and set it at the back of the stove. She covered her eyes and repeated the incantation. She had a gallon jug of spring water under the sink. From it she poured a glassful and slowly, very slowly, dropped the water on the plate. The drops sizzled and danced, but soon the plate was cool enough for her to bring back to the table. From a cupboard drawer she took a linen handkerchief, fitted it into another glass, and poured the cloudy liquid from the plate into it. "Linen it must be, not cotton," she warned me. "I forgot to tell you the prayer was the one for bedtime." The crude filtration over, there was left not quite an ounce of an almost clear liquid in the glass. She added a few drops of the oil of wintergreen and a teaspoonful of milk and then set the glass far back on the coolest part of the stove. "Now it sits a day, a night, and a day before all the water goes away and the powder is left. I'll save this for you when you come again." I asked her if I could have some of the stones. "Why not? You can practice making the powder."

I had the stones analyzed and got a surprise. They were specimens of amblygonite, a compound phosphate rock bearing iron, aluminum, and lithium. I looked up the literature on the preparation of lithium salts, and sure enough!—Aunt Jennie had followed a standard procedure. But there was no amblygonite, according to the geologists, in this part of the country.

You have no idea how long it took me to get the details from Aunt Jennie with all her irrelevant remarks and side comments. The amblygonite was brought to her by Anton Kiss, "a Gentile, but a fine man," from a quarry pit near the Passaic River. (The geologists didn't know everything, it seems.) Kiss brought a load whenever he came for his tonic. I saw him once, a strapping Magyar with a black handle-bar mustache, hale and hearty at seventy-nine. The oil of vitriol and the oil of wintergreen were supplied by Levine the druggist, still active in his store at eighty-one and a patron of Aunt Jennie's.

Of course, the incantations were meaningless in the preparation of lithium salicylate. Aunt Jennie thought they were necessary, and I didn't dare suggest they weren't. She was not rigid, however, about her apparatus. She used Pyrex and Corning ware, I discovered, as a modern advance over her old utensils.

Lithium for mania was interesting but of no moment to me. What was the use of rediscovering America? Now what I wanted to know was what was in Aunt Jennie's other medications. What did she have that, sans mysticism, would benefit mankind—and me?

Disappointment after disappointment. The medicine for straightening crooked bones was nonsense, merely a calcium mixture. She had three salves for skin ulcers: one was common zinc oxide in a rendered chicken-fat base; one was bread mold, the penicillin being suspended in clarified butter; one was made up of a watery suspension of gold shaved from the milled coins, a poor substitute for the gold-leaf treatment reported in the medical literature. The potion for dropsy was pounded foxglove mixed with cherry brandy, a novel and uneconomical way to prepare tincture of digitalis.

I've omitted all Aunt Jennie's mumbo jumbo: one salve had to be made only on a dark night, another at dawn, and the digitalis had to take ten days, each day stirred with a silver spoon, *mazel tov* being said ten times. I pretended to copy down the charms. Aunt Jennie looked at my notebook and marveled. "And even in English you can write the sacred tongue? Such wonders in America!"

I had to go slowly. I was dependent on Aunt Jennie's whims. I could neither cut short her reminiscences nor ask her for specific medications. Anne, my wife, complained that I was away from home too much. I missed playing with my boy. But I was willing to make sacrifices. I was certain that sooner or later amidst all the magical charms I'd find something spectacular.

One evening when I came, Aunt Jennie handed me a chopping knife and a wooden bowl. "Here. Chop. Chop even finer than for gefilte fish." She had ready a pile of salted meat. "Lazar the butcher brought me a fresh supply. I'll trim the meat and you'll chop it. We're going to make some new medicines."

I discovered why she lived so near to the slaughter-houses. Aunt Jennie made endocrine preparations: estrogens from minced ovaries soaked in almond extract; androgens from testes marinated in a mixture of roasted cattails (the plant type, not the animal), oil, garlic, and vinegar; desiccated thyroid from calves' thyroids blended with cinnamon and chopped cabbage leaves and dried in the oven. Her famed remedy for anemia was, as I'd expected, liver extract. Beef liver ("from pigs is better but pigs are not kosher") finely ground with kidneys and spleen, saturated with cherry brandy, evaporated in the sun, and then pounded in the mortar and pestle to a coarse powder. What good was all that to me?

One more try, I resolved, and then I'd give up the whole silly project. I got Aunt Jennie to give me the recipe for her abortifacient. That was very complicated. "Only from bulls can this be made and you need to have an expert butcher, not a plain slaughterer. He must cut out for you the bladder, the testicles, and all the parts around. Before, you had to make the pill the same day you got the parts but now, with freezers, you can keep them until you've got time. Grind everything in a meat grinder. Stir in a few drops of cherry brandy at a time and recite these three psalms." —and King David would turn over in his grave if he heard what Aunt Jennie called psalms— "and then throw in the pot a silver dollar. Wait until night, then take out the silver and rub it on this hand grindstone until the stone turns gray from the silver. Then put the grindstone in the pot and let it stand off the stove until it's cool. . . ." A few more complicated, weird steps and "what's left looks like glue, only black, and you mix it with dough to make a pill."

I had a sinking suspicion that I knew what Aunt Jennie made "to bring a woman around." I took one of the pills for analysis. I was right. Prostaglandin B, now in commercial production by a more rational method.

There was no question but that Aunt Jennie's remedies were effective. There were equally no question but that they were already well known and already preparable without voodoo and in less time. Aunt Jennie was a cookbook pharmacologist using materials without knowledge of the rationale for their use. The silver was bactericidal, for example, and the cherry brandy a mode of alcohol extraction, but all the mumbling and chanting was nonsense, totally unscientific. Modern chemistry had anticipated the crude formulas she had given me.

I went to see her for what I thought was the last time, bringing her a bottle of sweet wine as a gift. She insisted on having a glass with me and became garrulous. "The next thing we'll make is the medicine for gray hair, the one Tsilli, your great-grandma takes. I take it myself and see—my hair is as brown as the day I landed in America."

Fool that I was! I suddenly realized that Aunt Junnie's tonic was what I'd been looking for all the time. Anything that would prevent gray hair would make me a fortune. Gray hair was commoner than anemia or mania or unwanted pregnancies. The cosmetic industry was enormous. And Aunt Jennie's tonic was certainly effective. All the old men and women I knew of who took the tonic had not a gray hair in their heads.

"Let's start," I said enthusiastically.

She patted my hand. "Don't be in a hurry. We have to wait until Thursday for the new moon. Meanwhile I'll give you a little bottle you can test, like you say you do where you work." She handed me the familiar one-ounce bottle. "Only don't waste it. It's too hard to make. And don't take any yourself. You don't need it."

I had no intention of taking any although I knew great-grandma swallowed it with impunity. When I got home, I had an idea. Scotty, our Airedale, was thirteen years old, sluggish, his black and tan hair totally gray, cataracts filming his eyes; I knew his end was near but sentiment kept me from bringing him to the vet's to be put to sleep. I decided to see if the tonic was effective only in humans. I held Scotty's jaws apart and gave him a tablespoonful.

That was Sunday. On Tuesday Anne said, "Look at Scotty. He's actually getting frisky again." He was. He no longer lay apathetically near the radiator but roamed about the house sniffing and growling. He looked dirty, but I saw that the color was due to the darkening of the hair near the skin. On Wednesday I thought I noted an improvement in his vision. I got excited. I had him shorn. I gave him another tablespoonful of the tonic, all I had left. I had begun the analysis of the rest in my laboratory.

I was at Aunt Jennie's just before sunset on Thursday. I helped her clean up her supper dishes and set up her apparatus. And I made very careful notes.

She had a pile of meat she had taken from the freezer earlier. The meat was well thawed out, soft and mushy. She stripped a liver and three spleens of their outer membranes, chopped them finely, added dill and saffron, and covered the mixture with cherry brandy. She took other organs, among which I recognized only sweetbreads and brains, ground them up, added seven teaspoonsful of almond extract ("no more, no less"), four or five varied spices, and put them into a separate iron pot. She rubbed a gold piece with a lump of charcoal and then on a coarse grater. Fine shavings of the soft metal fell into the wooden bowl under the grater. "Enough to cover two thumbnails," she said. "You could use more but it's a waste." She stirred the shaved gold into the first pot, added more cherry brandy, and again stirred vigorously. "First comes the prayer, *Boruch Hai Ha-Olamin;* next, the *Shomer;* next, the *Shemai. . . .*" I didn't dare interrupt her by telling that I knew no Hebrew prayers, that I was an unbeliever. "All ten you must say while you're stirring." She looked out the window. "Aha! There's the new moon. We're lucky there are no clouds. Otherwise we'd have to wait a whole day. Now the *Rosh Chodesh,* and we're ready." She mumbled the prayer to be said on seeing a new moon, and washed her hands afterwards. "Also never forget the prayer for the washing of the hands." She combined the contents of the two pots. "Stir only with a wooden spoon." Then she took a very large linen napkin and ladled the mixture into it bit by bit over another wooden bowl. She tied the four corners of the napkin together and expressed the juice. "You're stronger. You squeeze." The filtering finished with about eight ounces of a dark brown alcoholic liquid, which she put into a pottery jug with a lump of charcoal. "Done! Now we have to wait until only half the juice is left. In Hungary we used to put it in a dark cool place and cover it with a heavy sheepskin, but here in America are iceboxes; so I just cover it with a clean rag and keep it in the icebox. It takes about ten days, sometimes two weeks, and the tonic is ready. Then you put it in a small bottle with a tight top and don't let air get at it until you're ready to use it. It can stay like that for a year on a shelf in the pantry."

Lots of mumbo jumbo, you see, with a little science: charcoal for clarification, evaporation of the alcohol, avoidance of air to prevent contamination, and the use of animal organs of high cellular content. But, and a big but, the tonic was effective. I cajoled another ounce from Aunt Jennie for more extensive analysis.

I got nowhere fast. The tonic was rich in sulfur, potassium, and phosphorus. The organic chains were complex unstable amides and amines. The proteins did not correspond to those that normally would be present in the organs Aunt Jennie used. I needed more data. I waited impatiently for the next new moon.

Meanwhile, Scotty's eyes began to clear; his hair grew back black and tan; he frolicked like a young pup. My wife and son were delighted with him. So was I. I brought him to the vet for a checkup. The vet wouldn't believe he was thirteen years old. He shrugged. "Well, Dr. Ross, I suppose if Moses could live to be a hundred and twenty, maybe your dog will live to be twenty." All he found was atrophy of the testicles, not abnormal at Scotty's age.

At the next new moon I asked Aunt Jennie for pieces of the organs she used. I painfully transliterated the prayers she chanted. She chuckled. "You know, my child, it took me too a long time to learn. I kept mixing up the prayers, putting the third before the first, and the fifth before the second, until I thought my brains would cook before I got them right. I couldn't write like you. With you it'll be easier."

It wasn't. I found that, besides the liver, brains, pancreas, and spleens I'd recognized, Aunt Jennie used adrenals and calves' thymus. Gold, naturally, was not in the final mixture; if it had any effect, it could only have been as a catalyst, which was highly unlikely. The proteins were again unclassifiable.

I worked on the tonic on my own time. I could have asked for advice and help from my superiors, but I wanted to keep the secret to myself. I dreamed of getting the Nobel Prize, once I had patented the basic ingredient and published my findings, as the man who would go down in history as the discoverer of the veritable elixir of youth.

For I knew that the tonic not only restored gray hair to its normal color. It had made Scotty young again. It kept my great-grandmother and my great-uncles and my grandfather hale and hearty at their advanced ages. It kept Lazar the butcher and Levine the druggist and Lawyer Greenbaum and Mrs. Schoenfeld and Mr. Gottfried and Zoltan Kovacs, the family handyman, from becoming senile. It was why Aunt Jennie had so many followers.

I tried everything in the books, but I could come to no definitive analysis. I started the other way around. I made alcoholic extracts of the various organs and combined them in several ways. No good. My experiments with aged dogs got nowhere. Only Aunt Jennie's tonic, prepared her own way, worked on them.

Aunt Jennie herself was no help to me. Why cherry brandy? Why not plum brandy? "Cherry brandy. That's all you can use." She let herself be persuaded once to use a fine French brandy. The resultant tonic looked and smelled different and was completely worthless. Why almond extract? "You don't need almond extract. The wise man, my teacher, squeezed from out of ground up kernels of peaches a kind of oil, but I found here in the stores you can buy the same thing, only from almonds, so why go through the forest when you can float down the river?" Why the gold, the iron pots, the wooden spoon? "You'll make me crazy yet with your questions. That's the way it was, that's the way it is, and that's the way it will be."

She was pleased, however, that I was such an earnest pupil. At great-grandma's funeral she told the family, "Lawyer Greenbaum wrote out a paper so Albert can have all my medicines when I'm gone." She was unaware that her tonic conferred longevity on its takers. She attributed her and her patrons' old age to the will of God.

I decided to systematize and rationalize Aunt Jennie's technique. I set up a laboratory in our basement and made contact with an abattoir to provide me with the necessary organs.

And then Aunt Jennie was killed. I was her heir. There was nothing she had that I wanted except her tonic. Of that she had exactly thirteen one-ounce bottles. I put them into a little house safe that I bought. They were my ace in the hole for my own use in case I couldn't duplicate the tonic.

I know that what I did then sounds callous. I used Aunt Jennie's patrons (including my own family) as experimental animals. I was driven by my ambition. I made variations and substitutions in preparing the tonic, trying to simplify the procedure and get at the basic substance.

New moons were ridiculous, a superstitious touch; the tonic should be preparable at any time. The prayers (taught me by a pious friend) were also unnecessary; they were purely a timing mechanism to denote the completion of the extractive process. My first batch of tonic made without the hocus-pocus was effective in dogs and humans.

I began to omit one ingredient at a time. The gold went first. The tonic seemed to be the same, but wasn't. It took me a month before I realized that my grandfather's death from pneumonia following a broken hip was not adventitious. Scotty's eyes began to film over and his hair turned gray. I tried substituting various gold salts. No go. My great-uncle Bernard failed rapidly. "Listen, what can you expect?" said my cousins. "He's seventy-five." Mrs. Schoenfeld died. So did Lawyer Greenbaum. I tried colloidal gold. Success! But now Scotty was dead, too.

Now I omitted first the dill and then the saffron. The absence of dill made no difference, but the tonic made without saffron had no value. The proportions of the four or five spices in the second pot could not be varied and all had to be used. I discovered that calves' thymus was essential; the source of the other organs (swine, beef, lamb) was unimportant. Zoltan Kovacs died of debility; I read Anton Kiss's obituary. I omitted first the liver, then the brains, and so on down the list. Brains, adrenals, thymus, and spleen were all I needed. Mr. Gottfried died of old age, and so did one by one my great-uncles. My experiments, you see, had to be confirmed by biological testing, and evidently the effects of the tonic wore off in a week.

At last I was ready to return to the analytic phase of my investigation. There were many tantalizing clues in the fabulous tonic. The inhibition of aging was probably not its only function. Take the spleen, for instance. The spleen was involved in immunological processes; maybe the tonic would solve the problem of tissue rejection in transplants. And saffron came from a crocus related to the variety which yields colchicine, a compound with strong chromosomal effects. And the adrenals were significant endocrine glands.

I'd had a series of colds. I decided to try the effect of

the tonic to build up my resistance. I took a tablespoon-ful.

The next day I was full of pep. My mind seemed to be working at top speed. I developed a new procedure for the synthesis of thiouracil and ran the preliminary tests. A couple of days later I was able to show my boss, Dr. Heinrichs, the result. He was enthusiastic. He shook my hand. He said I was brilliant. He assigned me to his stalled steroid project.

To make sure I'd live up to his expectations, that night I took another tablespoonful of the tonic. I slept like a baby, woke up singing, and realized that the tonic was a better stimulant than any of the amphetamines.

In twenty-four hours I solved Dr. Heinrichs' problem. He took me to see Dr. Kessel, the president, and de-manded that I get a new contract with a substantial raise lest I be lured away by another company.

From then on I took no chances. Every week I took a dose of Aunt Jennie's tonic. I put away my notebooks for my own experiments. I could make the tonic anytime now, and I had lots of time before me. I calculated that if my present acuity and originality of invention continued at the same rate, in a couple of years I'd be able to set my own terms as a pharmacologist and have my own laboratory with a staff of Ph.D.s to help in the analysis of the tonic.

I was amazed at my own successes. I had brilliant in-tuitions and pragmatic ability. Every project was a chal-lenging game. I got a bonus at the end of three months and another six months later.

The first intimation I had of trouble was with my sex life. My libido was definitely lessened. I attributed that to my working so hard and to fatigue. I was peppy all day long, but by eight o'clock I was ready for sleep. Then suddenly I became impotent. That upset me. I went to a urologist. He found nothing wrong with me and said the impotence was psychogenic.

I didn't believe him. I suspected the tonic was the cause. I didn't take it for a month. No change, except that I lost the sparkle and initiative and flashes of genius that had made my work so outstanding. As soon as I started the tonic again, my work improved.

Not my home life. To the silent reproach caused by my impotence was now added open marital discord. Anne and I quarreled constantly. She accused me of extravagance, of flaring up over trivialities, of lack of interest in my son. She was right, not that I cared to correct myself. I was having too much fun. I was taking an active interest in sports as a participant, not as a spectator. I spent hours in the gym, on the tennis courts, and joined a Celtic soccer team across the river.

I lost my job because of my sports activities. Dr. Heinrichs cautioned me one day: "Albert, you're the head of a section now, but Dr. Kessel is very dissatisfied with the work going on there now. Not enough supervision, too much camaraderie, too many practical jokes that could turn out to be dangerous. And you've been taking too much time off." I gave him the Bronx cheer and resigned.

When I told Anne what I'd done, she burst into tears. "You ought to see a psychiatrist, Albert. You're not the same man I married."

She was wrong. I was the same. She wasn't. She had grown older. I hadn't, thanks to Aunt Jennie's tonic.

She left me two weeks later, saying she couldn't stand my irresponsibility and my childish rages. I wasn't affected by her departure. The way I saw it was—marriage was a convenient way of having sex, and sex was no longer a concern of mine. I had no doubt that if I stopped the tonic long enough my sex urge would return, but between incredible longevity and brief ecstasies, who wouldn't choose long life?

About that time I noted that my scrotal sac was shrinking, my testicles were smaller, and my axillary hair was thinning out. I went back to shaving only twice a week. But my belly became flat and hard, and my muscles developed tremendously.

I became a boxer. Amateur, of course. But willing to pick a fight with a casual stranger and knock him out with a quick blow to the jaw, like in the movies. I became known to the police as a brawler.

I skipped support for my wife and son for a few months. Her brother, an attorney, hailed me into court and wanted me declared incompetent so that Anne could be appointed my guardian and have full charge of whatever funds I had. The court-appointed psychiatrists said I was not crazy, merely immature.

My money was running low. I made up a batch of the tonic and put an ad in a man's magazine: GRAY HAIR RESTORED TO NORMAL WITHOUT DYE. The response was fantastic. I sold two quarts (all I had) at ten dollars an ounce, and then made several gallons.

That one ad was enough. I had a steady clientele and they told their friends. I raised the price to twenty dollars and then to twenty-five and didn't lose a customer. I had grandiose ideas of taking over a factory to produce the tonic, of a big advertising campaign, and of being on Easy Street in no time without sweat.

I ran afoul of the Food and Drug Administration. Their chemists reported that the tonic was made up of organic extracts that could not possibly have an effect on gray hair. I was ordered to cease its distribution. I took a trip to Washington, showed my credentials as a pharmacologist, carried on and shouted at those stupid bureaucrats, demanded that they experiment with the tonic on aged animals, and made such a scene that I ended up in a hospital under observation with a diagnosis of possible paranoid psychosis.

I probably would have been released in two weeks had I not been so frightened at the prospect of being without the tonic. I raged and fought with the doctors and was formally committed to an insane asylum. Anne came down and had me transferred to an institution in New Jersey.

She refused to sign for my temporary release. "Get some treatment first, Albert. I'm going to wait until all those people who keep sending money for the hair tonic get discouraged. I'm kept busy returning the checks and cash."

The doctors made me furious. "A classic well-constructed paranoid delusion," they said. "Belief in the possession of an elixir of life is not uncommon."

All my pleadings were in vain. The doctors, smug as only doctors can be, paid no attention when I said that I was not a crackpot, that I really had a formula that prolonged life. I lost control of myself. I hit out at the attendants and refused to take the sedatives prescribed for me. The doctors had an answer for that—electroshock therapy.

After a dozen shocks I had enough sense left to recognize that I was being an idiot. The shock treatments not only left me sore physically but they also induced amnesia. I resigned myself to being a good calm patient. I stopped talking about the tonic. I made a silent resolve to reform. As soon as I got out, I'd go back to my original plan of analyzing the tonic and publishing my findings. I now understood why Aunt Jennie had said that the tonic was

not for me but only for older men and women. Its longevity effect came presumably after sex hormone production was at a low level. Before that time it was a stimulant, actually a true rejuvenator, but juvenility was a
menace, not a help, to normal adults. It had been so to
me, at least, judging from the way I'd been acting.

Most of the amnesia disappeared fairly rapidly, but
there were a number of things I couldn't recall. I didn't
worry too much about that. Chemical formulas, names of
drugs, salting-out procedures—I could find them in textbooks any time. I had also forgotten some parts of Aunt
Jennie's recipe for the tonic, but fortunately the rational-
ized version was safely in my notebooks in the desk in the
laboratory at home.

Anne came to see me regularly. She was pleased at my
so-called improvement. "I took the liberty of speaking to
Dr. Heinrichs," she said, "And he assured me your old job
is open for you." I nodded and said nothing about the
tonic.

The day I was discharged she came for me. "I have a
surprise for you. I didn't know how long you'd be in that
place; so I sold the house and took an apartment. It's
very nice. You'll like it."

A chill went through me. "What did you do with the
laboratory setup?" I asked.

"I put everything in storage," she replied. "All the apparatus, I mean. I threw out a lot of junk you had there,
though."

Correct. Along with the old insurance policies and in-
voices for chemicals, she'd thrown out my notebooks.

I'm working again as a junior pharmacologist. About
once a month I make up a batch of Aunt Jennie's tonic,
but it's no good. It has no effect on aged dogs. There's
something I just can't recall. Those four or five, maybe
six, spices she added to the second pot. So far I've tried
dozens of spices and herbs. No luck.

But I'm not discouraged I have hope. Just last week I
read about cyanins being used to stimulate the growth of
tissue cultures in vitro. And cyanins are present in almonds. Any day now I'm sure to remember those spices.

TIMESTORM

EDDY C. BERTIN

This story, written in the author's native Flemish, won the Belgian "Sfan Award" as the best original story in the Lowlands language sector. Bertin, who is one of the most imaginatively promising young writers of the Continent, has appeared with original fantasy tales in English, too, and this is his own translation of his prize-winner: a story of the Utopian revision of world history.

Harvey Lonestall awoke with the weird feeling that he had just come into existence. His head felt strangely empty and unadjusted as if someone had recently put something inside which had only now first started thinking. It was a very unpleasant feeling.

"I suppose this is the way first sounds must feel from a newly recorded disc," he thought. When he sat up in bed, however, the feeling passed and reality took over. Harvey rubbed his eyes and glared at the hexagonal window in a corner of the room. A weak ray of sunlight came in through the shadowed glassplate. Well, the sun promised another enjoyably warm day. It would seem that the Weather Department had at last decided upon a nice day! With difficulty he extended his right arm and silenced the tiny clock, which kept on repeating in a soft, sweet, and immensely irritating female voice: "Ten o'clock. Time to get up. Ten o'clock. Time to get up . . ."

He managed to switch the voice off just before the first morning commercial. It seemed a good hour for getting up on a Friday, the first day of the weekend. Four days of blessed rest, away from the "push-and-check-and-push" factory, as they called it. Of course, on Tuesday he'd have to restart working, but he didn't feel like thinking of that right now. He threw his legs off the antigravbed. The vibrator was activated immediately, the floor was comfortably warm and vibrated softly under his wrinkling toes. He stood up.

The sun disappeared. It didn't go out softly, as the lamps in his room used to, but it suddenly and completely blinked out of existence. With the sun, his room, the antigravbed, and the whole world disappeared.

The timestorm began in another galaxy, too far away from our Sol even to be seen with the strongest telescopes. It had been created by a collision of two driftsuns. At the instant of collision, while one of the suns was already going nova and exploding, during a millionth of a second, a crack came into existence in the familiar fabric of space and time. The antispace/antitime fragment existed only for an immeasurable instant, but this was enough. A cyclone of partly disintegrated matter and imploding energy, at war with all the fundamental laws of nature, threw its greedy tentacles out across past and future.

When he regained consciousness, he was lying face down on the floor and colored rainbow specks were dancing insane patterns on the irises of his eyes. Carefully he stood up and shook his head. He felt weak and dizzy. What exactly had happened? He remembered getting out of bed, and then . . . nothing! How had he become unconscious? Why? He immediately decided to see a psychmed this very morning! He'd take the instaphone and then . . .

Where was that damned thing?

Where was he? He looked around him, seeing nothing in the impenetrable cloak of darkness. A sudden spell of dizziness took him by surprise and he almost lost his balance. He felt as if he were hanging on a slender thread at the edge of a deep ravine, and an animal instinct of crushing panic kept him from moving. He had an unclear, vague memory of falling into a dark pit, just wide enough for him to pass through, but which seemed to go on and on through eternity. His fingers searched his body, but found no marks or bruises. Only his arms hurt a bit, but there was nothing broken or even severely painful. Maybe he had slipped while getting out of the antigravbed and bumped his head on the floor? But the floor was made of pseudofoam plastic—besides, the mecstabilizers should have broken his fall in any case. So where was he now?

Everything in the immediate—but what is immediate in time and space—neighborhood of the timestorm was absorbed in the rotating cyclone of antiparticles. The rip in time didn't exactly expand itself, rather it moved in jumps through the matter-time continuum. Space and distance had no real meaning for a phenomenon which in itself was a curse against the laws of the universe through which it moved. The timestorm flashed through hyperspace, only here and there finding momentary contact with the dimensional universe. The results of those impact points were two novas in Orion, and changes in the orbits of several small satellites in Messier-31, before two shards of the timestorm touched Earth.

Harvey pushed the NA-button on his wrist watch and a soft green light came into being. The cellar! He was in his own damned cellar! How had he gotten here? Besides, how was it possible that everything was still in darkness? He remembered getting up at ten o'clock, so, by this time, everything down here should have been brightly lit and the little workrobs should be busy everywhere. Where were those cursed lazy things? But, he felt, this way of reasoning was insane—a robot couldn't be lazy—it was only a machine, a perfected, expensive, and very accurate machine. He looked down at his watch and a new surprise came. Half past four? Impossible! The thing must have been damaged by his fall. Then he saw the date: April 9, half past four. But today was April 10th!

Something was very, very wrong. Was he really awake at all? He felt the pain in his arms and the vertigo in his head, but impressions such as those have been experienced in dreams also. What if he had only dreamed that he had awakened on April 10th? Then, in reality, he should still be lying on his antigravbed in his sleeping room and soon now the alarm would sweetly start calling, "Ten o'clock. Time to get up. Ten o'clock . . ." followed by the today's sponsor's message.

Soon now . . .
What was the thing waiting for?

The interchange working between parts of the four-
dimensional universe and the antistructure of the timestorm loosened small fragments of the timecyclone, which
were soon absorbed in far star clusters. Two of those
timeshards touched Earth during a fraction of a second
on April 10, 2113, before their next jump carried them
into the burning heart of a far sun in Andromeda. Harvey
Lonestall's house was the meeting point on Earth with the
antistructural phenomenon, but Harvey himself never knew
that he had been part of the timestorm.

Harvey took a few uncertain steps forward and fell.
And kept on falling. He wanted to shriek, but he didn't
seem to have any body left; if he had it did not react to
the panic instructions of his brain. It was as if someone
had taken off the top of his skull and exposed his naked
brains to the coolness and glare of outer space. He
seemed to be gliding along a silver thread which lost itself
somewhere in a colossal sparkling web of pulsating energy
patterns. Frightening images of strange forms and colors
appeared and passed away beside him at lightning speed
as his mind and body were partly disintegrated into atoms
and reassembled again until the mad terror became too
much and cloaked everything in blessed darkness. Unconscious, Harvey Lonestall fell through the timestorm.

The first thing he noticed when awakening for the
second time was that his wrist watch stood still. The hands
were frozen at half past four, and, though nothing seemed
to be broken, they did not move. He fixed his eyes on the
hands but they remained motionless. At least he again felt
hard substance under his body and fingertips, but the terrifying feeling of falling into nothingness was still burning
his mind. When the rotating, dizzy feeling finally went
away, he looked up. Immediately he closed his eyes and
slowly began counting from one to one hundred. Then he
dared open his eyes again.
Nothing had changed from what he had seen the first
time. The circular room on whose floor he was lying was
still there, and so were the incredible machines whose bulk
filled the walls and occupied most of the ceiling. This
wasn't a dream any more; he didn't possess the necessary

imagination to dream up something like this. The metal floor was cold and the coldness penetrated through his airy clothes to his body. He stood up. The nausea and vertigo had gone away, but he felt strangely deprived of weight, as if gravity was not as strong here as it should be. He passed his fingertips over the floor—cold metal and no vibrators to warm it up. Then he looked around at the machines that occupied the room. All kinds of switches, handles, levers and buttons, dials and control lights, but nothing in any way familiar. One would at least expect some kind of action in a room full of alien machinery, but here nothing moved. Not a single light winked, no needle moved across a dial. He heard an unspecific droning, but it seemed to come from nowhere in particular and formed an almost unnoticeable background noise.

Harvey looked up. There was a circular opening in the ceiling from which a metal ladder ran down to the floor. He shook it and it appeared strong enough to hold his weight. Holding on with both hands, he mounted unsteadily. The room above was exactly identical with the one he had just left, a circular room, another ladder and another opening in the ceiling. Again walls and ceiling were filled with frozen machines. The same monotonous noise was everywhere, and so was the light whose source almost seemed to come from the walls and machines themselves. But something was different—between two bulky machines, Harvey spotted something which could only be a small window. Eagerly he approached the round glass-covered opening and looked outside.

A psychic shock of vertigo threw him backward. His entrails did their best to get out through his throat, and his breath moved as a mad steamhammer through his brain. Because outside the window was . . . *nothing*. A bottomless infinite emptiness, no view, no stars, just . . . *nothing*. Even the expanse could not be guessed because there were no orientation points; it was a depth in more than three dimensions, an experience which clawed at his stomach and filled his brain with its total emptiness. He closed his eyes and reclined against one of the cold machines, waiting for the beating of his heart to slow down. Then he mounted the ladder to the next room, cautiously avoiding another look through the window at the void which lurked beyond.

That next room was empty, except for a strange structure in the center of the floor and a closed side-door. This seemed to be a kind of terminal in the climb for there was no ceiling ladder. It was apparently the highest point of the strange "building" or "tower" in the middle of some-where-nowhere where he had been brought by God knew what uncanny means.

He took a good look at the strange thing in the middle of the room. It appeared to be some kind of control apparatus, composed of two tables covered with switches and dials placed on both sides of a type of chair. From this seat, one could easily reach the two control panels. Between these two and eyes' height above the chair, another weird mechanism reached down from the ceiling, as might the arm of a dentist's drill. Two metal tentacles, each ending in one finger and interconnected by a confusing web of threads and contacts, held a cylinder of glass-like substance between them, suspended above the seat. The thing was no more than twenty centimeters long with a diameter of about five centimeters. Beside one of the switch-tables three similar objects were lying.

Harvey took one of them in his hands; it seemed almost weightless. It was not made of glass as he had supposed but of some sort of transparent material which gave off a metallic sound when he ticked against it with his finger-nails. Was it possible for a metal to be so strong that it could be made into layers thin enough to be transparent? No, in his world this was not possible, but neither was anything at all he had seen in this place.

The ends of the cylinder showed irregular indentations, probably through which they were connected and fastened to the two tentacle-arms of the apparatus. Inside the cylinder there was something resembling a golden thread. He peered closer and saw a seemingly endless series of extremely thin golden spirals, turning around themselves, parallel to each other. He tried to follow their lines but they always came back to the same place, forming a helix. The spirals ran to the end of the cylinder and turned back inside themselves to restart their ways. A Moebius strip, a voyage without beginning or end, a snake eating itself by its tail.

He couldn't resist sitting down in the chair, which was soft and adapted slightly to his body. There was a big switch right beside his hand. The glass-metal cylinder now hung exactly before his eyes. Logically seen, he was taking an uncalculated risk bordering on the reckless, but unbelievable things tend to heap upon each other until they go past the limits of endurance and reach their breaking point. Harvey pulled the switch.

Slowly and gradually the light disappeared from the room, as if all the walls softly were extinguished. The background noise became stronger in volume and a weird, shrill squeaking sound issued from the machine. A few control lights came on and a needle began running over a strip of plastic, making irregular dots on it. Immediately Harvey put the switch back into its original position. The sound stopped and the light came back into the walls. Well, he thought, there doesn't seem to be an immediate danger to this. With the courage of despair, he again switched on the machine.

As in a dream the lights disappeared, slowly slipping away from the room, and were replaced by a strange blurred sort of glimmer coming from the cylinder. The phantom light spread around him and created a milklike cloud of fog which seemed prisoner of a steady throbbing movement. Slowly but regularly the cylinder began turning on its axis, and out of it came a helix of uncountable small spirals, weaving themselves around the apparatus, forming a bizarre asymmetric figure of which he himself was the center. Strange colors and shapes followed immediately by sounds and smells began to infiltrate upon his consciousness; they dispelled with the room and the seat and also with Harvey's own thinking personality. He felt himself flowing away absorbed by the dreamlike helix.

Strong daylight swept inside through the small window, behind which he was kneeling. The room in which he found himself seemed to be some sort of storeroom or attic. He was looking outside, or rather the body in which Harvey Lonestall found himself, was looking outside.

The clamor of the enormous crowd below, which had collected along both sides of the broad street, came upwards from the street as raw clouds of sound. The heat was throbbing in the air as an enormous heart beat, and he smelled the sweat, which was irritatingly itching below his armpits. The first cars appeared in the distance, and cheers went up from the crowd below. Harvey tried to analyze this new situation. He was an intruder in someone else's body, but the stranger was oblivious to his presence. Harvey ordered the left hand to open and close, and the hand carried out his order. So he even had control over this body, but again without being noticed. Probably

the owner of the body thought—if he noticed it at all—
that he himself had decided to open his cramped fingers
for a second, and then close them again. But where was
he now?

Looking around at the room, some sort of stockroom,
he noticed a number of boxes and crates. On one near
him he saw stencilled the name: Dallas Book Repository,
Dallas, Texas. Dallas? That was a city which had existed
at one time in one of the states which had been part of
the U.S.A. What was he doing here? Then Harvey noticed
the numerals.

They ran right before his eyes, straight across everything he could see of the city and the crowd, a horizontal
row of figures that seemed to be burned into the very
essence of the air, seconds, minutes, hours, days, months,
years, as an enormous chronometer. He could decipher,
". . . 10:001963 . . ." in a flash, before the uproar of the
crowd drew his attention to what was happening below.
The body that housed Harvey's mind stood up from its
crouching position and took something from the floor beside it. The body, with Harvey as a stupefied spectator,
put the rifle in position against its shoulder, and through
the telescopic sight of the gun the face of a man appeared, a face Harvey recognized from the old history
films. The man was smiling broadly and waving to the
crowd, just before the shots were fired. The butt end of
the rifle shook against Harvey's shoulder. The man in the
car was thrown by the bullet; his bleeding head fell in the
lap of his shocked wife. The assassination of John Fitz-
gerald Kennedy had occurred.

A white shroud crawled lazily across the street; it made
the attic room disappear, thickened until it was an impenetrable grayish cloud of foggy fingers. Out of the fog,
small golden spirals came toward Harvey, turning and
turning around him, until they also were gone.

Harvey Lonestall was sitting in the chair; the helix had
stopped. In an automatic reflex, his hands pulled the
switch back.

He watched the helix closely and now noticed the long
series of incredibly small code ciphers on it. Coordinates
in time and space? What exactly had happened? Was this
a perfected kind of library? But everything had seemed
to be perfectly real, the heat, the smells, the sounds,
even the rebound of the rifle. A kind of time travel then,

to study past events from the person of the participants
while they were happening? Then Harvey remembered that
the body of the murderer had obeyed his simple command.
He had nonetheless remained a spectator, mystified and
astounded. But suppose he had ordered the rifleman not to
squeeze the trigger, or to turn it on someone else?

What kind of bizarre device was this? Had it all been a
matter of hallucination, a kind of dream voyage created
by the hypnotic influence of the moving golden threads?
There was only one way to find out. Carefully he took the
cylinder out of the tentacles of the machine. It loosened
immediately and fell in his hands. He put it with the
others and took another, which he placed between
the metal fingers. Then he sat down again and connected
the machine. The familiar process repeated itself, with the
white fog and the dying lights.

Then he was in the control room of a flying machine, a
very old airplane from what he could tell. In his time, it
would have been an expensive and fragile museum piece.
There were others with him, uniformed men whose faces
were hidden behind their glasses. The man at his right
side turned. "Now?" he whispered. Harvey nodded. He
looked down. They seemed to be flying above a long strip
of land, one side of which bordered the sea. Suddenly the
earth rose toward him in a whirling white cloud with a
heart of unimaginable brilliance. The displacement of air
threw the flying machine sideways and an intolerable heat
could be felt even in the control space. The brightness of
the sun below hurt his eyes through his dark glasses, and
he had to turn his face away even after the initial glare
had died down. "Farewell, Hiroshima," he whispered.
Through the flower of fire he could see the running black
numerals, ". .09:08:001945 . . ." Then the white petals of
the flower rose around the machine in a shroud of grayish
tentacles, crawling along his sides, and finally leaving him
again seated in the chair before a now unmoving cylinder.

Another scene out of a famous past . . . the first atomic
bomb on . . . what was the name his aviator had murmured? Some place which had been once at war with the
U.S.A. It had been a long time since he had watched history films from that period. But again he had been there
himself, he could still feel the coldness of the instrument
panel under his working fingers, the pressure of the head-
phones against his ears.

The third cylinder transported him into a misty darkness. He was walking through a forest of enormous trees with long tenuous leaves reaching to the ground like crawling green fingers. He was staggering under the weight of his outfit, and his feet were wading through mud and pools of slime and small plants that seemed to possess an eerie mobility, trying to move out of his way when he passed them. Above him the sky was hidden behind clouds. With normal eyes it probably would have been impossible to walk through this darkness without stumbling, but the infra-red glasses gave him good help. He was carrying something heavy in his hands, which he supposed to be some sort of weapon. Except for the plowing sound of his own feet, there wasn't the slightest noise to be heard in this weird jungle. Then suddenly there was light—too much of it and of the wrong color. A poisonous green flame flared up at his right side. In a reflex movement, obtained through years of special training and practice, he threw himself forward on the ground, rolled over and was already opening fire with the gun in his hands. The weapon was noiseless but very effective. Sparkling rays of fire mowed through the dark in a wide arc; with a crackling sound some of the trees took fire, their leafed arms suddenly alive with twitching as the flames licked at them. Through the flames an enormous dark thing came rolling toward him, green hellish fire sprouting from the three eyes atop the colossus.

Immediately Harvey was back in the seat, his neck and hands covered with the sweat of fear. Instinctively his fingers had acted on their own, and, by pulling the switch, had safely brought him back before the attacking monstrosity had reached him. He had had time, however, to recognize the enemy. A Dirval, one of the fighting robots the enemy had used when they had eliminated the entire population of the Venusian colonies, a walking tower of metal and fire vents. He recalled seeing them in the news emissions, some five years back in his time, when the Blackdon Pact had been signed, dividing the colonized parts of Venus in even sectors.

These things were more than just history films. The fear had felt too real, he could still taste the damp air of the Venusian jungle, smell the burning plants and feel the heat of the firing gun in his clamped hands. Whatever this machine was, it was much more than just a short vision into the past.

Nor could he forget the fact that, though he had preferred to remain a silent spectator in the bodies he had visited, he had possessed the power to utilize his own will over them. He had had the power to stop whatever had happened. If he had wanted to, the assassin's finger would not have pulled the trigger, the bomb would not have been dropped. Things became dizzy before his eyes as all the consequences of this thought began to filter through his mind. This machine gave complete *control* over everything that had happened; he was in some sort of control tower in which time itself could be manipulated, changed, in which perhaps time itself had been created! The cylinders were here, they existed. Someone, something must have made them, someone must have built this machine, this tower. But what for?

His mind rebelled, refused to dwell further on the problem. He had the feeling that he stood upon the threshold of a discovery which he knew in advance would fill his mind with helpless terror. It seemed almost as if his subconscious had already put the different elements together and it was his conscious mind that did not want to accept the conclusion.

He remembered the rows of ciphers which had seemed written in the air and which were also to be found on the cylinders. Exact coordinates in time, situating the events precisely. He could relive the whole event again and again, he could *live* it all again, many times, as often as he chose to put the cylinder in the caressing arms of the machine, as many times as the golden helix would absorb him into its private time world.

The cylinders in some alien way contained . . . no, they *were* life; real life linked them; thinking and acting human beings that could be controlled and used without ever being aware of this manipulation. If this surmise was correct, he now stood before the seat of a power which had complete control over the whole of mankind's civilization, a godlike power possessing unimaginable capacities. But . . . a god who had two hands and two feet, and a humanoid body? The dimensions of the chair were as if made for a human being.

He decided to set aside the search for an answer, and fixed his attention now on the door. As far as he knew, beyond the door should be the absolute nothing of which he had caught a glance through that circular window two floors below. But a door leading into nothing would have no reason for being. He touched the door and nothing happened. No photoelectric cells reacted when his finger broke the contact ray, no warmth cells either to open the door when he approached, as was usual in his world and time. He pushed the door and without any sound it opened. A long corridor stretched before him, both walls lined by thousands of pairs of metal arms, rising out of the walls. Each pair held a cylinder between them.

At regular intervals coordinates in big ciphers had been painted on the walls. A library, it flashed through Harvey's mind, a colossal library of life cylinders. Each one like a microfilm which can be looked at at will, and then put away again.

He began walking along the corridor, from time to time having a short look at the stored cylinders. These were all situated in a time period ranging from 1997 to 2077, and their coordinates varied from a few seconds to eighty years. Then, between the arms with the cylinders, doors appeared, about every thirty steps one door would open on a new corridor with cylinders, and new side doors opening on new corridors with more doors opening on more corridors.

It was utterly impossible, yet it existed. Through how many dimensions the corridors ran, Harvey could not guess. They should cross each other, but somehow they never did even though they all seemed to be constructed at straight ninety degree angles to each other. Always there were cylinders, millions, billions of them, all neatly stored away on their exact coordinates. All life which had ever walked the earth and maybe all life that ever would had its counterpart here in one of the weird cylinders. Because the past and the future had to be one, it could not be otherwise after what he saw here. Past, present, and future were simultaneous and continuing, and they all were placed right around this center outside of space and time, this semi-chaotic towerlike building in the heart of the absolute void.

Was life artificially created here, or were the cylinders exact copies made after real life, but used to control and direct the originals? What had been first, the cylinder or the life; what had been first, the chicken or the egg from which the chicken hatched? Or did everything begin and end at the exact time-shard of *being*?

He walked for what seemed an eternity through the never-meeting corridors, walked past millennia of history and futures, and on regular intervals found other ladders going downwards to circular rooms in which he found projection machines. There must be many, many projectors, and many, many towers, he thought, as silent sentinels into nothing, but internally connected by mile-long storage corridors for the cylinders.

Then, while nearing one of the doors, he heard voices. Immediately Harvey froze. They were high-pitched squeaking voices. Cautiously he approached and listened. Then he saw that the door stood partially open, and he peered inside. This control chamber was much bigger than all the former rooms. It housed at least ten projectors as far as he could see. Only three of them were being used, humanoid beings were lying relaxed in the seats, while the cylinders were rotating and clouds of golden-white fog enshrouded the viewers. Other men stood talking or were manipulating the machines on the walls, while others were busy at long tables at obscure tasks.

Harvey watched the creatures closely, seeing they were in fact different from human beings, though they were definitely humanoid. It wasn't only their clothes, which were gleaming metallike garments covering their bodies from neck to feet. They were taller than normal people, very slenderly built, almost spiderlike in bodily structure. Their hands and fingers were so thin they almost seemed like short tentacles; their heads were more elliptoid. On the back of the skull a ridge ran from the neck to the shoulders, almost as if they carried something just under the skin. Their ears were pointed and erect, and they seemed completely hairless. The almost Asiatic eyes had no brows, but otherwise they had the characteristics of humans; two eyes, one nose, one mouth, two arms, and two legs.

Much to his surprise he could understand everything that was being said, as if they spoke in his own language, though he knew that they did not.

"Molvan is controlling 001925," one of them was saying. "He is now watching Hitler, who became the leader of the National Socialist Party. We are trying to prevent the attack the Vvorn have planned during his meeting. Balcaers is speeding up the construction of the V1 and V2 missiles at Peenemunde, and he will try to introduce the V3 also. We have managed to discover and eliminate the Vvorn sabotage project there, but Balcaers prefers to control the whole operation personally."

"Noted on Kontro—23:12:001997 Q2E," one of the sitting beings answered. "How is Loidan getting along with Hopkins?"

"Fogor, how far is Loidan with the Hopkins coordinates? Please put a check on him immediately."

"Matthew Hopkins has met his partner. At the moment, they are questioning three suspected witches at Bathsvill, two of these will have to pass the water test and perish. The third one will survive the test, admit everything they want during the next interrogation, after which they will burn her. There is a slight reaction from some of the villagers, but fear, horror and hatred against the suspected carriers of dark powers prevail. Loidan does not expect any trouble from there."

"Contact Loidan again with the out-coordinator and let him give Hopkins a bit more inspiration with his methods."

"Done. Loidan acknowledges receipt of your orders. One witch dead during this interrogation, two to be hanged on the gallows. Noted down on Kontro—23:-12:001006 RR7."

"Good, not the slightest sign of any intervention of the Vvorn. Maybe they do not think this coordinate important. Haigghan is still working on Nero's personality. After he will have finished with him, no one will recognize the Peaceful Emperor. Haigghan is turning him into a sadist who will pass into world history because of his inhuman cruelties. Coordinates on Kontro—16:3:0062:7:35."

"Maighar! An inter-coordinate memo from Bucor. He has discovered the intervention project of the Vvorn, building up to the Waterloo crisis in Western Europe in 001800. It will need a tremendous set of control-research missions to discover the small units of Vvorn interference and eliminate them there. Is Waterloo worth the trouble?"

"No, I don't think so. Well, try it in any case. Maybe Coorin can occupy himself with it. How far is it with the construction of the sneg-gun?"

"Finished, Maighar. Here, have a look at it; isn't it a beauty? Not much bigger than the palm of your hand, a very simple mechanism, you just pull the trigger. No fire, no smoke, no sound, but it starts an intercellular disintegration action in the victim. Complete destruction of the body cells within a few seconds."

"Good, exactly what we need. But in which coordinate shall we introduce it? Late in 001940? No, too early for that kind of weapon. How about the conflicts at the Slate-settlement on Mars? Or perhaps halfway through the Venusian Wars?"

"No, I wouldn't advise that either. In that coordinate, the use of the gun will not receive enough attention for development and use; it would become a guerrilla weapon and never be used on a major scale. The results would stay buried in the Venus jungles. I suggest we introduce it in the Russian-Chinese conflicts, say in coordinate 001985."

"We shall see. I will have someone check on that coordinate. Maybe Loidan, after he has finished with the Hopkins case, can test a few responsive conditions and see in which the introduction of the sneg-gun will bring the best results. Meantime, you had better take the gun to the arsenal in tower VYR-3; that thing is too dangerous to idle around here."

Harvey raced away and hid in a side corridor. What he had overheard had made the truth come up inside him and it tasted raw and bitter. Now he had to admit what he had not dared face before.

War, hate, destruction, the primitive desire to murder in the human animal . . . they were not real, not inbred by nature, but artificially created here in these control rooms outside of Time and sent out across the ages. These aliens seemed as children, amusing themselves in a game of war on an intertime scale. They created the situations which led to bloody slaughters, made the weapons and introduced them whenever it best suited their insane logic. Probably they were made in the chosen time-coordinate by some weapon-maker or other, who was surprised at his own ingenuity. Mankind, so proud of its civilization and culture . . . no more than a set of pawns in this enormous chess game!

But these beings themselves? What profit did they get out of it? Was there a goal somewhere for them? Or was it only . . . an amusement? A diverting game for their morbid pleasure?

One of the beings passed Harvey's hiding place. The long, slender alien walked lightly past, with spiderlike movements of his long legs. The sneg-gun hung carelessly in his one hand. Harvey acted automatically, without bothering to think out his actions. Soundlessly he began following the creature, approaching it as a hunter stalks his prey. Then, when he was very close, he covered the remaining distance with a few jumps.

The alien turned with the speed of lightning, the carelessly carried gun flashing between his spread fingers and the muzzle already turning toward his attacker. But he was too late. The cylinder in Harvey's hand came crashing down on the creature's skull with full force. Something made a crackling noise—the being uttered an almost soundless squeak. The gun fell from its opened fingers as it clawed at its head. It fell sideways on the floor, made a few movements with its arms and legs, then was still.

Harvey did not hesitate. He grabbed the gun from the floor and retraced his steps back to the big control chamber. The weapon fitted perfectly in his hand, he had only to stretch his fingers a bit to reach the trigger. Though he had never seen it before, its use was perfectly simple.

"I still do not understand it," the creature that had been addressed as Maighar was saying. "The Vvorn built this labyrinth. It took us years to find the coordinates' guide and discover how to use the time capsules. The Vvorn must have foreseen our coming in some way or other and placed their traps. After all, we are—"

At this moment, Harvey stepped inside the room and the beings turned toward him. Their long features didn't register any emotion, but their surprise at the intruder's entrance showed in their rigid postures.

"So," Harvey said, "you didn't build this thing after all? But you damned well love to use it for your own amusement, don't you?"

"A . . . a living being," one of the humanoids whispered, "and it speaks our language!"

"A man," the creature Maighar said, "a man like ourselves, but from a much older coordinate. At first sight I'd place him in the 002000 coordinate, though I could be wrong, and he could be from a bit earlier. And he doesn't speak our language, just as we don't speak his. Time is one here, our brains automatically translate his words, just as he immediately understands ours. How did you get here, stranger?"

"I don't know, but I do know very well what I'm going to do here with your whole devil's building. I still don't know which insane goal you are trying to achieve by using these machines here. But I'm going to put an end to it. My God, all the horrors and pains you've created and seeded out across the centuries of mankind's history! It makes me retch, it almost seems too horrible to be true. But it is. But no longer!"

The creature smiled, a significant drawing up of its cruel lips, without real mirth. "You don't know anything, stranger," it said with its high falsetto voice. "How do you dare to judge that which is completely unknown to you? You judge without understanding, without even knowing any reason for our actions. We have come here from a future which is too far from your time even to be expressed in your terms. We are fugitives from that distant future, and our escape has cost us twenty-four dead. Only eighteen of us have managed it to the coordinates' tower. You can't stop us, human, and once you'll have learned everything, there will be no need for you to stop us. You won't want to. We have escaped from the time empire ruled by the Vvorn to . . ."

The word was a trigger to something buried deep in Harvey's brain, it loosened all his hatred, opened the gates to a storm of fury. He vaguely heard one of the aliens shriek, "Watch out, he has the sneg-gun!" as a red veil rose before his eyes, a bloody cloud of hate. Again his mind fell through a slimy pit, and from all the walls, a strange, soft voice whispered, "Kill! Kill! Kill!"

He didn't bother to ask whose voice was whispering to him; he pulled the trigger. A stony expression came into Maighar's eyes. He opened his mouth in a silent scream, then his body fell forward, his hands clasped to his stomach. His shaking body seemed to become fluid, boneless, it melted away into a pulpy mess. The others jumped at Harvey, but he was at too great a distance from them. He kept the trigger pulled in, and let the muzzle of the gun wander around the room in circles. It was so dreadfully easy, the creatures fell down as puppets from which he had cut the lead-ropes. They made a few high-pitched sounds and then were silent. When he finally stopped, they were no more than a mass of slime on the floor, which disintegrated further into nothingness.

Harvey went to the three projectors which were in use and shot the beings who sat in their chairs, leaving their minds prisoners in the far times where they had lingered. Eighteen, Miaghar had said, they had come here with eighteen. He had killed one in the corridor, three in the projection machines, and eight here in this room. He began to search the room and soon found the coordinates' guide they had spoken of, and a complete set of schemes of the time towers. Without much trouble or difficulties he soon discovered the remaining six humanoids at work in other projectors. They were unarmed and unknowing of his existence, and he shot them without mercy.

He seemed to have no human feelings left, there was nothing in him except burning hatred for those creatures who had called themselves "human" but who had been responsible for ages of pain, torture, persecution, and warfare. He executed them as the murderers they were, butchered them as he would mad animals. He never thought again about the voice out of the depths of his mind which had urged him to kill. He felt strangely empty after he had finished, almost as if the killing had taken something from him.

Then he began to study the coordinates and finally began adapting the world and time. He soon found out that his body functioned as an automaton in this world of no-time. It needed neither food nor sleep. Finding the needed cylinders proved a children's game with the guide. He started with a few simple experiments with relatively unimportant cylinders, then began building the world he wished for mankind, the better world it merited.

On a battlefield in 1915, a run-of-the-mill soldier died in a bomb attack. He had been born in Austria in 1889, and had been given the name Adolf Hitler. The Third Reich never blossomed into existence. Rogof Szivosky became the victim of an assassin's bullet the day before his political party grasped the power which resulted in World War III. Igor Valinsky took his position and through diplomacy was able to prevent the war. By his politics he also prevented the revolt of the Venusian colonies ten years later which had given rise to the Venusian Wars.

On a Sunday morning on June 28, 1914, exactly two minutes to ten, a man from the crowd suddenly threw himself before the gun fired at the Austrian heir to the throne. The incident created some political difficulties but they all quieted down by 1916. On the night of August 5, 1888, a black-cloaked man in Whitechapel suddenly died of a heart attack. The lancet knife hidden in his hands would never be used to cut the throat of the streetwalker Emma Smith and the man would never sign his letters in blood with "Yours truly, Jack the Ripper."

One hundred years earlier, a promising student, born in Corsica in 1769, became involved in a scandal and was thrown out of the military school in Paris. Napoleon Bonaparte would never climb up the career ladder to emperor. A pregnant woman had a bad fall in Paris in May 1740 and a miscarriage resulted. The child who would have become the Marquis de Sade was never born. The man who didn't agree with the Roman Church on many points never grew up as young Luther fell into a pool in 1489 and drowned.

Further and further, Harvey Lonestall went back into time, learning more and more how to effect big changes by small pawns, kneading the past as a sculptor a formless mass of clay, placing new players on the enormous chessboard of time, and removing others. Slowly he replaced war by peace, hatred by love. He finished what he considered his masterpiece by giving indigestion to the first caveman who tasted meat and so made sure that the man never wanted to touch it again, and neither would his descendants and the descendants of those. . . .

The man called Harvey Lonestall looked over his creation, checking the last and final coordinates, and was sure he had won over time. He could not have understood that in a universe where past, present, and future are one, there could only be one real victor: time itself. Maybe he would have understood it (and probably gone mad immediately) if he had searched for the specific cylinder in which he would have found himself in his own body as it fell through the timestorm and woke in the time tower. But an instinctive defense mechanism prevented him from searching for that cylinder.

Through the coordinates' guide he found the exact coordinates of the timestorm which had torn him from April 10, 2113, and after smashing most of the projectors, he used the last functioning one to bring himself back to his own time.

He awoke in a world which was as alien to him as the time tower had been when he had arrived there. This was a clean world whose only buildings were wooden shacks where the land, the water, and the air were clean of pollution, and where even the wheel had not yet been invented. He did not need long to adapt to the friendly vegetarian people who lived in this new world. He shared their society and lived among them for four years, happy in a free world where all conflicts were talked out to each other's satisfaction, where there were no words for anger and hate, and where weapons and warfare were things unimaginable.

And, of course, *this* earth was completely unprepared and unable to defend itself when the first ships of Vvorn appeared in the skies, out of the depths of an immense, big, and vicious universe. . . .

TRANSIT OF EARTH

ARTHUR C. CLARKE

Your editor sat with Arthur C. Clarke on the panel of judges of the IX Festival of Science Fiction Films at Trieste and was impressed then with the fact that Clarke is as well-grounded in solid hard science as he is in science fiction. Evidence of that will be found in this projection of a decade hence—a possible true event-to-come.

NOTE: *All the astronomical events described in this story take place at the times stated.*

Testing, one, two, three, four, five. . . .

Evans speaking. I will continue to record as long as possible. This is a two-hour capsule, but I doubt if I'll fill it.

That photograph has haunted me all my life; now, too late, I know why. (But would it have made any difference if I *had* known? That's one of those meaningless and unanswerable questions the mind keeps returning to endlessly, like the tongue exploring a broken tooth.)

I've not seen it for years, but I've only to close my eyes and I'm back in a landscape almost as hostile—and as beautiful—as this one. Fifty million miles sunward and seventy-two years in the past, five men face the camera amid the Antarctic snows. Not even the bulky furs can hide the exhaustion and defeat that mark every line of their bodies, and their faces are already touched by death.

There were five of them. There were five of us and, of course, we also took a group photograph. But everything else was different. We were smiling—cheerful, confident. And our picture was on all the screens of Earth within ten minutes. It was months before *their* camera was found and brought back to civilization.

And we die in comfort, with all modern conveniences —including many that Robert Falcon Scott could never have imagined when he stood at the South Pole in 1912.

Two hours later. I'll start giving exact times when it becomes important.

All the facts are on the log, and by now the whole world knows them. So I guess I'm doing this largely to settle my mind—to talk myself into facing the inevitable. The trouble is, I'm not sure what subjects to avoid and which to tackle head on. Well, there's only one way to find out.

The first item: In twenty-four hours, at the very most, all the oxygen will be gone. That leaves me with the three classical choices. I can let the CO_2 build up until I become unconscious. I can step outside and crack the suit, leaving Mars to do the job in about two minutes. Or I can use one of the tablets in the med kit.

CO_2 buildup: Everyone says that's quite easy—just like going to sleep. I've no doubt that's true; unfortunately, in my case it's associated with nightmare number one.

I wish I'd never come across that damn book—*True Stories of World War Two*, or whatever it was called. There was one chapter about a German submarine, found and salvaged after the war. The crew was still inside it— *two* men per bunk. And between each pair of skeletons, the single respirator set they'd been sharing.

Well, at least that won't happen here. But I know, with a deadly certainty, that as soon as I find it hard to breathe, I'll be back in that doomed U-boat.

So what about the quicker way? When you're exposed to a vacuum, you're unconscious in ten or fifteen seconds, and people who've been through it say it's not painful— just peculiar. But trying to breathe something that isn't there brings me altogether too neatly to nightmare number two.

This time, it's a personal experience. As a kid, I used to

do a lot of skin diving when my family went to the Caribbean for vacations. There was an old freighter that had sunk twenty years before, out on a reef with its deck only a couple of yards below the surface. Most of the hatches were open, so it was easy to get inside to look for souvenirs and hunt the big fish that like to shelter in such places.

Of course it was dangerous—if you did it without scuba gear. So what boy could resist the challenge?

My favorite route involved diving into a hatch on the foredeck, swimming about fifty feet along a passageway dimly lit by portholes a few yards apart, then angling up a short flight of stairs and emerging through a door in the battered superstructure. The whole trip took less than a minute—an easy dive for anyone in good condition. There was even time to do some sight-seeing or to play with a few fish along the route. And sometimes, for a change, I'd switch directions, going in the door and coming out again through the hatch.

That was the way I did it the last time. I hadn't dived for a week—there had been a big storm and the sea was too rough—so I was impatient to get going. I deep-breathed on the surface for about two minutes, until I felt the tingling in my fingertips that told me it was time to stop. Then I jackknifed and slid gently down toward the black rectangle of the open doorway.

It always looked ominous and menacing—that was part of the thrill. And for the first few yards, I was almost completely blind; the contrast between the tropical glare above water and the gloom between decks was so great that it took quite a while for my eyes to adjust. Usually, I was halfway along the corridor before I could see anything clearly; then the illumination would steadily increase as I approached the open hatch, where a shaft of sunlight would paint a dazzling rectangle on the rusty, barnacled metal floor.

I'd almost made it when I realized that this time the light wasn't getting better. There was no slanting column of sunlight ahead of me, leading up to the world of air and life. I had a second of baffled confusion, wondering if I'd lost my way. Then I realized what had happened— and confusion turned into sheer panic. Sometime during the storm, the hatch must have slammed shut. It weighed at least a quarter of a ton.

I don't remember making a U-turn; the next thing I

recall is swimming quite slowly back along the passage and telling myself, "Don't hurry—your air will last longer if you take it easy." I could see very well now, because my eyes had had plenty of time to become dark-adapted. There were lots of details I'd never noticed before—such as the red squirrelfish lurking in the shadows, the green fronds and algae growing in the little patches of light around the portholes, and even a single rubber boot, apparently in excellent condition, lying where someone must have kicked it off. And once, out of a side corridor, I noticed a big grouper staring at me with bulbous eyes, his thick lips half-parted, as if he were astonished at my intrusion.

The band around my chest was getting tighter and tighter; it was impossible to hold my breath any longer—yet the stairway still seemed an infinite distance ahead. I let some bubbles of air dribble out of my mouth; that improved matters for a moment, but, once I had exhaled, the ache in my lungs became even more unendurable.

Now there was no point in conserving strength by flippering along with that steady, unhurried stroke. I snatched the ultimate few cubic inches of air from my face mask—feeling it flatten against my nose as I did so—and swallowed it down into my starving lungs. At the same time, I shifted gear and drove forward with every last atom of strength.

And that's all I remember until I found myself spluttering and coughing in the daylight, clinging to the broken stub of the mast. The water around me was stained with blood and I wondered why. Then, to my great surprise, I noticed a deep gash in my right calf; I must have banged into some sharp obstruction, but I'd never noticed it and even now felt no pain.

That was the end of my skin diving until I started astronaut training ten years later and went into the underwater zero-g simulator. Then it was different, because I was using scuba gear, but I had some nasty moments that I was afraid the psychologists would notice and I always made sure that I got nowhere near emptying my tank. Having nearly suffocated once, I'd no intention or risking it again.

I know exactly what it will feel like to breathe the freezing wisp of near vacuum that passes for atmosphere on Mars. No, thank you.

So what's wrong with poison? Nothing, I suppose. The

stuff we've got takes only fifteen seconds, they told us. But all my instincts are against it, even when there's no sensible alternative.

Did Scott have poison with him? I doubt it. And if he did, I'm sure he never used it.

I'm not going to replay this. I hope it's been some use, but I can't be sure.

The radio has just printed out a message from Earth, reminding me that transit starts in two hours. As if I'm likely to forget—when four men have already died so that I can be the first human being to see it. And the only one for exactly one hundred years. It isn't often that sun, Earth and Mars line up neatly like this; the last time was in 1905, when poor old Lowell was still writing his beautiful nonsense about the canals and the great dying civilization that had built them. Too bad it was all delusion.

I'd better check the telescope and the timing equipment.

The sun is quiet today—as it should be, anyway, near the middle of the cycle. Just a few small spots and some minor areas of disturbance around them. The solar weather is set calm for months to come. That's one thing the others won't have to worry about on their way home.

I think that was the worst moment, watching *Olympus* lift off Phobos and head back to Earth. Even though we'd known for weeks that nothing could be done, that was the final closing of the door. It was night and we could see everything perfectly. Phobos had come leaping up out of the west a few hours earlier and was doing its mad backward rush across the sky, growing from a tiny crescent to a half-moon; before it reached the zenith, it would disappear as it plunged into the shadow of Mars and became eclipsed.

We'd been listening to the countdown, of course, trying to go about our normal work. It wasn't easy, accepting at last the fact that fifteen of us had come to Mars and only ten would return. Even then, I suppose there were millions back on Earth who still could not understand; they must have found it impossible to believe that *Olympus* couldn't descend a mere 4,000 miles to pick us up. The Space Administration had been bombarded with crazy rescue schemes; heaven knows, we'd thought of enough ourselves. But when the permafrost under landing pad three finally gave way and *Pegasus* toppled, that was that. It still seems a miracle that the ship didn't blow up when the propellant tank ruptured.

I'm wandering again. Back to Phobos and the countdown. On the telescope monitor, we could clearly see the fissured plateau where *Olympus* had touched down after we'd separated and begun our own descent. Though our friends would never land on Mars, at least they'd had a little world of their own to explore; even for a satellite as small as Phobos, it worked out at thirty square miles per man. A lot of territory to search for strange minerals and debris from space—or to carve your name so that future ages would know that you were the first of all men to come this way.

The ship was clearly visible as a stubby, bright cylinder against the dull gray rocks; from time to time, some flat surface would catch the light of the swiftly moving sun and would flash with mirror brilliance. But about five minutes before lift-off, the picture became suddenly pink, then crimson—then vanished completely as Phobos rushed into eclipse.

The countdown was still at ten seconds when we were startled by a blast of light. For a moment, we wondered if *Olympus* had also met with catastrophe; then we realized that someone was filming the takeoff and the external floodlights had been switched on.

During those last few seconds, I think we all forgot our own predicament; we were up there aboard *Olympus,* willing the thrust to build up smoothly and lift the ship out of the tiny gravitational field of Phobos—and then away from Mars for the long fall sunward. We heard Commander Richmond say, "Ignition," there was a brief burst of interference, and the patch of light began to move in the field of the telescope.

That was all. There was no blazing column of fire, because, of course, there's really no ignition when a nuclear rocket lights up. "Lights up" indeed! That's another hangover from the old chemical technology. But a hot hydrogen blast is completely invisible; it seems a pity that we'll never again see anything so spectacular as a Saturn or a Korolov blast-off.

Just before the end of the burn, *Olympus* left the shadow of Mars and burst out into sunlight again, reappearing almost instantly as a brilliant, swiftly moving star.

The blaze of light must have startled them aboard the ship, because we heard someone call out, "Cover that window!" Then, a few seconds later, Richmond announced, "Engine cutoff." Whatever happened, *Olympus* was now irrevocably headed back to Earth.

A voice I didn't recognize—though it must have been the commander's—said, "Good-bye, *Pegasus*," and the radio transmission switched off. There was, of course, no point in saying, "Good luck." *That* had all been settled weeks ago.

I've just played this back. Talking of luck, there's been one compensation, though not for us. With a crew of only ten, *Olympus* has been able to dump a third of her expendables and lighten herself by several tons. So now she'll get home a month ahead of schedule.

Plenty of things could have gone wrong in that month; we may yet have saved the expedition. Of course, we'll never know—but it's a nice thought.

I've been playing a lot of music—full blast, now that there's no one else to be disturbed. Even if there were any Martians, I don't suppose this ghost of an atmosphere could carry the sound more than a few yards.

We have a fine collection, but I have to choose carefully. Nothing downbeat and nothing that demands too much concentration. Above all, nothing with human voices. So I restrict myself to the lighter orchestral classics; the *New World Symphony* and Grieg's piano concerto fill the bill perfectly. At the moment, I'm listening to Rachmaninoff's *Paganini Variations,* but now I must switch off and get down to work.

There are only five minutes to go; all the equipment is in perfect condition. The telescope is tracking the sun, the video recorder is standing by, the precision timer is running.

These observations will be as accurate as I can make them. I owe it to my lost comrades, whom I'll soon be joining. They gave me their oxygen so that I can still be alive at this moment. I hope you remember that, 100 or 1,000 years from now, whenever you crank these figures into the computers.

Only a minute to go; getting down to business. For the record, year 1984, month May, day 11, coming up to four hours, thirty minutes, Ephemeris Time . . . *now*.

Half a minute to contact; switching recorder and timer to high speed. Just rechecked position angle to make sure I'm looking at the right spot on the sun's limb. Using power of 500—image perfectly steady even at this low elevation.

Four thirty-two. Any moment, now. . . .

There it is . . . there it is! I can hardly believe it! A tiny black dent in the edge of the sun, growing, growing, growing. . . .

Hello, Earth. Look up at me—the brightest star in your sky, straight overhead at midnight.

Recorder back to slow.

Four thirty-five. It's as if a thumb were pushing into the sun's edge, deeper and deeper—fascinating to watch.

Four forty-one. Exactly halfway. The Earth's a perfect black semicircle—a clean bite out of the sun—as if some disease were eating it away.

Four forty-eight. Ingress three-quarters complete.

Four hours, forty-nine minutes, thirty seconds. Recorder on high speed again.

The line of contact with the sun's edge is shrinking fast. Now it's a barely visible black thread. In a few seconds, the whole Earth will be superimposed on the sun.

Now I can see the effects of the atmosphere. There's a thin halo of light surrounding that black hole in the sun. Strange to think that I'm seeing the glow of all the sunsets—and all the sunrises—that are taking place around the whole Earth at this very moment.

Ingress complete—four hours, fifty minutes, five seconds. The whole world has moved onto the face of the sun, a perfectly circular black disk silhouetted against that inferno, ninety million miles below. It looks bigger than I expected; one could easily mistake it for a fair-sized sunspot.

Nothing more to see now for six hours, when the moon appears, trailing Earth by half the sun's width. I'll beam the recorded data back to Lunacom, then try to get some sleep.

My very last sleep. Wonder if I'll need drugs. It seems a pity to waste these last few hours, but I want to conserve my strength—and my oxygen. I think it was Dr. Johnson who said that nothing settles a man's mind so wonderfully as the knowledge that he'll be hanged in the morning. How the hell did *he* know?

Ten hours, thirty minutes, Ephemeris Time. Dr. Johnson was right. I had only one pill and don't remember any dreams.

The condemned man also ate a hearty breakfast. Cut that out.

Back at telescope. Now the Earth's halfway across the disk, passing well north of center. In ten minutes, I should see the moon.

I've just switched to the highest power of the telescope —2,000. The image is slightly fuzzy but still fairly good, atmospheric halo very distinct. I'm hoping to see the cities on the dark side of Earth.

No luck. Probably too many clouds. A pity—it's theoretically possible, but we never succeeded. I wish . . . Never mind.

Ten hours, forty minutes. Recorder on slow speed. Hope I'm looking at the right spot.

Fifteen seconds to go. Recorder fast.

Damn—missed it. Doesn't matter—the recorder will have caught the exact moment. There's a little black notch already in the side of the sun. First contact must have been about ten hours, forty-one minutes, twenty seconds, E.T.

What a long way it is between Earth and moon— there's half the width of the sun between them. You wouldn't think the two bodies had anything to do with each other. Makes you realize just how big the sun really is.

Ten hours, forty-four minutes. The moon's exactly halfway over the edge. A very small, very clear-cut semicircular bite out of the edge of the sun.

Ten hours, forty-seven minutes, five seconds. Internal contact. The moon's clear of the edge, entirely inside the sun. Don't suppose I can see anything on the night side, but I'll increase the power.

That's funny.

Well, well. Someone must be trying to talk to me. There's a tiny light pulsing away there on the darkened face of the moon. Probably the laser at Imbrium Base.

Sorry, everyone. I've said all my good-byes and don't want to go through that again. Nothing can be important now.

Still, it's almost hypnotic—that flickering point of light, coming out of the face of the sun itself. Hard to believe that even after it's traveled all this distance, the beam is only a hundred miles wide. Lunacom's going to all this trouble to aim it exactly at me and I suppose I should feel guilty at ignoring it. But I don't. I've nearly finished my work and the things of Earth are no longer any concern of mine.

Ten hours, fifty minutes. Recorder off. That's it—until the end of Earth transit, two hours from now.

I've had a snack and am taking my last look at the view from the observation bubble. The sun's still high, so there's not much contrast, but the light brings out all the colors vividly—the countless varieties of red and pink and crimson, so startling against the deep blue of the sky. How different from the moon—though that, too, has its own beauty.

It's strange how surprising the obvious can be. Everyone knew that Mars was red. But we didn't really expect the red of rust—the red of blood. Like the Painted Desert of Arizona; after a while, the eye longs for green.

To the north, there is one welcome change of color; the cap of carbon-dioxide snow on Mt. Burroughs is a dazzling white pyramid. That's another surprise. Burroughs is 25,000 feet above Mean Datum; when I was a boy, there weren't supposed to be any mountains on Mars.

The nearest sand dune is a quarter of a mile away and it, too, has patches of frost on its shaded slope. During the last storm, we thought it moved a few feet, but we couldn't be sure. Certainly, the dunes *are* moving, like those on Earth. One day, I suppose, this base will be covered—only to reappear again in 1,000 years. Or 10,000.

That strange group of rocks—the Elephant, the Capitol, the Bishop—still holds its secrets and teases me with the memory of our first big disappointment. We could have sworn that they were sedimentary; how eagerly we rushed out to look for fossils! Even now, we don't know what formed that outcropping; the geology of Mars is still a mass of contradictions and enigmas.

We have passed on enough problems to the future and those who come after us will find many more. But there's one mystery we never reported to Earth nor even entered in the log. The first night after we landed, we took turns keeping watch. Brennan was on duty and woke me up soon after midnight. I was annoyed—it was ahead of time—and then he told me that he'd seen a light moving around the base of the Capitol. We watched for at least an hour, until it was my turn to take over. But we saw nothing; whatever that light was, it never reappeared.

Now, Brennan was as level-headed and unimaginative as they come; if he said he saw a light, then he saw one. Maybe it was some kind of electric discharge or the reflection of Phobos on a piece of sand-polished rock. Anyway, we decided not to mention it to Lunacom unless we saw it again.

Since I've been alone, I've often awaked in the night and looked out toward the rocks. In the feeble illumination of Phobos and Deimos, they remind me of the skyline of a darkened city. And it has always remained darkened. No lights have ever appeared for me.

Twelve hours, forty-nine minutes, Ephemeris Time. The last act's about to begin. Earth has nearly reached the edge of the sun. The two narrow horns of light that still embrace it are barely touching.

Recorder on fast.

Contact! Twelve hours, fifty minutes, sixteen seconds. The crescents of light no longer meet. A tiny black spot has appeared at the edge of the sun, as the Earth begins to cross it. It's growing longer, longer. . . .

Recorder on slow. Eighteen minutes to wait before Earth finally clears the face of the sun.

The moon still has more than halfway to go; it's not yet reached the midpoint of its transit. It looks like a little round blob of ink, only a quarter the size of Earth. And there's no light flickering there anymore. Lunacom must have given up.

Well, I have just a quarter hour left here in my last home. Time seems to be accelerating the way it does in the final minutes before a lift-off. No matter, I have everything worked out now. I can even relax.

Already, I feel part of history. I am one with Captain Cook, back in Tahiti in 1769, watching the transit of Venus. Except for that image of the moon trailing along behind, it must have looked just like this.

What would Cook have thought, two hundred years ago, if he'd known that one day a man would observe the whole Earth in transit from an outer world? I'm sure he would have been astonished—and then delighted.

But I feel a closer identity with a man not yet born.

I hope you hear these words, whoever you may be. Perhaps you will be standing on this very spot, one hundred years from now, when the next transit occurs.

Greetings to 2084, November 10! I wish you better luck than we had. I suppose you will have come here on a luxury liner—or you may have been born on Mars and be a stranger to Earth. You will know things that I cannot imagine; yet somehow I don't envy you. I would not even change places with you if I could.

For you will remember my name and know that I was the first of all mankind ever to see a transit of Earth. And no one will see another for one hundred years.

Twelve hours, fifty-nine minutes. Exactly halfway through egress. The Earth is a perfect semicircle—a black shadow on the face of the sun. I still can't escape from the impression that something has taken a big bite out of that golden disk. In nine minutes, it will be gone and the sun will be whole again.

Thirteen hours, seven minutes. Recorder on fast.

Earth has almost gone. There's just a shallow black dimple at the edge of the sun. You could easily mistake it for a small spot, going over the limb.

Thirteen hours, eight.

Good-bye, beautiful Earth.

Going, going, going, good-bye, good——

I'm OK again now. The timings have all been sent home on the beam. In five minutes, they'll join the accumulated wisdom of mankind. And Lunacom will know that I stuck to my post.

But I'm not sending this. I'm going to leave it here for the next expedition—whenever that may be. It could be ten or twenty years before anyone comes here again; no point in going back to an old site when there's a whole world waiting to be explored.

So this capsule will stay here, as Scott's diary remained in his tent, until the next visitors find it. But they won't find me.

Strange how hard it is to get away from Scott. I think he gave me the idea. For his body will not lie frozen forever in the Antarctic, isolated from the great cycle of life and death. Long ago, that lonely tent began its march to the sea. Within a few years, it was buried by the falling snow and had become part of the glacier that crawls eternally away from the pole. In a few brief centuries, the sailor will have returned to the sea. He will merge once more into the pattern of living things—the plankton, the seals, the penguins, the whales, all the multitudinous fauna of the Antarctic Ocean.

There are no oceans here on Mars, nor have there been for at least five billion years. But there is life of some kind, down there in the badlands of Chaos II, that we never had time to explore. Those moving patches on the orbital photographs. The evidence that whole areas of Mars have been swept clear of craters by forces other than erosion. The long-chain, optically active carbon molecules picked up by the atmospheric samplers.

And, of course, the mystery of Viking 6. Even now, no one has been able to make any sense of those last instrument readings before something large and heavy crushed the probe in the still, cold depths of the Martian night.

And don't talk to me about *primitive* life forms in a place like this! Anything that's survived here will be so sophisticated that we may look as clumsy as dinosaurs.

There's still enough propellant in the ship's tanks to drive the Marscar clear around the planet. I have three hours of daylight left—plenty of time to get down into the valleys and well out into Chaos. After sunset, I'll still be able to make good speed with the head lamps. It will be romantic, driving at night under the moons of Mars.

One thing I must fix before I leave. I don't like the way Sam's lying out there. He was always so poised, so graceful. It doesn't seem right that he should look so awkward now. I must do something about it.

I wonder if *I* could have covered three hundred feet without a suit, walking slowly, steadily—the way he did to the very end.

I must try not to look at his face.

That's it. Everything shipshape and ready to go.

The therapy has worked. I feel perfectly at ease—even contented, now that I know exactly what I'm going to do. The old nightmares have lost their power.

It is true, we all die alone. It makes no difference at the end, being fifty million miles from home.

I'm going to enjoy the drive through that lovely painted landscape. I'll be thinking of all those who dreamed about Mars—Wells and Lowell and Burroughs and Weinbaum and Bradbury. They all guessed wrong—but the reality is just as strange, just as beautiful as they imagined.

I don't know what's waiting for me out there and I'll probably never see it. But on this starveling world, it must be desperate for carbon, phosphorus, oxygen, calcium. It can use me.

And when my oxygen alarm gives its final ping, somewhere down there in that haunted wilderness, I'm going to finish in style. As soon as I have difficulty in breathing, I'll get off the Marscar and start walking—with a playback unit plugged into my helmet and going full blast.

For sheer, triumphant power and glory, there's nothing in the whole of music to match the *Toccata and Fugue in D Minor*. I won't have time to hear all of it; that doesn't matter.

Johann Sebastian, here I come.

GEHENNA

BARRY N. MALZBERG

As one who has had to ride the New York subways all the days of his life, one can say that the title of this typical Barry Malzberg tale is thoroughly justified—even if the subway itself is not really the *raison d'être* of the narrative.

A

Edward got on the IRT downtown local at 42nd Street for Greenwich Village. The train stopped at 33rd Street, 27th Street, 17th Street, and Christopher Circle. As it turned out he met his wife at this party.

It was a standard, Greenwich Village all-of-us-are-damned gathering. She was sitting in a corner of the room, her feet bare, listening to a man with sad mustaches play a mandolin. Edward went over to say hello to her. She looked at him with vague disinterest and huddled closer to the mandolin player, who turned out—on further inspection—to be her date for the night. But Edward was persistent—his parents had always told him that his fearfulness was his chief detracting characteristic—and later that night he got her address.

Two days later he showed up with a shopping cart filled with gourmet food and asked her if she would help him eat it. She shrugged and introduced him to her cats. Three weeks later they slept with one another for the first time and the week after that the mandolin player and he had a fight, at the end of which the mandolin player wished them well and left her flat forever. Edward and Julie were engaged only a few days after that and during the month he married her in Elkton.

They went back to New York and started life together. He gave up mathematics, of course, and became an accountant. She gave up painting and took to going to antique shops once a week, bringing back objects every now and then. It was not a bad life, even if it had started out, perhaps, a bit on the contrived side.

Three years later Edward opened the door and found Julie playing with their year-old daughter, shaking a rattle and putting it deep into the baby's mouth. The scene was a pleasing one and he felt quite contented until she looked up at him and he saw that she was crying.

He put down his briefcase and asked her what was wrong. She told him that their life had been an utter waste. Everything she wanted she had not gotten—everything that she had gotten she did not want. She was surrounded by things, she told him, she had prepared herself as a child to despise. And the worst of it was that all of it was her own fault. She talked of divorce but only by inference.

Realizing that the fault was all his, Edward said that he would check up on some suburbs, get them a nice-sized house and some activities for her during the day. And so he did—all of it and they were very happy for a while if gravely in debt—until he came home from the circus one night with his daughter and found that Julie, feet bare, had drowned herself in the bathtub.

B

Julie got on the IRT downtown local at 42nd Street for Greenwich Village. The train stopped at 32nd Street, 24th Street, 13th Street and the Statue of Christ. As it turned out, she met her husband at this party. It was a standard Greenwich Village we-are-finding-ourselves party and he came in late, dressed all wrong, his hands stretching his pockets out of shape. He was already very drunk.

She was there with a boy named Vincent who meant little to her but who played the mandolin beautifully and sang her love songs. If the songs were derivative and the motions a trifle forced—well, it was a bad period for both of them and she took what comfort she could. But when her husband-to-be came over and spoke to her—his name was Edward as it turned out—she could see beyond his embarrassment and her misery that a certain period of her life and of the mandolin player's was over. He wanted her telephone number but because she didn't believe in telephones she gave him her address instead while Vincent was off changing his clothes. She told him that she was very unsure of herself.

Three days later, while she was still in bed, he came with flowers and candy and told her that he could not forget her. With a smile she invited him in and the first time was very good—better than it had been with Vincent, anyway. Edward was gone when Vincent came later that evening and she told him that she had been lusting after the sea all her life—now she at least had found a pond. Then she told him what she and Edward had done. He wept and cursed her. He told her that she had betrayed everything of importance, the small reality they had built together—but she was firm. She said that lines must be drawn for once and for all between the present and the possible.

After that she saw nothing of either Vincent or Edward for a week. Then Edward came with a suitcase. He said he had moved out of his parents' home and had come to marry her. She did not marry him right away but they lived together for some weeks—one evening she found a note in her mailbox, just like that, saying that Vincent had committed suicide.

She never found out who had sent the note and she never told Edward anything. But a week later they were married in Yonkers and went to a resort upstate, where they were happy for a few days.

They came back and bought furniture for her flat. He dropped out of astronomy and became an industrial research assistant—or something like that.

For a long time her days were simple—they were, as a matter of fact, exactly like the days she had known just before she met Edward—and the nights were good, pretty good anyway. Then she became pregnant in a difficult sort of way and eventually the child, Ann, was born—a perfect child with small hands and a musical capability. Edward said that they would have to find a real home now—he was very proud—but she said that the old life could keep up, at least until Ann was ready for school. But one night he came home early, very excited and—just like that—

told her that he had found them a home in the suburbs. She told him that this was fine. He said that he was very happy, and she said the same.

They moved to the suburbs and were content for a while, what with car pools and bridge and whatnot, as well as good playmates and a healthy environment for Ann. But Edward, for no reason, began to get more and more depressed and one morning when she awoke to find his bed empty, she went into the bathroom to find him slumped over the bathtub, his wrists open, blood all over the floor, a faint, fishlike look of appeal in his stunned and disbelieving eyes.

C

Vincent got on the IRT downtown local at 42nd Street for Greenwich Village. The train stopped at 37th street, 31st Street, 19th Street, and Christ Towers. As it turned out, he lost his girl at this party. It was a standard Greenwich Village look-how-liberated-we-are kind of party and it was a strange thing that the two of them went separately since the 42nd Street stop was the nearest to both of their apartments. But she believed in maintaining her privacy in small, damning ways.

She was sad that night, sad with a misery he could not touch, much less comprehend. It had been a good time for both of them—they had been going together for the four months since she broke off with his closet friend—and he played her songs on his mandolin—promises of lost and terrible loves, promises of a better future, songs of freedom and loneliness; and she loved his mandolin. She told him that she found her whole soul in his music.

So he was playing songs for her at the party this night, not even wanting to be there, hoping that they could go back to her flat and put the mandolin beside the bed and make their kind of love, when he saw that she was looking at another man in the corner of the room—a man of a different sort from the rest of them, since he was the only one who was not already drunk. The man was looking back at her and in that moment Vincent knew that he was quite doomed, that he and Julie were quite finished.

To prove it to himself he left his instrument on her knee and went to the bathroom. When he came back they sprang apart like assassins and he knew that the man had her address. There was nothing to do, of course, but to leave the party and he helped her with her coat, put his mandolin over his shoulder and led her down the stairs. Halfway to the street he told her that she had betrayed them. She did not answer, later murmured that she could not help herself, much less another person—but she would make this night the best of all the nights that she had ever given him.

And so she did, all night and into the dawn while her cat stroked the mandolin, making wooden sounds, rolling the instrument around and around on the floor. In the morning he left her—and took his clothing—and then he did not see her at all for a few days. When he came back there was a different look on her face and the man was in her bed, lying next to her.

He did not care—he had lost any capacity for surprise when she had come from his closest friend, broken enough to need him. He only wanted to meet the man named Edward (who might become his closest friend too) but the man did not want any part of him at all and there was a very bad scene—a scene that ended only when Vincent knocked the man to the door and smashed him there to the floor.

But he never saw her again, victory or not. He had no need to—everything that needed proof had been proven. But he thought of her often and many years later, when he killed himself by leaping from a stranger's penthouse, his last thought as he felt the dry wind and saw the street coming at him was of his old mandolin, her solemn cat and the night she had given him her best because she had already partaken of his worst.

D

The child Ann—who had very sensitive and gentle hands—became a young woman who was drawn at odd moments to the windows of pawn shops in which she saw old mandolins—and once, for a week, she took flute lessons. But she had no money and less patience—that last was her biggest fault, along with a lack of assertiveness— and she dropped them.

Now she is going to a party in Greenwich Village. She does not know what will happen to her. The night is still a mystery. She is still young enough to scent possibilities in the wind—tonight may hold some finality, although one never knows. See her, see her—she is in the Times Square stop of the IRT—the engineer sounds a song in the density.

She counts the stops and waits. The train stops at 34th Street, 28th Street and 14th Street. Now it is at Christopher Street and Sheridan Square.

ONE LIFE, FURNISHED IN EARLY POVERTY

HARLAN ELLISON

For an author justly famed for his imaginative vigor and his bold challenge to the world to come out and fight, this is unusual. For one thing it represents Harlan Ellison in what seems to be a retrospective and even self-deprecating mood, and for another it touches upon a hobby of his few know of—he likes toy soldiers; a trait he shares with the editor of this anthology.

And so it was—strangely, strangely—that I found myself standing in the backyard of the house I had lived in when I was seven years old. At thirteen minutes till midnight on no special magical winter's night, in a town that had held me only till I was physically able to run away. In Ohio, in winter, near midnight—certain I could go back.

Not truly knowing *why* I even wanted to go back. But certain that I could. Without magic, without science, without alchemy, without supernatural assistance; just *go back*. Because I had to, I needed to . . . go back.

Back; thirty-five years and more. To find myself at the age of seven, before any of it had begun; before any of the directions had been taken; to find out what turning point in my life it had been that had wrenched me from the course all little boys took to adulthood and set me on the road of loneliness and success that ended here, back where I'd begun, in a backyard at now-twelve minutes to midnight.

At forty-two I had come to the point in my life I had struggled toward since I was a child: a place of security, importance, recognition. The only one from this town who had made it. The ones who had had the most promise in school were now milkmen, used-car salesmen, married to fat, stupid *dead* women who had themselves been girls of exceeding promise in high school. *They* had been trapped in this little Ohio town, never to break free. To die there, unknown. I had broken free, had done all the wonderful things I'd said I would do.

Why should it all depress me now?

Perhaps it was because Christmas was nearing and I was alone, with bad marriages and lost friendships behind me.

I walked out of the studio, away from the wet-ink-new fifty-thousand-dollar contract, got in my car and drove to International Airport. It was a straight line made up of in-flight meals and jet airliners and rental cars and hastily purchased winter clothing. A straight line to a backyard I had not seen in over thirty years.

I had to find the dragoon to go back.

Crossing the rime-frosted grass that crackled like cellophane, I walked under the shadow of the lightning-blasted pear tree. I had climbed in that tree endlessly when I was seven years old. In summer, its branches hung far over and scraped the roof of the garage. I could shinny out across the limb and drop onto the garage roof. I had once pushed Johnny Mummy off that garage roof . . . not out of meanness, but simply because I had jumped from it many times and I could not understand anyone's not finding it a wonderful thing to do. He had sprained his ankle, and his father, a fireman, had come looking for me. I'd hidden on the garage roof.

I walked around the side of the garage, and there was the barely visible path. To one side of the path I had always buried my toy soldiers. For no other reason than to bury them, know I had a secret place, and later dig them up again, as if finding treasure.

(It came to me that even now, as an adult, I did the same thing. Dining in a Japanese restaurant, I would hide small pieces of *pakkai* or pineapple or *terriyaki* in my rice bowl and pretend to be delighted when, later in the meal, my chopsticks encountered the tiny treasures down in among the rice grains.)

I knew the spot, of course. I got down on my hands and knees and began digging with the silver penknife on my watch chain. It had been my father's penknife—almost the only thing he had left when he died.

The ground was hard, but I dug with enthusiasm, and the moon gave me more than enough light. Down and down I dug, knowing eventually I would come to the dragoon.

He was there. The bright paint rusted off his body, the saber corroded and reduced to a stub. Lying there in the grave I had dug for him thirty-five years before. I scooped the little metal soldier out of the ground and cleaned him off as best I could with my paisley dress handkerchief. He was faceless now, and as sad as I felt.

I hunkered there, under the moon, and waited for midnight, only a minute away, knowing it was all going to come right for me. After so terribly long.

The house behind me was silent and dark. I had no idea who lived there now. It would have been unpleasant if the strangers who now lived here had been unable to sleep and, rising to get a glass of water, had idly looked into the backyard. *Their* backyard. I had played here and built a world for myself here, from dreams and loneliness. Using talismans of comic books and radio programs and matinee movies and potent charms like the sad little dragoon in my hand.

My wristwatch said midnight, one hand laid straight on the other.

The moon faded. Slowly, it went gray and shadowy, till the glow was gone, and then even the gray after-image was gone.

The wind rose. Slowly, it came from somewhere far away, and built around me. I stood up, pulling the collar of my topcoat around my neck. The wind was neither warm nor cold, yet it rushed, without even ruffling my hair. I was not afraid.

The ground was settling. Slowly, it lowered me the tiniest fractions of inches. But steadily, as though the layers of tomorrows that had been built up were vanishing.

My thoughts were of myself: *I'm coming to save you. I'm coming, Gus. You won't hurt any more . . . you'll never have hurt.*

The moon came back. It had been full; now it was new.

The wind died. It had carried me where I'd needed to go. The ground settled. The years had been peeled off.

I was alone in the backyard of the house at 89 Harmon Drive. The snow was deeper. It was a different house, though it was the same. It was not recently painted. The Depression had not been long ago; money was still tight. It wasn't weather-beaten, but in a year or two my father would have it painted. Light yellow.

There was a sumac tree growing below the window of the dinette. It was nourished by lima beans and soup and cabbage.

"You'll just sit there until you finish every drop of your dinner. We're not wasting food. There are children starving in Russia."

I put the dragoon in my topcoat pocket. He had worked more than hard enough. I walked around the side of the house. I smiled as I saw again the wooden milk box by the side door. In the morning, very early, the milkman would put three quarts of milk there, but before anyone could bring them in, this very cold winter morning in December, the cream would push its way up and the little cardboard caps would be an inch above the mouths of the bottles.

The gravel talked beneath my feet. The street was quiet and cold. I stood in the front yard, beside the big oak tree, and looked up and down.

It was the same. It was as though I'd never been away. I started to cry. Hello.

Gus was on one of the swings in the playground. I stood outside the fence of Lathrop Grade School, and watched him standing on the seat, gripping the ropes, pumping his little legs. He was smaller than I'd remembered him. He wasn't smiling as he tried to swing higher. It was serious to him.

Standing outside the hurricane fence, watching Gus, I was happy. I scratched at a rash on my right wrist, and smoked a cigarette, and was happy.

I didn't see them until they were out of the shadows of the bushes, almost on him.

One of them rushed up and grabbed Gus's leg, and tried to pull him off the seat, just as he reached the bottom of his swing. Gus managed to hold on, but the chain ropes twisted crazily and when the seat went back up, it hit the metal leg of the framework.

Gus fell, rolled face down in the dust of the playground,

and tried to sit up. The boys pushed through between the swings, avoiding the berserk one that clanged back and forth.

Gus managed to get up, and the boys formed a circle around him. Then Jack Wheeldon stepped out and faced him. I remembered Jack Wheeldon.

He was taller than Gus. They were *all* taller than Gus, but Wheeldon was beefier. I could see shadows surrounding him. Shadows of a boy who would grow into a man with a beer stomach and thick arms. But the eyes would always remain the same.

He shoved Gus in the face. Gus went back, dug in and charged him. Gus came at him low, head tucked under, fists tight, arms braced close to the body. He hit him in the stomach and wrestled him around. They struggled together like inept club fighters, raising dust.

One of the boys in the circle took a step forward and hit Gus hard in the back of the head. Gus turned his face out of Wheeldon's stomach, and Wheeldon punched him in the mouth. Gus started to cry.

I'd been frozen, watching it happen, but he was crying—

I looked both ways down the fence and found the break far to my right. I threw the cigarette away as I dashed down the fence, trying to look behind me. Then through the break and I was running toward them the long distance from far right field of the baseball diamond, toward the swings and seesaws. They had Gus down now, and they were kicking him.

When they saw me coming, they started to run away. Jack Wheeldon paused to kick Gus once more in the side; then he, too, ran.

Gus was lying there, on his back, the dust smeared into mud on his face. I bent down and picked him up. He wasn't moving, but he wasn't really hurt. I held him very close and carried him toward the bushes that rose on a small incline at the side of the playground. The bushes were cool overhead and they canopied us, hid us; I laid him down and used my handkerchief to clean away the dirt. His eyes were very blue. I smoothed the straight brown hair off his forehead. He wore braces; one of the rubber bands hooked onto the pins of the braces, used to keep them tension-tight, had broken. I pulled it free.

He opened his eyes and started crying again.

Something hurt in my chest.

He started snuffling, unable to catch his breath. He tried to speak, but the words were only mangled sounds, huffed out with too much air and pain.

Then he forced himself to sit up and rubbed the back of his hand across his runny nose.

He stared at me. It was panic and fear and confusion and shame at being seen this way. "Th-they hit me from in back," he said, snuffling.

"I know. I saw."

"D'jou scare'm off?"

"Yes."

He didn't say thank you. It wasn't necessary. The backs of my thighs hurt from squatting. I sat down.

"My name is Gus," he said, trying to be polite.

I didn't know what name to give him. I was going to tell him the first name to come into my head, but heard myself say, "My name is Mr. Rosenthal."

He looked startled. "That's *my* name, too. Gus Rosenthal!"

"Isn't that peculiar," I said. We grinned at each other, and he wiped his nose again.

I didn't want to see my mother or father. I had those memories. They were sufficient. It was little Gus I wanted to be with. But one night I crossed into the backyard at 89 Harmon Drive from the empty lots that would later be a housing development.

And I stood in the dark, watching them eat dinner. There was my father. I hadn't remembered him being so handsome. My mother was saying something to him, and he nodded as he ate. They were in the dinette. Gus was playing with his food. *Don't mush your food around like that, Gus. Eat, or you can't stay up to hear* Lux Presents Hollywood.

But they're doing "Dawn Patrol."

Then don't mush your food.

"Momma," I murmured, standing in the cold, "Momma, there are children starving in Russia." And I added, thirty-five years late, "Name two, Momma."

I met Gus downtown at the newsstand.

"Hi."

"Oh. Hullo."

"Buying some comics?"

"Uh-huh."

"You ever read *Doll Man* and *Kid Eternity?*"

"Yeah, they're great. But I got them."

"Not the new issues."

"Sure do."

"Bet you've got *last* months. He's just checking in the new comics right now."

So we waited while the newsstand owner used the heavy wire snips on the bundles, and checked off the magazines against the distributor's long white mimeographed sheet. And I bought Gus *Airboy* and *Jingle Jangle Comics* and *Blue Beetle* and *Whiz Comics* and *Doll Man* and *Kid Eternity*.

Then I took him to Isaly's for a hot fudge sundae. They served it in a tall tulip glass with the hot fudge in a little pitcher. When the waitress had gone to get the sundaes, little Gus looked at me. "Hey, how'd you know I only liked crushed nuts, an' not whipped cream or a cherry?"

I leaned back in the high-walled booth and smiled at him.

"What do you want to be when you grow up, Gus?"

He shrugged. "I don't know."

Somebody put a nickel in the Wurlitzer in his booth, and Glenn Miller swung into "String of Pearls."

"Well, did you ever think about it?"

"No, huh-uh. I like cartooning, maybe I could draw comic books."

"That's pretty smart thinking, Gus. There's a lot of money to be made in art." I stared around the dairy store, at the Coca-Cola posters of pretty girls with pageboy hairdos, drawn by an artist named Harold W. McCauley whose style would be known throughout the world, whose name would never be known.

He stared at me. "It's fun, too, isn't it?"

I was embarrassed. I'd thought first of money, he'd thought first of happiness. I'd reached him before he'd chosen his path. There was still time to make him a man who would think first of joy, all through his life.

"Mr. Rosenthal?"

I looked down and across, just as the waitress brought the sundaes. She set them down and I paid her. When she'd gone, Gus asked me, "Why did they call me a dirty Jewish elephant?"

"Who called you that, Gus?"

"The guys."

"The ones you were fighting that day?"

He nodded. "Why'd they say elephant?"

I spooned up some vanilla ice cream, thinking. My back ached, and the rash had spread up my right wrist onto my forearm. "Well, Jewish people are supposed to have big noses, Gus." I poured the hot fudge out of the little pitcher. It bulged with surface tension for a second, then spilled through its own dark-brown film, covering the three scoops of ice cream. "I mean, that's what some people *believe*. So I suppose they thought it was smart to call you an elephant, because an elephant has a big nose . . . a trunk. Do you understand?"

"That's dumb. I don't have a big nose . . . do I?"

"I wouldn't say so, Gus. They most likely said it just to make you mad. Sometimes people do that."

"That's dumb."

We sat there for a while and talked. I went far down inside the tulip glass with the long-handled spoon, and finished the deep dark, almost black bittersweet hot fudge. They hadn't made hot fudge like that in many years. Gus got ice cream up the spoon handle, on his fingers, on his chin, and on his T-shirt. We talked about a great many things.

We talked about how difficult arithmetic was. (How I would still have to use my fingers sometimes even as an adult.) How the guys never gave a short kid his "raps" when the sand-lot ball games were in progress. (How I overcompensated with women from doubts about stature.) How different kinds of food were pretty bad-tasting. (How I still used catsup on well-done steak.) How it was pretty lonely in the neighborhood with nobody for friends. (How I had erected a facade of charisma and glamour so no one could reach me deeply enough to hurt me.) How Leon always invited all the kids over to his house, but when Gus got there, they slammed the door and stood behind the screen laughing and jeering. (How even now a slammed door raised the hair on my neck and a phone receiver slammed down, cutting me off, sent me into a senseless rage.) How comic books were great. (How my scripts sold so easily because I had never learned how to rein in my imagination.)

We talked about a great many things.

"I'd better get you home now," I said.

"Okay." We got up. "Hey, Mr. Rosenthal?"

"You'd better wipe the chocolate off your face."

He wiped. "Mr. Rosenthal . . . how'd you know I like crushed nuts, an' not whipped cream or a cherry?"

We spent a great deal of time together. I bought him a copy of a pulp magazine called *Startling Stories* and read him a story about a space pirate who captures a man and his wife and offers the man the choice of opening one of two large boxes—in one is the man's wife, with twelve hours of air to breathe, in the other is a terrible alien fungus that will eat him alive. Little Gus sat on the edge of the big hole he'd dug, out in the empty lots, dangling his feet, and listening. His forehead was furrowed as he listened to the marvels of Jack Williamson's "Twelve Hours to Live," there on the edge of the fort he'd built.

We discussed the radio programs Gus heard every day: *Tennessee Jed, Captain Midnight, Jack Armstrong, Superman, Don Winslow of the Navy.* And the nighttime programs: *I Love a Mystery, Suspense, The Adventures of Sam Spade.* And the Sunday programs: *The Shadow, Quite, Please, The Mollé Mystery Theater.*

We became good friends. He had told his mother and father about "Mr. Rosenthal," who was his friend, but they'd spanked him for the *Startling Stories,* because they thought he'd stolen it. So he stopped telling them about me. That was all right; it made the bond between us stronger.

One afternoon we went down behind the Colony Lumber Company, through the woods and the weeds to the old condemned pond. Gus told me he used to go swimming there, and fishing sometimes; for a black oily fish with whiskers. I told him it was a catfish. He liked that. Liked to know the names of things. I told him *that* was called nomenclature, and he laughed to know there was a name for knowing names.

We sat on the piled logs rotting beside the black mirror water, and Gus asked me to tell him what it was like where I lived, and where I'd been, and what I'd done, and everything.

"I ran away from home when I was thirteen, Gus."

"Wasn't you happy there?"

"Well, yes and no. They loved me, my mother and father. They really did. They just didn't understand what I was all about."

There was a pain on my neck. I touched a fingertip to

the place. It was a boil beginning to grow. I hadn't had a boil in years, many years, not since I was a . . .

"What's the matter, Mr. Rosenthal?"

"Nothing, Gus. Well, anyhow, I ran away, and joined the carny."

"Huh?"

"A carnival. The Tri-State Shows. We moved through Illinois, Ohio, Pennsylvania, Missouri, even Kansas . . ."

"Boy! A carnival! Just like in *Toby Tyler or Ten Weeks with the Circus*? I really cried when Toby Tyler's monkey got killed, that was the worst part of it, did you do stuff like that when you were with the circus?"

"Carnival."

"Yeah. Uh-huh. Didja?"

"Something like that. I carried water for the animals sometimes, although we only had a few of those, and mostly in the freak show. But usually what I did was clean up and carry food to the performers in their tops——"

"What's that?"

"That's where they sleep, in rigged tarpaulins. You know, tarps."

"Oh. Yeah, I know. Go on, huh."

The rash was all the way up to my shoulder now. It itched like hell, and when I'd gone to the drugstore to get an aerosol spray to relieve it, so it wouldn't spread, I had only to see those round wooden display tables with their glass centers, under which were bottles of Teel tooth liquid, Tangee Red-Red lipstick and nylons with a seam down the back, to know the druggist wouldn't even know what I meant by Bactine or Liquid Band-Aid.

"Well, along about K.C. the carny got busted because there were too many moll dips and cannons and paperhangers in the tip . . ." I waited, his eyes growing huge.

"What's all *thaaat* mean, Mr. Rosenthal?"

"Ah-ha! Fine carny stiff *you'd* make. You don't even know the lingo."

"Please, Mr. Rosenthal, please tell me!"

"Well, K.C. is Kansas City, Missouri . . . when it isn't Kansas City, Kansas. Except, really, on the other side of the river is Weston. And busted means thrown in jail, and . . ."

"You were in *jail?*"

"Sure was, little Gus. But let me tell you now. Cannons are pickpockets and moll dips are lady pickpockets, and paperhangers are fellows who write bad checks. And a tip is a group."

"So what happened, what happened?"

"One of these bad guys, one of these cannons, you see, picked the pocket of an assistant district attorney, and we all got thrown in jail. And after a while everyone was released on bail, except me and the Geek. Me, because I wouldn't tell them who I was, because I didn't want to go home, and the Geek, because a carny can find a wetbrain in *any* town to play Geek."

"What's a Geek, huh?"

The Geek was a sixty-year-old alcoholic. So sunk in his own endless drunkenness that he was almost a zombie . . . a wetbrain. He was billed as The Thing, and he lived in a portable pit they carried around, and he bit the heads off snakes and ate live chickens and slept in his own dung. And all for a bottle of gin every day. They locked me in the drunk tank with him. The smell. The smell of sour liquor, oozing with sweat out of his pores, it made me sick, it was a smell I could never forget. And the third day, he went crazy. They wouldn't fix him with gin, and he went crazy. He climbed the bars of the big freestanding drunk tank in the middle of the lockup, and he banged his head against the bars and ceiling where they met, till he fell back and lay there, breathing raggedly, stinking of that terrible smell, his face like a pound of raw meat.

The pain in my stomach was worse now. I took Gus back to Harmon Drive and let him go home.

My weight had dropped to just over a hundred and ten. My clothes didn't fit. The acne and boils were worse. I smelled of witch hazel. Gus was getting more antisocial.

I realized what was happening.

I was alien to my own past. If I stayed much longer, God only knew what would happen to little Gus . . . but certainly I would waste away. Perhaps just vanish. Then . . . would Gus's future cease to exist, too? I had no way of knowing; but my choice was obvious. I had to return.

And couldn't! I was happier here than I'd ever been before. The bigotry and violence Gus had known before I came to him had ceased. They knew he was being watched over. But Gus was becoming more erratic. He was shoplifting toy soldiers and comic books from the Kresge's and constantly defying his parents. It was turning bad. I had to go back.

I told him on a Saturday. We had gone to see a Lash La Rue Western and Val Lewton's *The Cat People* at the Lake Theater. When we came back I parked the car on Mentor Avenue, and we went walking in the big, cool, dark woods that fronted Mentor where it met Harmon Drive.

"Mr. Rosenthal," Gus said. He looked upset.

"Yes, Gus?"

"I gotta problem, sir."

"What's that, Gus?" My head ached. It was a steady needle of pressure above the right eye.

"My mother's gonna send me to a military school."

I remembered. *Oh, God*, I thought. It had been terrible. Precisely the thing *not* to do to a child like Gus.

"They said it was 'cause I was rambunctious. They said they were gonna send me there for a *year* or two. Mr. Rosenthal . . . don't let'm send me there. I didn't mean to be bad. I just wanted to be around you."

My heart slammed inside me. Again. Then again. "Gus, I have to go away."

He stared at me. I heard a soft whimper.

"Take me with you, Mr. Rosenthal. Please. I want to see Galveston. We can drive a dynamite truck in North Carolina. We can go to Matawatchan, Ontario, Canada, and work topping trees, we can sail on boats, Mr. Rosenthal!"

"Gus . . ."

"We can work the carny, Mr. Rosenthal. We can pick peanuts and oranges all across the country. We can hitch-hike to San Francisco and ride the cable cars. We can ride the boxcars, Mr. Rosenthal . . . I promise I'll keep my legs inside an' not dangle 'em. I remember what you said about the doors slamming when they hook'm up. I'll keep my legs inside, honest I will. . . ."

He was crying. My head ached hideously. But he was *crying!*

"I'll *have* to go, Gus!"

"You don't care!" He was shouting. "You don't care about me, you don't care what happens to me! You don't care if I die . . . you don't—"

He didn't have to say it: *you don't love me.*

"I do, Gus. I swear to God, I do!"

I looked up at him; he was supposed to be my friend. But he wasn't. He was going to let them send me off to that military school.

"I hope you die!"

Oh, dear God, Gus, I am! I turned and ran out of the woods as I watched him run out of the woods.

I drove away. The green Plymouth with the running boards and the heavy body; it was hard steering. The world swam around me. My eyesight blurred. I could feel myself withering away.

I thought I'd left myself behind, but little Gus had followed me out of the woods. Having done it, I now remembered: why had I remembered none of it before? As I drove off down Mentor Avenue, I came out of the woods and saw the big green car starting up, and I ran wildly forward, crouching low, wanting only to go with him, my friend, me. I threw in the clutch and dropped the stick into first and pulled away from the curb as I reached the car and climbed onto the rear fender, pulling my legs up, hanging onto the trunk latch. I drove weaving, my eyes watering and things going first blue then green, hanging on for dear life to the cold latch handle. Cars whipped around, honking madly, trying to tell me that I was on the rear of the car, but I didn't know what they were honking about, and scared their honking would tell me I was back there, hiding.

After I'd gone almost a mile, a car pulled up alongside, and a woman sitting next to the driver looked down at me crouching there, and I made a *please don't tell* sign with my finger to my freezing lips, but the car pulled ahead and the woman rolled down her window and motioned to me. I rolled down my window and the woman yelled across through the rushing wind that I was back there on the rear fender. I pulled over and fear gripped me as the car stopped and I saw me getting out of the door, and I crawled off the car and started running away. But my legs were cramped and cold from having hung on back there, and I ran awkwardly; then coming out of the dark was a road sign, and I hit it, and it hit me in the side of the face, and I fell down, and I ran toward myself, lying there crying, and I got to him just as I got up and ran off into the gravel yard surrounding the Colony Lumber Company.

Little Gus was bleeding from the forehead where he'd struck the metal sign. He ran into the darkness, and I knew where he was running . . . I had to catch him, to tell him, to make him understand why I had to go away.

I came to the hurricane fence and ran and ran till I

found the place where I'd dug out under it, and I slipped down and pulled myself under and got my clothes all dirty, but I got up and ran back behind the Colony Lumber Company, into the sumac and the weeds, till I came to the condemned pond back there. Then I sat down and looked out over the black water. I was crying.

I followed the trail down to the pond. It took me longer to climb over the fence than it had taken him to crawl under it. When I came down to the pond, he was sitting there with a long blade of saw grass in the mouth, crying softly.

I heard him coming, but I didn't turn around.

I came down to him, and crouched behind him. "Hey," I said quietly. "Hey, little Gus."

I wouldn't turn around. I wouldn't.

I spoke his name again, and touched him on the shoulder, and in an instant he was turned to me, hugging me around the chest, crying into my jacket, mumbling over and over, "Don't go, please don't go, please take me with you, please don't leave me here alone . . ."

And I was crying, too. I hugged little Gus, and touched his hair, and felt him holding onto me with all his might, stronger than a seven-year-old should be able to hold on, and I tried to tell him how it was, how it would be: "Gus . . . hey, hey, little Gus, listen to me . . . I *want* to stay you *know* I want to stay . . . but I can't."

I looked up at him; he was crying, too. It seemed so strange for a grown-up to be crying like that, and I said, "If you leave me *I'll* die. I will!"

I knew it wouldn't do any good to try explaining. He was too young. He wouldn't be able to understand.

He pulled my arms from around him, and he folded my hands in my lap, and he stood up, and I looked at him. He was gonna leave me. I knew he was. I stopped crying. I wouldn't let him see me cry.

I looked down at him. The moonlight held his face in a pale photograph. I wasn't fooling myself. He'd understand. He'd know. I turned and started back up the path. Little Gus didn't follow. He sat there looking back at me. I only turned once to look at him. He was still sitting there like that.

He was watching me. Staring up at me from the pond side. And I knew what instant it had been that had formed me. It wasn't all the people who'd called me a wild kid, or a strange kid, or any of it. It wasn't being poor or being lonely.

I watched him go away. He was my friend. But he didn't have no guts. He didn't. But I'd show him! I'd really show him! I was gonna get out of here, go away, be a big person and do a lot of things, and someday I'd run into him someplace and see him and he'd come up and shake my hand and I'd spit on him. Then I'd beat him up.

He walked up the path and went away. I sat there for a long time, by the pond. Till it got real cold.

I got back in the car, and went to find the way back to the future, where I belonged. It wasn't much, but it was all I had. I would find it . . . I still had the dragoon . . . and there were many stops I'd made on the way to becoming me. Perhaps Kansas City; perhaps Matawatchan, Ontario, Canada; perhaps Galveston; perhaps Shelby, North Carolina.

And crying, I drove. Not for myself, but for myself, for little Gus, for what I'd done to him, forced him to become. Gus . . . Gus!

But . . . oh, God . . . what if I came back again . . . and again? Suddenly, the road did not look familiar.

OCCAM'S SCALPEL

THEODORE STURGEON

Theodore Sturgeon has made an issue for years of the right of science fiction writers to be received as mainstream authors and not relegated to any special category "ghetto." In spite of which, this story still had to appear in the pages of a standard sf magazine. However, he could have a point here, for the question is whether this is rightfully a science fiction story or one which merely uses certain parts of the sf stockpile to make a valid suspense tale.

I

Joe Trilling had a funny way of making a living. It was a good living, but of course he didn't make anything like the bundle he could have in the city. On the other hand he lived in the mountains a half mile away from a picturesque village in clean air and piney-birchy woods along with lots of mountain laurel and he was his own boss. There wasn't much competition for what he did; he had his wife and kids around all the time and more orders than he could fill. He was one of the night people and after the family had gone to bed he could work quietly and uninterruptedly. He was happy as a clam.

One night—very early morning, really—he was interrupted. *Bup-bup, bup, bup.* Knock at the window, two shorts, two longs. He froze, he whirled, for he knew that knock. He hadn't heard it for years but it had been a part of his life since he was born. He saw the face outside and filled his lungs for a whoop that would have roused them at the fire station on the village green, but then he saw the finger on the lips and let the air out. The finger beckoned and Joe Trilling whirled again, turned down a flame, read a gauge, made a note, threw a switch, and joyfully but silently dove for the outside door. He slid out, closed it carefully, peered into the dark.

"Karl?"

"Shh."

There he was, edge of the woods. Joe Trilling went there and, whispering because Karl had asked for it, they hit each other, cursed, called each other the filthiest possible names. It would not be easy to explain this to an extraterrestrial; it isn't necessarily a human thing to do. It's a cultural thing. It means, I want to touch you, it means I love you; but they were men and brothers, so they hit each other's arms and shoulders and swore despicable oaths and insults, until at last even those words wouldn't do and they stood in the shadows, holding each other's biceps and grinning and drilling into each other with eyes. Then Karl Trilling moved his head sidewards toward the road and they walked away from the house.

"I don't want Hazel to hear us talking," Karl said. "I don't want her or anyone to know I was here. How is she?"

"Beautiful. Aren't you going to see her at all—or the kids?"

"Yes but not this trip. There's the car. We can talk there. I really am afraid of that bastard."

"Ah," said Joe. "How is the great man?"

"Po'ly," said Karl. "But we're talking about two different bastards. The great man is only the richest man in the world, but I'm not afraid of him, especially now. I'm talking about Cleveland Wheeler."

"Who's Cleveland Wheeler?"

They got into the car. "It's a rental," said Karl. "Matter of fact, it's the second rental. I got out of the executive jet and took a company car and rented another—and then this. Reasonably sure it's not bugged. That's one kind of answer to your question, who's Cleve Wheeler. Other answers would be the man behind the throne. Next in line. Multifaceted genius. Killer shark."

"Next in line," said Joe, responding to the only clause that made any sense. "The old man is sinking?"

"Officially—and an official secret—his hemoglobin reading is four. That mean anything to you, Doctor?"

"Sure does, Doctor. Malnutritive anemia, if other rumors I hear are true. Richest man in the world—dying of starvation."

"And old age—and stubbornness—and obsession. You want to hear about Wheeler?"

"Tell me."

"Mister Lucky. Born with everything. Greek-coin profile. Michaelangelo muscles. Discovered early by a bright-eyed elementary school principal, sent to a private school, used to go straight to the teachers' lounge in the morning and say what he'd been reading or thinking about. Then they'd tell off a teacher to work with him or go out with him or whatever. High school at twelve, varsity track, basketball, football and high-diving—three letters for each —yes, he graduated in three years, *summa cum.* Read all the textbooks at the beginning of each term, never cracked them again. More than anything else he had the habit of success.

"College the same thing: turned sixteen in his first semester, just ate everything up. Very popular. Graduated at the top again, of course."

Joe Trilling, who had slogged through college and medical school like a hodcarrier, grunted enviously. "I've seen one or two like that. Everybody marvels, nobody sees how easy it was for them."

Karl shook his head. "Wasn't quite like that with Cleve Wheeler. If anything was easy for him it was because of the nature of his equipment. He was like a four-hundred horsepower car moving in sixty-horsepower traffic. When his muscles were called on he used them, I mean really put it down to the floor. A very willing guy. Well—he had his choice of jobs—hell, choice of careers. He went into an architectural firm that could use his math, administrative ability, public presence, knowledge of materials, art. Gravitated right to the top, got a partnership. Picked up a doctorate on the side while he was doing it. Married extremely well."

"Mister Lucky," Joe said.

"Mister Lucky, yeah. Listen. Wheeler became a partner and he did his work and he knew his stuff—everything he could learn or understand. Learning and understanding are not enough to cope with some things like greed or unexpected stupidity or accident or sheer bad breaks. Two of the other partners got into a deal I won't bother you with—a high-rise apartment complex in the wrong place for the wrong residents and land acquired the wrong way. Wheeler saw it coming, called them in and talked it over. They said yes-yes and went right ahead and did what they wanted anyway—something that Wheeler never in the world expected. The one thing high capability and straight morals and a good education doesn't give you is the end of innocence. Cleve Wheeler was an innocent.

"Well, it happened, the disaster that Cleve had predicted, but it happened far worse. Things like that, when they surface, have a way of exposing a lot of other concealed rot. The firm collapsed. Cleve Wheeler had never failed at anything in his whole life. It was the one thing he had no practice in dealing with. Anyone with the most rudimentary intelligence would have seen that this was the time to walk away—lie down, even. Cut his losses. But I don't think these things even occurred to him."

Karl Trilling laughed suddenly. "In one of Philip Wylie's novels is a tremendous description of a forest fire and how the animals run away from it, the foxes and the rabbits running shoulder to shoulder, the owls flying in the daytime to get ahead of the flames. Then there's this beetle, lumbering along on the ground. The beetle comes to a burned patch, the edge of twenty acres of hell. It stops, it wiggles its feelers, it turns to the side and begins to walk around the fire—" He laughed again. "That's the special thing Cleveland Wheeler has, you see, under all that muscle and brain and brilliance. If he had to—and were a beetle—he wouldn't turn back and he wouldn't quit. If all he could do was walk around it, he'd start walking."

"What happened?" asked Joe.

"He hung on. He used everything he had. He used his brains and his personality and his reputation and all his worldly goods. He also borrowed and promised—and he worked. Oh, he worked. Well, he kept the firm. He cleaned out the rot and built it all up again from the inside, strong and straight this time. But it cost.

"It cost him time—all the hours of every day but the four or so he used for sleeping. And just about when he had it leveled off and starting up, it cost him his wife."

"You said he'd married well."

"He'd married what you marry when you're a young block-buster on top of everything and going higher. She was a nice enough girl, I suppose, and maybe you can't blame her, but she was no more used to failure than he was. Only he could walk around it. He could rent a room and ride the bus. She just didn't know how—and of course with women like that there's always the discarded swain somewhere in the wings."

"How did he take that?"

"Hard. He'd married the way he played ball or took examinations—with everything he had. It did something to him. All this did things to him, I suppose, but that was the biggest chunk of it.

"He didn't let it stop him. He didn't let anything stop him. He went on until all the bills were paid—every cent. All the interest. He kept at it until the net worth was exactly what it had been before his ex-partners had begun to eat out the core. Then he gave it away. Gave it away! Sold all right and title to his interest for a dollar."

"Finally cracked, hm?"

Karl Trilling looked at his brother scornfully. "Cracked. Matter of definition, isn't it? Cleve Wheeler's goal was zero—can you understand that? What is success anyhow? Isn't it making up your mind what you're going to do and then doing it, all the way?"

"In that case," said his brother quietly, "suicide is success."

Karl gave him a long penetrating look. "Right," he said, and thought about it a moment.

"Anyhow," Joe asked, "why zero?"

"I did a lot of research on Cleve Wheeler, but I couldn't get inside his head. I don't know. But I can guess. He meant to owe no man anything. I don't know how he felt about the company he saved, but I can imagine. The man he became—was becoming—wouldn't want to owe one damned thing. I'd say he just wanted out—but on his own terms, which included leaving nothing behind to work on him."

"Okay," said Joe.

Karl Trilling thought, *The nice thing about old Joe is that he'll wait. All these years apart with hardly any communication beyond birthday cards—and not always that—and here he is, just as if we were still together every*

*day. I wouldn't be here if it weren't important; I wouldn't
be telling him all this unless he needed to know; he
wouldn't need any of it unless he was going to help. All
that unsaid—I don't have to ask him a damn thing. What
am I interrupting in his life? What am I going to interrupt?
I won't have to worry about that. He'll take care of it.*

He said, "I'm glad I came here, Joe."

Joe said, "That's all right," which meant all the things
Karl had been thinking. Karl grinned and hit him on the
shoulder and went on talking.

"Wheeler dropped out. It's not easy to map his trail for
that period. It pops up all over. He lived in at least
three communes—maybe more, but those three were a
mess when he came and a model when he left. He
started businesses—all things that had never happened before, like a supermarket with no shelves, no canned music,
no games or stamps, just neat stacks of open cases, where
the customer took what he wanted and marked it according to the card posted by the case, with a marker hanging on a string. Eggs and frozen meat and fish and the
like, and local produce were priced a flat two percent
over wholesale. People were honest because they could
never be sure the checkout counter didn't know the prices
of everything—besides, to cheat on the prices listed would
have been just too embarrassing. With nothing but a big
empty warehouse for overhead and no employees spending thousands of man hours marking individual items, the
prices beat any discount house that ever lived. He sold
that one, too, and moved on. He started a line of organic
baby foods without preservatives, franchised it and moved
on again. He developed a plastic container that would burn
without polluting and patented it and sold the patent."

"I've heard of that one. Haven't seen it around, though."

"Maybe you will," Karl said in a guarded tone. "Maybe
you will. Anyway, he had a CPA in Pasadena handling
details, and just did his thing all over. I never heard of a
failure in anything he tried."

"Sounds like a junior edition of the great man himself,
your honored boss."

"You're not the only one who realized that. The boss
may be a ding-a-ling in many ways, but nobody ever
faulted his business sense. He has always had his tentacles
out for wandering pieces of very special manpower. For
all I know he had drawn a bead on Cleveland Wheeler
years back. I wouldn't doubt that he'd made offers from

time to time, only during that period Cleve Wheeler wasn't about to go to work for anyone that big. His whole pattern is to run things his way, and you don't do that in an established empire."

"Heir apparent," said Joe, reminding him of something he had said earlier.

"Right," nodded Karl. "I knew you'd begin to get the idea before I was finished."

"But finish," said Joe.

"Right. Now what I'm going to tell you, I just want you to know. I don't expect you to understand it or what it means or what it has all done to Cleve Wheeler. I need your help, and you can't really help me unless you know the whole story."

"Shoot."

Karl Trilling shot: "Wheeler found a girl. Her name was Clara Prieta and her folks came from Sonora. She was bright as hell—in her way, I suppose, as bright as Cleve, though with a tenth of his schooling—and pretty as well, and it was Cleve she wanted, not what he might get for her. She fell for him when he had nothing—when he really wanted nothing. They were a daily, hourly joy to each other. I guess that was about the time he started building this business and that, making something again. He bought a little house and a car. He bought two cars, one for her. I don't think she wanted it, but he couldn't do enough—he was always looking for more things to do for her. They went out for an evening to some friends' house, she from shopping, he from whatever it was he was working on then, so they had both cars. He followed her on the way home and had to watch her lose control and spin out. She died in his arms."

"Oh, Jesus."

"Mister Lucky. Listen: a week later he turned a corner downtown and found himself looking at a bank robbery. He caught a stray bullet—grazed the back of his neck. He had seven months to lie still and think about things. When he got out he was told his business manager had embezzled everything and headed south with his secretary. Everything."

"What did he do?"

"Went to work and paid his hospital bill."

They sat in the car in the dark for a long time, until Joe said, "Was he paralyzed, there in the hospital?"

"For nearly five months."

"Wonder what he thought about."

Karl Trilling said, "I can imagine what he thought about. What I can't imagine is what he decided. What he concluded. What he determined to be. Damn it, there are no accurate words for it. We all do the best we can with what we've got, or try to. Or should. He *did*—and with the best possible material to start out with. He played it straight; he worked hard; he was honest and lawful and fair; he was fit; he was bright. He came out the hospital with those last two qualities intact. God alone knows what's happened to the rest of it."

"So he went to work for the old man."

"He did—and somehow that frightens me. It was as if all his qualifications were not enough to suit both of them until these things happened to him—until they made him become what he is."

"And what is that?"

"There isn't a short answer to that, Joe. The old man has become a modern myth. Nobody ever sees him. Nobody can predict what he's going to do or why. Cleveland Wheeler stepped into his shadow and disappeared almost as completely as the boss. There are very few things you can say for certain. The boss has always been a recluse and in the ten years Cleve Wheeler has been with him he has become more so. It's been business as usual with him, of course—which means the constantly unusual—long periods of quiet, and then these spectacular unexpected wheelings and dealings. You assume that the old man dreams these things up and some high-powered genius on his staff gets them done. But it could be the genius that instigates the moves—who can know? Only the people closest to him— Wheeler, Epstein, me. And I don't know."

"But Epstein died."

Karl Trilling nodded in the dark. "Epstein died. Which leaves only Wheeler to watch the store. I'm the old man's personal physician, not Wheeler's, and there's no guarantee that I ever will be Wheeler's."

Joe Trilling recrossed his legs and leaned back, looking out into the whispering dark. "It begins to take shape," he murmured. "The old man's on the way out, you very well might be and there's nobody to take over but this Wheeler."

"Yes, and I don't know what he is or what he'll do. I

do know he will command more power than any single human being on Earth. He'll have so much that he'll be above any kind of cupidity that you or I could imagine— you or I can't think in that order of magnitude. But you see, he's a man who, you might say, has had it proved to him that being good and smart and strong and honest doesn't particularly pay off. Where will he go with all this? And hypothesizing that he's been making more and more of the decisions lately, and extrapolating from that— where is he going? All you can be sure of is that he will succeed in anything he tries. That is his habit."

"What does he want? Isn't that what you're trying to figure out? What would a man like that want, if he knew he could get it?"

"I knew I'd come to the right place," said Karl almost happily. "That's it exactly. As for me, I have all I need now and there are plenty of other places I could go. I wish Epstein were still around, but he's dead and cremated."

"Cremated?"

"That's right—you wouldn't know about that. Old man's instructions. I handled it myself. You've heard of the hot and cold private swimming pools—but I bet you never heard of a man with his own private crematorium in the second sub-basement."

Joe threw up his hands. "I guess if you can reach into your pocket and pull out two billion real dollars, you can have anything you want. By the way—was that legal?"

"Like you said—if you have two billion. Actually, the county medical examiner was present and signed the papers. And he'll be there when the old man pushes off too—it's all in the final instructions. Hey—wait. I don't want to cast any aspersions on the M.E. He wasn't bought. He did a very competent examination on Epstein."

"Okay—we know what to expect when the time comes. It's afterward you're worried about."

"Right. What has the old man—I'm speaking of the corporate old man now—what has he been doing all along? What has he been doing in the last ten years, since he got Wheeler—and is it any different from what he was doing before? How much of this difference, if any, is more Wheeler than boss? That's all we have to go on, Joe, and from it we have to extrapolate what Wheeler's going to do with the biggest private economic force this world has ever known."

"Let's talk about that," said Joe, beginning to smile.

Karl Trilling knew the signs, so he began to smile a little, too. They talked about it.

II

The crematorium in the second sub-basement was purely functional, as if all concessions to sentiment and ritual had been made elsewhere, or canceled. The latter most accurately described what had happened when at last, at long long last, the old man died. Everything was done precisely according to his instructions immediately after he was certifiably dead and before any public announcements were made—right up to and including the moment when the square mouth of the furnace opened with a startling clang, a blare of heat, a flare of light—the hue the old-time blacksmiths called straw color. The simple coffin slid rapidly in, small flames exploding into being on its corners, and the door banged shut. It took a moment for the eyes to adjust to the bare room, the empty greased track, the closed door. It took the same moment for the conditioners to whisk away the sudden smell of scorched soft pine.

The medical examiner leaned over the small table and signed his name twice. Karl Trilling and Cleveland Wheeler did the same. The M.E. tore off copies and folded them and put them away in his breast pocket. He looked at the closed square iron door, opened his mouth, closed it again and shrugged. He held out his hand.

"Good night, Doctor."

"Good night, Doctor. Rugosi's outside—he'll show you out."

The M.E. shook hands wordlessly with Cleveland Wheeler and left.

"I know just what he's feeling," Karl said. "Something ought to be said. Something memorable—end of an era. Like 'One small step for man—' "

Cleveland Wheeler smiled the bright smile of the college hero, fifteen years after—a little less wide, a little less even, a great deal less in the eyes. He said in the voice that commanded, whatever he said, "If you think you're quoting the first words from an astronaut on the moon, you're not. What he said was from the ladder, when he poked his boot down. He said, 'It's some kind of soft stuff. I can kick it around with my foot.' I've always liked that much better. It was real, it wasn't rehearsed or memorized or thought out and it had to do with that moment and the next. The M.E. said good night and you told him the chauffeur was waiting outside. I like that better than anything anyone could say. I think he would, too," Wheeler added, barely gesturing, with a very strong, slightly cleft chin, toward the hot black door.

"But he wasn't exactly human."

"So they say." Wheeler half smiled and, even as he turned away, Karl could sense himself tuned out, the room itself become of secondary importance—the next thing Wheeler was to do, and the next and the one after, becoming more real than the here and now.

Karl put a fast end to that.

He said levelly, "I meant what I just said, Wheeler."

It couldn't have been the words, which by themselves might have elicited another half-smile and a forgetting. It was the tone, and perhaps the "Wheeler." There is a ritual about these things. To those few on his own level, and those on the level below, he was Cleve. Below that he was mister to his face and Wheeler behind his back. No one of his peers would call him Wheeler at all, ever. Whatever the component, it removed Cleveland Wheeler's hand from the knob and turned him. His face was completely alert and interested. "You'd best tell me what you mean, Doctor."

Karl said, "I'll do better than that. Come." Without gestures, suggestions or explanations he walked to the left rear of the room, leaving it up to Wheeler to decide whether or not to follow. Wheeler followed.

In the corner Karl rounded on him. "If you ever say anything about this to anyone—even me—when we leave here, I'll just deny it. If you ever get in here again, you won't find anything to back up your story." He took a complex four-inch blade of machined stainless steel from his belt and slid it between the big masonry blocks. Silently, massively, the course of blocks in the corner began to move upward. Looking up at them in the dim light from the narrow corridor they revealed, anyone could see that they were real blocks and that to get through them without that key and the precise knowledge of where to put it would be a long-term project.

Again Karl proceeded without looking around, leaving go, no-go as a matter for Wheeler to decide. Wheeler followed. Karl heard his footsteps behind him and noticed with pleasure and something like admiration that when the heavy blocks whooshed down and seated themselves solidly behind them, Wheeler may have looked over his shoulder but did not pause.

"You've noticed we're alongside the furnace," Karl said, like a guided-tour bus driver. "And now, behind it."

He stood aside to let Wheeler pass him and see the small room.

It was just large enough for the tracks which protruded from the back of the furnace and a little standing space on each side. On the far side was a small table with a black suitcase standing on it. On the track stood the coffin, its corners carboned, its top and sides wet and slightly steaming.

"Sorry to have to close that stone gate that way," Karl said matter-of-factly. "I don't expect anyone down here at all, but I wouldn't want to explain any of this to persons other than yourself."

Wheeler was staring at the coffin. He seemed perfectly composed, but it was a seeming. Karl was quite aware of what it was costing him.

Wheeler said, "I wish you'd explain it to *me*." And he laughed. It was the first time Karl had ever seen this man do anything badly.

"I will. I am." He clicked open the suitcase and laid it open and flat on the little table. There was a glisten of chrome and steel and small vials in little pockets. The first tool he removed was a screwdriver. "No need to use screws when you're cremating 'em," he said cheerfully and placed the tip under one corner of the lid. He struck the handle smartly with the heel of one hand and the lid popped loose. "Stand this up against the wall behind you, will you?"

Silently Cleveland Wheeler did as he was told. It gave him something to do with his muscles; it gave him the chance to turn his head away for a moment; it gave him a chance to think—and it gave Karl the opportunity for a quick glance at his steady countenance.

He's a mensch, Karl thought. *He really is. . . .*

Wheeler set up the lid neatly and carefully and they stood, one on each side, looking down into the coffin.

"He—got a lot older," Wheeler said at last.

"You haven't seen him recently."

"Here and in there," said the executive, "I've spent

more time in the same room with him during the past month than I have in the last eight, nine years. Still, it was a matter of minutes, each time."

Karl nodded understandingly. "I'd heard that. Phone calls, any time of the day or night, and then those long silences two days, three, not calling out, not having anyone in——"

"Are you going to tell me about the phony oven?"

"Oven? Furnace? It's not a phony at all. When we've finished here it'll do the job, all right."

"Then why the theatricals?"

"That was for the M.E. Those papers he signed are in sort of a never-never country just now. When we slide this back in and turn on the heat they'll become as legal as he thinks they are."

"Then why——"

"Because there are some things you have to know."

Karl reached into the coffin and unfolded the gnarled hands. They came apart reluctantly and he pressed them down at the sides of the body. He unbuttoned the jacket, laid it back, unbuttoned the shirt, unzipped the trousers. When he had finished with this he looked up and found Wheeler's sharp gaze, not on the old man's corpse, but on him.

"I have the feeling," said Cleveland Wheeler, "that I have never seen you before."

Silently Karl Trilling responded: *But you do now*. And, *Thanks, Joey. You were dead right.* Joe had known the answer to that one plaguing question, *How should I act?*

Talk just the way he talks, Joe had said. *Be what he is, the whole time.*

Be what he is. A man without illusions (they don't work) and without hope (who needs it?) who has the unbreakable habit of succeeding. And who can say it's a nice day in such a way that everyone around snaps to attention and says: *Yes, SIR!*

"You've been busy," Karl responded shortly. He took off his jacket, folded it, and put it on the table beside the kit. He put on surgeon's gloves and slipped the sterile sleeve off a new scalpel. "Some people scream and faint the first time they watch a dissection."

Wheeler smiled thinly. "I don't scream and faint." But it was not lost on Karl Trilling that only then, at the last possible moment, did Wheeler actually view the old man's body. When he did he neither screamed nor fainted; he uttered an astonished grunt.

"Thought that would surprise you," Karl said easily. "In case you were wondering, though, he really was a male. The species seemes to be oviparous. Mammals too, but it has to be oviparous. I'd sure like a look at a female. That isn't a vagina. It's a cloaca."

"Until this moment," said Wheeler in a hypnotized voice, "I thought that 'not human' remark of yours was a figure of speech."

"No, you didn't," Karl responded shortly.

Leaving the words to hang in the air, as words will if a speaker has the wit to isolate them with wedges of silence, he deftly slit the corpse from the sternum to the pubic symphysis. For the first-time viewer this was always the difficult moment. It's hard not to realize viscerally that the cadaver does not feel anything and will not protest. Nerve-alive to Wheeler, Karl looked for a gasp or a shudder; Wheeler merely held his breath.

"We could spend hours—weeks, I imagine, going into the details," Karl said, deftly making a transverse incision in the ensiform area, almost around to the trapezoid on each side, "but this is the thing I wanted you to see." Grasping the flesh at the juncture of the cross he had cut, on the left side, he pulled upward and to the left. The cutaneous layers came away easily, with the fat under them. They were not pinkish, but an off-white lavender shade. Now the muscular striations over the ribs were in view. "If you'd palpated the old man's chest," he said, demonstrating on the right side, "you'd have felt what seemed to be normal human ribs. But look at this."

With a few deft strokes he separated the muscle fibers from the bone on a mid-costal area about four inches square, and scraped. A rib emerged and, as he widened the area and scraped between it and the next one, it became clear that the ribs were joined by a thin flexible layer of bone or chitin.

"It's like baleen—whalebone," said Karl. "See this?" He sectioned out a piece, flexed it.

"My God."

III

"Now look at this." Karl took surgical shears from the kit, snipped through the sternum right up to the clavicle and then across the lower margin of the ribs. Slipping his fingers under them, he pulled upward. With a dull snap the entire ribcage opened like a door, exposing the lung.

The lung was not pink, nor the liverish-brownish-black of a smoker, but yellow—the clear bright yellow of pure sulfur.

"His metabolism," Karl said, straightening up at last and flexing the tension out of his shoulders, "is fantastic. Or was. He lived on oxygen, same as us, but he broke it out of carbon monoxide, sulfur dioxide, and trioxide and carbon dioxide mostly. I'm not saying he could—I mean he had to. When he was forced to breathe what we call clean air, he could take just so much of it and then had to duck out and find a few breaths of his own atmosphere. When he was younger he could take it for hours at a time, but as the years went by he had to spend more and more time in the kind of smog he could breathe. Those long disappearances of his, and that reclusiveness—they weren't as kinky as people supposed."

Wheeler made a gesture toward the corpse. "But—what is he? Where—"

"I can't tell you. Except for a good deal of medical and bio chemical details, you now know as much as I do. Somehow, somewhere, he arrived. He came, he saw, he began to make his moves. Look at this."

He opened the other side of the chest and then broke the sternum up and away. He pointed. The lung tissue was not in two discreet parts, but extended across the median line. "One lung, all the way across, though it has these two lobes. The kidneys and gonads show the same right-left fusion."

"I'll take your word for it," said Wheeler a little hoarsely. "Damn it, what *is* it?"

"A featherless biped, as Plato once described homo sap. I don't know what it is. I just know *that* it is—and I thought you ought to know. That's all."

"But you've seen one before. That's obvious."

"Sure. Epstein."

"Epstein?"

"Sure. The old man had to have a go-between—someone who could, without suspicion, spend long hours with him and hours away. The old man could do a lot over the phone, but not everything. Epstein was, you might say, a right arm that could hold its breath a little longer than he could. It got to him in the end, though, and he died of it."

"Why didn't you say something long before this?"

"First of all, I value my own skin. I could say reputation, but skin is the word. I signed a contract as his personal physician because he needed a personal physician—another bit of window-dressing. But I did precious little doctoring—except over the phone—and nine-tenths of that was, I realized quite recently, purely diversionary. Even a doctor, I suppose, can be a trusting soul. One or the other would call and give a set of symptoms and I'd cautiously suggest and prescribe. Then I'd get another call that the patient was improving and that was that. Why, I even got specimens—blood, urine, stools—and did the pathology on them and never realized that they were from the same source as what the medical examiner checked out and signed for."

"What do you mean, same source?"

Karl shrugged. "He could get anything he wanted—anything."

"Then—what the M.E. examined wasn't—" he waved a hand at the casket.

"Of course not. That's why the crematorium has a back door. There's a little pocket sleight-of-hand trick you can buy for fifty cents that operates the same way. This body here was inside the furnace. The ringer—a look-alike that came from God knows where; I swear to you I don't—was lying out there waiting for the M.E. When the button was pushed the fires started up and that coffin slid in—pushing this one out and at the same time drenching it with water as it came through. While we've been in here, the human body is turning to ashes. My personal private secret instructions, both for Epstein and for the boss, were to wait until I was certain I was alone and then come in here after an hour and push the second button, which would slide this one back into the fire. I was to do no investigations, ask no questions, make no reports. It came through as logical but not reasonable, like so many of his orders." He laughed suddenly. "Do you know why the old man—and Epstein too, for that matter, in case you never noticed—wouldn't shake hands with anyone?"

"I presumed it was because he had an obsession with germs."

"It was because his normal body temperature was a hundred and seven."

Wheeler touched one of his own hands with the other and said nothing.

When Karl felt that the wedge of silence was thick enough he asked lightly, "Well, boss, where do we go from here?"

Cleveland Wheeler turned away from the corpse and to Karl slowly, as if diverting his mind with an effort.

"What did you call me?"

"Figure of speech," said Karl and smiled. "Actually, I'm working for the company—and that's you. I'm under orders, which have been finally and completely discharged when I push that button—I have no others. So it really is up to you."

Wheeler's eyes fell again to the corpse. "You mean about him? This? What we should do?"

"That, yes. Whether to burn it up and forget it—or call in top management and an echelon of scientists. Or scare the living hell out of everyone on Earth by phoning the papers. Sure, that has to be decided, but I was thinking on a much wider spectrum than that."

"Such as—"

Karl gestured toward the box with his head. "What was he doing here, anyway? What has he done? What was he trying to do?"

"You'd better go on," said Wheeler; and for the very first time said something in a way that suggested diffidence. "You've had a while to think about all this, I—" and almost helplessly, he spread his hands.

"I can understand that," Karl said gently. "Up to now I've been coming on like a hired lecturer and I know it. I'm not going to embarrass you with personalitities except to say that you've absorbed all this with less buckling of the knees than anyone in the world I could think of."

"Right. Well, there's a simple technique you learn in elementary algebra. It has to do with the construction of graphs. You place a dot on the graph where known data put it. You get more data, you put down another dot and then a third. With just three dots—of course, the more the better, but it can be done with three—you can connect them and establish a curve. This curve has certain characteristics and it's fair to extend the curve a little farther with the assumption that later data will bear you out."

"Extrapolation."

"Extrapolation. X axis, the fortunes of our late boss. Y

axis, time. The curve is his fortunes—that is to say, his influence."

"Pretty tall graph."

"Over thirty years."

"Still pretty tall."

"All right," said Karl. "Now over the same thirty years, another curve: change in the environment." He held up a hand. "I'm not going to read you a treatise on ecology. Let's be more objective than that. Let's just say changes. Okay: a measurable rise in the mean temperature because of CO_2 and the greenhouse effect. Draw the curve. Incidence of heavy metals, mercury and lithium, in organic tissue. Draw a curve. Likewise chlorinated hydrocarbons, hypertrophy of algae due to phosphates, incidence of coronaries . . . All right, let's superimpose all these curves on the same graph."

"I see what you're getting at. But you have to be careful with that kind of statistics game. Like, the increase of traffic fatalities coincides with the increased use of aluminum cans and plastic tipped baby pins."

"Right. I don't think I'm falling into that trap. I just want to find reasonable answers to a couple of otherwise unreasonable situations. One is this: if the changes occuring in our planet are the result of mere carelessness— a more or less random thing, carelessness—then how come nobody is being careless in a way that benefits the environment? Strike that. I promised, no ecology lessons. Rephrase: how come all these carelessnesses promote a change and not a preservation?

"Next question: What is the direction of the change? You've seen speculative writing about terra-forming'—altering other planets to make them habitable by humans. Suppose an effort were being made to change this planet to suit someone else? Suppose they wanted more water and were willing to melt the polar caps by the greenhouse effect? Increase the oxides of sulfur, eliminate certain marine forms from plankton to whales? Reduce the population by increases in lung cancer, emphysema, heart attacks and even war?"

Both men found themselves looking down at the sleeping face in the coffin. Karl said softly, "Look what he was into—petrochemicals, fossil fuels, food processing, advertising, all the things that made the changes or helped the changers—"

"You're not blaming him for all of it."

"Certainly not. He found willing helpers by the million."

"You don't think he was trying to change a whole planet just so he could be comfortable in it."

"No, I don't think so—and that's the central point I have to make. I don't know if there are any more around like him and Epstein, but I can suppose this: if the changes now going on keep on—and accelerate—then we can expect them."

Wheeler said, "So what would you like to do? Mobilize the world against the invader?"

"Nothing like that. I think I'd slowly and quietly reverse the changes. If this planet is normally unsuitable to them, then I'd keep it so. I don't think they'd have to be driven back. I think they just wouldn't come."

"Or they'd try some other way."

"I don't think so," said Karl. "Because they tried this one. If they thought they could do it with fleets of spaceships and super-zap guns, they'd be doing it. No—this is their way and if it doesn't work, they can try somewhere else."

Wheeler began pulling thoughtfully at his lip. Karl said softly, "All it would take is someone who knew what he was doing, who could command enough clout and who had the wit to make it pay. They might even arrange a man's life—to get the kind of man they need."

And before Wheeler could answer, Karl took up his scalpel.

"I want you to do something for me," he said sharply in a new, commanding tone—actually, Wheeler's own. "I want you to do it because I've done it and I'll be damned if I want to be the only man in the world who has."

Leaning over the head of the casket, he made an incision along the hairline from temple to temple. Then, bracing his elbows against the edge of the box and steadying one hand with the other, he drew the scalpel straight down the center of the forehead and down on to the nose, splitting it exactly in two. Down he went through the upper lip and then the lower, around the point of the chin and under it to the throat. Then he stood up.

"Put your hands on his cheeks," he ordered. Wheeler frowned briefly (how long had it been since anyone had spoken to him that way?), hesitated, then did as he was told.

"Now press your hands together and down."

The incision widened slightly under the pressure, then abruptly the flesh gave and the entire skin of the face slipped off. The unexpected lack of resistance brought Wheeler's hands to the bottom of the coffin and he found himself face to face, inches away, with the corpse.

Like the lungs and kidneys, the eyes—eye?—passed the median, very slightly reduced at the center. The pupil was oval, its long axis transverse. The skin was pale lavender with yellow vessels and in place of a nose was a thread-fringed hole. The mouth was circular, the teeth not quite radially placed; there was little chin.

Without moving, Wheeler closed his eyes, held them shut for one second, two, and then courageously opened them again. Karl whipped around the end of the coffin and got an arm around Wheeler's chest. Wheeler leaned on it heavily for a moment, then stood up quickly and brushed the arm away.

"You didn't have to do that."

"Yes, I did," said Karl. "Would you want to be the only man in the world who'd gone through that—with nobody to tell it to?"

And after all, Wheeler could laugh. When he had finished he said, "Push that button."

"Hand me that cover."

Most obediently Cleveland Wheeler brought the coffin lid and they placed it.

Karl pushed the button and they watched the coffin slide into the square of flame. Then they left.

Joe Trilling had a funny way of making a living. It was a good living, but of course he didn't make anything like the bundle he could have made in the city. On the other hand, he lived in the mountains a half mile away from a picturesque village, in clean air and piney-birchy woods along with lots of mountain laurel and he was his own boss. There wasn't much competition for what he did.

What he did was to make simulacra of medical specimens, mostly for the armed forces, although he had plenty of orders from medical schools, film producers, and an occasional individual, no questions asked. He could make a model of anything inside, affixed to or penetrating a body or any part of it. He could make models to be looked at, models to be felt, smelled and palpated. He could give you gangrene that stunk or dewy thyroids with real dew on them. He could make one-of-a-kind or he could set up a production line. Dr. Joe Trilling was, to put it briefly, the best there was at what he did.

"The clincher," Karl told him (in much more relaxed circumstances than their previous ones; daytime now, with beer), "the real clincher was the face bit. God, Joe, that was a beautiful piece of work."

"Just nuts and bolts. The beautiful part was your idea—his hands on it."

"How do you mean?"

"I've been thinking back to that," Joe said. "I don't think you yourself realize how brilliant a stroke that was. It's all very well to set up a show for the guy, but to make him put his hands as well as his eyes and brains on it—that was the stroke of genius. It's like—well, I can remember when I was a kid coming home from school and putting my hand on a fence rail and somebody had spat on it." He displayed his hand, shook it. "All these years I can remember how that felt. All these years couldn't wear it away, all those scrubbings couldn't wash it away. It's more than a cerebral or psychic thing, Karl—more than the memory of an episode. I think there's a kind of memory mechanism in the cells themselves, especially on the hands, that can be invoked. What I'm getting to is that no matter how long he lives, Cleve Wheeler is going to feel that skin slip under his palms and that is going to bring him nose to nose with that face. No, you're the genius, not me."

"Na. You knew what you were doing. I didn't."

"Hell you didn't." Joe leaned far back in his lawn chaise—so far he could hold up his beer and look at the sun through it from the underside. Watching the receding bubbles defy perspective (because they swell as they rise), he murmured, "Karl?"

"Yuh."

"Ever hear of Occam's Razor?"

"Um. Long time back. Philosophical principle. Or logic or something. Let's see. Given an effect and a choice of possible causes, the simplest cause is always the one most likely to be true. Is that it?"

"Not too close, but close enough," said Joe Trilling lazily. "Hm. You're the one who used to proclaim that logic is sufficient unto itself and need have nothing to do with truth."

"I still proclaim it."

"Okay. Now, you and I know that human greed and

carelessness are quite enough all by themselves to wreck this planet. We didn't think that was enough for the likes of Cleve Wheeler, who can really do something about it, so we constructed him a smog-breathing extraterrestrial. I mean, he hadn't done anything about saving the world for our reasons, so we gave him a whizzer of a reason of his own. Right out of our heads."

"Dictated by all available factors. Yes. What are you getting at, Joe?"

"Oh—just that our complicated hoax is simple, really, in the sense that it brought everything down to a single cause. Occam's Razor slices things down to simplest causes. Single causes have a fair chance of being right."

Karl put down his beer with a bump. "I never thought of that. I've been too busy to think of that. *Suppose we were right?*"

They looked at each other, shaken.

At last Karl said, "What do we look for now, Joe— spaceships?"